Slashback

"Cal Leandros, who is half human and half Auphe (a monstrous version of elves), and his human brother, Niko, make their living by hunting the supernatural creatures who prey on humans. Now a serial killer with ties to Spring-heeled Jack is on the prowl, and he has a grudge against Cal. The eighth addition to this urban fantasy series (after *Doubletake*) should please Thurman's many fans."

—*Library Journal*

"This combo thriller and mystery will send your readers back into the stacks looking for more from this *New York Times* bestselling author." —*Booklist*

"This dark and dynamic urban fantasy series continues to not only maintain but exceed the expectations of its fans."

—Smexy Books

"A roller-coaster ride of horror and humor."

—Bookshelf Bombshells

"[The Leandros brothers] are back in style in a way that surpasses the last book on every level."

—Bookin' It Reviews

"Thurman does her usual stellar job of combining wisecracks and violence, but the relationship between Cal and Niko remains the heart of the series." —*RT Book Reviews*

"The book quickly became a page-turner, just like all of the previous books have been. This is a great series and I highly recommend it to readers who like gritty and violent urban fantasy with undertones of noir humor."

—Fang-tastic Fiction

Doubletake

"Rob Thurman conjures up one of the grittiest tales of the Leandros brothers yet." —SFRevu

continued . . .

"Another wonderful addition to an intriguing series."

—Night Owl Reviews

Blackout

"Thurman delivers in spades . . . as always, a great entry in a series that only gets better with each new installment."

—SFRevu

Roadkill

"Readers will relish this roller-coaster ride filled with danger. . . . The unexpected is the norm in this urban fantasy."

—Alternative Worlds

Deathwish

"Thurman takes her storytelling to a whole new level in *Deathwish*. . . . Fans of street-level urban fantasy will enjoy this."

—SFRevu

Madhouse

"Thurman continues to deliver strong tales of dark urban fantasy."

—SFRevu

Moonshine

"[Cal and Niko] are back and better than ever . . . a fast-paced story full of action."

—SFRevu

Nightlife

"A roaring roller coaster of a read . . . [it'll] take your breath away. Supernatural highs and lows, and a Hell of a lean over at the corners. Sharp and sardonic, mischievous and mysterious."

—*New York Times* bestselling author Simon R. Green

THE TRICKSTER NOVELS

The Grimrose Path

"Thurman's comic timing is dead-on [and] well-targeted in Trixa's cynical, gritty voice . . . a fast-paced urban adventure that will have you cheering."

—Fresh Fiction

Trick of the Light

"Rob Thurman's new series has all the great elements I've come to expect from this writer: an engaging protagonist, fast-paced adventure, a touch of sensuality, and a surprise twist that'll make you blink."

—#1 *New York Times* bestselling author
Charlaine Harris

"A beautiful, wild ride, [and] a story with tremendous heart. A must read."

—*New York Times* bestselling author Marjorie M. Liu

THE KORSAK BROTHERS NOVELS

Basilisk

"Thurman has created another fast-paced and engaging tale in this volume. . . . Fans of great thriller fiction will enjoy *Basilisk* and the previous novel *Chimera* quite a bit."

—SFRevu

"*Basilisk* is full of excitement, pathos, humor, and dread. . . . Buy it. You won't be sorry. It is one heck of a ride!"

—Bookshelf Bombshells

Chimera

"Thurman delivers a fast-paced thriller with plenty of twists and turns. . . . The characters are terrific—Stefan's wiseass attitude will especially resonate with the many Cal Leandros fans out there—and the pace never lets up, once the two leads are together. . . . Thurman shows a flair for handling SF/near-future action."

—SFRevu

"A touching story on the nature of family, trust, and love lies hidden in this action thriller. . . . Thurman weaves personal discovery seamlessly into the fast-paced action, making it easy to cheer for these overgrown, dangerous boys."

—*Publishers Weekly*

"A gut-wrenching tale of loss and something so huge that the simple four-letter word 'hope' cannot begin to encompass it. . . . *Chimera* grabs the reader's attention and heart immediately and does not let go. . . . This is a masterpiece of a good story and great storytelling."

—Bitten by Books

Downfall

A Cal Leandros Novel

Rob Thurman

A ROC BOOK

ROC
Published by the Penguin Group
Penguin Group (USA) LLC, 375 Hudson Street,
New York, New York 10014

USA | Canada | UK | Ireland | Australia | New Zealand | India | South Africa | China
penguin.com
A Penguin Random House Company

First published by Roc, an imprint of New American Library,
a division of Penguin Group (USA) LLC

First Printing, August 2014

REGISTERED TRADEMARK—MARCA REGISTRADA

ISBN 978-0-451-46529-0

Printed in the United States of America
10 9 8 7 6 5 4 3 2 1

Never give a sucker an even break.

—Latin proverb

This book was written to Robin Goodfellow and for Robin Goodfellow. In respect for all the times he hid behind the curtain, saving the day if not also the world with unseen cons, scams undiscovered, and deceptions none could begin to fathom. For his unparalleled trickery and a loyalty unmatched, I devote this long overdue limelight to him.

Without his tireless if grumbling efforts, the Leandros brothers would never survive long enough to entertain us.

If you reread the first eight books of the series, look more closely this time. Goodfellow's tricks are everywhere—unnoticed by readers and characters alike—and always have been.

Flectere si nequeo superos, Acheronta movebo.
— Virgil (19 BC)

If Heav'n thou can'st not bend, Hell thou shalt move.
— Alexander Pope (1728)

If I cannot move Heaven, then I will raise Hell.
— Clarence Darrow (1910)

If I can't tear down Heaven, I'll raise fucking Hell.
— Cal Leandros (2014)

Never give a sucker an even break.
— Latin proverb

There's a sucker born every minute.
— David Hannum (1869)

Prologue

Cal

They said if you couldn't tear down Heaven, then you'd have to raise fucking Hell.

I thought they, the infamous and forever "they," were shortsighted.

Why couldn't I do both?

That's what I thought absently, caught by the spectacle of fire when the sun fell from the sky. Heaven was falling, and Hell was rising to meet in mutual destruction. I wondered if I'd get a free apocalyptic hot dog with those fireworks?

My brother would say the sun was only setting, the same as it had done every day before us and the same as it would do every day after us. He'd go on to point out it had set on the days when the planet was a barely cooled mass of lava and no living thing was there to see the sun at all. He was like that, my brother. Full of words, full of

*knowledge, full of things he had never seen but could vi-
sualize more clearly than what I could manage with what
was right in front of my face. He was the smartest man—
not to mention the most willing to share any and every
fact whether you wanted to hear it or not—that I knew.*

But this time he would've been wrong. Now, at this
moment and for me alone, the sun was falling. Heaven
was falling, and so was I—falling as I'd always known I
would do. Falling because sometimes that's the only
choice. Falling, but not falling alone—my brother
wouldn't allow that. Considering where we were, I was
damn glad to have that choice and that presence at my
side. We stood tall in the tower, surrounded by a thousand
teeming monsters, serpentine and scaled in snow-blind
white, eyes as bloody murder red as the dying sun, and
with curved dark metal fangs as long as my hand. They
were never still, a constant undulation of hills and valleys.
If I could stand in the middle of the Arctic with nothing
but mound after mound of ice as far as the eye could see,
it would be like this.

Of course the Arctic might have less mutilation, blood,
and death than was circling us now.

Fuck if it isn't the details that get you every time.

Am I right?

Yeah . . . thought so.

I took one last look at an indigo sky, a fiery orange and
vermilion veil settling over the dark horizon, and then focused back on the giant scarlet pyre that inched downward. Falling for me. Waiting for me. Waiting for Caliban.

Caliban, who had once been something new and something old and something unlike anything on this earth.

But the earth wasn't everything. I was no longer unique,
and Niko was right. It wasn't Heaven but the sun that
called my name. It knew who I was—what I was and what
I was not. Completely human, no. Wouldn't that be bor-

ing? Wouldn't that be dull? But I wasn't entirely—there is such a thing as too much fun—a manically gleeful monster either. I was monster enough, though, and, in a way, human enough as well—at least for this.

I wasn't alone in my monster cred.

Some of us monsters, part or pure, had a talent, both stunning in theory and terrifying in reality. We could make the fabric of reality our bitch, tear it in two like the cheapest of tissue paper and pass through. We could travel to where we'd been, even if it had only been the once . . . and some of us could travel to any place we could see.

And I could see, my eyes full of the sun's fire.

Damn straight, I could see.

Strange. I always thought I'd die in the dark—at night, when the monsters most typically come out.

Not so.

For the monsters or me.

"Are you ready?" my brother asked.

I knew what Niko saw when he looked at me. Red eyes instead of gray. Silver hair, not black. It didn't matter. It never had to him. That made me the luckiest bastard in the world. I dropped my guns—who needed weapons when you were one? The smile I gave him was all teeth. Not happy, but not afraid. Satisfied, definitely. Vengeful as hell—yes, yes, yes. I'd known this was coming. I'd known how our lives would end since I was ten years old. Now, fifteen years later, I was inevitability made flesh. "We haven't made a last stand in a while. Think we can make this one stick?"

"We can." Niko smiled back. His sword was dripping with black blood, but his eyes showed only peace and determination. He'd known the same as I how our lives would play out; it had only taken him longer to see. Hope was impractical, but it was also a damn stubborn son of a bitch when it came to brothers. "Time for a new game, *little brother," he said with a familiar lifetime-long fond-ness. "Time to hitch another ride."*

Yeah, I was the ticket to ride all right.

And my rides? No one did rides like I did.

I looked back at the sun. Nik was right. It was time. Off into the sunset we'd go.

Reaching for the sun, I took that ride.

1

(Rescheduled due to unforeseen circumstances.)

Goodfellow

Ten days ago

There's a sucker born every minute.

Engrave that on every brain cell. Write it on every neuron firing in your ... Wait.

Was that a sniper on the roof? Across the street from the bar where I was reaching for the door handle, what was that I saw in the deepest of shadows? A sniper with a gun that could destroy a tank? Yes, it was. Ares, God of War, save me from human idiots who'd kill a newly born rabbit with a nuclear warhead to overcompensate for their one-inch dick and the shriveled raisins that made up their testicles. It was beyond annoying.

And the night had only begun. I had drinking ahead of me, along with a gloriously dire internal monologue that I'd been planning for days. One that had it been external rather than internal would make all those about me fall to their knees at the glory and the tragedy of it. I'd taken the precaution of writing some of it down to prevent what would be a catastrophic loss to history if I somehow lost the future opportunity to speak it aloud.

Gamou.

Nonetheless, it seemed there were other things to take care of first. I'd return to the bar and my soliloquy . . . now that I considered it, some would think that sounded somewhat conceited even for me. Soliloquy . . . hmmm. My thoughts, then, for the judgmental, I meant, and they were barely self-centered thoughts at that. No, not ego-centric and narcissistic at all. Thus, I merely had to do away with the sniper while keeping the opening line of my fateful and earth-shaking contemplations prepared in my mind. . . .

There's a sucker born every . . .

Hephaestus's sweaty pits and fiery forge, did the streetlights deceive me? Was that a rocket launcher propped up beside the roof-dwelling idiot sniper?

I let go of the doorknob and made my way across the street, loved and hidden by the dark as I ever was when I wished to be. Obviously this train of thought would have to be continued later. Although suckers and idiots . . . They weren't all that different, were they?

I didn't have to memorize that.

(Goodfellow: the rest of the chapter has been re-scheduled due to oblivious Cal's irritating and unforeseen circumstances and my solution of them—as always.)

2

Caliban

Ten days ago

It's what's on the inside that counts.

Remember that.

It'll come up later. Pop quizzes aren't out of the question.

Not that I was thinking that now. I had other things on my mind. Someone trying to kill me was one of them.

It wasn't that someone was trying to kill me was anything to get excited about, not really. That had been happening half of my life. Most of the supernatural world didn't like me—or didn't like my kind. To them we were one and the same and were treated as such. Attempted murder, mutilation, or a one-Cal massacre, it was part of life. Truthfully, it was hard to scrape up any actual annoyance, much less get pissed off about it anymore. It was the same as complaining about rush-hour traffic: pointless and likely to make things worse when your cabdriver lost his shit and tried to stab you in the eye.

As someone was already doing their best to stab me in the eye or close enough, I didn't need to add to that particular theoretical scenario. Yeah, it wasn't the homicidal mayhem aimed at me that had my temper exploding. It was the large shard of mirror thrown at my face that disturbed me—disturbed me enough in fact that while I'd only planned on using the axe I was carrying for a threat or two, I'd now changed my mind. If they wanted to play "Here's Johnny!" then who the hell was I to deny their scaly little bitch hearts?

If they weren't Stephen King fans, I'd be damned disappointed.

Here's a fun fact about me: I wasn't into mirrors, whether they were bolted to the wall, mounted on an oversexed puck's ceiling, or broken in a bathroom with a large triangular-shaped piece of it flying toward me like a quicksilver blade.

Mirrors. Not a fan.

Nothing ever good could came of one. For that matter nothing good came *in* one or *out* of one.

But this was my luck we were talking about, and it always took a nosedive at the Ninth Circle, a supernatural bar where I worked. The place put the fight in bar fight; that had been a fact from day fucking one. I had things thrown at me and my face in particular all the damn time. Occupational hazard. It was usually beer bottles, chairs, or even other patrons—you never knew. So, normally, having anything, knives included, tossed at me with vicious accuracy wouldn't faze me.

The fragment of mirror did.

What I thought I saw reflected in it was worse.

Shit.

One moment I was investigating—otherwise known as hoping to break up a fight and kick ass—in the bathroom, and the next I was dodging impalement. We only had the one bathroom. *Paien*—monsters—didn't care about separation of gender when it came to dumping bodily fluids, and as many species had more than two genders anyway, you couldn't please everyone. One bathroom would have to do.

I walked in with the fire axe, the one used frequently but never for fires, which we kept behind the bar, and ended up in a four-way bitch-fest between two succubae, one lamia—better known as a leech on two legs in my book, and one wildly grinning shirtless puck. I didn't care he was bare from the waist up. I counted myself lucky he had pants. I'd unwillingly—so very unwillingly—seen more than my fair share of naked pucks in my life. Only half-naked, like this one, that was a gift from above.

I was guessing from the trickster's grin, the succubae's bared snake fangs, and the lamia's pulsating ... You know what? Here's an interesting evolutionary fact that most natural creatures and supernatural creatures have evolved from the same blob of cells before taking different forks in Darwin's path. A swamp leech is distantly related to the *paien* humanoid leech masquerading as a woman, at least in how they both feed. Wide-open circular mouths ringed all the way around with teeth and a blood-seeking, hungering pulsation behind those teeth that would make you think more than twice about swimming in anything but a perfectly clear pool with an incredibly high saline content ... and with a spear gun.

Or like me, who'd seen far too many mouths of lamia attached to their victims and sucking them dry, I didn't swim at all. Trust me, I didn't miss it.

Back to what I'd been thinking when I first walked in: The succubae wanted payment for services rendered to the puck. The lamia had been taking a bathroom break and simply wanted to eat the puck, as they are uncommon and the uncommon are generally considered a delicacy; and the puck was doing as all pucks do. He was skipping out on his bill, wreaking fucking havoc, and enjoying the hell out of himself.

The two succubae, covered in glittering midnight blue snake scales with storm-cloud black and silver hair, grabbed the lamia and tossed her into the large rectangular mirror on the wall—some *paien* are vain, but mostly they like to know what's sneaking up behind them. Hence the mirror. As the lamia was thrown through the air to hit and hit goddamn hard, the mirror shattered explosively. I ducked, the puck—pucks always know the better part of valor is watching their own ass—hid in a stall, and the lamia ended up lying crumpled on the floor. "Ladies," I drawled. "You know the rules: Charging clients or eating clients"—no one cared which—"is done in the alley *outside* the bar. Leeches and sex slurpers are no exception."

The lamia took offense to the leech remark, not that I knew why. Once they fastened those round mouths and latched on, they paralyzed you and then they liquefied and sucked out everything contained in your sack of skin that wasn't bone. If you don't like the name, don't spread the fame. Regardless, they never seemed to see the truth in that, and this one was no exception. Hissing in a lamia's customary homicidal outrage—which I admit they did damn well—seven on a scale of one to ten in making your eardrums ache, she oozed up to a sitting position and snatched up a large shard of mirror to fling it at my face.

That was when I saw it.

There it was—maybe—in the shimmering surface before it tumbled and I threw myself to one side. I ended up with a painful slice across my forehead and a complete lack of patience. "Fine," I spat. "You've been down-graded from ladies to bitches." I lifted the axe, often used, well sharpened, and shining as bright as the edge of a brand-new guillotine. The lamia's anger fled at the silver gleam, leaving her oddly deflated, her black eyes showing wild wariness as she peered up through the long dark hair that covered most of her face to cascade along with her floor-length black dress like a pool of poison on the dirty tile around her.

"You know what a friend once told me the Good Book says?" I grinned with dark cheer. "Thou shall not suffer a bitch to live."

"That's not quite how the quote goes," came a deep, disapproving voice from behind me that I really didn't want to hear right now. "Trust me, Caliban." I didn't. I went with ignoring him instead.

The succubae were running. I didn't care about them. They started this, but they'd been smart enough not to throw anything at me that might slice off my face ... or make me feel something more painful. They got a free-bie this time. The lamia? No freebies for her and her mirror and what she'd made me see.

Making me see? Making me see *that*?

It wasn't that. It wasn't. Nononono.

Death was too easy for her, but it was all I had.

I had started to heave the axe downward when a large hand caught the wooden handle just below the metal head and yanked me backward. "Let her go," Ishiah ordered. "I can't keep docking your pay whenever you maim or kill a patron. You've been working for free for three weeks now."

"Pigeons like you are cheap. What can I say?" I muttered under my breath before turning and letting Ishiah, my boss, an ex-angel or peri as the *paien* called them, take the axe. "It wasn't my fault that she'd started a fight with a piece of glass and I was going to end it with a four-foot-long axe. That was purely poor planning on her part." I waved a hand at my T-shirt. It was black with small red letters you'd have to be way too far into my personal space to make out. They spelled out IF YOU CAN READ THIS ... YOU'RE ALREADY DEAD. I took my personal space seriously. "I'm responsibly labeled. What more do you want?"

I was trying to distract myself by bitching to Ish, but it wasn't working. I couldn't forget what I might have seen in that glass. It could've been a trick of the light. It could be nothing. There was time enough for that later. Like maybe never. If I was lucky. Unfortunately I was never lucky. I pushed it all away and moved on to dealing with my boss.

"What I want, but doubt I will ever get, is an employee who is less bloodthirsty than all my patrons put together." Ishiah had let the weight of the axe carry it to hang inches above the floor. He was swinging it slowly, barely moving it, all in all, but I got the picture.

"Yeah, yeah. Ruin my fun." I walked over and knocked on the stall door where the puck had fled. "You in there. We already have one puck in town. Robin Goodfellow. I don't know whether he'd throw you a party to reminisce about the orgy days of yore or kill you for poaching on his territory. Want me to call and ask?"

Pucks didn't care for other pucks, being identical physical clones of one another. With the enormous ego each and every one of them had, two of them in one city was one too many. They either disliked each other, loathed each other, or hated each other with a homicidal fury. It depended on the pucks and their particular past. Added to that, Goodfellow, he was old. He said he'd been around before dinosaurs, when the stars were the size of your fist, and the daytime sky was purple with the birthing gas of a new world. Or so he said. He could've been lying. To a puck, a lie was a work of art. Truth, except on rare occasions, was an insulting lack of effort on your part.

I hadn't been sure about the dinosaur issue, but I'd finally accepted it was true enough. My kind, half of what lived in my genes, had also apparently hunted dinos for sport. Not for food, for fucking *fun*. When it came to telling tales, there was one thing and only one that Robin didn't lie about: the Auphe. When Nik and I were kids and hadn't known what the monsters were that followed us from town to town, we'd called them Grendels thanks to Niko's love of Beowulf. When we were a little older, we'd been clued in to what the true name of the bogeyman that did more than follow us; that had hid under our bed, in our closet, and outside every window of every house we'd lived in.

Auphe.

What humans had once hilariously, maybe hysterically painted into mythology as elves. See an Auphe face-to-face and survive it . . . that would make you hysterical, delusional, and more than a little mad. Storybook elves were as to Auphe as goldfish were to great white sharks—sharks with a thousand metal teeth in a hypodermic needle grin. They weren't pretty, they didn't ride horses, they didn't wear golden armor. They didn't wear clothes at all. The only use for a horse they would have would be to eat it. They had roamed the world, an albino, scarlet-eyed, clawed naked *animal* that Mother Nature had for some reason gifted with a brain. A twisted, psychopathic brain, but with the talent of cunning and speech and plans for genocide all the same.

Too bad that hadn't worked out for them. On the other hand, lift a cold one that it had turned out for me. Genocide didn't look too good on most résumés, but in this case, I didn't have one goddamn qualm. No one cried a single tear over their extinction.

I most definitely hadn't. They had been what had birthed the half of me, what had stamped my monster card and let me mix with the *paien* while bringing my human half along as my plus one. *Paien* thought humans were boring and often only good for eating, but they absolutely hated the Auphe. It could be because the Auphe had thought the same thing about *paien*—they were a meal, nothing more and nothing less. No better than a human. No more challenge than week-old roadkill. Although the Auphe, like cats and three-year-olds, did like to play with their food. That explained that while *paien* might loathe that half of me, they didn't often fuck with it either.

Thanks to Robin's history lesson to my brother and me on everything that we didn't know about the Auphe, which was that selfsame everything, I'd learned several years ago that if I stood up to a monster, most would slink away before I needed to pull a weapon. Goodfellow might lie for fun and profit, but I believed him about my murderous ancestors. If he said he'd once seen an Auphe rip off the head of a velociraptor, turning it into a prehistoric Pez dispenser, then he had.

It meant something that there was someone to go to who knew the truth about the beginnings of my family tree—the first killers to walk this rock. It meant something that a born con man had taken two overgrown wildly suspicious delinquents, picked up on their clueless nature, their panicked need to escape the monsters that followed them, and filled them in on what was really watching them with scarlet eyes. What was watching *me*.

Who I was.

What I was.

Ignorance is not bliss. Ignorance is being a defenseless pigeon right as the hawk hits you in a splatter of blood and feather. With the truth, if it was possible to survive, you'd have a chance to try. Damn straight it meant something, meant almost everything that Robin was the only one in our lives that had laid it out for us and told us that ugly truth. Ugly or not, it had saved our lives.

Robin knew all the truths there were, I suspected, making my brother and I damn lucky he'd lived this long.

It meant something entirely different to the puck hiding in the stall and lucky wasn't it. Robin liked my brother and me, but he didn't give a rat's ass about any pucks other than himself. In the *paien* world the older you were, the more powerful you were ... and, as a bonus, often the more of a drooling, psychotic whack job you were. Goodfellow, most likely the second puck ever created, and almost as old as the Auphe, wasn't insane, but that didn't stop him from keeping the rest of the pucks on their toes, wondering if he would snap any moment, trap them with a thousand and one tricks not a single other trickster had yet to come up with, eat their faces, and then make artistic outdoor decorations with their bones. He had no problem encouraging that train of thought.

I loved that about Robin. He had one helluva sense of humor.

"Hey." I knocked on the stall door again, asking, "If you had to spend your afterlife as some kind of trinket, what would it be? My nana, for instance"—I didn't have a nana, but it made for a good story—"collects wind chimes, the kind made of natural materials. Wood, stone—oh, and bone. She says nothing sounds like bones do when they rattle in the wind. Her birthday is in a month. You might not know it, but Goodfellow lately has been heavy into arts and crafts, you know, in between the orgies. I was thinking of asking him if he could make Nana—"

The door slammed open and the puck was out of the

bathroom and gone. A flash of brown hair, green eyes, and leather pants and then nothing. It was nothing I was very grateful for. "Don't let Robin wear leather pants," I told Ishiah. "I like my eyes. I need them. I don't want them to go *Ark of the Covenant* on me and melt down my face."

"You are not in the minority of that issue, trust me," Ishiah snorted. "You should've seen him back in the day in a toga. No, the kilt was the worse. No, wait. When he dressed up as a handmaiden with Loki when they were trying to pass Thor off as the fertility goddess Freyja. That was ..." He stared past me with glazed eyes and a look more haunted than any house built over a Native American burial ground in all the best cheesy movies. "I don't want to talk about this any longer."

Shaking off the memories, the peri folded up his white-and-gold-feathered wings. They instantly disappeared. They always came out if there might be a fight. He'd once said it was for flight, maneuverability, and another way of knocking weapons from people's hands. I'd called bullshit and told him he was the feathered version of a blowfish. He was trying to puff himself up to look more badass.

He'd replied that he was an ex-angel of the Lord and his levels of badass couldn't be measured by mere human means. I threw down the "I'm not human" card, the "the Auphe were on earth long before you were" card, and rounded it off with the "my bad-assery had gotten me the nickname of Unmaker of the World and yours gets you anally perched on Christmas trees every year" card. And when I emphasized that yes, I meant anally, not annually, everything had gone downhill from there.

That no one knew that a resulting knock-down, drag-out fight would spill several bottles of common cleaning solutions that then could conceivably mix into an explosive that caused the temporary loss of part of the roof was a lack of education and not my problem. I never claimed chemistry was my best subject.

That was my first week of docked pay.

"Hey, Robin knows Loki and Thor? Loki and Thor are real?" For Nik and his love of mythology and me and my love of radically incorrect (but screw accuracy—look at those giant Amazonian Wonderbreasts) comic books and superhero movies, the concept was equally cool. "He hung out with the God of Mischief and Chaos and that other surfer dude with the hammer?" Then I homed in on the important part. "He dressed up like a bridesmaid? Goodfellow?" That was a bit of mythology Niko had told me that I'd for once enjoyed, although neither of us knew Robin had been there. "Oh, damn. I am going to give him shit *forever*."

"Best not. He might tell Loki and Norse gods care about the Auphe the same as most *paiens*—not at all. And certain trickster gods such as Loki in particular have a special hatred for them."

"Are you saying if Goodfellow invited him to New York, I might end up in a bridesmaid dress for the rest of my natural life?"

"He's not that kind of trickster. He prefers his lessons short and to the point. You'd spend the rest of your life as a puddle of blood, bone fragments, and liquefied spleen," he said dryly, "in a jar on his mantel with you still conscious and aware despite your souplike consistency until he eventually tired of listening to your splashing and burbling."

Okay, that I could do without. Stay away from Loki. I got it. I gave in as Ishiah provided me with a light shove toward the bathroom door. "The lamia sliced you fairly deep. Go home. We don't want you bleeding all over the bar tonight."

I was mopping at my forehead with a wad of paper

towels and gave in with a grumble. He was right. Head wounds, no matter how minor, bled like crazy, and when you worked in a bar that catered to vampires, Wolves, revenants, *vodyanoi*, lamia, and too many other ghoulies to count, you didn't want to hang around leaking blood until someone finally snapped and fell off the wagon. It didn't have to be blood drinkers. Blood could also trigger rage, the smell of prey, and all kinds of other things Ishiah wouldn't want to put up with.

Normally I would've run home. It's far, but if I did run it, I could skip the ten miles in the morning. But smelling of blood and having difficulty with my usual emergency mode of travel, I took a cab. It had a mirror too, not like the one in the bathroom—the bright sliver that had tumbled through the air showing in brilliant detail things I didn't want to see. That I probably hadn't seen, had only imagined. This one now was your typical dark rearview mirror. I would've had to lean forward to see anything at all in it.

I didn't.

I wasn't ready. I wish we could've stuck with the Norse god discussion, because I wasn't prepared to think about this. Not mirrors, reflections, any of it. I wouldn't be ready at home either, but there I could turn on all the lights. Be in a safe place. If there was anything to see at all, and there probably wasn't. I have good vision, but I'd only a split second to see my warped reflection in the shard the lamia had thrown at me. That isn't enough time to see anything more than a trick of the light.

Right?

Right.

I checked the locks on the door to our place. No signs of anyone trying to pick it, although they'd have better luck taking a crowbar to it. Niko was serious about his locks after several break-ins of the less than human type, who had no interest at all in stealing our TV. Stealing our lives or livers or both, yes, but our electronics were safe. Looking up at the second-floor window, I could see the metal bars and glass were intact. Good to go.

Opening the four locks on the door of our apartment, I walked in and locked up behind me as automatically as I'd done since I was seven or eight. There were as many human monsters in the world as there were Grendel/ Auphe and Niko had taught me how to stay safe early on. I'd learned defensive moves with a kitchen-fucking-Ginsu knife he'd stolen at a flea market almost before I'd learned to tie my shoes. Hey, my life was worth more than laces. That's what Velcro is for, asshole.

I dumped my jacket on the floor. My double shoulder holster I left on, as well as the knife in each boot, and the holster at the small of my back. Most accidents happen in the home. If a flesh-crazed zombie cockroach was going to come after me—and it wouldn't be the first time— I wanted to be prepared.

I liked our place, the best by far we'd ever had. It had been converted from a garage and was about the space of four good-sized apartments. Promise, Niko's one and only, had taken a small amount of money from her five late husbands, which told you how much money they had had to consider this investment small. She had it redone and rented it to us for practically nothing, which was exactly in our price range most of the time: practically nothing. Sometimes we were flush and sometimes we were flushed. It was the nature of the business.

Paying assholes hostage money and making sure to get the hostage back. Paying assholes ransom money, then killing them if the hostage was already dead, and returning the money to the family. Kidnapping children-eating assholes, holding them for ransom, and then dropping them off thirty-story buildings. That was one of my favorites. Exterminating poison-spitting pixies. That was the least of my favorites. Fucking pixies. Clearing a pack of kishi out of a Kin neighborhood as kishi howled at a frequency that made Mafia Wolf ears bleed. Blowing up a mausoleum to get rid of a ghoul. Granted, doesn't show a lot of respect for the dead, but once ghouls eat enough of the dead, they move on to the living. Nipping that in the bud is in everyone's best interest. Not to mention explosives. I had a no doubt unhealthy—but who cared?—love of explosives.

It was a dirty business. Even if Niko tried to keep us on the more moral side of it, it was also a business that someone would be paid to do. It might as well be us. We were familiar to the extreme with the *paien* population—the monsters that humans have no idea exist. A kelpie living in a Central Park pond had killed ten pony lovers who tried to push it out of the water to safety before we put it down. You'd have thought the blood-soaked mane, unnaturally glowing bog green eyes, and three rows of piranha teeth would've made a person think twice, but nope.

People . . . too stupid to live, . . . yeah, that's all. Too stupid to live.

I was dragging my feet with all the crap that had nothing to do with what was lurking in the depths of my murky subconscious, looking for a way . . . any way to hide. No putting it off any longer; that would only make what I'd imagined worse. If I had seen it at all. It could've been an illusion caused by the speed of flying glass and my jerking movement to try to avoid it. It *could* be nothing. It didn't have to be what I'd automatically assumed. I only had to look and get it over with and then I could laugh at my paranoia. Even if it was from the fetal position under my bed, it was still laughing. That counted.

I walked down the hall and into the bathroom. For all
the size of the open area of kitchen, living room, gym,
and then add on the two bedrooms, the bathroom
seemed small and getting smaller the longer I stood in it
staring at the ragged green towel. It was partially rolled
to wedge on top of the medicine cabinet with the rest
falling over to hide the mirror. I'd put it up one day years
ago in a different place, but no matter where we moved,
the position of the towel never did. And Niko never
commented on it. Hell, Niko, to save me the humiliation,
was the one to put it up.

I don't like mirrors, as I'd thought in the bar. By now
that's not news, right? It certainly wouldn't be news to
anyone who knew me—really knew me, I mean. Three or
four people, which wasn't a long list, but I had no desire
to add to it. The more on your list, the more likely you'll
fuck up and let the wrong person in. In my world, you
often find out who that wrong person is a second or so
after he buries a dagger in your back. I didn't care for
that, and it made an awkward fit when it came to my
jacket. They say it's not paranoia if people are really out
to get you. What do they say when there are people . . .
creatures whose sole purpose in being *born* is to get you?

Ah well. Things weren't likely to change.

Popularity is for pussies anyway.

So, yeah, I had a handful of people who knew my
thing about mirrors. The not-liking thing. It wasn't a phobia. It absolutely was not . . . anymore. Not that it would
matter if it were. I was a low-maintenance guy. I shaved
by feel and pulled my not-quite-shoulder-length hair
back into a ponytail. If my hair grew out too long, my
brother cut it for me. He'd started after the first time he
caught me trimming it with a KA-BAR serrated combat
knife. All in all, it was under control. All hygienic chores
would be, and were, done reflection-free. No mirrors re-

quired. And if I missed a patch shaving, no one at the place I bartended would mention or notice for that matter. The clientele were a little more than hairy and/or furry themselves. Living without mirrors was a helluva lot more doable than looking into one.

But, let me repeat, not a phobia.

Unfortunately tonight I did need a mirror. Niko wasn't here to help me out. He was out with his vampire ball-and-chain Promise. Not that he would call her that, nor would he do anything to stop her from dislocating my arm if she heard the not so affectionate nickname. Sadly, it even wasn't true. They were one of those meant-to-be couples. Romeo and Juliet, minus all the angst and suicide. Paris and Helen of Troy, without the war, mass destruction, and stupidity of a guy who couldn't keep his dick in his pants . . . under his ancient leather miniskirt—whatever. Brad Pitt and Angelina Jolie, but lacking the litter and the ability to be a living tour of Nations of the World ride at Disneyland, Alien and the Predator if . . . nope, that was perfect. Same interests, same hobbies, and one had fangs while the other a deep, *deep* appreciation of deadly weapons.

A disgustingly perfect couple who didn't deserve to have their night interrupted over a slight mental malfunction I'd picked up years ago. They should be on Promise's sofa, drinking wine and surfing Transylvanian Web sites for orphaned vamp babies to adopt. They should have at least that first part of a night together, as the second part never could or would happen.

My brother had always put me first in his life, probably a result of raising me himself. Nik had once let it slip, and only then because it had been the first, last, and only time he'd been too drunk to self-censor, that our mother, Sophia, hadn't bothered to pick me up out of the birth-blood-streaked bathtub she'd delivered me in. She'd cut the cord with a rusty steak knife and stepped over me to stagger out of the tub. After telling Niko "Here's that pet you've been nagging me for," she went to her room to fall into bed with a bottle of whiskey. With that stellar maternal reaction, I doubted she'd given me any further thought other than to look at me with an eye calculated as to whether I was small enough to flush down the toilet. But too bad for Sophia. Niko said I'd been born small, about five pounds. Five pounds isn't much, yet still larger than your average dead goldfish.

With Promise being more understanding about Niko and my *Titanic*-sized case of codependency than . . . hell . . . any woman, vampire or human, I wasn't going to crash their alone time. Naughty time. Pervy time. Whatever time they had going on, it didn't matter. I could handle this myself.

First I'd check the cut to see if it needed stitches. I'd done stitches enough times I wouldn't see anything in the mirror but the slice to the skin. It had long become pure reflex, done on enough different body parts, my brother's as well as my own, that I didn't need to pay attention. When that was done, I could focus on the mirror itself for a second or two to see if anything looked . . . off.

Easy.

I reached toward the mirror and ripped down the towel as I fumbled for the first aid kit, one of several stashed around, under the sink, spotting the box of syringes while I did so. That was a different situation. I might dread the mirror, but I was pinning a lot of hopes on those syringes and the new bottles in the refrigerator that went with them.

But time for that later.

With gauze and peroxide I wiped the dried and fresh blood from the slice that ran from the far end of my right eyebrow in an almost directly horizontal line to my hairline, keeping my eyes on it and only it. It was a red, seeping mess, but once I had it cleaned, it turned out not to be that deep and only a few inches long. It might not even scar. Wouldn't that be a shock, considering the scarred mess my hands, chest, and ribs were? I applied several butterfly bandages and it looked good. A little blood would ooze past the antibiotic cream a half Auphe with a hyped-up immune system like me didn't actually need, but otherwise it could've been worse.

The worse, of a different sort, was what I was preparing for now.

I dropped my eyes to study the sink as I pulled the ponytail holder out of my hair. It was a nice sink—no cracks in the glazing, the first one we'd had in the city where the water came out clear instead of rusty orange. I'd much rather look at it than the mirror. "Coward," I exhaled before stiffening my shoulders and raising my gaze. My hair, now free of the holder, fell thick and black as my mother's own had been. Dark and depthless as it always was . . . except for one solitary gleam. I felt my stomach burn as I raised slow fingers to tease out that glitter I'd seen in the broken piece of hell's own reflection at the bar.

One silver-white hair.

It was tucked down in the lower layer and only chance, the flickering light of the bar's bathroom, a flying sliver of mirror, and my own suspicious pessimism had let me see it. It could be natural. I'd already thought that. Black hair often goes prematurely gray or white. Sophia's hadn't. I was twenty-five now. She'd been thirty-eight when the Auphe burned her alive in our decrepit trailer, but she'd died with hair as black as her burned corpse. She could've been lucky, if dying a pretty much well-deserved death with your natural hair color could be called lucky. Her mother or father could've gone gray younger. I wouldn't know. I'd never met them, but . . . I had to have hope. Faith was a lying whore who'd kicked me to the curb me long ago, but Promise and Goodfellow had proved charity existed. Why not a little hope to prove the trio wasn't a mirage?

The hair was between my thumb and forefinger—only the one. I didn't see any more of them. One premature silver-white strand, it was normal. So fucking *normal* that I should be pissed at getting that worked up. Niko would snort at my idiocy. Goodfellow would buy me the cheapest box of hair dye he could find at the drugstore. They would . . . I dragged my fingers down the bright thread and felt the snag of serrated hooks too small to be seen by the naked eye. It stung, a hundred tiny bites.

Hope had given me my answer. Hope was a bitch, same as her sisters, because the Auphe had white hair. They had silver-white hair that burned and bloodied your skin when you snagged a hand in the fall of it as you jerked back their head to cut their throat. It bit and had a texture slick at first touch and then jagged, altogether strange compared to human hair.

I yanked at it, pulling it free from my scalp. It didn't come easy like human hair either. It came stubbornly with a root stained with a clot of blood and a pain that didn't only annoy; it pissed me the hell off. It showed in my eyes. Not from their narrowing in anger, but that the gray of them glittered with small flashes of ember red. They would, wouldn't they? The Auphe had white hair and the Auphe had eyes as red as the Nile had once run in the First Plague of Egypt.

The beginning of the end. There was no stopping it now.

My life, as I knew it, was over.

As one healer had told me: Auphe genes always win.

He didn't say it to be cruel, although Rafferty's bed-side manner was fairly crappy; he said it for two reasons. First, it slipped out, I thought, he was that surprised I looked completely human except for paler skin than normal. Second, it was true. The Auphe had been the apex predator of the entire world for millions of years. They didn't have a recessive gene in them. I might have started out half human, but that hadn't lasted too long. That had shown in ways that weren't visible.

When I was young, I hadn't thought like other kids did. I didn't understand them or people in general. Rules, expectations, right and wrong. None of that came natu-rally. Practicality, expediency—that was what I had been born knowing. For Niko's sake I had memorized the school's rules, society's rules, and for him I followed them when it was convenient.

It wasn't always.

But what did they say? Charged but never convicted? That was good enough for me.

Then I became older. Then I was snatched away for two years to Tumulus Hell, and then I came back ... then, then, then. I couldn't remember those two years, but I'd changed. Age and subconscious trauma, a tanta-lizing good time for all. That's when the occasional bouts of temper started. As a kid, it had never been personal. If you were in my way and I had to punt your balls to the sky to move you, I didn't enjoy it ... much. It just had to be done. After Tumulus and two years of age and raging hormones, I began to appreciate the little things like that. If I had to take down a monster for the good of the neighborhood ... think of the children, right? Why not have fun while you were doing the "right" thing?

On and on marched the Auphe genes overriding my human ones, and there was no stopping it. After the in-crease in violence then came the loss of control now and again . . . and perhaps one or two complete losses of sanity. No big deal, you understand, because I could push those away, make myself forget them.

It was a different game now. The Auphe had always played to fucking win, and their DNA did the same. The difference being as a six-year-old taking Dodgeball to a *Lord of the Flies* level because rules were inexplicable and winning was all that mattered was just a freaking strange-ass kid. Now I was a man, one who ran with the supernatural, the *paien*, and now everyone would see it. Not only smell it, sense it, observe it in the way I moved. No, the time had come when they would *see* it. With less than a glimpse, with a fraction of a glance, they would see.

If they could see it, I would be it.

Remember that pop quiz I'd warned about at the bar?

"It's what's on the inside that counts?"

Wrong.

There was another half Auphe in the world besides me. Grimm. He'd asked me once what would I do when I finally looked as Auphe on the outside as he knew me to be on the inside. He would find that saying hilarious. I mean, he wasn't wrong. Is it fucking hilarious or what? People actually *say* that. It's what's on the inside. . . . What would they say if they knew what actually was on my inside, when the hereditary remains of the first murderer to walk the earth finally destroyed the dwindling human genes of its descendant and showed its true face?

What would they say when someday the red sparks grew like a lethal wildfire in my eyes until there was no gray left at all—only blood and flame?

What would they say when the Auphe inside and outside finally matched? Because that was what was happening. I couldn't change the way I looked and not change the way I *was*. When the outer monster appeared, it would magnify, explode, and raise all fucking hell with the inner me. There was no escaping that. I wouldn't be half Auphe any longer. There'd be no more uneasy partnership with what I wished I was, what I actually was, and what I would soon be. I'd be pure Auphe, and the entire *paien* world including my family and friends knew that would make me a mobile slaughterhouse. Murder walking.

Cal would die and Caliban would be free.

Prisms and splinters of silver and glass rained around my feet. This was about the fifth mirror I'd shattered in my life. What did that add up to? Thirty-five years of bad luck. I laughed, but it wasn't as dark and bitter a laugh as I'd expected. Then again, why cry over milk that had been spilled before I was born, a biblical flood of it from my very moment of conception? I grinned without humor or maybe only the kind of humor a human couldn't see or understand. Time was running out, no matter what the mirrors wanted to charge me.

Thirty-five years of bad luck. Yeah, right. I laughed again. I should live so long.

And everyone else?

Everyone else should pray that I didn't.

3

Goodfellow

Where was I before I was rudely yet inevitably interrupted. Ah . . . yes.

There's a sucker born every minute.

Engrave that on every brain cell you have, if you don't already know it. And if you do not know it, then you haven't got a single brain cell to inscribe. You are brain-dead. Do everyone a favor and find an empty grave to settle into, as that is all you're good for.

In the utmost seriousness, you will not hear any words more wise or more important in your life. Grip them tightly and do not forget. They may save your life someday.

There's a sucker born every minute . . . and you might be one.

I hadn't come up with the saying. That it hadn't been me, Robin Goodfellow, shames me still, but someone beat me to it. I'd no doubt been buying a pair of leather pants at the time. Ah, those were the days. I had said something similar long before that saying made the rounds. Of course I had.

"Pithekous richnei perittomata san anthropoid richnoun chemata."

It was Latin, my second favorite language, for "People throw money like monkeys throw feces." It loses a bit in translation, but it was quite popular, oh, a few thousand years ago. Some of my fellow pucks used it to this day. Most everyone else had forgotten it. How fleeting fame. As quick to come and go as virginity. What can one do . . . but enjoy it while it lasts?

Whatever the reason—I was almost positive it had been leather pants—a human, in fact, had said that, had beat me to it. If there were one thing to admire about humans, aside from their obsession throughout time with all things sexual, it would be their innate grasp of the obvious. They really put it out there, didn't they? The obvious. The sex I was scheduled to think about in seven more minutes left me time now to concentrate on that: the *obvious*.

What was uncelebrated instinct to my kind, mortals had been forced to learn and then had embellished and gilded until it was a monument so massive it pierced the heavens themselves. It wasn't enough to rip off those hobbled by morality; they had to slap a thick coat of sugary icing on it to hide what they'd done. Maybe some sprinkles while you were at it. You had to create an establishment out of it. Stick a franchise on every corner.

The art of the con, when had it become such an acceptable and, worse yet, *legal* career choice? All of that wrapped around one single concept: the blind, the naïve, the Pollyannas . . . the suckers.

Humans, they could take the fun out of anything— even being a used car salesman.

The time I was taking off from running the car lot might inspire me. It could be time for a new career or new for this millennium. Lawyer perhaps. Shakespeare hadn't been wrong there. As a matter of fact, I think that I *was* Shakespeare's lawyer when he wrote "The first thing we do, let's kill all the lawyers." He wasn't wrong. When I'd finished billing him he didn't have a pot to piss in. He didn't even have a coin with which to buy something to drink to create piss.

Those were the days.

I took another swallow of my wine and pulled at my tie with my free hand. I drank beer on the rare occasion—when working a deal with the salt of the earth (of course a forty-five percent interest rate is normal on a car loan. Would I lie to you?) I tried not to choke on my wine on memories of my last sale, at least for a while. Humans. No challenge at all.

I also drank beer with friends, family really, who couldn't afford what I normally imbibed in great quantities and liked to attempt to bring me down to their level via beer swilling, pizza gorging, and intolerably idiotic television in which even the eye candy couldn't save your sanity.

That the attempts actually worked on occasion didn't surprise me. These particular friends had spent lifetimes upon lifetimes returning to wear away at my spectacular taste. I was forced to give credit where credit was due as much as I hated that anyone could manipulate a trickster, much less a supreme trickster such as me. Then again, if I, fully aware, let them do it, was it manipulation at all?

As, despite myself, let them I did.

For a trickster, that was an unfathomable sacrifice. Yet they were my truest and oldest of friends. When you'd lived long enough to forget thousands of years as if they were only a moment and could recall a world long before humans evolved, friends such as those mattered. When they reincarnated time and time again throughout eternity simply to keep me company—or that's how I chose to think of it as everything *is* about me—they more than mattered. Of course my company was incomparable. Tagging after me through the endless years was absolutely understandable.

I took another drink, blind to the exquisite color of the grape. Loyalty, sadly, wasn't everything.

Unfortunately they, unlike me, were the same as all humanity: suckers.

Not in all ways, not even in many ways, but in one very specific way and they never learned. They never learned. *Skata.*

What I was to do about that, I didn't know. Yet.

But I would know, as I was brilliant that way. I took another swallow and raised an eyebrow in appreciation. Oh, excellent. A distraction. Even in a "fulfilling monogamous relationship" or whatever the freaks called it, I was still allowed to look, and look I did.

A dryad swept past me in a scent cloud of apple blossoms and honeysuckle. My seven minutes until pornographic thoughts were to be given their due weren't up yet, but I could push up the timeline and appreciate her lithe lines and exquisite curves. She gave me a coy look that didn't require the bucket of pheromones splashed liberally in the air around her. I gave her my perfected "I would lift you and five of your sisters to sexual nirvana but, despair to the world, my mighty cock is shackled with the chains of fidelity" apologetic expression. Other species and cultures are often astounded by how much a puck can emote in one lowering of a brow combined with one regretful but minute tightening of our lips. Other species and cultures are so dim and dull that I don't know how they exist, not dying of boredom with their childlike and clumsy physical manifestations of emotion. They may as well physically vomit their feelings upon everyone around them. But, as the superior race and creature on this earth, I had to ignore that argument or I'd be along . . . except for other pucks. I shuddered at the notion.

Infinitely worse.

The dryad had shaken her fall of jade green hair and sighed in disappointment at the loss of a sexual experience that would've ruined her for all other trees. I couldn't blame her for her depression clear to be seen as she moved to the far side of the bar laughing with a few nymph friends and cuddling up with an enormously large reddish brown Wolf—a ruse to hide her pain, I knew. I felt mildly guilty and sent a drink her way as an apology for my "condition."

I tucked away the scarlet and silk sliver of arousal as well as the emerald and silver necklace I'd slipped from her neck without her having a clue—you couldn't be the trickster you should be if you didn't keep a larcenous and thieving hand in. I returned my focus to the very expensive wine that they kept behind the bar especially for me. Today had absolutely not been a beer day. Forget that it was what I was expected to drink by those who knew my current fake identity:

Rob Fellows, car salesman extraordinaire, shaking hands, slapping backs, tossing down a brewski with the guys. It was part of the job description. However, gods forbid if Bacchus, who'd finally given up AA as a long-lost cause, found out. To drink a wine before its time was a killing offense in his pickled brain. The shock of a Bud Lite might drain the immortality right out of him. If it didn't, he would boot my unbelievable ass into the next century.

And we didn't want to disappoint the ladies and fine gentleman, now, did we? My ass was a work of art. Damaging it would be like drawing on Michelangelo's *David* with brightly colored markers. A crime against man and any number of pantheons of gods.

If one worshipped a god . . . and that god didn't happen to be me.

Sometimes, when I let myself forget why I'd quit it, which wasn't often, the Fall of Troy saw to that, I missed the god con: the temples, the marble statues of me in all my unclothed glory, the priestesses and priests none of whom were virgins in my service—that should go without saying. I missed the offerings of gold and jewels, honey cakes and wine. Then there was the sound; I've never been able to explain it. The indrawn breath of those who knelt, seeing their god for the first time. It was a softly reverent and a song of adoration for me and me alone. I was their world.

The orgies were nice too.

Very, *very* nice indeed. *Primo. Phantastike. Ausgezeichnet. Spectaculaire.* I took another sip of wine as the bar faded around me and ancient Rome surrounded me with its scents and sounds, the taste of grapes, the songs of my worshippers, and the feel of their warm skin against mine, covering every inch. Soft fingers in my hair, clever fingers cupping my . . .

The feather that dropped in my wine just in time for me to almost drink and choke on it jolted me back to the Ninth Circle—a bar that had not one speck of marble, gold, or honey cakes in it anywhere. *"Kolo,"* I hissed, leaning back from the assault to fish the red-soaked white-and-gold feather out of my glass. "What is wrong with you? Do you attempt to poison all your customers this way?" It wasn't completely out of the question. "Or am I special?"

Naturally I was special, but that had nothing to do with my currently defiled wine. Still, I had been defiled by similar feathers frequently over the last year, defiled in the most positively carnal sense, and I went on to drink the wine with only a shrug.

"That was your orgy face," my attacker said with grim disapproval. "We agreed. You can look all you wish, you can reminisce about the good old days when there was no STD you didn't seek out, but you don't make the orgy face while you do it. Also, is that blood on your collar and a rocket launcher leaning against your stool?"

Which was wholly unfair as I, a puck, could not catch any sexual diseases. Oh, perhaps there had been the one case of the pixie version of chlamydia during which my penis did radiate pink, yellow, and green for a month, but that had been over a thousand years ago at least. I'd been pixie-free since. Considering the size of my cock, causing it to be mistaken for the Aurora Borealis for those thirty days, it was for the best that the glow of rainbow colors passed quickly. Thousands of years didn't change the fact that tourists were annoying as hell, or, as Cal would say, a bitch and a half.

Not to mention that I couldn't go near the ocean without confused whales, dolphins, and other sea life beaching themselves. It had not been a good month.

I hissed in annoyance and gestured imperiously at one of the peris beyond the bar for a glass of water and a cloth to dab at the blood. This was my fifty-sixth favorite shirt. How unbelievably inconsiderate could one be to bleed on Dolce and Gabbana? "Yes, it is a rocket launcher. You might want to dispose of it before Cal returns to work and humps it with the love that dare not speak its name." I flashed a smug grin at the peri leaning across the bar from me. "And you only know that's my orgy face as you were spending your time outside the temples and villas marking down the naughty and nice for a god who didn't even create me."

I pushed my glass toward him for a refill. "In this day and age I believe they'd call that stalking. Romantic really. You with your flaming sword. Me with the only sword I'll ever need." I gave my best salacious smirk. "We could've had so much amazing hate sex if you'd removed that pillar of salt out of your ass sooner."

Dark eyebrows lowered in annoyed menace, but gray-blue eyes were bright with humor and the scar on his jaw tightened, which was a good indicator he was fighting back a smile. "I was only showing common sense, you randy goat. As they say, you lie down with dogs, you get up with pixie herpes. And where did you get the rocket launcher?"

"It was not herpes," I snapped, keeping my voice low. No one gossiped like *paien*. "And you weren't hanging about then with your schoolgirl crush and sermons on how to remove the greed, lust, avarice, sloth, gluttony, fornication—basically all the fun from my life."

Ishiah, retired angel and full-time pain in my ass, but mostly in the very best of ways, studied me and did smile this time. "I always had an eye out for you, Robin, no matter where you were."

Monogamy, it was a hard road to walk, particularly considering the rest of the puck race thought me perverse and disgusting for it, but at times like this, I couldn't regret it. Over a year now and I wouldn't change it.

"Always?" This time my grin was wider and far more wicked. "Was I often nude when you spied on me? How did that make your angel naughty parts feel? More holy? Less holy? Not holy at all?"

"You know how you made them feel last night." He deposited the freshly filled wineglass in front of me. "Don't fish for compliments."

"Don't fish . . ." I shook my head and dropped my chin in my hand. "Three thousand years since you've shown up in my life and it's like you don't know me at all."

"Yet I know when you're brooding. Which is worrying. I sent Cal home early, so I was hoping for a brood-free rest of the night." He pulled back pale blond hair into a short tail and tied it off as around us the bar hummed with the gruff tones of werewolves, the sibilant tongue of lamias and succubae, the disheartened bubbling of *vodyanoi* who still smelled of the East River. It was a typical night.

"I wasn't brooding. I was thinking of orgies. You yourself said so," I contradicted, and took a large swallow of wine that showed no respect for the vintage at all.

"In between moping. Why are you moping?" he demanded with a scowl no one, not Hades the ice-hearted god of the underworld himself, could call sympathetic. Ishiah was correct, though. He did know me, and he knew that thrown a line of sympathy, I'd use it to verbally tie him in daisy chains of denial and skip the conversation altogether. He might be an ex-angel, but I was much older than him and had walked the earth a million years before his God had stumbled across the place. My tongue was a deadly weapon and not always in an enjoyable manner.

Although ninety-nine percent of the time it certainly was.

"I'm taking a break from the business," I said abruptly. He'd find out sooner or later. It might as well be now.

I'd put my best manager in charge of the car lot until I returned—if I returned, another shark like me . . . but one in puppy dog clothing. Soulful brown eyes, a sheepish grin, and an "aw, shucks" accent had little old ladies and big hulking men falling all over themselves to throw money at him. They never got quite close enough to see that the flesh of his last meal hadn't cleared his tonsils yet. He was wasted on humanity. He'd have made a great trickster—buy a lemon, learn an important life lesson.

"Hmm." Ishiah leaned closer to ring a fingernail against the crystal of the wineglass, then closer yet still until I felt his warm breath against the sensitive skin behind my ear. "Are we celebrating you temporarily shedding the responsibility of a moral, decent, and contributing member of society or at least the closest you can possibly come?" He tilted his head, and there was the sensation of the singing nerves of teeth scraping across the line of my jaw. Not quite a bite, but not quite the absence of one either. It caused my first genuine smile of the day, and I suspect he knew it. Easing back far too soon, he raised his eyebrows to wait for my answer.

"Not quite. I do sell lemons, but I do not pay taxes, which removes the moral, decent, and contributing part of your question. And it's not a vacation, as much as I'd like to spend a month or two on several nude beaches." There was only a little mockery in the portion about nude beaches as I knew Ish would sooner fight another rebellion in Heaven than display himself on the most entertaining of beaches. I swiveled back and forth on the stool to give Ishiah a broad and no doubt lecherous smile. I can dial back the lechery, if my life depends on it in the utmost sense of the word, but that wasn't often. And with the pictures of beaches and a naked angel in my head, now wasn't one of those times.

It wasn't my fault. He *had* started it.

"Then if it's not a vacation, what are you planning?" He folded his arms to lean on the scratched and stained wood of the bar top beside me.

I felt my dirty grin melt away along with my momentary good mood and dipped my finger into my glass. Sketching the symbol for infinity on the bar in a red that shouldn't have looked like blood yet did, I studied it and then exhaled harshly. "It's time ... or it will be soon."

He gave a dark frown. It was more for me, I thought, than for what was coming. He knew how attached I was. "Are you certain?"

"Over a thousand lives watching them die now? Yes, I'm certain. Especially this time." I stared at the symbol for all that is and all that will always be and was not comforted in the slightest. Reincarnation wasn't the consolation one imagined.

"Do they know?" He shifted, a thoughtful expression crossing his face to disappear as quickly as it had come. "Cal was here earlier, working. He got banged up a bit and I sent him home. He seemed ... not tense at first. Distracted perhaps. But after the fight, more of a disagreement compared to most nights, he was very much on edge—as if something happened. Something I missed. And usually when he's threatening to cut someone in half with an axe, he's more cheerful."

"Sometimes they sense it." As many lives as they'd lived, they should. I exhaled and shook my head, as when they did suspect what was coming, the end never changed. "Sometimes they don't. It doesn't matter if they do or not. They never fight to retreat from it. They always fight their way to throw themselves through it. Warriors. In almost every life, they are warriors," I scoffed, "and as such they have no brain cells, only skulls sloshing with honor and adrenaline-fueled death wishes." I wiped away the double loop sketched in wine with a gesture more careless and violent than was necessary.

"And there never is a way through it?" A heavy hand rested on the nape of my neck. "Or a way to convince them to step back, just once?"

"No." I bowed my head and felt the heat of his palm sink through the muscle and into my spine itself. This was the first time in all my life that I hadn't been alone in this. "Not yet. A puck who can't talk someone out of certain death—over nine hundred times at least. I disgust myself."

And I had tried. In the names of all the gods and goddesses that had once ruled, I had tried. But Niko, in all his variations, never lacked an unbreakable conviction in whatever cause he chose, and Cal . . . Cal had never been able to let anything go. And that was in addition to his almost gleeful lack of self-preservation. If reincarnation was meant to teach them lessons, they were very slow students.

This time was the worst of them all. In other lives, I'd seen ways out before, not always, but fifty percent of the time at least. They involved cowardice, desertion, backstabbing, and a wholly self-centered sense of self—all good things to pucks—but all things Niko refused to be a part of, and where Niko went, Cal never failed to follow. That had been before. Now the battle was coming to them, not vice versa. They could run forever and still might not escape it. And they wouldn't run. When they were boys they had, when they hadn't known what they were running from, but they were men now. They'd decided their running days were over. No matter how it all ended.

Selfish *bastards*. Running wouldn't work this time, but could they not at least *try*?

Although there had been the one time Cal had been chosen to be a eunuch for Queen Jezebel's harem, and he had no qualms about running then, the ass.

Niko and I had been on horses when we rescued him from the palace guard. He'd started running and hadn't stopped until we were half a mile outside the city before swinging up on the horse to settle behind Niko. I'd laughed harder than I had in ten years. The crazed son of a bitch who backed down from nothing and no one, yet at several points he had out-*run* our horses who were at a full gallop.

This from the man who'd once told David regarding Goliath, "Hey, Jewish kid, I'm bored. You want me to take this asshole for you?"

Perhaps if I hired someone to threaten to castrate him now, he would run. I sighed. No, he would merely shoot them. Things weren't so simple these days.

The warm weight of Ishiah's hand slid down to the middle of my back. Without my noticing, he'd moved around the bar to stand behind me. "But Niko and Cal, they never knew before—that death wasn't the end. That they came back. Time and time again. That you would be waiting for them. That you miss them when they're gone, questionable taste aside. That they need to do right by you. Perhaps that can be the difference. Perhaps this time you can convince them they need more than someone fighting at their side. They need planning, plotting, scheming. They need what you do best."

Angels of the Lord—not mine, but regardless—were made to be convincing with voices that rang with faith and truth. Unfortunately I'd been born with feelings of a devious nature that I was forced to admit would've filled me with cold chills at that faith and truth, if they hadn't warred with and lost against how unbelievable the sex was with Ishiah. Not to mention the lust, the blatantly carnal desire . . .

The new handcuffs we'd just used last night.

"It's your orgy face again." He grimaced.

"No, that face was for you and you alone." I gave him a sharp-edged grin.

He returned it with enthusiasm. I was proud. It wasn't everyone who could tempt an angel and then corrupt him thoroughly after he retired. "Smug bastard," he grumbled, sitting on the stool beside me, shoulder to shoulder. "What is coming for them, then? Who is it?" he asked. "I can guess, but I do hate the mockery that inspires in a trickster if I guess wrong."

I tapped one finger against the bar. "Grimm and the Bae." Caliban's utterly insane half Auphe cousin and his offspring he'd created to replace the now extinct Auphe. He'd been out of sight for months now. He'd had time to heal from our last battle and was more than past due back to torture Cal some more. I was surprised he'd waited this long

My second finger tapped down. "The Vigil, which by the way is where I obtained the rocket launcher." I'd left the sniper rifle. It was garbage. The Mossad would've turned up their noses at it. "One of them was on the roof across the way about an hour ago waiting for Cal to leave." Since Iahiah had sent him home early, the Vigil had missed him. Luck . . . ever a lady for me. I nudged the weapon with my foot. "Boys and their big bad toys. He had more than this and was, as they say, armed for bear." I'd disposed of him. As big and bad as he'd thought he was with his portable armory, he wasn't close to being as bad as I was. "Oddly, he was going commando."

"Carrying that, it isn't a stretch to think he was in commando mode," Ishiah replied, handing the weapon over the bar to one of his fellow peris to hide from sight.

"Hm? Oh no. I meant he was going commando as in no briefs or boxers. Curious, that. If you're going into battle, one would think you'd desire to keep your package of goods tightly secured and safe," I contemplated.

"You mean he was . . . Why did you even look?" Ishiah demanded, face flushing with embarrassment or anger. With an ex-angel, who knew which emotion it was?

"Curiosity mainly." What a bizarre question . . . to a

puck at any rate. "Also I was searching for hidden ID. Did you know that I once smuggled over the border Gabriel's Trumpet in my—" Ishiah's hand slapped over my mouth. As if that wouldn't be ludicrous if true. I did need to invest huge amounts more time toward developing his sense of humor.

That was currently beside the point, however. As the man on the roof had been human, and the only humans who knew about *paien* or the Auphe were the Vigil and the Rom. The Rom, all of them now, were aware of Cal and Niko and thanks to a decimated Sarzo Clan. They knew to stay away from them. It was easy enough to guess, ID or no—that meant he was Vigil.

Cal's understandable, but very real, fuckup, of flashing an especially nasty piece of the supernatural world in broad daylight on a sidewalk of humans. And humans, aside from the rare exception, didn't know about us. They couldn't know. If they did, they would kill us. They would try to kill all of us, every last *paien* on this world. That was how man was. If you didn't understand it, kill it. If they were more powerful than you, build even more horrible weapons and absolutely kill it. But the war would be bloody and the humans wouldn't escape unscathed, not from us or from their shiny new instruments of hell.

Unscathed or not, win they still would by sheer numbers alone.

The Vigil existed to prevent all of that: discovery and the most likely ensuing war. Naturally, if it came down to war, they were an all-human thousand-year organization with more information, and actually accurate information, on *paien* than *paien* themselves probably had, which would not be in our best interest. Preventing a war *was* in everyone's best interest, however, but ours most of all. They had not ever been happy with Cal, but he'd proved useful in wiping out the Auphe and he kept under the radar, so they were satisfied.

I wondered if they knew about Grimm and his Bae offspring. Unlikely. Grimm was clever. If he took over the world, it would be done before anyone knew it had happened.

Cal wasn't like Grimm. Nik had been in danger and if Cal had thought anything at all before gating in front of those people, it would've been "watch the light show and fuck you and the three-legged donkey you staggered in on." I understood it. I knew saving Niko was all that mattered to him at that moment, but the Vigil would not understand or care. They wouldn't be happy with Cal now. They would conclude that he had to go. They weren't entirely wrong that Cal had been foolish and reckless, but, same as Cal, I didn't care. It had been to save Niko. The Vigil could kiss my superb ass.

Cal was my friend and I would do anything to keep him. It wouldn't be the first war I'd fought in. It wouldn't even break the top two hundred.

Before I could tell Ishiah about threat number three, a wave of terrified howling erupted, filling the bar and the night air outside. Perfect timing. That one I'd expected, and expected now or yesterday, but close enough to the same. Every Wolf was headed for the door in a panic, clawing at the wood to escape, smashing through the small window to run, to flee the city before it was too late. They were the packless ones. The subcontractors for the Kin, better known as the werewolf Mafia, and now, from the citywide howls, they were nothing. The hunted. Prey. The new Alpha had risen.

Caliban's ex-homicidal fiend with benefits had finally forced all the Kin to submit. Or die. The kid truly did know how to pick the chicks.

My third finger hit the bar by Ishiah. "And Delilah." I

had informants, but I also had a sense for a rise of power—the smell of it, the taste of it, the recognition of the perfect time for it—all those and more. All had told me the same.

I'd seen this coming as well. Tricksters aren't too successful if they don't keep their eyes open to squirrel away nuggets of information to use for cons, for blackmail, or to sell. I'd noticed the bitter infighting in the Kin, I knew who the cause of it was, and I knew who I'd put my money on coming out on top . . . and when. The ruthless, the crazed sociopath, they win every time.

I knew because I'd done the same before many times, long ago.

Sat on a hundred thrones.

"Wonderful. I'm thinking my Kin protection money just doubled." Ishiah already had a shot glass of tequila in his hand, and he tapped it to my glass. He threw it back, then grunted, "I hate to say it, but what a bitch."

That she was.

But to give credit where credit was due . . . she did excel at it.

All hail the new queen.

4

Caliban

Around three a.m., an hour or so after the Kin howl of triumph, Nik found me as I was tying knots in the top of garbage bags and growling with a furry tail popped out of one weak seam. Stuffing it back in, I reached for the duct tape on the floor beside where I crouched and sealed the heavy-duty—my ass—garbage bag full of werewolf. "Hey, Cyrano," I said absently, not bothering to look up as yet another seam split. Goddammit. I waved a hand toward the kitchen breakfast bar. "I made you breakfast."

He closed the door and locked it behind him, no asking how I knew it was him and not some random flesh eater. My brother knew I could smell him a block away in the city—five miles away in the countryside. The Auphe gift that keeps on giving. A predator's sense of smell was the least of it.

Glancing down at the two bagged but not tagged

Wolves I was wrapping up, he raised his eyebrows. "I suppose I do not have to ask if you heard the Howl." The call passed from Wolf to Wolf to Wolf, traveling miles, to cities, states, then the entire country, carrying the news. The Kin belonged to Delilah now, and Delilah was a stone-cold killer. Stay out of NYC. That was the Howl.

Howl with a capital H because it was like that Disney movie with all the Dalmatians. Hundred and one, right? I paused a second and concentrated on the hazy childhood memory of that.

Good old Disney, who lied psychotically about nearly every supernatural creature they stuck in a movie. Set the bar high when you were a kid and then swung that same bar at your skull when you grew up and faced the real deal. Like mermaids. Cute on TV. In real life they have miniature shark teeth, drown you, tuck your body into an underwater nook, and when you're good and decomposed, they eat you.

Thank you, Disney, for the scar of that mermaid bite mark on my back.

The Howl seemed to be fairly accurate so far, and that was something. "Yeah, the 'Twilight Howl,' or was it Bark?" I grinned up at him this time. "I think it's a little more homicidal with Mafia werewolves than cute and fluffy spotted dogs." I finished taping the last bag.

Delilah and I, while we'd once been fiends with benefits, had been on the lookout for an opportunity to kill each other for a while now. I, because she'd tried to slaughter my friends and brother. Delilah, as she was the single Wolf who didn't mind screwing an Auphe. Rather liked it, I was pretty sure, as it was dangerous and Delilah loved danger. None of the other Wolves approved, though, including her now all-female Mafia. They worshipped her for taking down the top male Alpha and for being All Wolf, but they had their limits. Fucking an Auphe was one of them. Nobody loved the Auphe. If this was a Lifetime made-for-TV movie, the sobbing would abound.

Delilah would try to kill me. Sooner or later. We'd both been working on killing each other for months now. She'd get around to it personally one day. She'd taken over the entire werewolf Mafia of NYC and she had things to do. Killing me was one of them, without question, but down the list some. Instead she settled for sending me three newly anointed female Kin to do it for her. She knew it wouldn't work, didn't want it to work, as she wanted to do it herself. It would be seen as an effort on her part until then.

And Delilah, hell, she might be able to pull that off. I was good, but so was she.

I'd always known how good she was and smart, but it hit home with what happened before Niko had come home. I knew she'd suggested it. No other Wolf would've thought of it.

What had caught me off guard was it didn't happen that way. It didn't. They don't knock on the door. They'd have broken in through the second-floor window to slink in. They'd have tried to surprise me outside before I got through the door. They hadn't done those things, the normal things . . . in our world. They'd showed up half an hour later and knocked.

Me? I'd been stupid. I hadn't bothered to inhale their scent when I'd opened the door, because monsters? Monsters don't knock. Or so I was under the impression.

I'd opened the door, Glock in hand. I was perplexed at what stood there, then caught on, and couldn't have been less in the mood for this shit. Fur and round gold eyes that belonged in the forest instead was hovering above a sidewalk. Yeah, I'd been stupid, no lying to myself about that, but not completely idiotic. I'd been prepared. A human knocking at your door can kill you if he's armed well enough.

The three of them, in varied stages of wolf, had rushed through and taken me to the floor. There were claws, fangs, and growling—it reminded me of some absolutely unbelievable sex Delilah and I had had more than once. You can have good memories whether the person involved is a psycho killing nightmare or not. Strange, but true. I'd been relieved none of the Wolves were silver-blond like Delilah. When I put her down, I'd do it because it needed to be done. I didn't want substitutes that I could pretend were her. When I ended her life, I wanted to see it in her eyes, no one else's. She'd tried to kill people who mattered to me, *everyone* who mattered to me, to gain points with the Kin. Forget what we'd had before, I wanted to see the realization, fear, and haze of death in the red-gold of her setting sun eyes—clouding as I watched. The other Wolves didn't, wouldn't matter.

The first one who had been on me had dark-brown hair, to her waist, a filmy down of it on her face that crept down her entire body, which was easy to see as her clothes were in tatters and rags on the floor as she'd shifted further into Wolf. She had spring grass green eyes and claws longer than her fingers. She was beautiful in the way nature alone can create beauty. The fact that she'd been trying to bury her claws in my throat was too bad. I shot her in the head, between those amazing pale green eyes.

Dark dishwater blond had been the second one. Another All Wolf, capable of only partial shifting, most of them. She didn't have claws, but her fangs angled toward me would've made a shark piss the Atlantic. I'd shot her in the mouth three times and finished her with a coup de grace to the back of her head when she'd turned to either run or crawl inch by inch to breathe her last. Wolves weren't my favorite monsters, but leaving one to skulk off to die in a corner, I wouldn't do that.

Monsters of almost any kind don't deserve that.

The last had hair the color of the darkest ink, eyes round and pale blue as barely bloomed flax. Except for her eyes, you'd have thought her human, not a Wolf or a member of the All Wolf cult at all. Nails, neat and tidy, the same color as her eyes, grew eight inches at least and had stabbed toward my own eyes. I'd kicked her back and aimed my gun at her chest. Her small but perfect breasts were covered by a silk shirt the same blue that she coveted elsewhere . . . as were her pants and her boots spangled with sky-colored topaz stones, and then there was her gun. It wasn't every day you saw a Wolf with a gun. Even her gun had been blue. I knew some guns came in sunshine yellow or bright pink, Rugers, Walthers, Mossbergs, Colts, and Tauruses, but light blue? Not available. Custom job, I'd swear on it.

"That must've cost big bucks," I'd said to her as she stood over me while I lay on my back where the first Wolf had knocked me flat.

"Money is money, but style is much more. How one represents one's self."

I suppose that was why she hadn't shifted any further. This chick loved her clothes, and destroying them if she didn't have to . . . as in having a gun . . . wasn't going to happen. That gun, by the way, was a Ruger. I'd recognized it in less time than she'd taken to aim at my chest.

Mine, not as colorful, was aimed at her head—same as the first two. Practice, practice, practice. "Style doesn't mean much to me." I tightened my finger on the trigger. "And I represent myself with my aim, which means more than blue boots, shiny stones, and a custom-painted gun."

She could have shot me in the chest and I might have died; chances are I would've died, but not necessarily instantly depending on her aim. I also could have fired simultaneously, as practice was my life. That practice would've put a bullet in her brain. She'd die, no way out of that. I might live. I might not, but she wouldn't know one way or the other—she wouldn't have known if she'd done her Alpha Delilah proud or not, as she'd be dead.

Disappointing Delilah was one thing. Disappointing Delilah and not living to inform her of the situation was worse. Delilah would want to know. Poor Delilah, too busy taking over the Kin and killing those she didn't trust or think worthwhile, that wasn't leaving her time to kill me herself. Just yet.

"If I get you first," I asked casually, "can I have your boots? My neighbor loves all that sparkly crap like that."

She snarled, a bizarrely upper-class snarl—I'd not seen an upper-class Wolf before, and I'd thought it was more over the thought of me looting her boots from her dead body than killing her.

"You can always run?" As that would be one less body for me to clean up, and with the day I'd had, it would be worth it.

She didn't run. She retracted her claws, the fingernail polish a little worse for wear, tucked her gun in her boot, and then turned her back on me and walked away. Damn, she had balls. I hadn't minded and not only over the cleaning-up issue. It was Delilah I wanted dead, not the other female Wolves she'd gathered to her. If anything, I applauded them. The Kin refused female Alphas, refused those of the All Wolf cult. The Lupas deserved to rule. If you weren't the unbeatable killer Delilah was, the males would have the female Wolves in strip clubs or worse. They'd been disgusted by the All Wolf, considering them the lowest of the low. They deserved what the female

Wolves gave them. I hoped it was nasty and inventive. Knowing Delilah, it would be.

I hadn't thought twice about that.

I didn't bother reliving the fight a second time. It hadn't been worth reliving the first.

"Delilah didn't waste any time sending a few messengers over in case I did miss the Howl. Messengers, assassins, whatever. I don't think she was that serious, though, only sending three. This is most likely revenge for the fact that the birthday present I gave her when we were screwing was a bag of doggy chews." I nudged the body curled in the Hefty bag on the floor. "We need more garbage bags. Extraduty. I had to double-bag these."

"You think?" Niko hung up his long leather coat with care on the wall-mount hook. His holster that was made to hold his katana along his back, under that coat, and out of sight he leaned against the wall. He slept with the katana under the bed. I didn't judge. I slept with a gun under my pillow and a knife under my mattress. And I had, at least with the knife, since I'd been ten years old.

"Think? About the revenge for the doggy chews or the garbage bags?"

"You should've killed her, you know," he said, shaking his head at the garbage bags of dead Wolf. "Or let me. We all knew about her ruthlessness and her ambition. We all knew this day would come when the Kin would bow before her."

I was actually rather proud of her for that. The Kin did not accept female Alphas and they did not accept All Wolf Alphas. Delilah was as female as they came and I didn't regret all the times she'd proved that to me. I didn't know why people, even the Kin, forget the female of any species is the most dangerous. They are treacherous and fearless and won't hesitate for a second to do what has to be done. Rules are for the weak in their eyes.

Delilah was also All Wolf, the speciest movement that worked to prove that werewolves needed to drop the "were," lose the ability to shift to human, and go back to what they'd been before evolution took that "looking like humans part of the time will fool them and let us catch and eat them faster" branch. All Wolf rejected evolution's logic there. They wanted to be all wolf, all the time, no human taint. All Wolves only bred with other All Wolves to up the wolf genetic quotient every time. The results were werewolves that mostly couldn't shift all the way to human. They were stuck halfway between human and wolf when they moved among people, with furry ears, gold eyes, sharp teeth, all usually concealed by hoodies. They didn't mind. They had a goal, and in another hundred, five hundred, a thousand years, they'd get there. But for now, what Delilah had done. . . .

Un-fucking-precedented.

A female All Wolf Kin Alpha, along with the enormous number of all-female All Wolves she'd spared when taking out a random pack. It was very Amazonian, and if I'd watched *Xena* when I was a little kid, which I didn't—fuck you very much—I'd think that was pretty goddamn hot.

"I should've killed her sooner," I agreed. I'd had at least two wide-open opportunities and every intention of doing it. She'd betrayed me, after all, and while I was used to that, no big deal really, she'd betrayed my brother and my friends, and that shit didn't fly. "I wish I'd killed her." And I did. For all that she fascinated me—that was nothing compared to protecting my own. "But something always came up. I hesitated the first time, for fucking old times' sake, I guess." I grinned. "Literally. With the fucking, in case you missed that."

Nik, long dark blond braid swaying with the movement, swatted me on the back of the head as he walked by to the kitchen. "Yes, I believe I did 'get that,' foul-mouthed brat."

"And the second time we were fighting something bigger and badder than her and we needed her help." I stood from my crouch and gave one bag a solid kick. It stayed whole. God bless duct tape. "But now? Puppy love is over. I'd take her out in a second, if . . ." I was fighting the urge not to. As much as I told myself I would take her out for what she'd tried to do to my family, that nothing and no one could stop me, I was lying to myself.

I couldn't. Not now. I'd waited too long.

Investigating a covered plate he'd pulled from the oven set at low heat, Nik caught my gaze. His eyes were the same gray as mine—minus the irregular come-and-go streaks of Auphe red—and I couldn't wait for that conversation. I'd started physically, fucking *physically* turning into one of the worst monsters that ever lived. Homicidal insanity couldn't be far behind. How was your day?

"You would?" He was testing me. He had been my entire life.

"You know I would and I should have already, back then, screw her help." I folded my arms and leaned against the back of the couch, my sweatpants and T-shirt threadbare and my mind almost equally so after what I'd seen in the mirror.

"And I know you caught my 'if.' It's too late," I added. "Delilah is more than the Kin Alpha. She's the leader of the All Wolf movement, and the Lupa rebellion." Lupas were what wolves had come to call the all-female packs. "If I kill her, all her brainwashed flunkies will hunt us down. And from the howl"—which had covered the entirety of New York City and much farther—"there are

more of them than even we could possibly handle." She
must've been recruiting on the sly from Kin packs in
other major cities. Delilah was buckets of crazy, but she
was astounding when it came to strategy.

Niko reached under the bar and pulled a stool to the
kitchen side so he could sit and face me. "That's true.
There are too many, but I'm surprised you thought of
the consequences to that extent." He pointed a fork at the
bagged Big Bad Wolves surrounding me. "Especially as
she sent you a personal message." He looked down at his
uncovered plate and gave a curious sniff. Niko was only
human—"only" meaning "the most dangerous human
alive," a human who had, per a mouthy puck, lived a thousand lives, all of them as warriors, one of them as Achilles
himself. And wasn't that strange? Niko was not only reincarnated from Achilles, but he was also descended from
him. He was descended from himself. It made my head
hurt thinking about it.

The result was worth it, though. My brother was a born
fighting machine. But that didn't matter when it came to
casseroles. Although Niko had somehow carried lifetimes
of fighting, experience compounded into one of the more
lethal and deadly men around in this particular existence,
his nose was still a plain human nose. Larger than average, yeah, but that didn't mean it worked any better.

"Consider it an early breakfast or a late night snack,
whichever, but it's a breakfast casserole," I explained.
Once I heard the Howl, I'd known he'd be home fairly
quickly to keep the wolf from our door, so to speak.
"One half is Spanish with tomatoes, free-range eggs, chil-
ies, and the usual. The other half, since you've been
swinging back and forth between vegetarian and vegan
lately, is a lot of tofu and soy masquerading as cheese,
meat, eggs, and so on." Killing Wolves and cooking all
within an hour, was I talented or what?

Nonplussed, Niko glanced warily at me and took two bites, one of each side. "It's . . . good."

I should've been insulted, but, hell, I'd been known to set Pop-Tarts on fire and not the kind of combustion that a fire extinguisher can put out, but full-on NYFD aiming hoses, firemen staggering out covered in blackened soot, and all looking at me horrified as if I'd walked out of the pages of a Stephen King book. I wasn't a fire starter. I was forgetful, and timers weren't worth my attention or they confused me. Whatever. Suck my dick.

"Now tell me who actually made this." Nik took another bite, a large one, and I counted the whole attempt as a success.

"I did. I took lessons." I ducked my head, half-embarrassed, and stared down at garbage bag number one—the brown, green-eyed Wolf, would've been great at frontal assault, but with a gun jammed in your face, great becomes useless. She was the one with the enormous claws and stuck that way thanks to the All Wolf interbreeding. I'd idly wondered at the time how she opened pickle jars with paws and claws instead of hands.

Considering what I'd seen in the bathroom mirror, I should've asked her.

I cleared my throat and continued. "Lucy . . . Lucienne, she's a chef . . . next door taught me how a couple weeks ago. I thought it'd mean more to you if I was the one who cooked it." It had taken a week and a half exactly to get right, but I'd known for weeks, hadn't I? I'd felt it coming. The darkness that was a tsunami aimed at Nik and me, the wave twenty stories high. It brought death. It brought the end.

I didn't know how I was aware that our time or at least mine in this life was coming to an end. I had no idea why I could feel it or be this convinced, but I could. It felt like déjà vu.

I'd had no real visible sign or hint this was all coming—the Lupa Wolves ascending over the city—I'd completely missed it despite the fact that Delilah's fondest birthday wish was my guts on a platter. That my Auphe side was becoming external and would inevitably drag the inner core of me to match, I'd only noticed tonight. I'd always known in the past that Grimm, with a bowl of popcorn, would show up eventually whenever it did happen to catch my physical side show. Whenever I turned, he would try to turn me, then full Auphe, again, either to his side or an even more ruthless side, my side. I hadn't, however, known that time was now. I hadn't known specifically any of this until now, thanks to one silver hair. I wasn't shocked at my obliviousness; I wasn't that observant unless something was currently chewing through my abdomen to get to the tasty parts.

The only thing that I had noticed was that Goodfellow had been giving me some extremely pointed and intense stares when I wasn't looking . . . and when I was. That was more terrifying than the Grim Reaper himself knocking at my door. Not counting *that* weirdness—and I tried very hard not to—I'd not seen anything, but I'd felt something in my gut all the same. Deep within, my subconscious, home to the more Auphe pieces of me, might have noticed something my conscious hadn't. The silver hadn't shown up in my hair yet, but my Auphe genes felt it coming. Noticed enough to give me a warning.

Playtime is over.

The Auphe in me celebrated its true self taking over, and it mourned I was determined to stop it with my death being a Black Friday Sale deal with appeal. As the Auphe in me was the main problem, it could take its woe and suck it up.

The only bright spot in this was that when I died, I was dragging that part of me kicking and screaming with me. The Auphe died with me. Grimm would be around, but he was still half with no grasp of what a true Auphe was. I could screw him and screw the Auphe in me. With that somewhat happily vengeful thought, I moved away from the couch and propped elbows on the breakfast bar and watched my brother eat. Besides, "over" was a relative term. The feeling of dread didn't come with a convenient timer to help me out. I did have to die—the mirror couldn't be denied—but who knew how long I had? It could be weeks, months, maybe if I was lucky even a year, depending on how long I could keep control. I might have to go the hoodie route myself depending on how quickly my hair and eyes changed, but if a Wolf whose hands were stuck in mutated paws that couldn't open pickle jars could pull it off, so could I.

I couldn't depend on luck, though. I'd learned that before my ABCs. That meant that I needed to do all I could for Nik before it was too late. I couldn't convince him my end wasn't his. That had been certain since the days when my first word had been his name and my first wobbling toddler steps had been toward him, not toward the woman who had sold her womb and had despised what had slid out of it.

If I couldn't convince him to let me go alone—and I knew that was nonnegotiable in all the ways that there were ways—then I could make sure his last days were the best I could make them. Voilà ... breakfast, which was much more difficult than simply killing something for him. I knew he'd appreciate that the effort of the first far exceeded the effort of the latter.

"Lucy taught me to make it. I had to pay her, singed my damn fingers over and over. And the wretched, evil tofu. Just looking at that crap made me want to ..." I shut up. This was a present. A gift, and you didn't ruin one of those by bitching. "Anyway, she's a helluva lot meaner than you. I had to learn fast if I wanted to keep my fingers. So it had better be the best breakfast casserole you've ever had."

"It is. I so solemnly swear." This time he pointed the fork with a piece of red and yellow dripping goo at my forehead and the now-cleaned shallow gash. "Don't tell me you're docked another week's pay or we may have to live off your casserole for the next two weeks." Then his lips curved wickedly as his eyes narrowed slightly. "Hmm. I'm glad you're not vain, baby brother. It looks like you're going gray already."

Shit. I grabbed a handful of hair on each side of my head and pulled them forward. There it was, on the right this time. Another single silver strand that I knew hadn't been there two hours ago when I shattered the bathroom mirror. So much for waiting until after Nik's meal to break the news. After a quick jerk and a sharp pain, I placed the white hair between us on the sand-colored countertop. Blood smudged the root the same as it had with the first one. Wasn't that the Auphe all over? You couldn't even rip a handful of their hair free without a battle to the bloody death.

Niko frowned at the strand before running his finger over it lightly, promptly losing most of the Greek-Rom olive tint to his skin. I didn't blame him. I knew what he had felt—the unnatural bite and scrape of unseen barbs. If I hadn't been born already Auphe-pale, I'd have lost a little color too.

"Cal?"

"I know." Shrugging, I sat down heavily on a stool of my own. I dropped a more or less triangular-shaped piece of mirror I'd retrieved from the bathroom floor onto the counter. You only figure out you're going to need a mirror after you've broken the only one you own. I added, "I first saw it at work a few hours ago. I had some red in my eyes too." I smirked a little, because, hell, at this point, why not? "You know, the kind that Visine doesn't get out? A few flecks in each iris, but they disappeared once my enormous initial freak-out faded."

I pushed the fragment of mirror, facedown, to and fro. "It's okay, Cyrano," I assured him earnestly. As earnest as I could be. It wasn't an emotion I used often, but I needed it now. "Auphe genes always win. We've known that forever now, right?"

Not forever as other people would think it, but for a few years. And in our life a few years was practically forever.

My brother stared at me blankly, the lines of his shoulders and jaw as tense as I'd ever seen them. I should've kept my mouth shut, I thought with vicious recrimination. I should've lied for all that we rarely ever lied to each other. Hadn't since we were kids, but he shouldn't have to hear this. He shouldn't have to know. Wasn't it enough that I did? Then again, he was going to see it, see me change sooner or later, and how to explain that away? Sometimes there are no options. That should've made me feel better.

It didn't.

Nik stayed frozen that way for one excruciatingly long moment, long enough for my gut to roil in a riptide of rage and grief for him. It wasn't fair and it wasn't right, for all that we had known it was coming someday. Like the world itself—it wasn't *fair*. Nik who thought he could fix anything for his brother, but he knew this . . . no one could fix this. He shouldn't blame himself for not doing the impossible. It wasn't . . . it wasn't . . . My inner fury faded somewhat as I saw it. I saw him. I saw all the tension in him melt away as if it had never been. In an instant, he went from stone to as relaxed as he'd been minutes before. Eyes warm, he gave me a rueful smile that said that life was no different now than it had been yesterday or the day before—and it wasn't.

My brother, he knew everything. And he knew this too. He knew how it was and how it'd always been. Our whole lives had been lived as if each day were our last.

This was the same.

It didn't mean he'd give up; Nik didn't have that in him. But he wouldn't insist on carrying the weight alone like he once would have, and he wouldn't let it break him. We'd both learned our lesson there.

He continued with his breakfast, ordering casually, "Stop pulling them out. You'll end up bald. Not to mention that it's unsanitary, especially when I'm trying to eat." Unsanitary. Not the end of us or possibly the end of the world. It was unsanitary. Of course it was.

"There is some good news. I'm not rabid on the inside. I feel more like I did years ago. If I had to look like an Auphe on the outside but get to stay human on the inside, it'd be worth it. Face it, neither one of us knows exactly what'll happen. But anything is better than unsanitary, right?" I wiped a hand across my mouth and nose to cover my amused and relieved snort.

Niko disregarded all sanitary issues as he went on after me without pause. "Tomorrow . . . today rather . . . we have to check out the new drug." The drug, epinephrine, was Niko's idea based on my reactions in the past and was meant to return me to a somewhat more Auphe state, in a way. It was ironic, but in our lives more than somewhat necessary and an Auphe talent that was as useful as deadly. We were concentrating on useful, but I'd rather think about it later, as I had plenty to think about now. More than enough. I'd consider the pros and cons of it for the tenth time when I used it, and that was hours yet. Sleep came first.

"Then we have that job chasing down a *Bakeneko*.

You'll enjoy it. They can throw fireballs and unhinge their jaws like a python to swallow a human whole. They can walk upright on their hind legs if they desire. Interesting creature." Man-eaters who could throw fireballs? Niko wasn't giving me a hard way to go. This was almost a present. He knew that I would have a good time. "Although this one is younger, not as strong or large as an adult, and tends to eat children."

That was not a present, but if we killed it, we'd save some future victims. There would be kids who'd live to grow up; that was something. Not to discount the fireballs. I wanted to see the fireballs.

"I do enjoy fire," I confirmed in the wildest of understatements. I enjoyed it more when I was the pyromaniac in charge, but being on the receiving end was fun for a challenge now and again. Arson—it wasn't a compulsion, but it was an entertaining hobby.

"How does it lure kids out where it can steal them?" I questioned curiously. "I wasn't the brightest kid, but I wouldn't have gone with a man-sized cat that walked on its hind legs and threw fire. But I was a little introverted"—hardly that, I thought, grinning to myself—"who's to say?"

"The *Bakeneko* can also talk," he answered, the words somewhat absent and vague. "What they say to children isn't documented anywhere unfortunately."

Finishing about half of his breakfast, which was more than I expected considering the topic of conversation, Nik tapped long fingers on the edge of the plate. The drumming seemed random but was either a rhythmic pattern of Morse code or a riff by some long-dead guy whose music caused healthy people to lapse into comas instead of vice versa. It was inevitable, though. I'd grown up seeing the same signs. That's how Nik's mind worked, logical inside and out. I was lucky this particular outside show of logic wasn't expressed through two hours of katas.

"You're changing on the outside, fast or slow." He put a special weight on "slow." "We can't be sure without a healer, but we knew it would come one day. Rafferty always had a bedside manner that would make even the AMA cringe, but he balanced it out with almost always being right." Stopping the tapping, he pushed the plastic dish out of the way and focused on me in a way no one else ever had. Read me like no one else ever could because no one else had spent my entire life watching over me. "But on the inside?" he asked. "You said you haven't changed, except perhaps for the better. More control."

I hadn't. He would've noticed. The man noticed if I said I was going out to watch a game with Goodfellow when I meant I was going out to get laid by a forest nymph in Central Park. And that wasn't lying . . . that was . . . ah . . . privacy.

How'd I catch on that he knew? The small can of bug spray—termites aren't particular in choosing one type of wood over another more personal kind—and the condom—both hit me in the back of the head every time I was halfway out the door. I only slept with nymphs mainly as they couldn't breed with an Auphe or a half Auphe. There were spores and pollen and I didn't much listen past that once Goodfellow gave me a list of female *paien* that I absolutely could not impregnate with a cute little bundle of flesh-eating baby Auphe.

This all meant that outside of the minor inconvenience of food-crazed aphids possibly attacking my dick, it was a given that Niko noticed everything about his little brother. For years I'd tried to convince him that a two-year difference between us didn't make me his sole responsibility. I was twenty-five, Jesus. I could take care of myself.

Well, hell, fine, there was the one time after getting laid by the nymph, I did accidentally stab that performance artist with the five-foot-long, three-foot-wide mass of dreadlocks in Times Square, but anyone would've thought he was a yeti. *Anyone.* And as an FYI for other performance artists at large: Do not scream in the ear of a man at nighttime in NYC as a part of your art. I know I'm what some would call excessively armed, but there are perfectly normal humans who would've blown his head off with whatever cheap piece of tin crap they had tucked in the back of their jeans. It was lucky I'd been trained not to flash a gun in a crowd and that his haystack pile of dreads and flailing limbs concealed any kind of guess at a vulnerable area for a killing blow. I think I stabbed him in the armpit. It was no lie that my knife smelled that way when I was cleaning it later.

Completely off the subject, I know. The guy lived . . . Nik checked the paper. Nik was also the one who wanted to know why I couldn't smell the difference between a hygiene-challenged human and a yeti. That meant we spent a week tracking down a yeti in the Catskills—a *yeti*, America wasn't the great melting pot for humans alone—just so I could memorize its scent. And this all started with Nik knowing I planned on getting a little nymph action before I even did.

Big brothers could dish out some scary omniscience shit.

This time that was a good thing, as it also meant that when I told him, "No. Like I said, I've felt fine. Normal anyway. I'm not saying I don't want to kill monsters who piss me off, but they always deserve it and it's no different than, hell, the best I've been in years," he knew I wasn't lying. "Minus the fake yeti, not my fault, my homicidal urges have been surprisingly low." Trying to kill the slimy lamia at the bar wasn't out of the ordinary. She started it. She fed off humans and killed them in the process. She wouldn't have been missed or mourned.

It was surprising, though, the past month, how I'd reverted to a younger, less psychotic personality.

My inner Auphe, the part of me that didn't show, liked a side order of violence frequently. It was a bitch to rein in, and it was a bitch and a *half* when I was less than successful at doing it. I gave a mental shrug. I gave it my best shot and was mostly successful unless provoked. That I was very easy to provoke—I didn't know if that was the Auphe or just me. Eh, what could you do? I took Nik's fork and a biteful of what was left on the plate. I was glad he'd liked it because ... Christ. I barely choked it down and let the fork fall with a clatter.

"My control has been good," I confirmed. The past month my monster within had been remarkably well behaved. Weirdly so. I ran a finger along the scars that ringed my wrists. They weren't pretty. Were scars ever? Sometimes ... yes. It looked as if I'd been chained up by a crazed serial killer, and I had been. But a few slugs from a shotgun to loosen the chain allowed me to rip my hands through the still-entirely-too-tight links. Metal fragments had embedded in my wrists. Once they'd healed, they left thickened, angry red and gouged depths of glossy white flesh around my wrists like barbwire bracelets were my personal fetish. I didn't mind, though; not many of us did, not in our world—unless you were an overprotective brother.

Scars meant you walked away. Scars meant you won. Scars meant the one that chained you was dead and gone and you'd laughed as he'd plummeted all the way to hell.

"Do you think what Jack did to you"—Niko touched a finger tip to my temple—"could that be causing this?

The Auphe in you trying to come out in other ways since you can't travel?"

Jack. The original Spring Heeled Jack who'd been killing since the 1800s. He hadn't been a he, but a them—a two-in-one killer, although they'd functioned as one and it was simpler to think of them as one, not a killer-combo meal. Truth or not. A *paien* parasitic storm spirit attached to and feeding off the energy of an angel. A true angel, with all the power that went with it, not the retired, lacking in the phenomenal cosmic power kind the peris were. Not like Ishiah, who could make a sword turn to flame for old times' sake, but that was pretty much it.

Yeah, good old Jack, who'd taken Nik right out from under my nose for his newest sacrifice.

Once they were separated from each other, the storm spirit parasite attached to the angel that had combined to become Spring Heeled Jack had been both easy enough to kill. Oddly, the angel half had been the easiest. One shotgun blast to a crystalline tortured and twisted form did the trick, and I don't think the angel was sorry to die. He wasn't what he'd once been. The storm spirit had mutilated him into something vile and insane, something that thought a murderer was the same as an underage prostitute selling her body to keep starvation at bay. Both sinned. Both would be skinned, the flesh burned, and sent up to God as an offering Old Testament–style. Although back then those sacrifices had been mostly lambs and sheep—a goat for variety—Jack had held to stricter standards.

Jack got to keep the skin. He who offers the sacrifices on high in the scent and smoke of roasting meat shall keep the skin for himself as reward for serving God. So said the Bible.

Amen.

And you thought reading wasn't a laugh a fucking minute.

Jack had used the power of the storm spirit to give me a DIY electroshock treatment during my incredibly crappy rescue attempt. He knew what I was, what I could do—tasted it in my blood. He thought cooking my brain would keep me from gating/traveling out of the chains and upstairs to where he was about to kill Niko. I could still feel the dry ice burn of hands pressed to both temples and the storm that was Jack flaring suddenly inside me. I saw the lightning and then I *was* the lightning. The floor had vanished beneath me as I hung suspended in midair, arms and legs splayed as I seized, convulsion after convulsion.

I didn't remember anything more after that until I woke up chained in the basement. And Jack had been right . . . he had fixed me but good. I couldn't gate. I couldn't tear a hole in the world and escape my chains. There was no walking through the space between reality, nothingness, and back again to stand between my brother and our would-be killer. Unfortunately for Jack, he had concentrated on my supernatural talents, which was far from all I had. I'd grown up as a teen with the only special abilities of gutting you with a kitchen knife or, if you were human, using all that Nik had taught me to beat the shit out of you—hand to hand.

I had a brief flicker of nostalgia for the good old days when I knew of only one monster in the world and kitchen utensils could solve all my problems. Then it had been time for work, and when that work was done, I could play. All work and no play, Jack hadn't known what that meant. Jack hadn't known anything but punishment and death in the name of his Lord. Jack hadn't known what a shotgun was either . . . as he'd left me mine on the floor within reach.

It had worked as well as a gate.

Nik's fingers looped around my scarred wrists and I

mused, "Sometimes the human ways work just as well." I'd survived without gates since Jack's death, and if it weren't for Grimm, I'd continue to endure. Unfortunately, there was Grimm and he'd figure it out sooner or later that I was crippled in the gating department. That's when it would come crashing down.

His thumbs rubbed absently across the more raised scars as if he could wipe them away. He'd done that since they had healed. I didn't think he was aware of the habit these days—he'd done it that often. Like I said . . . overprotective. I didn't mind. A brother who loved me. How could I mind that?

"I don't know if the Auphe is showing more on the outside to make up for the fact that I can't gate since Jack fried my brain. But I don't feel any different. If it wasn't for"—I pulled one wrist free of his grip and waved a hand in front of my face to indicate my hair and eyes—". . . if not for that, I'd say I feel good. Relaxed." As relaxed as I'm capable of was closer to the truth, but I took what I could get when it came to that attitude. It was often hard to come by in my adult years. "But that might have less to do with what Jack did to me and more with what happened in the other church basement. What I did."

That had satisfied the Auphe in me, the human in me, and the brother in me. No part of me had a problem with it. That gratification could be lingering.

Before I found Jack, I'd found his followers, zealots, insane killing nut jobs, call them what you want, the assholes, in one of the churches I was searching for Jack and my brother. An angel, twisted as he was, where else would he go? His happily homicidal little cult had stood between me and that information. They'd stood between me and Nik. That hadn't been acceptable.

My demonstration on how unacceptable had been to the point.

It hadn't ended well for them. The coroners must have spent a week minimum soaking them up with a sponge. When I can make gates, I can build one to walk through to someplace a block away, a hundred miles away, a Hell's dimension away . . . or I can build a gate *inside* a member of a psychotic sect who wouldn't tell me where my brother was. There were fourteen of them, with knives and bared teeth. They were almost as vicious and feral as me . . . on a good day. It wasn't a good day that day. I opened thirteen gates and tore those bastards to shreds. The last one, the one I left to talk, spilled all. And then he joined his friends.

When I was a kid, five years old I think, I thought there was a difference between humans and monsters. Both could hurt you and both could be evil, but killing monsters was different from killing humans. Years later, when I was ten and in the attic of a completely human serial killer, I figured out why I'd thought something so stupid.

Monsters are much easier to spot. They can be beautiful, but unreal. Otherworldly. They can also be a hideous, horrifying, putrefaction that somehow lives and *moves*. Seeing one of those is enough to make you want to vomit and deny its reality, deny that somehow the world had created this.

Humans, though, humans look normal. They smile. They ruffle the hair of children and pat dogs, laugh as a long canine tongue swipes across their faces. They slap you on the back and offer to help you move your furniture into your new apartment. They might offer you a soda too . . . hot, sweaty work, right? And they could possibly spike your soda, drag your unconscious body into their place next door, and dismember you in their bathtub. With monsters you know where you stood. But humans—they keep their nightmare selves hidden.

Monsters had the decency to warn you. People . . . they didn't.

In the end, I'd learned. If you lived to kill, maim, or torture for no reason other than your own personal entertainment, I'd put you down and I didn't give a shit what you looked like or what species you were when I did it. When it came my turn, if that's what I became, I hoped someone did the same for me.

A hypocrite I was not.

Those fourteen acolytes of Spring Heeled Jack that I killed would've kept spreading his word and his work whether he was gone or not. You steal, you die. You lie, you die. You commit adultery, you die. You work on the Sabbath (rough on the people who work in the hospitals), you die. And on and on. Everyone knows the Big Ten, and mitigating circumstances weren't a concept these guys had a grasp on at all. They were no less a disease than Jack had been and they had to go before their poison infected others, before innocent people began to die every day.

I hadn't lied to Nik about it. I hadn't lied to Nik about anything since I was ten maybe, once when I was fourteen if lies of omission counted. He raised me, and lying was no way to pay him back. Plus, when I needed a moral compass—and, holy shit, did I ever—then my brother was the perfect person to provide it.

"You think ridding the world of fourteen would-be serial killers has made you . . . mellow?" Niko was on his feet and covering the rest of the casserole with plastic wrap to put in the fridge. His eyes were on me, however, eyebrows lifted doubtfully. "I don't think so."

He wasn't wrong now that I thought it through. In the past the more violence I was forced into, the more I craved. Maybe this had just been a good month and I was in a mood to match it. Good moods were unusual

for me, but so were good months. No looking a gift horse
in the mouth.

"Okay. The hair and eye thing has something to do
with my fried brain, then." I yawned, not bothering to
smother it. "Can we talk about this in the morning? Because I know in the morning for you is four hours away.
And that doesn't come close to qualifying as a nap in my
book."

He relented and why not? I'd cooked for him—
unheard-of effort there. I'd bagged my own kills if I hadn't
had the chance to toss them in the Dumpster outside yet.
I found out that I was changing physically into an Auphe
and hadn't had the type of reaction ending up with me
setting the couch on fire with my completely illegal but
fun-as-hell flamethrower. I was dealing ... for now.

Gold star for me.

"Go to bed," Nik said. "I'll see what we can do about
the Wolves for you and in four and a half hours we'll be
in the park, injecting you with somewhat illegal drugs in
hopes of repairing your talent for shortcuts before
Grimm puts two and two together." Peering around the
open refrigerator door, he pointed out, "This has happened before, remember? You were bitten by those
Egyptian spiders with the amnesia venom and all the
Auphe portion of your genes immediately concentrated
on fixing your lost memories."

They had, leaving me more human than I'd been
since ... hell ... conception. I remembered that, how it
felt to be human for the first time in my life. I wished I
didn't. You don't know what you're missing if you've not
had it at all.

But once the Auphe genes had done their job, I was
restored. I returned to normal. Not human—that had
never been my normal, whether I'd looked that way or
not.

"Meaning if we fix the gating issue, I could stop changing physically?" I slid off the stool and started toward the hall before hesitating. "What if it works the other way? What if I can gate again and I keep changing? The genes keep going like Rafferty said they eventually would?" What if this had been the trigger that kicked the slow-moving genes into high gear for good. If so, I'd be more Auphe—a damn sight more Auphe, inside and out. If that happened, I'd be *all* Auphe sooner or later.

I'd always known that, but I'd been crossing my fingers for it to be later. "It might be better to leave the gating thing alone." Like I'd said, people didn't know that what's on the outside does sometimes count more than the inside—when you're an Auphe.

"Don't give up on me, little brother." Niko was unflinching. He always had been. In light of all this festive new evidence, he was the same. "I don't give a damn what you look like now or might look like later. I'm not giving up on you no matter what a thousand healers say."

"Because I'm your favorite brother?"

He gave me a glare that was the color of a perfect storm. "Because I'll kick your ass if you do. We don't give up. In our entire lives, we haven't once given up when we had every reason to."

No, we hadn't. When anyone else would have, we hadn't. "I still think it's because I'm your favorite brother." Giving your brother, your only brother, a hard time was the law. It was one of the few I obeyed. Besides, who needs to admit genuine emotion when you have sarcasm?

Niko didn't keep up his half of the brother dynamic. He didn't bitch back and he didn't pretend to kick my ass, although he actually could kick my ass. Instead he leaned around the refrigerator and pushed me on my way into the hall toward the bedrooms.

"Grimm," was all he said.

Yet again, he was right. If Grimm found out I couldn't gate, I wouldn't have a chance to worry about buying hoodies to cover unusually silver hair or sunglasses to cover equally unusual eyes, glowing the red of a crematorium's flames.

I couldn't ignore this problem. Hoodies and sunglasses wouldn't cut it. If I couldn't gate, I would be useless to Grimm. Worse, I wouldn't be *interesting* to Grimm. I would be worthless and boring, and Grimm didn't do well with either of those. Grimm faithfully followed the often-quoted philosophy, if slightly altered to suit him: If you can't chase it, eat it, fuck it, or laugh at it . . . then kill it, piss on its body, and walk away.

If Grimm killed me because I was boring, not only would it piss me off, but no one would care if I looked human, Auphe, or like a mutated aardvark.

Gating. I could do that. I didn't have much choice.

I'd had the traveling ability for years, gating with ease until the recent case of a lightning-induced knot tied in my brain. I now had drugs stolen in bulk from several pharmacies. I had an idea that Niko had theorized to test out. And, last but not least, when it came to Grimm, I had more motivation than the second-to-last member of the Donner Party.

Gating.

Piece of cake.

Hell, yeah.

Four hours, forty-five minutes, and one new silver hair later, I was trying to bury myself in a pile of leaves in the southern woods of Central Park while a second bullet slammed above me into the tree I was using as entirely inadequate cover.

There was no piece of cake. Not at all. Not unless the

cake was microscopic and packed inside the first sniper round that missed my head by millimeters before I'd dived to the ground. That's right, things were so damn dire that I was forced to convert to the metric system to indicate how fucking close my head came to exploding like a blood-filled cantaloupe.

I'd seen Niko leap up into a tree not far from me like a damn human jaguar. He was at the tree, up, and gone into the red-and-gold leaves before my eye could barely catch the movement. I wanted to whisper in an annoyed hiss at him what a great idea to avoid the boggles on the other end of the park only to be shot by some member of the NRA whose truck had gotten keyed, whose dog had died, whose girlfriend had dumped his ass on a picnic in the park, fixing this spot forever in his meth-addled mind, and who had finally catastrophically lost his shit. But the guns in his truck? Those he hadn't lost.

I couldn't do that, though, as it would give my position away . . . or more away than it already was, and this was not an out-of-town redneck looking for double-wide trailer, beer-soaked vengeance as much as I wished it were. This was a professional sniper. This guy had been to war, honed his skills, and learned to love them. He was not the kind of guy who put on too much female deer urine, passed out in a whiskey coma, and ended up humped to death by an eight-point buck while out hunting. This sniper was trained, alert, and probably had a kill list longer than my dick. I already had his attention. I didn't want more of it.

When we'd arrived at the park and run a few miles into the woods to make sure no one would see, we tried out Niko's idea to cure my gating problem. In the past, before I had picked up on how to gate whenever I wanted, it had taken a rush of adrenaline—the kind that often comes with the knowledge that if you don't move now, you're going to die the kind of gruesome death that would have Frank Miller himself hurling. That was how I'd made my very first gate and several later on. Since I wouldn't believe Niko was about to kill me and it was risky to run around looking for something that could kill me and would kill me if my traveling didn't come back online, Nik had come up with the next best thing. Epi-Pens Basically an instant shot of five hundred micrograms of adrenaline. I wouldn't be facing death, but my heart and other systems would feel like they were. It seemed reasonable, imitating what your body would do in a potentially fatal situation.

It hadn't worked.

I'd pulled down one side of my sweatpants to jam the delivery port against my outer thigh—Nik had read the instructions to me nearly two hundred times—and clicked the needle home. I waited for a full minute and tried to make a gate. Nothing. My heart rate picked up a little, but not much, and with the Auphe being immune to almost any poison, I shouldn't have been surprised that artificial adrenaline wouldn't do the trick. I'd been about to say so to Nik when the first bullet was fired. After that it had been hiding in leaves, cursing gun laws that didn't understand that while I needed guns for fighting monsters, everyone else should be armed with nothing but a slingshot or maybe a good-sized stick.

Niko was still out of sight among the topaz, ruby, and amber billowing clouds that made up the autumn foliage. Knowing him, he was leaping from tree to tree like goddamn Tarzan, not caring if he got himself shot as long as he saved me. I wondered for a second if I could get an electric shock collar at the pet store for him for when he got that "no greater love hath a man than to lay down his life . . ." gleam in his eye and give him a healthy zap. It would be in his best interest, honestly. During that second, while I was also guesstimating the collar measurement of my brother's neck, I had managed to get three more EpiPens out of the front pockets of my lightweight black jacket and injected all of them this time. For a moment my pulse pounded hard and fast and then staggered while my chest ached with sharp, stabbing pains. I thought I'd given myself a heart attack. I could see my death, facedown in the brown and yellow grass, foam spilling over my blue lips. Eyes fixed while hands froze clawing at the dirt.

Like I hadn't faced worse images, real ones, than that in kindergarten. Someone would have to try a little harder than that to scare me. And the elephant sitting on my chest? That pain? Pain was good. Pain let you know you were still alive to feel it.

Wake up, I prodded mentally at the base of my brain. The lizard brain where all the survival emotions, all the truly nasty emotions lived. The truly entertaining ones.

My heart rhythm was steadying and my chest pain fading, but I felt something better than all that. I felt the prickle at the back of my neck, under my skin, slithering veins of fire up into my skull. It was there all right. Sleepy but awake for now and . . . curious.

Time to play?

I bared my teeth happily at the echo. That's right. Time to fucking play.

Narrowing my eyes to slits, I scanned the area slice by visual slice beyond the trees, past a small clearing, and into the trees past that. There it was. There was the glitter of a sniper's scope. I wormed my hand inside my jacket, my hand on the grip of my Desert Eagle, as I strained to see every detail . . . the scope, the leaves covering the shooter as mine had covered me, the dark brown watch cap pulled low over his ears to better blend into the trees around him . . .

And then I was gone.

I shot him in the head, just behind his ear. I'd appeared behind him haloed with my gate—bruise purple, corpse gray, deadly lightning—surrounding me. It was quicker than building one to walk through. It hadn't made a difference, though. He'd been almost as quick and I'd known there was no chance of hitting him in a nonlethal area as he'd started to whip over and off his stomach. There was no time for that or for asking who he was and why he'd tried to kill Niko and me. It wasn't if I didn't already know. The fact that he was too fast and too good, nearly as good as Niko, played a part too. Hesitation in that case is not your buddy.

I was impressed and maybe even a little unsettled. "A .375 CheyTac with subsonic rounds," I said, prodding the gun respectfully with the toe of my sneaker. "That is a helluva lot more gun than he needed for us. I guess we should be flattered." Niko was moving up to my side. He dropped down from a tree like I'd known he would. He could keep up with me most of the time, silver medal easily, whether I gated or not. The dead guy on the ground came in third, but a bronze medal was nothing to be ashamed of ... unless you were buried with it.

I crouched down to check for ID, not that I needed it, but Nik had taught me to be thorough. I didn't expect to find any, and I wasn't disappointed. No wallet, brown hair, brown eyes that were dead and blank, already dimming. Average height, average weight, average jeans, shirt, and jacket. Even the tags had been cut from his clothing, his boxer briefs too. The most average man alive—well, not alive anymore. He'd have blended in anywhere. "Bastard," I sighed. "If I have to stick my hand down your pants, I expect at least a Walmart tag for the trouble."

"It worked."

I looked up at Niko's half question/half statement.

"The epinephrine."

"Yeah, it did. You're the genius you're constantly telling me you are." I slapped the side of his knee and stood, putting the Eagle back under my jacket out of sight as we jogged away from the body. "It took four maximum doses and my pulse is up there." Nothing like a human's would be, which was encouraging. "But it worked."

"Four doses."

I could see his ambivalence: satisfied it worked and not at all satisfied it had taken so much. He already had my wrist snared in an unbreakable grip and was monitoring my heart rate. He knew the side effects better than I did. "But we don't know if it'll keep working or you'll have to inject yourself every morning or with every single gate."

"We'll find out. I'll be a lab rat for a good cause." And not getting killed by Grimm was a damn good cause. "If I do have to inject it every time, we'll also have to find a better injection system, a needle long enough to go through my jeans. I can't be pulling down my pants to stick it in my thigh in the middle of a fight. Goodfellow would find it fucking hilarious, but me, not so much." Leaves fell around us as we ran, the rain of them gloriously bright and beautiful because of, not in spite of, their death.

"Who do you think that guy was?" I asked after several more long strides. It was a senseless question, the kind you ask when you know the truth but wish you didn't. We both were perfectly aware of the only kind of ordinary yet incredibly skilled human who would want me dead. Hell, the only other human I associated with aside from the hot dog guy these days was Nik.

The hand stayed on my wrist, Niko still counting. "You know who he was."

Yeah, I did.

"Un-fucking-lucky for one," I muttered. "He was good with an even better gun." But I'd been better. I kicked up enough of the bright-colored fallen foliage to imitate a phoenix as I ran faster. No one held a grudge like a paramilitary organization.

You might forget your fuckups, although saving Nik would never be a fuckup to me, but you can bet those who tally the fuckups never forgot them. . . .

Or you.

5

Goodfellow

"The Vigil is after Cal."

I had a deep and abiding camaraderie, a friendship undeniable with Niko. In every one of his lives that I'd encountered him, I'd found him to be intelligent, loyal, noble, brave, an excellent fighter, the best possible human to have watching your back, and incredibly sexy even in only a slave's loincloth. What was I thinking? Especially in only a loincloth. Yet there were times, rare as a virgin in a Roman whorehouse, true, but there did exist the uncommon occasion when I would've greatly enjoyed breaking an urn, a small piece of statuary, or, in these times, a chair over his head.

I slid farther down on my couch designed for twenty people or one puck and one possessive mummified dead cat. Salome rasped a purr, sounding as if she were choking on a pound of Egyptian sand, while draped over my knee. There was no heartbeat in her still chest, and after years, I had yet to get used to that. I rubbed tired eyes and then raised my best incredulous gaze to his stubborn one. I hated the stubborn one. It was akin to a stew of obstinacy and righteousness seasoned with a demand deadly enough it had you giving in when the first two wouldn't have swayed you at all. Particularly when he had his sword out . . . as he did now. Curse my self-preservation instincts.

"You don't possibly think this surprises me," I said skeptically. "If you tell me that it surprises *you*, I will be forced to downgrade you from 'the smart brother.'" Straightening from my weary sprawl, I put Salome on the floor to go find her fellow dead cat companion, Spartacus. Cal had gifted me with him after killing the murderous mummy that had made the both of them. I thought he was hoping for an unholy spawning and a litter of more zombie cats. That would be my luck.

Niko continued to loom, katana at his side, waiting. He knew words were my weapon, but they were also my weakness and, of all others, Niko best knew how to use that against me. Silence, I loathed it, and he knew it. "He gated in broad daylight when he was trying to save you from Spring Heeled Jack!" I snapped, spreading my arms wide to indicate all the unbelievable lunacy that act entailed. I had hundreds of informants in the city and I hadn't needed to talk to one of them to know that the Vigil would come after Cal after that idiotic move he'd made. The Vigil had made their rules clear. Humanity, as a whole, could not know of *paien* of the supernatural— outside horrible reality shows. Neither were they wrong. If humanity knew of us, there were enough of them to kill us all or lead to a fear-based, on their side, war if nothing else.

"Broad daylight!" Yes, it was a repetition and I was

more skilled with any language to make that unnecessary, but ... by Menoetius, most reckless and crazed of the Titans, sometimes even Niko didn't listen.

"It was more toward twilight actually and irrelevant." Face smooth, eyes calm, he lifted the katana and tapped the point not quite idly on the thick slab of rock crystal that constituted my coffee table.

"Fine. It was dim. It was dusk. The fact remains it wasn't dark. People could see, which leads us to another very unpalatable fact: He did it in front of at least twenty people!" I dropped my arms. Nothing could stretch far enough to show the amount of idiocy that went into that. This wasn't ancient Greece. Mount Olympus wasn't the current tourist attraction and gods and goddesses didn't disappear into the ether on a daily basis in the sight of whoever they chose. Those days were gone.

"Much as it pains me to admit, I'm not quite capable of seducing those twenty witnesses and using my immeasurable stamina and infinity of sexual positions to put them all in orgasm-induced comas, catatonic at the knowledge nothing in this life will ever match a mere fifteen minutes with me." I continued with little that could be construed as a good mood. "We were fortunate as it was that he was quick enough that no one caught it on their phone. Therefore it's not at one million hits on YouTube. It wasn't on television. There was the infinitely amusing hallucinogenic gas theory, as you couldn't blame it on swamp gas in *gamou* New York City, so someone was doing their part in covering it up." The Vigil at their best.

"But it remains, Cal lost control in public. No, that's not true. Cal didn't have any control to begin with when he was searching for you and Jack and care he did not. And don't for a moment underestimate me by assuming I don't know about a basement full of partially disintegrated bodies that happened less than twenty minutes later," I sniped, "which, I'm assuming, is how he did find Jack and you, the mandatory sacrifice in these over-wrought scenarios, the helpless golden-haired ninja-in-need." I'd pay for that description sooner or later, but it would be worth it. I went on to voice the obvious. "Even brainwashed people talk when other people around them begin to explode like one hundred and fifty pounds of raw meat wrapped around a stick of dynamite."

"They were not good people. Bad things tend to happen to not good people." There was a minute shift of his shoulders, the most dismissive of shrugs. "Also irrelevant." The sword tapped against the stone again.

"I think the Vigil would agree with you there. I can say with a fair amount of certainty that they have found Caliban irrelevant to life and plan on relieving him of it altogether," I said with bitter force. I couldn't help it. Always ... *always* they made it so difficult to keep them alive.

There was a nearly invisible flicker of fear behind Niko's calm. Present, then vanished in the smallest fraction of a moment. No one would've seen it aside from me or Cal, but no one had known Niko for most of human history save the two of us.

Sighing, I waved a hand in his direction. "You are beyond fortunate I remember how you looked in a loin-cloth. Put away your toy and sit down while I get us both something to drink. Then we can play our little game I've become so fond of over the years."

Rising to my feet, I went to my bar. I wavered between the truly hard liquor and wine. Achilles had grown up drinking wine as if it were water, as had Alexander as well. Arturus drank a piss-poor beer-ale mix the memory of which made me cringe to this day. Niko in this life didn't drink often at all, but there were exceptions. This would qualify. I went with wine and handed him the glass. He had sat on the coffee table, katana sheathed, back ruler straight, appearing stoic as one could be yet cripplingly afraid, although he'd refuse to admit it to anyone, Cal and me included. Always had he been this way. The strong one—afraid to be afraid.

My living room was more than large enough that I could sit on the couch without invading his personal space, and I did. I dropped down opposite him and clinked my glass against his. He took a swallow and questioned with one raised eyebrow, "Game? What game?"

Tossing back half my glass, no decorous swallows for me, I answered impatiently, "The game we so often play. You ask, 'Robin, will you help us on this utterly doomed and certainly suicidal quest?' And I say, 'You're mad. Insane. A demon resides in your head and we must find a physician to do a nice trepanning, drill a hole in your skull and let it out. Now, go away and leave me to drink and whore in peace.'"

I drained my glass with my next swallow and then pointed the crystal goblet at him. "Whereupon you prevail on honor that I do not possess and accuse me of an inherent courage I would consider worse than a venereal disease and eventually say that you cannot do it without me. You cannot do it without your friend."

I'd brought the bottle of wine with me and poured myself another glass. "Of course I'm not able to resist that. I never have been. The 'cannot do it without me' part, yes. That I can resist. I'm brilliant. Naturally there are many things that cannot be done without me." I watched the liquid in my glass swirl as I tilted it from side to side. "But when you say 'friend,' I am defenseless." I put the now empty bottle down on the couch beside me and concentrated on drinking my wine more slowly this time. "I'll assist with the Vigil. You knew that before you walked through my door." With a key I was beginning to regret having given him.

A hand touched my knee, heavy and comforting. "I have never meant it like that, Robin, I swear. I have never meant to use your friendship." His gaze was steady on mine. "I depend on you like Cal depends on me. Sometimes, like now, I am lost and you're the only one I know who might have a map. And if you didn't or couldn't help, you'd still be my friend. Our friend. That will never depend on what you can do for us. It depends solely on you being you."

He leaned back, removing his hand, and giving me one of his smiles that occurred so infrequently. "Not to mention, who else can drive Cal into hiding simply by threatening nudity?" I drank my wine, for the first time in eight hundred years or so speechless. Niko went on easily, blatantly giving me a chance to recover. "And when did you ever see me in a loincloth?"

"A slave auction in the southern part of Britain," I said promptly, the taste of grape on my tongue. "You'd been captured probably in what is Ireland now. Tribes fighting tribes. Whoever was captured alive ended up as a slave. Unfortunately that was the way of the world then. But you were apparently not agreeable to being a slave." No, Niko didn't have it in him to give in, to not make them earn every single inch they dragged him along. "Barely seventeen at the most, you were fighting your captors every step of the way. You had reddish blond hair and skin much more pale than yours is now. You did have the same nose, however."

I smiled at the memory, the first flare of excitement at finding him again. "I'd learned to recognize you both by then, no matter the color of your hair or skin. Your temperaments oddly rarely change"—this life was the most dramatic change I'd seen by far . . . thanks to the Auphe genes in Cal—"and are wholly unmistakable. I bought you and gave you your freedom."

"What about Cal?" Niko questioned, rolling the wineglass between both hands. "Did you buy him too or did I go back home to find him?"

There was the end of the pleasant part of that recollection, too many lifetimes for me to barely recall. Niko wouldn't remember at all. That was how his particular rebirth worked.

As I was not reincarnated, I was not as fortunate as Nik in losing those memories, the good ones or the ones that made for sleepless nights. I'd been around before the spoken word existed. When they developed one by one, language after language, I had learned them all. I hadn't only seen what Niko of that incarnation had done then, I'd also understood what he'd said. Paying the slaver, who I would get back at some day for putting a man such as Niko in chains, I'd unlocked those same chains and told Niko he was free.

He hadn't known I was there. His eyes had been wild as his head whipped about, looking . . . searching. He found it in a nearby gawking tribesman. He had then called out a name in a voice ragged and torn before lunging at the tribesman, seizing the knife from his belt, and cutting his own throat all in one swift continuous movement. It happened so fast that no one could stop it—not Zeus, not God, Odin, or Allah, certainly not me.

He had crumpled at my feet and bled to death in seconds. With my hands wrapped around his neck trying in vain to stop the flood, I'd learned my lesson. If one brother was found, *watch* him until the other is in sight. The name he had said with black guilt and blacker despair, it would be that of his brother—the Cal of this time.

Kneeling in the mud, hands and arms up to my elbows

coated in scarlet, I'd bent my head and buried my face in dirty red hair. I stayed that way until he was as cold as the ground beneath us and the blood on me dried to a maroon crust. It had been a hundred and ten years since I'd seen him last, and to lose him in a matter of minutes . . . well . . . I wasn't going to let that go, was I?

I'd done what I did best, brushing off the death by claiming to be a sentimental fool who hated to see a pet die. I'd talked and drunk and laughed and sucked information out of every man in that tribe until I'd narrowed it down to the three possible men who had killed a five-year-old Cullen during the raid. They'd all gathered around while one swooped down to grab him as he ran toward his brother, who was shouting for him across the field. The one, whichever one it had been, had held the little boy upside down by his legs and cut his throat. Slaughtered him like a pig in the very same way Niko, with remorse-driven purpose, had slaughtered himself.

I hadn't been able to find which of the three held the blade that took that Cal's life and, for all intents and purposes, had taken Niko's as well. It didn't matter that I didn't know, because I'd killed all three. One had held the knife, but the other two had watched and laughed. They all deserved what I gave them. It wasn't quick as say the slitting of a child's throat was. It wasn't like that at all. Once they'd drunk enough to pass out, I stole a horse and cart to take them out of the village far enough that there would be no interruptions, and then I took my time. I couldn't remember if it was two days or three, but in vengeance of a five-year-old child and a seventeen-year-old young man, neither of whom I would be able to rejoin this time, I doubted it had been long enough.

Not nearly.

"Robin?"

I left the past where it belonged and finished my wine

before giving Niko's expression of concern a brightly wicked smile. "Yes. You went home to him and took me along with you. Cullen was his name then." That was true. It was the last thing Niko had said before drowning in his own blood. I didn't know what his own name had been, but Cullen meant cub and so I'd thought of Niko as Phelan—wolf—when I returned those three days later to bury him.

Phelan and Cullen, another two I hadn't been able to save.

"There was a grand celebration." I saw it that way sometimes, imagining laughter, firelight, the smell of roasting chickens, and that terrible ale. I pictured a small boy who threw himself into my lap and gave me a handful of sticky honeycomb for bringing his brother home to him. Everyone knows pucks lie. Few know why we lie. They don't know that the truth can be so unbearable that you'd rather lie to anyone, yourself most of all. I stretched my smile wider. "Dancing and drinking all night and well into the next day. If human females were fertile with pucks, I would no doubt have impregnated half your village."

Niko snorted, convinced, and why wouldn't he be? I hadn't invented the lie, but I'd been second in line behind the one who had. "Thank you."

I leered. "For not impregnating half—"

"For helping with the Vigil," he interrupted, trying for annoyed, but you didn't have to be a puck to hear the affectionate humor in his voice. "Delilah and the Kin are after Cal as well. She sent a few Wolves after him the night of the Howl, but I think we can handle them."

Yawning—it had been a long day already—I dismissed with "I've taken care of that as well. You don't have to worry about Delilah and her puppies anymore, not for a while. A few weeks, a month—I'll let you know."

"Why? And how would you know this?" His fingers wrapped around the edge of the rock table that was his seat. Not in a suspicious clench, but in a hopeful and loose grip.

"Trust me. The Kin is handled for a time and when Delilah and they are back on Cal's trail, I will let you know."

He nodded and gave me that emotion pucks hardly ever receive. Faith. "Very well." Curiously, it was now he who looked as if he needed a little faith of his own. "I need to get back home. We might have found a solution for Cal's gating problem today, but last night he noticed he had gotten a little more . . ." He hesitated. "Auphe. A few white hairs. Specks of red that come and go in his eyes. So far it has nothing to do with him gating. It started the night before that and he's handling it well. No rages. No massacres, but I'd like to keep an eye on him."

He stood, took his glass to the kitchen to carefully rinse it out as the most polite of guests do, thanked me again, and was out the door before I was able to close my mouth. Speechless now for the second time in eight hundred years. It could not be fathomed. Yes, my brother was physically turning into the most murderous creature spawned in the mists of time and I should check to make certain he consumed his microwave meal instead of our neighbors. What? Pardon? Should I have mentioned that sooner? Was the "no massacres" comment not reassuring?

I let myself twist sideways and then fall backward on the couch, vaguely hoping Salome and Spartacus might eat me and put me out of my misery. Not that they ate, being dead and all, but they weren't above killing large mammals, Great Dane–sized mammals. Puck-sized mammals. At least I didn't have to concern myself with the Vigil as much as Cal had brought it on himself. It was

rather insulting that Niko thought I'd wait for him to ask
for my aid. As I'd told Ishiah last night, I'd known the
Vigil was a threat, and I'd known about the shooting in
the park this morning five minutes after it had happened.
The hundreds of my informants had come in handy then.
I was a trickster. I knew almost everything there was to
know . . . in this city, if not the majority of the world.

"Help with the Vigil," he'd requested.

I laughed, perhaps a little deranged and more than a
little arrogant.

Zeus on High.

I'd taken care of the Vigil *hours* ago.

Fingers woke me from my nap, wandering their way
through my hair, tracing their way lightly across my
scalp, before pulling free and flicking my earlobe with
stinging force. Loving, I'm certain, but stinging as well.
"*Ganbay llebaa*, it's time for me to go."

It wasn't Aramaic that Ishiah spoke, but it was a close
enough variation for anyone to gather the gist of what
he said when he bothered to speak at all. I did like them
laconic and mysterious. Denying you have a type is the
same as lying about your favorite sexual position or particularly naughty kink: You're the only one who loses out
in the end.

"Ish." I scowled in sleep-soaked recognition while
rubbing my ear before I snapped to a hyper state of vig-
ilance I'd learned over too many battles. It was a lesson
well learned long before I'd fought in history's first genuine war. One should always be alert. Now, in particular,
was a time to keep that in mind. I had many irons in the
fire and only two hands to juggle them. Readiness was
all. Relax for one heartbeat alone and death could be
upon you or upon those more important than you.

I opened my eyes, released my ear, and rolled over

onto my back to offer a comfortably loose and forgivingly drowsy grin to him as he leaned, resting his folded arms on the back of the couch. Although the lack of anxiety was a lie and the comfortable ease was false, it was the best intentioned of deceptions. A gift better than the truth. Ishiah knew part of my plans, but not all of them, not yet. Nor did he know quite how risky they were, how dependent on every single thing falling perfectly into place. Let him keep his peace of mind a little longer.

"Ganbay llebaa," I echoed with a more salacious flavor to the words. "Thief of your heart." A closer approximation would be "heart thief" with the implication that the theft had been devious, not entirely desired, yet unexpectedly welcome. It was a complex and ancient language. Ishiah knew that his version would be even more appreciated and closer to a puck's first love: our ego.

"Do you tell the other peris that's what you call me? Do they know the romantic and poetic soul that lurks behind their boss's sour expression and foul temper?" I asked, reaching up to seize a strand of his hair that had fallen loose around his scarred face. I liked it that way. It reminded me of the first time I'd seen Ishiah, in some nameless battle, smiting demons or those who'd partaken of shellfish or pork or they who had labored on the Sabbath. I couldn't remember the insignificant details of it all having concentrated rather obsessively on him, who had then been an angel.

The light blond hair had been wild in the wind created by the thrashing of his muscular white-and-gold wings. Or I'd guessed at the time that was the color of the feathers under the ubiquitous layer of desert sand. That combined with what very little angels had worn in those days—to call it a loincloth would be generous— with the contrast of dark eyebrows and a pugnacious jaw ridged by scar tissue was positively created to catch my attention. Lust at first sight, I was quite used to by then and more than willing to admit it to him once the smiting was done. And admit it quickly I had.

It you do not ask, you do not receive. I *knew* Ishiah had plagiarized that from me and put his own twist on it before passing it on to a scribbling monkey named Luke or Matthew or Roscoe. Whoever.

It was too bad plagiarism was the least annoying result of that situation. Ishiah had been my first angel. I'd heard of them for years, of course, yet not crossed paths with one. Ishiah had managed to replace my happy-go-lucky lust with fury in one sentence. He was gifted in that manner.

"Or," I continued, "do you tell them you call me an oversexed, disease-ridden, humping, sinning goat who would burn in Hell for all eternity while forced to consume my own flaming intestines if only you had the jurisdiction? You remember? As you told me when we first met?" I released his hair to take a handful of his shirt and pull him over the back of the couch and on top of me. From a distance his eyes were blue-gray, a rainstorm on the horizon, but up close they were blue. Clear blue but for a single large speck of gray next to the pupil of his right one. I ran my thumb along his stubborn chin. I couldn't see the bristle, but I could feel the invisible prick of it against my skin. A hundred years as an ex-angel and he still forgot to shave some days.

With an impatient huff, he moved in for a kiss, warm and with enough hungry bite to it to banish that fragment of desert-worn history running through my mind. After a year, the slide of tongue, the teeth nipping just short of painful, the unique taste of rain and ozone. He'd left Heaven, but the sky he'd flown in and its more dangerous moods still burned in him. The taste and feel were familiar enough to revel in with the added comfort of knowing I had all the time in the world. It was also thoroughly addicting and left me craving more. Now. Immediately. Perhaps never to stop.

Sadly, what I wanted and what the world was delivering at my doorstep were poles apart. I had all the time in the world, but others did not.

I licked a stripe across the slightly salty skin of his throat before slapping him firmly on his ass, not as awe-inspiring as mine naturally, but as close as one could come without being me. "Yes, time for you to go. We don't have long." His frown was darkly resigned. The gray-and-blue that studied me was clouded with hesitation and worry. But other things as well . . . better things . . . things meant only for me and not for the dangerous circumstances that surrounded us. My lips curved. "Aren't you thankful I taught you tongues are for more than talking, *aetos-mou*?"

My eagle. He pretended that the name meant nothing, but he had yet to fail to smile when I called him that . . . as opposed to the time he cut me off from sex for a week when I called my turtledove—in front of Niko, who understood Greek. Niko, despite his not especially vast sense of humor, had found it rather amusing, enough so to choke on his tea. Niko had been more entertained and me not at all when Ishiah stood firm on the no sex punishment. A hard lesson learned.

Unfortunately not the type of hard lesson for which I had a great deal of enthusiasm, a greater amount of equipment, and a safe word.

Pity.

"Ass." He kissed me, quickly this time, and then sat up. "They don't ask what I call you, the other peris. They see it in my eyes whenever I watch you walk into the bar."

Words such as that should heat you from within, not make you feel as if you're tempting fate. I hid them away that I alone and not the fickle finger could find them. With that, I shoved Ishiah to his feet. "If you can't get this done, if someone wants to take issue with you over this"—brutal and violent issue—"tell me now. We'll find another way." Sitting up, I ran a hand over my hair, smoothing down what Ishiah's fingers no doubt had teased into a mess of which only Einstein would've approved. "I don't trust them."

"They are me or rather I was once them. You do trust me." He'd hidden his wings and now stood straight and tall, the ex-soldier he was.

"Yes, yes, I trust you." I grimaced as he tried and failed to not look as if I'd given him the keys to ten absolutely street-*illegal* Lamborghinis with that one simple word. But in a way, I had. Pucks didn't have a word for trust in our mother tongue; it was that foreign a concept. We had to coopt the term from other languages. Trust from a puck meant . . . it was . . . I couldn't. I didn't have the luxury to think about that, not now when I least could afford being distracted. And Ishiah was the very definition of distraction.

"But I don't trust them, whether you were once them and whether they are uncannily good at locating people." And of that we were in desperate need as my earthbound informants weren't as effective as those who could fly. "And you shouldn't either."

I held up an imperious hand—I'd taught that to Caesar—as he started to speak. "You think that you know them, but you don't. You knew them a long time ago. Do not assume all will be the same. They aren't your kind any longer. Try to be prepared for it, that's all I ask." For now, that's all I asked. When he returned, I'd ask for removal of clothing and a vigorous round of Kama Sutra bingo, but at present a healthy sense of suspicion and caution to keep him unharmed was all I required.

"What you want is in everyone's best interest. Heaven's as well. They'll see the positive side of cooperation," Ishiah promised. He promised it with a defiant glare that didn't bode well for our potential allies if they disagreed with him. He was young, to think logic made such a difference. I forgot that at times. He was four thousand years old, give or take, but I was millions of years and I knew what he did not. Logic was a fantasy. Reason and common sense were the unicorns of the thinking world. Glorious and wonderful for the most naïve to imagine, but did they exist?

It depended on who you asked.

Virgins didn't count.

I hoped he was correct, because if we couldn't find this particularly talented individual that Niko, Cal, and I all knew, none of this counted for anything. I followed Ishiah to the door, where he suddenly stopped, turned, and leaned forward to rest his forehead against mine. As he closed his eyes, one hand came up to tightly cup the back of my neck. We stayed that way for minutes, maybe longer. His breath was warm against my ear, steady and even, until it finally hitched slightly. "So . . . time for your best lie?" My breezy and casual attitude when he'd woken me up hadn't fooled him as much as I'd hoped.

"I can do this. All of it," I promised. Including the schemes he knew nothing of yet, which was for the best if he hoped to concentrate on his own mission. "Everyone has a weak spot.

"Everyone is a sucker, one way or the other, and I haven't met a sucker I couldn't take since day one," I added with the unshakeable arrogance and cold confidence of Hob the Elder and the Younger, the first and second trickster to walk the earth. "I *can* do this."

It was true. I could . . . or I would die trying. That wasn't a lie unless it was a white one. I hid any doubts using all my skill from the time when rivers were far more often made of lava than water. No one would see them, including those who knew more of me than most.

He nodded with visible relief, reassured and full of faith. The faith wasn't my fault. That came from Above. By no means would I teach anyone such a disastrously simplistic and deluded concept—not if I wanted them to survive for very long. I'd been working on that with him, trying to shove him into reality, but he was stubborn. Hopefully there would be a future to work on it more. I kissed him again, slapped his ass one more time for luck—and because it truly was one fine ass—and he left.

He left, shutting the door behind him, without seeing the feather I'd plucked from wings of invisibility to have it turn to gold-dusted ivory resting in my hand. Ridiculous. Sentimental. All the things pucks were not. I tucked it down inside my shirt, pulled in a deep breath, and switched gears. I ruthlessly forced myself back to my birthright—the engineer of deserved downfalls. Scourge of any sucker who crossed my path. And was there anyone who wasn't a sucker? To me? No. I was Goodfellow. There was no trick I hadn't pulled, no lie I hadn't invented. Grimm thought the Auphe played games. I had learned to cheat before games *existed*. It was time to remember that. I smiled to myself, tasting the past victories—sweet and sharp like blood—of those games on my tongue, before moving my thoughts to the next step.

Now . . . what did I have next on my list?

Ah yes.

RV parks.

6

Caliban

"Shit, okay, that's a big needle."

Niko's sideways glance at me was full of long-suffering patience stretched to a saint's limits and ten times beyond. It was the look that had me all but hearing the Vatican knocking at our door to give my brother the thumbs-up on miracles confirmed—canonizing is a go—and I folded instantly. "Hey, not that big. Sorry. It must be low blood sugar affecting my eyesight.... I'll eat something. Some pizza rolls maybe while you work with those completely, absolutely normal-sized needles. Perfect for the job."

"Hmm." Nik continued working on upgrading the epinephrine injectors to ones that could pierce denim and flesh in one go, which, I didn't care what his expression said, meant one big fucking needle. He was settled in a sterile drape-covered area on the floor between the

couch and our sparring gym mats. I didn't know why he
bothered with sterility, as my boosted Auphe immune
system hadn't once found an ordinary, human-style in-
fection it couldn't beat.

That was bullshit. I knew why he was fixated on con-
trolling the things that he could, as thanks to me, there
were so many he couldn't control that we'd both lost
count. His brother was turning into an Auphe and they
don't make a pill for that, do they? No, they do not. Instead he'd work on improving the adrenaline injection
system because longer needles are easy to obtain if you're
willing to go into the dark and nasty parts of the city. And
while his brother might not have had any type of infec-
tion in his life, that didn't mean we couldn't take precautions and keep that one hundred percent resistance at . . .
one hundred percent.

If Nik couldn't do anything else, he could do those
things. He knew more about coping mechanisms than
four out of five psychiatrists.

And if he was able to scare the shit out of me with a
giant freaking needle, that was a bonus I didn't begrudge
him.

Much.

I loaded the microwave as I watched him take apart
the autoinjectors. If I could've thought of anything to say
to make him feel better, I would have . . . but what? I'm
turning into an Auphe, more of one than I already am,
but no worries. I only killed one person today. You can't
beat that, can you?

That wasn't going to improve his mood.

The gating was still working at least. I'd gated three
times since the park. I'd felt a little strain at the fourth
one. Hopefully that would hold and I might only have to
shoot up once in the morning and be a gating madman
all day. Neither of us brought up the fact that if I grew

immune to the epinephrine and this adrenaline-gating experiment didn't keep working, Grimm would kill me. On the other hand, if it did keep working, there was a chance I could become more and more homicidal like I'd done in the past, until I killed Grimm, solving all our problems . . . unless I decided to kill Grimm and everyone else in the tristate area. Psychotic killing sprees were not as predictable as you'd like.

Not good. That's all I could think when mentally running through any of the scenarios and conversations Niko and I had gone over in covering them. Catastrophic, wrath of nature, acts of God not covered by insurance. These were the levels of "not good" I was anticipating.

The truest thing I could say would be if I managed to kill Grimm, then kill me. Save the world. Save yourself. Save everyone from what I might do. Let Promise and Robin carry you through the aftermath and live your life. Don't throw it away if I'm already gone. The truest thing . . . and if I said it, Niko would lose his mind. It would be on the inside where none of us could see. Quiet, hidden, and unrevealed to the rest of us. He'd do it, though, and follow me to my death anyway. Whatever I said or begged for on my knees would have less meaning than if he were deaf and blind. He did everything and anything for me, always had and always would, and it made me feel like an unshakable goddamn burden at times.

Other times, like now when the microwave dinged and I wondered if Niko would be shocked if I threw a plate of pizza rolls in his face, I felt as if he was the burden. He was the heavy weight that whispered in my ear that he had a lover, he had friends, he had an actual career teaching, and a life to live, but if I tripped up once and Grimm or bad genes or a crazed human militia group took me down, I was condemning him along with me. Couldn't he live for himself like normal selfish people?

I opened the microwave door, choking on the resentment and guilt, stared at the steaming pizza rolls, then at Niko as he tore apart medical apparatus. For me naturally. Always for goddamn me. I glowered back at the sizzling rolls again. They would decorate his face in a napalm equivalent of tomato sauce and pepperoni perfection if only I'd pick up the plate and . . .

"Problem?"

I laughed at Nik's question. It was full of the irritation, fatalism, and unfailing affection of a big brother. The remorse and bitterness stewing in me were gone as quickly as the first pizza roll I swallowed. I was an idiot. We had talked about this too many times in the past to bother mentally bitching to myself about it. I went first; he would come after me. So what? Did I think it would be different if the opposite were to happen? If Niko left me, was I capable of burying him, mourning, and moving on? Fuck, no. I couldn't begin to believe that.

We'd known this since we'd known anything at all. As kids and then teenagers and early twentysomethings, we'd had no one but each other. We'd locked into each other like puzzle pieces. A few years later, we did have more and that was . . . good. Something I'd not dreamed of and something incredibly amazing. We had a life. It was dangerous and usually crazy as hell, but it was a real life. Who'd have pictured that? Not me, but, real life or not, we'd had it for four or five years at the most and that didn't compare to the earlier twenty-odd years when we were the solitary certainty in each other's life.

That had set around us more solid than stone. When people and situations had come along in our path to change that, it was too late. We were whole in ourselves, stronger than anything outside us, and we wouldn't be changed. Not for any reason, no matter how convincing and valid that reason could be.

Sometimes nothing can be done. We are who we are. It's no one's fault.

Thanks to Robin I knew there were other lives. Different lives. That meant that back in ye olden times if my drunk ass had fallen off a horse and broken his neck, because that was absolutely how I'd shuffle off at least one mortal coil, then Nik would've had Goodfellow, probably a wife, and some little ninjas running around. He'd have had reason to go on. We wouldn't have had the cluster fuck of sociopath mother, packs of Auphe chasing us, and my monster genes to make our codependency stronger than gravity. I wanted Niko to have that chance, past or future lives to come. I couldn't imagine it for myself—then again my imagination wasn't the best, and that was the last problem I needed to worry about.

Past and future lives were covered. That let us give all our attention to this one. It wasn't a lap dance, but I'd take it anyway.

"No, no problem," I answered. "Want some commercially inedible food source before we go out on the job tonight?" I removed the plate from the microwave and waved it in his general direction in offering.

"I'll survive without. The thought is appreciated nonetheless." His face reflected polite dismissal, but the apology was semigenuine. And the day kept getting better and better. I wasn't dead yet and more pizza rolls for me—there was no downside. As I popped one in my mouth and hissed at the lava-temperature heat of the filling, Niko completed one EpiPen and set it aside. "Robin said he would help us with the Vigil."

I swallowed the nuclear meltdown that was the second pizza roll, and it started a raging wildfire in my stomach. It wasn't close to being a new sensation for me, and I picked up a third one that singed my fingertips. "Why?"

Niko had gone to Robin's to ask for his assistance with the Vigil; that wasn't news. The Vigil, however, were powerful and based in many of the larger worldwide cities. They were highly armed and trained humans who were determined that humanity and the supernatural should not meet, not shake hands, not party and not ever limbo together. I understood their point. At least half of the *paien* thought of humans as free-range, pluck-it-yourself chickens. That might seem harsh, but there weren't a fraction as many *paien* compared to humans, and most of them had been here first. I thought of them as lions . . . or tigers; there weren't many, this world belonged to them too, and with billions of humans, which side could afford to miss a few? It didn't hurt that most grazed on dopers, muggers, the types that lurked in places that no one would be if they didn't have reasons, bad reasons, to be there.

And if no one hired me to take out the ones that were the equivalent of rabid and munching on more wholesome folk, I wasn't that interested. There was a food chain, and if not paid to think otherwise, I respected it—unless the killing was done merely for sport and not survival. That wasn't in anyone's best interest. Otherwise, everything worked out fine as long as the *paien* used common sense and didn't reveal themselves to humans. Didn't let humanity know that, shocker, *they* weren't the top rung on evolution's ladder. Didn't take their blanket of obliviousness, shred it apart, and show the bloody teeth and claws that hid behind it.

Like I had done.

"Why?" Niko, sitting on the floor with legs crossed, repeated my question, and that was not a sign of pleasant things to come. I'd first heard it as a kid when I set a neighbor's trailer on fire. They weren't in it at the time and it had to be done. It wasn't as if arson was my *hobby*. But the bitching had gone on for weeks after and it all started with the same tone of "You have brain cells for a reason. Use them." "Did you say 'why'?"

I put the plate down with one hand before tossing the pizza roll from one to another in hopes of cooling it down. I only succeeded in burning the fingers of both hands instead of just the one. "The Vigil is right. I screwed up in the biggest, baddest way I could. I'm not sorry about what I did. You're alive and you might not have been if I hadn't broken the rules." Broken my brain, broken it all.

"But you're not their brother and you don't mean to them what you mean to me." I gave up and discarded the blazing roll back on the plate. "I get why they think I'm a risk. When it comes to you, I am. I always will be." I slammed the microwave door shut and leaned against the breakfast counter. "Robin knows that too, and he knows that getting in the crosshairs of the Vigil is not worth his life. It's my problem, not his."

My problem. Just once in my life I was going to get someone to believe that. Not Nik, I knew, but *someone*. It's my nightmare, not yours, stay away. Save yourself. I had one friend. I'd like him to live.

Just once . . . was it that much to fucking ask?

Niko had lowered his eyes to start working on the second EpiPen. "While I was at Robin's requesting help with the Vigil, he told me how he met us in one of our previous lives. I'd been a slave captured from another tribe in Ireland. He bought me, gave me my freedom. He hadn't thought for a moment whether or not to do it. I could see that," he said, hands working faster with repetition.

"He has been at our sides too many times we can't

remember, and that won't change. The Vigil or Grimm or the entire Auphe race, he won't abandon us. You don't doubt me. You shouldn't doubt him." His gloved hands reassembled the second device. "And we annihilated the entire Auphe race—twice—or did you forget?"

I knelt opposite him on the edge of the blue paper cloth spread on the floor. I didn't bother trying to explain it wasn't about doubt. He knew. I'd done the same before and dragged Robin into our mess when it was Niko who was in trouble. Yeah, I was hypocrite enough to expect people to have self-preservation when it came to helping me, to recognize who I was, what I was, and that it wasn't worth gambling their lives. At the same time I would risk others for Niko ... whether they volunteered or not. They could kick and scream all they wanted; I'd chalk up to A-plus enthusiasm and toss them under that bus if it would save my brother's life.

Nik wasn't me. He was good and, in his own way despite all the lives he'd taken and his lethal abilities, pure. I was not. But there was a common exclusive selfishness we shared. Niko was good, the best man I knew. It didn't change the fact that Niko would sacrifice anyone for me if it came to that. Anyone at all. Friend or lover.

I didn't much care that I wasn't good. I didn't agonize over the state of my conscience ... or the lack of the largest part of it. Not until long after I'd drowned it in blood, when it was far too late to make other choices. That was the difference that kept me quiet. If my brother could scratch out any scrap of denial for himself, I wouldn't take it away from him. How could I when I was the reason he'd compromise himself?

We'd both toss you under the bus—facts were facts— but Nik was the only one of us who'd feel bad about it.

Visually examining, but not touching, one of the completed autoinjectors with four times the normal dose and with the unfortunately necessary extra-long needle, I said, "Ireland? Green beer and leprechauns. If you were taken as a slave, where was I? Packed with enough muscle and rivers of ginger testosterone they had me standing at stud?"

"Obviously you're overdue a visit to a nymph. Pay me for the condoms this time or I'll give you a box of Saran Wrap for your dick instead. And, no, you were back at our village. You must've escaped capture. There was a celebration when Robin and I came home, he said, and then shared far too much information about all the women whose heartfelt gratitude didn't involve any clothing." He shook his head, a Pavlovian instinct with Goodfellow. His braid began to slip over his shoulder into the sterile field and he flipped it back. "He said your name was Cullen."

Cullen.

I felt my breath hitch and stop in my throat.

Cub.

The boy whose parents had died of the fever, but had his brother, grown tall and strong, to take care of him.

The brother who shouted my name … Cullen, Cullen … as strange men, big and dirty, flooded into our village.

The brother … *my* brother who told me to run to him, and I tried but he was far and my legs were short. I tried to call back before large, hard, hurting hands had snatched at me and harsh voices had jeered as I kicked desperately. He was far away but he was running. He ran faster than anyone in the village. I was proud and bragged about him at every race. My brother, it was my brother who ran faster than a stag. He would come for me and chase away these men. Stupid men.

I swung suddenly, the grass my heaven, the sky my ground. Everything was upside down, but I saw the bright copper shine of my brother's hair, his face twisted and hurt like it had looked when Mum had died half a day after Dada. Scared, my brother was scared. But that was all right. He'd been scared before, but he still loved me and took care of me. This would be the same.

Something cold slid across my throat and there was no air. I couldn't breathe and I couldn't cry out for help or say his name. I couldn't see him anymore, but I heard him scream for me when a red river flowed over my face, hiding everything from sight. I heard him as all was red and red until I finally fell into it. I fell into that red river that had somehow shadowed into black.

I didn't hear my brother after that.

I didn't hear anything.

I coughed and managed to pull in air. That it tasted of blood was imagination or memory, maybe both. Putting the injector down with numb fingers, I saw the glimmer out of the corner of my eyes, both left and right. More silver hair. The Auphe had had a grab bag of predatory goodies: unstoppable immune system, gates, absence of conscience, and now great memories too, it seemed. Racial memories, no doubt, and I was a special mix of races. Wasn't that the cherry on the damn top of it all? Whatever Great-great-great-great-homicidal-Grandpa had done, you would remember if you tried.

I stood. "You're right. If he wants to help, we should let him." If he'd offered to help after what had happened to Cullen, a little *kid*—if he could bear to keep helping us after that, who was I or anyone to say no or try to stop him?

"Now, about the *Bakeneko* we have to take out tonight? It doesn't matter if the Vigil is out to get us if we can't pay the rent. Play with your big-ass needles tomorrow. We should leave soon. Those pizza rolls aren't going to tide me over all night long." Circling around, I yanked at his braid. As a reward for not contaminating his precious sterile field, he stopped at the third autoinjector and went to take a shower before the hunt. When I heard the spray start and the sound of it hitting the sides of the shower as it scattered around when Niko stepped in, I stepped out. Outside the front door as the gloom of twilight began to creep in, I called Goodfellow.

"What is it, Caliban? I'm on the other line and I do not have time for this," came Robin's impatient snap.

Feeling more than snappish in turn, I snarled, "Cullen died."

Little Cullen, five winters old, with a big brother he worshipped. Little Cullen who'd not lived to see a sixth winter.

"I died before they took Niko. There was no party back at the goddamn homestead. No clowns and balloons. No goddamn kegger to welcome the two of you back," I challenged. "Why don't you tell me what really happened when you set Nik free?"

I'd heard it on a hundred cop shows. Once is chance. Twice is coincidence. Three times is a pattern.

We already had the once. Niko had been Achilles and had followed in my footsteps when I died as Patroclus.

I had a sick feeling now with Cullen that we went beyond chance. I felt what it had been like to be Cullen. I *had* been Cullen, and as Cullen I knew how my brother would react to watching my throat cut in front of him.

Not fucking well.

The voice on the other end of my phone went from harried to flat. "You remembered?"

"Not when he told me the story, because that was a lie, right? Only when he said my name was Cullen." I rammed fingers into my hair and wanted viciously to rip it out, every silver strand. "I get a new white hair every time I turn around. I'm guessing that combined with the memory of Cullen means that Auphe have racial memories, which is a good indicator my human half has them too, but I don't know or care. All I want to know is what happened to Nik. I was dead. Some bastards hung me upside down and bled me dry and he *saw* it. He saw them butcher me like a piece of meat. But later you found Nik. You bought him. I know you were lying about me waiting for him back home. What else did you lie about? He said you set him free. What happened then? What did he do?"

The air should've smelled of exhaust and hot dog fumes and the stench of too many people, but I smelled grass and trees and the smoke of a peat-fed bonfire. "What did he do, Robin?" I demanded again.

I had to know. This life was this life, and that was okay, because in other lives, Niko lived. If I died first, Nik lived on like normal people do. He survived. Whether it was fighting as a warrior or giving it up to marry, have kids, and be a farmer smelling of horse manure, I didn't care. I just cared that he lived. I wasn't the end of him. I wasn't the inevitable fucking end of him. It wasn't always my fault. It couldn't *always* be my fault.

There was the sound of a long breath let out, as harsh as some death rattles I'd heard, and the answer so emotionless it had to be a cover for the exact opposite. "What do you think? What he always does," he said without color or life. "What *you* always do."

What we always did.

That skipped straight over coincidence to pattern.

I'd thought it was this life that had us so intertwined and tied to each other. The circumstances—abusive mother, monster father, the constant threat of capture, death, and fates worse than all those combined. I'd been wrong. It wasn't because of the Auphe or Sophia or two years I'd lost to the Auphe hell that was Tumulus. It wasn't the unnatural genes in me either. Nik and I had been this way through our entire cascade of lives Robin had hinted at to us. We'd been brothers, cousins, comrades-in-arms, but always we'd been one.

Flawed because we were unable to stand alone or whole as others weren't because we were forever one.

I didn't know if we were damaged or if we were complete.

I didn't know.

I *had* to know.

"Shit." I spat, banging the phone against the side of my head. "Shit. Shit. Shit." I put the phone back to my ear and choked out, "I can't ... it can't always be ... me? Is it me that gets Niko killed? Is it me every time? Is it my fault?" No. Fuck, no. "Is it both of us? Do we take fucking turns? Robin, is it—"

His voice came back smooth and soothing, "Caliban, do you recall when we first met? When you were nineteen? How I hypnotized you to recall the two years you couldn't remember when the Auphe had you prisoner? How badly it went and how I told you not to let anyone hypnotize you again? No one. No more hypnosis. Not even me? That it took you too far until you were all but gone and I very nearly couldn't get you back? Do you remember?"

That was as apropos of nothing as you could fucking get. It made no sense. What was he talking about? What did that have to do with anything right now? "I remember." The words were thick and wet, my legs were giving out beneath me, and I didn't give a damn. "What does that have to do ... Screw it. It never changes, does it?" Did I want to know that? Did I really? Wasn't ignorance better? Despite my jumbled thoughts my mouth wouldn't stop. "Niko and me? It never *changes*. We always die too goddamn soon. We never have real lives. You said you both came back. You said Cullen was alive and—"

He cut me off, soft and calm. "I lied as I do. About the

hypnosis. I practiced. I thought I was the best, but I became better. Remember the nights months ago you came to my place to watch movies or come to my parties? When Niko was out with Promise? There were no movies and there were no parties. We talked instead. Or I talked, talked to make you safe. You don't remember that part, I made certain of it, but you did listen then. You need to listen now. Caliban, *obliviscaturque puer. Obliviscaturque* Cullen. Forget that boy. Forget Cullen. Forget his life. *Oblivisci omnia.* Forget it all. *Obedite custos.* Do you understand?"

Obey my guardian.

Forget.

Obltus.

Obey.

Odiemus.

"*Intellgeo.* I understand."

Someone's voice—it sounded like mine in a weird way and yet not quite—startled me. I was standing outside—what the hell? My back was braced against the concrete next to our door. I was practically on my ass, and my face was wet. I wiped at it curiously as I straightened until I was upright and looking up at the sky. Was it raining?

"Cal? Are you there?"

Huh. No rain. I took the phone away from my ear and looked at the screen. MOTHERPUCKER floated on a pale blue background. That was another "huh." Putting it back to my ear, I said, "Robin? Did I call you by accident?"

"I wouldn't be surprised," he huffed as if he couldn't decide to laugh or give me hell. "My number is only one digit away from 1-900-SXY-VRGN. I hope Niko doesn't go through your phone bill. I'd teach you all about burner phones and fake credit cards, but I'm busy at the moment. By the way, if I did have a 1-900 number, you couldn't afford it."

"Hey," I protested, not really sure what I was protesting, but it seemed the thing to do.

"Good night. And, Caliban? The truth is often highly overrated. Keep that in mind."

What was that? The fortune cookie of the day?

Before I could ask, there was a click and the phone went silent. I switched it off automatically and thought how close Robin's laugh sounded to jagged determination . . . and despair. But that made no sense. A third huh would've been too much for me to justify, even with my own low opinion of my IQ. I slid the phone back in my pocket and headed back inside, refusing to admit I didn't remember coming outside at all.

We were on the clock. Niko and I had a *Bakeneko* to kill.

Standing in a rain I couldn't see or feel on an outstretched hand wasn't going to make that happen, was it?

Why you would build a cookie-cutter neighborhood full of kids next to a junkyard, garbage dump, whatever, I don't know? But someone had done so. Or maybe the neighborhood came first, as brand-spanking-new as it looked, and the junkyard came second, bringing the *Bakeneko* with it.

It could be no one cared, that there were much worse places to live.

I knew how that felt.

When I was a kid, eleven, I thought—a year after Jack, our serial-killing neighbor—I'd have thought living in tiny gingerbread houses next to a junkyard would be paradise, much nicer than renting the dump across the street from the halfway house. Or Nik using the computer at school to check for sex offenders the first day every day we moved and once finding out ten out of fourteen houses on our block were marked. We'd caught the Greyhound bus after school that same day, stolen most of our mother's money—Sophia could stash anything and make it nearly impossible to find, which was why it was most and not all her cash—and we left the state.

She caught up with us a week later; she always did. After a fight with Niko shouting that I was only eleven, I was *not* a monster able to fight off a two-hundred-and-fifty-pound molester no matter what Sophia thought, and then Jack, Jack, Jack. What Jack had done to me—what Nik refused to say out loud: that Jack had chloroformed me, sliced my chest open with a scalpel in the start of J for his initial, and that he would have killed me if two unexpected things hadn't happened. I hadn't thought that after all that, she'd give in. The fact that Nik's fifteen-year-old face was blank and cold as he reached into the kitchen drawer to pull out a steak knife helped her make her decision. My brother who had rammed a knife into Jack's heart and I hadn't ever thought he regretted it. Sophia hadn't known that, but she'd been street-wise enough to know you can only push people so far.

There was a line and she'd recognized she was precariously balanced on it.

She'd actually gave him a twenty for food, recognizing and afraid of what she saw of herself in him. But his reasons were about protecting his brother. Hers were about protecting herself. Nik had already paid the deposit for the place, under the table thanks to his age and the fact that the place should've been condemned, but it was all the money we had. We ended up living in that apartment for a while. It was crawling with mold and scuttling with cockroaches, but it got a clean sweep when it came to sexual offenders. There were no swings or slides, not a sliver of grass, but it was the best Nik could do.

In comparison, a junkyard was the next best thing to a playground . . . as long as you had your tetanus shot. You could explore, build tree houses that, forget the name, sat on the ground and were made of abandoned cars, but it would've been close enough. But I was eleven, Nik wasn't much older, and there was no way Sophia would pay her hard-earned drinking, drug-buying cash for a small, brightly painted house not much bigger than the living room of the smallest apartment we'd once lived in. It could've been five hundred dollars more . . . two hundred dollars more; she wouldn't have done it.

"Kids, huh?" I jumped up and started climbing the chain length, hoping they hadn't gone all the way with the deluxe razor wire in the package. "It lives next to practically a Walmart full of them. All half off with a coupon for buy one, get the next one free."

Niko was following me, passing me truth be told, but who needs truth? "I wonder if it lures them in. I can't see that as possible. The fence is not your typical fence children would climb. It's nearly twelve feet tall and . . ."

"There's concertina wire," I finished with a groan. Concertina wire was cylindrical loops of razor wire— razor wire times two. I could see it glittering in the bright white moonlight like an ice-covered guillotine. I did hate razor wire with a passion, concertina more so. It only showed up when I was wearing something I liked and did not want ripped to shreds, like my jacket tonight.

"The children or the *Bakeneko* could've dug a hole under the fence in a less visible area." Niko reached into the pocket of his duster, hanging from the fence with one hand, tossed something to me, and then retrieved another for himself. They were wire cutters, the extremely expensive kind that even razor wire couldn't stand up to.

"Riiight. I was supposed to buy these a while back. Last month?" I started cutting and dodging the *spang* and slice of the wire in the air.

"Last year. But no worries. These are your next Christmas and birthday present and paycheck from the bar, assuming you ever get another one with your customer reviews." Nik had gone through the wire a helluva lot more quickly than I had and was now climbing down the other side, then jumping.

I'd made my last cut, tucked the clippers away, and was about to swing over the top before I caught the smell. It wasn't easy among the thousands of other scents in a junkyard, but I tried to stay familiar with the smell of those who hate me. "Nik, stop." But it was too late. He'd already soared down to land crouched with one hand planted on the ground. "Dogs."

Another deep breath brought a new scent to me as I plunged down after him. "And either a lot of cats or one big-ass cat."

Big-ass cat it was.

7

Caliban

The first thing a person should know when breaking into a junkyard is that (A) five Dobermans are overkill and (B) having their vocal cords severed so that they can't bark to alert intruders is animal cruelty of the highest order, and it's also cruelty to me when one buries his teeth in my leg because by the time I smelled and heard him coming, it was too late. His black coat soaked up the moonlight instead of reflecting it

I didn't want to hurt it. I liked dogs. They didn't like me, hated and were terrified of me depending on the dog and its aggression level. They smelled me, looked at me, and knew I was wrong. As far as I was concerned, that meant they had common sense. Cats, non-children-eating supernatural cats rather, liked me. But then cats liked to play with their food while it was still alive. Not the best recommendation or reference, but it is what it is.

I was about to swing my Desert Eagle to hopefully only knock the dog unconscious, as its grip on my leg changed from restraining me in place to having a snack. It chewed with enough enthusiasm that I had faith that it would make its way through flesh to bone in no time at all. I'd be doing a public service. There was nothing like gnawing on hard bone to keep teeth bright and tartar-free. Before I had a chance, it yanked its jaws away, teeth taking a little flesh as a souvenir, and lifted its head. Four more Dobermans had drifted out of the stacks of cars into a small opening of dead grass and an equally dead tree. They had been beginning to circle Nik. They weren't a threat, but no one wants to kill a dog. Those four Dobermans lifted their heads as my Lassie had and then all five as one raced back toward the maze of cars.

They didn't make it.

All five died in that peculiar and unnatural silence, clawed, bitten, set on fire, and all of them swallowed whole. It was disgusting. I'd killed too many monsters and some people as well, and none of it had made me feel as sick as this. The smell of burned dog hair, seared flesh, spreading blood . . . Jesus Christ, they were just dogs. No self-respecting monster had to kill a dog to survive.

"Mine."

Twisted paws with sheathing and unsheathing claws were spread wide to indicate Niko and me. To a *Bakeneko* humans were the meal of choice. Dogs weren't as tasty or it would've eaten them along with the kids. It slaughtered the Dobermans to have us for itself. Isn't it nice to feel wanted?

It would've been five feet tall . . . until it ate the dogs. Then it swelled to the size of a seven-foot-tall linebacker, beginning to stand on its hind legs as Niko had said it might. I'd have thought it awkward, but they weren't straight as a human's or crooked like a cat's. They were multijointed almost like an insect's. That it wasn't all the way up, continuing to rise from a crouch, had me guessing that once it did stand, it would be almost two feet taller. Nine feet tall and holy shit. It had fur—if something that had the wet-slime sheen of grave moss growing unpleasantly sleek on the buried decomposition beneath it could be considered fur. There were stripes the hue of ashes and the deep rust-black color of blood caked and dried on the floor of the abandoned slaughterhouse we'd passed driving into town. Its face was feline, close anyway, until it opened its mouth. I was waiting for the big boa constrictor/*Alien* unhinging scene, but that didn't happen.

It spoke.

"Where's my baby?" it crooned. It had the fangs of a cat, but each tooth was a fang, each the same length, and there were more than it needed . . . three or four times more.

"Mommy wants her baby." Every word was soaked with longing, sadness, and tears. "Baby needs to come to Mommy."

We'd wondered how it lured out the kids. Now we knew because I knew that voice; Niko knew it. It had its claws, mental ones, in our brains winding out a voice we'd never forget, a voice we'd heard on the first days of our lives. It was unreal. It could've been her. It was her, identical to the smoky, blue velvet, and whiskey melody. It was our mother as if she were right there.

It was too bad Sophia hadn't loved us a single moment in time. Too bad she was a bitch and a half. Too bad for you, *Bakeneko*.

It could've cried its fake river over the "heartbreak of its missing child," but if I'd been a kid and heard that voice saying those things, I'd have crawled out the window all right, but not toward it. I'd have gone to the other end of the house, out the window, and run like hell. I'd have known it was something monstrous or it was Sophia about to engage in a human kind of monstrosity. I'd take the first any time.

"Now we know." Niko was swinging his katana lightly back and forth. "How it tempted the children." They were the ones whose parents loved them.

Wasn't that a bitch that your mother's being one could've saved your life?

Confused at our immunity, it called a few more times as we started moving toward it, but not in a friendly "looking for my mommy" manner. It yowled, a screech that had both of us staggering for a moment that gave it time to try something else. If we wouldn't come to Mommy, Mommy would barbecue our asses.

Here's the second thing someone should know when hunting *Bakeneko*: They are assholes. The fireball throwing part is important, undeniable, and you should keep your eye out for the unhinging of the jaw in preparation to swallowing you, because I've looked down into that maw and it is not pleasant. That doesn't change the fact that I would like it to go on the record for monster killers who will come in our footsteps, *Bakeneko* equals asshole and that's the ball you shouldn't take your eye off if you plan to survive.

"It ate five Dobermans and my jacket is on fire."

I felt this needed pointing out, as it was also much larger than it had been before it ate the Dobermans and I liked my jacket. I'd bought it off a street vendor, but it was cool, had survived an entire year with me, which was unheard-of, and I might be emotionally invested in it . . . mildly. Okay, I loved that goddamn jacket, I wouldn't find another one that fit half as well while covering up my guns, and I was freaking furious about its demise.

Stomping on the scorched sleeve beneath my boot, I finished putting the flames out. Damn it. The whole thing was toast, nothing of it left. I still felt bad for the dogs too, but it wasn't like I could resurrect them any more than I could my jacket. Not to mention my jacket had not pissed on my leg before trying to rip it off with bone-crushing jaws. The dog had probably thought about it as it tried to chew its way through flesh and bone.

"To be fair—" Niko dodged a ghostly blue fireball and kept moving through the rusting rubble of the junkyard. "I told you they could walk on their hind legs, although I didn't know they could leap with such agility or I would've mentioned it."

"Leap?" I snarled as I tried unsuccessfully to aim both my Desert Eagle and my SIG at the blurry stripes of the gray of corpse flesh and the rusty brown of dried blood that streamed through the night air and our only break, the full moon. There weren't any trees to block what light that we did have. That was something. "It's not leaping, Nik. Frogs leap. It's levitating. Hell, it's fucking flying. There is nothing froglike in the way it moves. If there was, I'd have shot it already and PETA wouldn't be holding a candle-light vigil later for five fucking Dobermans. The furry children, Nik, think about them." I might have snapped, but this wasn't how I'd planned on this job going.

"I think it's a positive sign in your personal development how you've made it about the children and not about yourself . . . or your jacket that only coincidentally said 'Die, asshole. Die' on the back in font only a comic book editor could love." He kept moving, climbing over crumbled piles of brick overgrown with thick masses of vine I was hoping like crazy was poison ivy, poison oak, poison anything that would make Niko sorry he'd engi-neered the assassination of my jacket. And he had; I knew he had.

"That was luck. I only cared about how well it concealed my holsters." I regretted it as soon as I said it. It was a lie huge enough that the retaliation could only be the very same jacket with a rainbow and a glittering pony painted on the back. Niko would find it—he had his evil, sadistic ways. It would be less painful to admit to it now. "Fine. It was antisocial and hateful and that's why I liked it. You kill everything I love. Bite me." I fired both guns. I was close to ambidextrous, enough that if it moved at a normal speed I could nail it, but the *Bakeneko* knew nothing about normal. I hit it with the Eagle and that was accomplishment enough for me.

It tumbled through the air and hit in a pile of weeds and rotted wood and what looked like a washer or dryer or something domestic I didn't give a shit about. Its eyes focused on me, predatory and narrow, but not like a cat's. They were the eyes of a snake, the slit pupil narrower, more cold and moonlight flashing from the clear scales that protected them, before it disappeared into the high grass about twenty-five feet away with the limbs of a years-dead weeping willow drooping to veil it with brown, dried-out strands.

"Hide-and-seek. I'm not playing that game." I gated, disappearing before Niko could grab my arm, and grabbed it he would have. Once the *Bakeneko* was up and flying around again, we were screwed. We had to get it when it was down and for at least a few seconds not mobile. But that wasn't Nik's priority, not when I'd regained my gating ability just today. Gating when you were on top of your game was a rush you couldn't imagine until it hit you. Gating when you weren't on top of your game could melt your brain or it could wrap you in psychotic madness or it could kill you. You never knew. That killing you was often the best outcome told you how much you did not want to fuck with gates if you weren't MVP material.

That meant I had to make the hard call and I did.

I reappeared straddling the *Bakeneko*. I could taste the blood, feel it winding slowly from my nose, painting my lips, and running down the back of my throat. No big deal. I'd done this before. Too many swallows of copper and salt to count. This was nostalgia and nothing but. Both of my guns were pressed to the *Bakeneko*, one muzzle to its head, feline with pointed ears, slit-pupiled eyes, and a grotesquely gaping jaw that continued to un-hinge until I could see how it could swallow a full-grown man. It belonged in the Amazon, not here. The second muzzle was against its chest, covered with stripes of fur. Could be ash and blood. Could be something else. It could be color-coordinated as fuck. I didn't know and it didn't matter. It had eaten five Dobermans in less than three minutes. That's all I had to know. I needed to pull the triggers; that was all.

I did pull them. I didn't bother to think about it. By now, that reflex was more automatic than breathing. I pulled the triggers, but I didn't know if it did the job. I did hear the two shots. I didn't realize at first those two shots weren't mine. First a line of fire had traced across my back and almost simultaneously grazed my temple before I dropped to the ground and rolled onto my back, not that I wanted or planned to. I rested beside the *Bakeneko*. It was either already dead or smart and pretending to be. One or the other, I didn't know, as it remained motionless— and was still a dick.

My head hurt ... God, it hurt ... my back and head were as on fire as my jacket had been. I didn't know why or who or what ... Then I heard a man scream, followed by another voice, a woman this time, crying out, and finally several wolves howl in triumph. I stared at the moon and the sky and the few stars that stood out against a canvas of the deepest midnight velvet.

Nice. I didn't see stars often, not in the city.

Upstate. This was practically the wilderness. I shouldn't be surprised to hear the howl of a wolf or maybe a coyote.

Wrong . . . not a wolf, and a coyote was out of the question.

It was a Wolf. New York didn't have wolves, but they did have Wolves. They had the Kin. They had the werewolf Mafia and from the wet, grinding sounds of it, one of them was eating the man who'd shot me. I'd been shot. There was no mistaking that pain for any other. The burn of it was unmistakable.

"Cal." Niko was on top of me, a warm hand pressed to the side of my head. Why? Oh . . . the blood. He was trying to stop the blood. "Can you gate us home? Cal? Do you hear me? Can you get us home?"

A man and a woman, had to be Vigil, both with guns and night scopes to have hit me twice even in the light of the brilliant moon and Wolves with Vigil on their menu. That didn't make sense. All of them wanted us dead. I couldn't leave Nik to that. "Home," I slurred, raising a hand to grip Nik's shoulder and hang on tight. Home. The strain was worse this time. Noticeable the fourth time, not too great the fifth time, bad the sixth and final time. By now I was long used to the side effects of the game being on top of you instead of the other way around and none of it stopped me from taking us home. The Vigil. Wolves, and Nik. They couldn't have him or hurt him, and if he tried to protect me he could get hurt. He could die.

Fuck that.

I'd gate and the hell with the consequences. I had to. I couldn't let it be our fault. Not this time. Not again.

Cullen said so.

Cullen knew.

Cullen, whose brother was the fastest runner in the tribe.

Cullen, who was stubborn and wild and now that he knew, he wasn't going to forget. Whoever thought he could make him do that was wrong. Robin was wrong. Five winters, but five winters was enough to learn how to protect your family.

The purple lightning of the gate crashed around Niko and me. It would take us home. Take us someplace safe. Cullen approved of safe and told me to hurry up. Slow and safe weren't often the same and didn't I know anything?

Bossy little shit.

"I am telling you, Goodfellow, it was the Kin. Several of them from the sounds of it. Delilah's own took out a member of the Vigil to save Cal."

That would be Niko. I didn't understand what he was saying, not completely. I didn't think I understood what he was implying either. I was too dizzy and sick to my stomach to make sense of it. That didn't mean I didn't understand something else. I understood that he was the one person I knew who could try on optimism for a fit while buying a ticket for the *Hindenburg* or the *Titanic* and make it work. My brother, take a bow. I didn't know how he managed it, but he did.

"Perhaps," he continued, "she has changed her psychopathic mind about Cal and for whatever twisted reason wants to keep him alive."

My brother, the . . . wait. What? "Psychopathic? Twisted"?

That was entirely uncalled for. I'd been aware when I hooked up with her that she wasn't entirely sane, but who is? I wasn't entirely sane and aware right now, but no one was waving accusations in my direction, were they? She was nuts, but she'd always been nuts. Nothing to announce as new or in any way to blame on me.

"I am an enormous fan of rash assumptions." That was Robin. I recognized the sarcasm. "But let's keep this in the realm of possibility." And the brutal truth, I recognized that too.

"He's right," I murmured, pleased that the words sounded close to . . . well, words. I was proud. "Delilah . . . dead." I tried again. "Delilah wants . . . me . . . dead." I opened my eyes to see the ceiling of Niko's room, no scorching on his pristine beams like the soot-stained ones in my room. A pair of wide gray eyes and slitted green ones were both staring at me. The latter made me wonder what Robin was up to. "What?" I grumbled at him, and his suspicious gaze. "She hates me. If she's saving me, she has reasons. And not sexy reasons."

I did miss the sexy reasons. The murder and psychosis, I didn't miss as much when I knew any moment they could be aimed at me. If I did progress to full Auphe, inside and out, Delilah would like me more—give our fiends with benefits further consideration. Psychos . . . how fair was it that they had more fun?

"I can't believe she ever had sexy reasons regarding you, anytime, anywhere." Robin accepted a piece of blood-soaked gauze from Niko's hand and disposed of it out of sight. "Let's go with she was insane before and she's insane now and never will we know her reasons, as they're reasons of which reason knows nothing."

"That was a quote, Cal." Niko was pressing something, I was guessing more gauze, against my temple. "A highly mutilated, highly inappropriate quote, but a quote nonetheless." He knew I hated quotes unless they involved profanity, sarcasm, and maybe cannibalism. I hated them doubly when my head hurt as much as it did. Where was I anyway? Oh. The usual postfuckup location. I was on his bed, where I most often ended up when wounded, as it was cleaner than mine. Better for wound care or any minor surgeries. Joy. I swallowed, tasted the faint aftertaste of blood, and decided I was alive enough not to worry about minor issues ... such as anything anyone said while I was conscious. Except for one thing. . . .

"If I'm going to die, no quotes." I ran my tongue over the crust of dried blood on my teeth and felt the impossibly high thread count of Niko's sheets under the bare skin of my back, my shirt gone. "And if I'm going to live, no quotes. Where's my shirt?"

"The same place as your jacket." Niko's hand increased the pressure against my head. "A better world. Let them pass on in peace. You, however, were shot ... twice by the Vigil. They're mostly superficial wounds, but you need to be more careful in the future."

That wasn't right. I knew the cat-thing had been flying around worse than a high-hopping toad on speed. Being distracted by that and not picking up on a human assassin was not at all my fault. When it came down to it, I was certain that research was Niko's area and not knowing that a fireball-throwing, attack-dog-eating Asian cat creature could all but fly was his department. "No." I swiped a hand at the one he had resting against my temple. I missed, but that didn't mean I didn't try. "You said ... fireballs. You didn't say it could *fly*. You . . ."

That's when I felt it.

That was the thing about gates. If you couldn't build them, make them, create that wound in the world, you couldn't feel them either. With the epinephrine, I wasn't cured, but I was treatable. I'd been treated today. I'd traveled several times today. I could feel it when others traveled my way.

"Grimm."

I sat up, the hell with the blood and having been shot but not enough to kill me. None of that counted now. "Grimm." I looked around wildly as if I could see the whole city from the bed I was trapped in. "A gate. Grimm is in the city."

Worse. I felt it. He was close . . . so damn close.

"Grimm is here."

8

Goodfellow

I'd shown up at Niko and Cal's place fifteen minutes after Niko called me. The speed laws I'd had to break and the driver I'd had to bribe with a vacation to Barbados not counted in that trip. Cal was shot, Cal was down, Niko needed me, and I went. Money is nice, but when you're alone, it's a luxury that eases your way yet bars you from knowing if anyone wants you for you alone. Do they want your company or do they want the luxuries your company brings with it? Most pucks don't care. I had times when I didn't care. Like me for me or like me for what I can give you, what was the difference? I very probably didn't like you either, and while you were focused on my wealth, I was focused on your genitalia. But there was Niko, Cal, and Ishiah, and there I knew the distinction. There money meant nothing, blood was everything, and when they hurt, *you* hurt. I hadn't been born knowing that. Did I wish I'd not ever learned it?

Sometimes.

"He was shot." Niko's hands had already ripped Cal's shirt off, and then I ran into his bedroom. He was cleaning and taping down a dressing on a long but shallow furrow on his brother's pale-skinned back. "It had to be the Vigil."

This was why I loathed subcontractors. They were inevitably less than efficient.

He was rolling him back now and trying to stop the bleeding from the crease on Cal's right temple. Head wounds—they bled an ocean and at times you didn't know if they were barely anything or the swipe of Death's scythe itself. I pushed Niko's hands aside and held the gauze in place myself as he tunneled scarlet fingers into his tightly bound hair. Strands of the dark blond braid fell loose and turned the same red that stained his hands. "It was a *Bakeneko*—it was nothing. Relatively easy except for his stupid, idiotic jacket and I'd factored in the destruction of that. I was hopeful at least." He paced beside his bed. "But someone shot Cal. It had to be the Vigil. It was dark. There was only the moonlight to use to see. He . . . they had to have night scopes. I heard two of them scream, a man and a woman, when I heard Wolves take them down after they shot Cal. They attacked and *ate* the assassins. I could hear that too. Why would they when Wolves hate us . . . ? I have no damn idea of their motive. Fuck."

I wondered if Cal had any idea the cursing his brother was up to when he wasn't conscious to hear it and yet butter wouldn't melt in Niko's mouth when Cal could know what he was saying. I used to think that he was trying to be a good influence, but now I thought Niko had a bit of trickster in him. He didn't curse when Cal would hear, because Cal would enjoy it. It was the smallest of evils, but I approved nonetheless.

Neither Niko nor Cal was enjoying anything at the moment unfortunately. "Let me." Niko sat on the side of the bed and replaced my hands with his. I didn't fight him. We both needed something to do and I was already doing my part whether I was the only one who knew or not. He lifted the gauze, frowned at the still-pulsing blood, and reapplied pressure. "I am telling you, Goodfellow, it was the Kin. Several of Delilah's own took out two members of the Vigil to save Cal."

That's when Cal woke up and offered a more realistic if not necessarily more accurate commentary on what had happened. I wanted to smirk at words that were so very Cal—not sexy reasons indeed—but I couldn't. He looked . . . he didn't appear right. I knew if he didn't seem right to me, it was worse to Niko. Cal's black hair was streaked in several locations with strands of silver and his eyes were gray hosting a rattlesnake pattern of scarlet. It was enough to lose hope at the sight, but Cal, his words, his actions . . .

He was the same. For now.

I'd seen him give in to his Auphe side before, more than once. I'd seen what it was when he went feral and rabid and was lost to his humanity. I'd seen Cal at his worst.

This wasn't it. He looked more Auphe, yes, but inside, he was as Cal as he'd ever been. And when he said Grimm's name, that Grimm had come, he said it with anger, not anticipation. When he said Grimm . . . cousin/brother/Auphe . . . he was saying stop him, keep him away, not bring him to me, not let us fight/join/flip a coin on the fate of the world.

Cal didn't want any part of Grimm and that said it all.

He remained Cal.

I gently touched the dried blood on Cal's upper lip that had come from gating too much with too little. Our cub. With the next gate the blood might come out of his ears. Zeus, I hoped not, but we didn't have a choice. I bent down and whispered calmly in his ear too low for Niko to hear, "Cal." Niko did not need to know this. Niko would make me incredibly sorry if he knew I'd hypnotically conditioned his brother, whether it was for emergencies or not. I was sorry, but emergencies didn't come much worse than Grimm.

"Take Niko and you to where you lived when you were thirteen years old." It was an age plucked at random but before the Auphe had taken him. Bound to be safer than what was happening now. "Now. Do not come back until tomorrow at the very soonest. *Odiemus.*" Obey.

He lifted his eyes to mine blankly and did what I'd taught him over this past year. "Cal, *odiemus. Ego enim iam parere.*"

His lips framed the words that didn't have the breath behind them to say aloud as I'd taught him. A secret wouldn't stay that way long if Niko heard his lazy baby brother speaking Latin. But I didn't have to hear the words. I read his lips and knew them all the same. Zeus, I was screwed. Never such a mess as I had made. It wasn't this Cal who'd spoken. It wasn't this Cal that made it clear I wasn't in charge forever.

I'd conditioned Cal to the hypnosis, but what had I missed? All the other Cals of all his other lives should be long gone, sleeping deep down that I couldn't reach them. But who had recently appeared out of the past, whole and intact, because of a lying piece of *skata* of a story I'd told Niko? Who obviously wasn't going to let himself be forgotten regardless of what I'd told Cal to do so at his panicked call when he'd remembered earlier?

Cullen. Cullen who was Cal before Cal himself was.

Ego enim iam parere.

Cullen obeyed, but only for now.

Whatever I might command, whatever amount of hypnosis I laid upon Cal would have to get by Cullen first from now on. And as Cullen was Cal once upon a time and Cal was Cal period—stubborn as Hades, neither bowed before anyone, not even me, unless I tricked him. I'd tricked Cal into hypnosis. Cullen hadn't been an issue, not a cloud on the horizon of this past year, not until I made him one with that damn story.

"Ego enim iam parere."

He obeyed . . . but for now, not forever.

"You won't have to," I promised as quietly as before. "It's coming to an end, and this time around, in this life we all win. I swear it. Three times three." Three times three, a bond even a puck won't break.

This time I said in English and loud enough for Niko to hear me, "Cal, gate!"

The combination of Cullen/Cal must've believed in my oath, and I hoped he kept believing it or life would get more difficult, if that were possible. The purple and black and gray swallowed him, his brother, and most of the bed. They were gone, far from here. I had no idea where. That lack of knowledge was best for all of us.

Hopefully both Niko and Cal would assume Cal had gated wildly, barely conscious, and taken them randomly to a place from their childhood, which meant far from here. Whatever their reaction, I could hold on to the satisfaction that I'd been right, little good that it did me. If any situation called for hypnotic-forced gating, Grimm was it. Not that he'd been all I'd thought of months ago when I started this: Grimm, Delilah and the Lupa, the Vigil. If there was a worst-case scenario, a puck had long ago thought of it, written it up, and submitted it as a screenplay. I'd come up with fifteen more scenarios in which hypnosis could be a saving grace, such as Cal beginning to remember Tumulus on his own and his two years there and the insanity or catatonia that would follow. I hadn't ranked the scenarios correctly or guessed who'd be fighting me on the other side, but I'd known eventually someone undefeatable would.

Something or someone always did and always had done so.

Gods, this had better be worth it, as I was *done*. I was pulling every underhanded trick out of my jockstrap this time. This was going to go my way and no one was going to stop me.

There were many times in the past that I'd known what was coming but refused to admit it as I'd thought I couldn't stop it. I wasn't doing that any longer. I was older and wiser. Once I'd respected my friendship with Niko and Cal enough to let them make their own decisions about their lives and about their deaths. If you love something, set it free ... yes, well, if the cliché of that didn't make one vomit, then the added incredible idiocy, naïveté, and sheer laziness of that saying impressed me not at all. I'd seen how letting Niko and Cal make their own decisions had worked out for them in the past.

If free will had ever had a manual, the two of them had thrown it away.

I'd seen death come far sooner than necessary again and again. Achilles and Patroclus. Alexander and Hephaestus. Arturus and Caiy. Phelan and Cullen. That had been only four lives among a thousand. I could name them for hours, a graveyard of death before its time. Cal had been right in his pissed-off and panicked call to me, half of it. They were karmic *gamou* dominoes. When one died, the other either immediately or very soon after followed. It wasn't always Cal, as he feared, though. Niko had gone first many a time himself with Cal following as swiftly as he could.

That meant two things. The first, I was tired, so very tired of it all. This in turn led to the second conclusion: Their major-decision-making days were over. They were humans, mostly. *Humans.* Why had I ever thought them capable of thinking anything through? I was a puck. I was a *trickster* and there was no more denying that. Fate was dealing the cards to Cal and Niko, but I would be the one playing their hand. I was born and bred for this. Whether the brothers knew it or not, they were sitting this one out and I was doing what came as naturally as the beat of my heart.

I watched what was left of the bed collapse onto the floor. It was a mess. But that was not my problem. I had no plans of cleaning it up.

"Grimm," I said, leaning back in my chair with hands locked behind my head. Beyond the bedroom door, the hall was dark . . . except for a pair of bright red eyes.

I gave my best salesman smile.

It was the same one that had Eve picking Eden's apple tree bare to give them all to me. "Here. Have a bite of the fruit of knowledge," I'd offered with an appropriately devious smile as I tipped her with the last one. She had needed knowledge with her body—the beta version always leaves vast realms for improvement. With that knowledge, I'd heard a few angels gossip, would come shame at her nudity. She *needed* a little shame . . . let's not lie, a great deal of shame. I was doing her a favor. She needed to be covered up, and the sooner the better. She made the Neanderthal female downstream munching on her own lice look like a vision of beauty and desire.

My grin widened as the crimson eyes drifted closer down the hallway, now with the sheen of metal claws sparking in the halo of the bedroom light. Getting the customer in the door was the difficult part. After that, it was all over. That car was sold. "Come on in. Sit a spell." I ran my tongue over my teeth. Slick. Full of predatory shine.

Smiling like the shark I was.

"Let's make a deal."

It was three days, not one, before I saw Cal and Niko again. What with being shot, superficially or no, concussed, and having gated too many times on too little epinephrine, Cal hadn't been in the best of shape. Or as Niko had put it when he'd called me extremely early the next morning after the shooting from some dive motel in Arkansas:

"Be armed when we arrive home. I want to kill you with a clean conscience."

I didn't fail to smile fondly whenever Niko threatened me with bodily harm.

He'd seen me fight Auphe, the last troll, revenants, boggles, goddesses, zombies of two different types, and much more. I'd convinced him on occasion to spar with me as well and he generally agreed if I swore a solemn oath to keep at least my pants on. He'd given up on the shirt and refused to listen to my lecture on the history of naked Greco-Roman wrestling.

Clothed or unclothed, he knew who the better fighter was. Niko was one of the best, if not the best, human fighters alive today, but I was me. In my first fight I'd been armed with a rock. Yes, the rock was the first weapon. When the spear was first invented, I was ecstatic. I was vastly tired of wielding granite and getting blood and brain tissue splashing back on me during battles. Say what you want about preverbal man, he loved to fight. The *paien* around at the time weren't any different.

Niko knew what I could do. That didn't mean he would back down. That had been true before he was a nearly undefeatable warrior. Stubborn *nothos.*

He hadn't always been the best among humans, and wouldn't that make him, highly offended, choke on his protein drink? It was true, as thoroughly he would deny it. Niko, a grim child with little in the way of choice, had learned and relearned to fight in this life for Cal. As he grew, he also worked to be the honorable man. Every day he embraced it. Honor and conceit, he would say, do not go together.

Yet, know it or not, he was so very conceited regarding his fighting skills that when I defeated him sparring, his face would go blank, his lips pressed tight against each other, all holding back his enormous annoyance. He'd glare at his sword as if it were the one at fault then take it to the rack of twenty-four swords mounted on the sparring area wall and place it at the bottom in a sheath with a deliberate misquote of Sun Tzu painted upon it: Even the finest sword will fail you.

The first time it happened I'd turned to Cal who, as usual, was slouched on the sofa. "The sheath of shame," he drawled. "It'll be punished until it rotates back to the top before it's forgiven." He'd flipped a page in a comic book . . . pardon, graphic novel. "Niko's kind of nuts about his weapons"—he gave me a quick smirk as Niko's back was to us—"and batshit about losing."

Ah, Niko, enjoy your conceit. You've earned it. Punishing your swords might be somewhat odd, but your personal life is your own.

Defamed swords or no, sparring with him to subtly train him out of adequate dojo-taught habits into far more successful ones came with incredible ease. That hadn't been the case long ago when Niko carried a pointed stick meant to be a spear and Cal a torch to set the attackers on fire. I'd first come to realize that these two particular humans kept appearing in my life, from decades to hundreds of years apart, sometimes looking similar, sometimes not, but forever with the same somewhat irritating personality, Cal, and unbreakable nature, Niko.

I do admit humans didn't get interesting until they developed into an upright form, lost that matted fur, and eventually gained a primitive culture and language. They had known less words than your current treat-trained Pomeranian, but it was an improvement nonetheless. It still had taken me another thousand years or so to recognize the two humans following me from life to life and another five hundred years before I decided what to do about it.

The first time I had approached these peculiar humans who followed me from death to life and back again, it was pure curiosity. This was before war and cities. This was a time a stranger could be cautiously welcomed provided he brought food. I'd not interacted with humans before, but I'd observed their customs. I brought a great deal of food and was instantly the most popular person in the camp. It had taken me about two hours to become fluent in their language, surprisingly complex as it had come to be from that of their ancestors. I also brought them alcohol, the first they'd tasted. It was fermented mare's milk, no favorite of mine, but there were no grapes in this region and I made do. It was a success. Cal—Kree as he was called then—became my new best friend right as he toppled over and passed out across my lap as we sat in the dirt. I laughed and patted him on the back.

I'd lied to myself. It hadn't been curiosity that had brought me to meet them.

It was loneliness.

I had lived more years than I thought could exist, and it seemed I would keep living through them. If there was an end in sight, I could not see it. I didn't want to live them alone.

Patting Kree's limp form one last time, I leaned against the shoulder of the man/boy who went everywhere with him. I leaned and felt the warmth of another person in more years than I knew. "You are a good brother to watch and protect Kree as you do." Kree had a temper and no fear, which could be a problem that some people didn't care for. That would be nothing new in all the future days to come.

Val shrugged. He was big for the younger age that sat smoothly on his face. His hair could've been dark blonde, light brown, or dark brown. With not enough water to keep them all alive, the people of the tribe didn't waste it on bathing. Their hair in matted twists tied back with cords of more goat skin, it was impossible to guess anyone's hair color ... except Kree. His was black, a dusty, filthy black, but black all the same.

"I don't know that he is my brother." He ate another bite of the food I'd brought, face lightening at the taste of dates I'd picked far from here. "Everyone lies with everyone. We are too few to take one mate only. We need to grow."

I could see that, but I could see what I had since I'd come into their camp. Val watched Kree as if he were a child of four summers rather than the same age that Val appeared to be. Fifteen summers for each of them, perhaps sixteen. If they lived to be twenty, that would make them legends in this part of the desert.

Four or five more years and I would be alone again.

They'd come again—I'd seen that—puzzling from a distance or retreating if they approached me, but their rebirths didn't fall in a pattern. Sometimes a hundred

years, sometimes a thousand right before I forgot they'd
existed. That wasn't acceptable, four or five years. I
needed longer with them. I might grow bored of them or
loathe them, but I first needed that chance to know for
certain.

"Val," I said, carefully moving an unconscious Kree off
my lap and onto more dirt for a nice nap. I did a quick
check of his movements and eyes. Val had drunk the
mare's milk as all the others had, but not as much. I had
seen when he felt the intoxicating effect on him and
passed the still two-thirds-full skin to Kree. He wanted to
stay alert. If no one else in the camp felt that responsibility, he did. It was a good sign for what I had in mind.

"Val," I repeated. "How would you like to learn to
fight and fight well?"

"Fighting is but waste. Waste of blood and lives when
all the people could join together, share what we have."
From his dark expression I could tell he thought that's
how it should be, but not how it would be.

"You're correct, but, Val, there are too few of you in
this land to make that a reality. It would be a long time
before that has a hope of happening. I can teach you
though. Teach you to defeat any enemies you might have
here. You could live longer; you could keep Kree alive
longer. You could live long enough to join the tribes, to
force a peace, that no more children die fending off attackers with sticks." It was manipulative, but not a trick.
Val did want that, all of it, and if I received what I wanted
as well, where was the harm?

It was one of the better decisions I'd made.

Niko as Val hadn't been anything special then except
for his determination in the days when in warm weather
people wore nothing but desert ocher paint and thought
horses were for eating not riding. Yes, a very long time
ago. He'd had raw talent, but this was long enough ago

that humans hadn't yet organized murder and they didn't have a word for war. Nor a concept. There were too few of them, no cities to speak of yet. Wars are not made of fifty men and boys fighting over a cluster of ragged tents.

In those days, rocks lashed to a thick wooden handle to smash skulls and spears that were no more than stone-sharpened lengths of wood—basically a pointy stick—were the only human options. I kept my *paien* metal weapons hidden and worked with what was available to Val.

That's how it began.

Finding someone who knew enough to teach you to fight was unheard-of then. The battles hadn't been large enough. There was a new leader every day with the corpse of the previous one, head crushed, feeding the scavengers. No one would waste their time training you—if there were someone worthy to be a teacher. There was not. Survive one skirmish and that was blind luck. Surviving two made you a wise veteran. I'd not seen anyone make it through a third one in my wanderings. One learned on their own by fighting for their life.

Until I had come along.

The first to share food, mare's milk, and fighting skills.

Val had been the start of it, and I was teaching him even now. I had found him and his brother every time after their deaths as Val and Kree. Niko had gone on to become among the best of whoever he was with at the time—tribes, nomadic raiders, protector of small clans living in houses built of mud, finally towns and cities, palaces, and temples. Thanks to his first instruction from me, his continued education in each following life, and his innate will to protect.

In every life I taught him and in every life he improved. I was just now realizing Niko improved *too* much. He didn't start with a blank slate in each life. Well, he did, but within weeks he was fighting at a level most would take years to accomplish—in a year, he had the skill of decades of daily battles. I hadn't thought about that before, more concerned with finding the newly incarnated him and Cal, and then more concerned with trying to convince them to do anything possible to stay alive, the reckless idiots.

I'd carelessly thought he was unequaled in this life thanks to being descended from Achilles—the most skilled human warrior I'd ever seen, having the genes of an epic warrior passed down from the Rom, generation to generation in the Vayash clan who'd wandered Greece at the wrong time. But it was more—of course with Achilles and reincarnation, he was basically descended from himself—I doubt he enjoyed thinking about that procreational peculiarity. In the other lives, though, without Achilles, he'd gotten better and better, learned more quickly than a human could.

Cal said the Auphe had racial memory. Perhaps the only difference between them and humans was that the Auphe could mentally access those memories, whereas with humans it was locked away in the subconscious, showing up in instinct and muscle memory. Picking up an old skill in a fraction of the time that it had once taken you long before this new life. It was undeniable Niko couldn't be the fighter he was in the short number of years he'd had to learn. He was too young. He could be good, but good wouldn't bring down an Auphe, and Niko had brought down more than one.

He was all that he'd ever been, accumulating what he gathered in each life into the unbelievable skill he possessed today. He was ... Achilles, yet impossibly more. It was astonishing. Phenomenal.

Naturally, I was still better.

That went without saying. I was Goodfellow.

But I had also been and remained his instructor, whether he knew it or not, and I was proud of my student. To see him cut an army in half practically on his own. To see what I'd created in him with my teachings. To see the perfect human warrior.

It wasn't my fault—no one could say it was—that I hadn't been able to teach Cal an Ares-blessed thing.

A teacher is only as good as his student. Cal had invariably wanted the minimum skill to keep him alive, as he needed his other valuable time to drink, get in fights, chase women, sleep, and generally enjoy the hell out of life. I had to respect that if not out-and-out applaud it.

Cal and I had weaved a decadent path of debauchery and sin across the world throughout history. While Niko could come close to keeping up with me in weapons, Cal came close to keeping up with me in everything else. There'd been a time that when I said, "Orgy," Cal didn't freeze up and flee; Cal had said, "Where? And let me grab the two fleetest horses in the camp."

Watching him in this life was . . . difficult. In most all others he'd been happy, horny, and human through and through, foulmouthed and laughing—someone who loved life. Now he rarely drank because of his alcoholic mother and Auphe tolerance. He avoided most sexual encounters unless they could be proved beyond all doubt not to produce more Auphe offspring. He fought, but it was with a bitterness that was the opposite of the fun-loving spirit with which he'd gone about it when he was completely human. He'd once fought for the thrill of it and usually everyone staggered home drunken, beaten to Hades and back at the end of the night, but alive. When he was a Viking, I'd been involved in innumerable alcohol-fueled brawls while watching his back every single night. Now when he fought, it was for a reason, not a hobby . . . or a much more vicious hobby than it had been. Cal was the only one to walk away still breathing from fights these days.

He did still sleep a good deal and thank the God of the Forge that guns had been invented, as those he used with genuine skill. This Cal . . . all his lives had been short as he'd earlier guessed and I cursed that . . . but at the same time, the majority of those limited lives he had reveled in. Not all—not Phelan and Cullen and there were others that ended no better—but most . . . most had been good lives.

Exceptional lives.

Mayfly ones, but exceptional yet brief enough to make me think of walking away the next time I found them. Spare myself the pain. I had thought about it, I admitted, as they were so fleeting, but I hadn't been able to do it.

I knew I never could.

"How is Cal?" I questioned Niko as I sat down at the computer, which rested on the desk by a window overlooking Central Park. I opened up my e-mail account I'd set up days ago with dual subjects of "RVs" and "Canada" and swallowed a sigh. When you knew all the tricksters in the world, your network was wide and effective but generated enough e-mails to make your eyes ache.

I'd clicked on the first e-mail and tried not to groan at the ignorance contained within. I knew Cal was all right. I knew that he was alive, I told myself as I deleted the e-mail.

If he hadn't been and the last gate had killed him, Niko wouldn't bother with warning me to arm myself. He would come for me from behind, honor discarded and nobility tossed aside. He would do whatever it took—there are warriors and then there are berserkers who will do anything it takes, no matter how horrific. Cal knew he was a killer, every life he'd known, whether he excelled or was at best mediocre at it. Niko knew the same, but Niko thought he was in control. Niko had rules and lines not to be crossed and a code, or so he thought. His blind spot was truly extraordinary.

I'd seen that in the Trojan War. Of all our time, I always thought of that life first . . . always. It had been the best in all the ways until it had been the very worst when Achilles went insane.

I'd seen him do, Zeus . . . when Patroclus fell and Achilles had charged the field, Death himself would've fled the atrocities. Uncountable numbers of soldiers are nothing against the willingness to do essentially anything and everything necessary for vengeance.

Niko didn't remember other lives as Cal could. He'd forgotten what he was capable of, but I hadn't.

That was how I knew Cal was alive and more or less fine. If he hadn't been, there'd be a good possibility I'd be reading my e-mails when Niko's sword buried itself in my back. "Is he sleeping, then?" I went on, not waiting for a response from Niko. He was taking too long to answer, and that wasn't the most positive of signs. I needed him back to normal. I needed them both back to as close to normal as could be hoped for right now.

Niko responded with a sharp bite, "Yes, he's asleep. He gated us to a field where a carnival we once lived at had been. He dropped, covered in blood from his mouth, nose, and ears. Luckily they'd built a motel since then by the road. I checked us in, cleaned him up, and now he won't wake up." Niko's control was wavering, but his anger wasn't. It was growing. "You told him to do this. To take us away. Now he won't wake up. Why did you do tell him to do that? He wasn't healthy enough to gate again. Why did you risk him like this?"

I had to be careful, as careful as you could be while conning everyone you knew.

Conning Niko, in addition, took more than being careful. It was beyond dangerous. Niko, who in this life was closest to Achilles than in any other before save the original. I knew how he'd possibly react—not well. Of all his past selves, why Achilles? I hadn't been able to reach any of them, a staggering one hundred percent failure rate, but Achilles had been my worst mistake. Achilles who seemed to have no fear—who you could believe was half god raised on high, yet had fallen the furthest. He'd had fear and doubt, but hid it away so deeply no one saw it.

Much like Niko.

But why would he show those darker emotions or keep them once I'd appeared in their lives? A living all-powerful god had claimed him as brother-in-arms and family closer than blood. He could let it all go, drop the weight from his shoulders. He had his cousin Patroclus to keep whole in battles and war and the Great God Pan at his side to help him do it—with that, how could he possibly lose? He thought that he no longer had anything to risk or capable of being lost.

Achilles, who I recalled so well. . . .

Achilles had been a hand's grasp away from being a god himself.

Achilles, although entirely human, had been even less than a hand's grasp away from being a monster, one equal to what Cal now assumed he himself could be.

I stared blindly at the computer screen and saw only blood.

When Cal . . . when Patroclus had died, that brutal and bloody death—it was one slow enough for Achilles to run to his side, to see the words bubbling through blood, to watch death come and seize Patroclus in a convulsion that came from a lack of oxygen as his lungs filled with blood.

"You were to keep him safe." He'd grasped the edge of my armor, shaking me with all his strength. I thought he'd hoped my neck would snap. "You are the Great *God* Pan and you swore to keep him safe." Turning away from me, he'd let go and shoved me back from resting on my knees to hitting the rocky ground hard enough I felt my spine wrench, a rib break, and a concussion flare in red mist behind my eyes when my head hit the hard surface. Achilles gave me a look made of dual sharp blades of disgust and betrayal before he spat blood-tinged saliva onto my chest where my heart beat under the armor.

I'd played the god game several times before, but I couldn't bear to again, not after that.

I struggled to sit up as I told Achilles that I'd tried, *never* would I have let this happen if I could've stopped it. I would've taken the blows myself if I had reached him in time. I had sworn to watch over him for Achilles. Swearing oaths in war is the most foolish and heartbreaking of things. It's futile. They can't be kept. Sometimes in battle you get separated—as much as you attempt not to. I'd seen Patroclus swept away in a wave of soldiers, Trojan and ours. I worried, but I wasn't desperate as I fought my way back toward him. He wasn't like Achilles in skill, but he scraped by enough to survive more battles than he had summers since his birth. He could take care of himself until I made it to his side.

He shouldn't have fallen.

Couldn't have fallen.

He should stand up, let me take the blow in his place; I'd told Patroclus the same. That here, watch, I'd remove my armor. I had done so and tossed the breastplate as far across the stone and sand as I could. Slit my throat, puncture my lung, skewer my heart with his sword, I'd demanded, though that wasn't a mercy I deserved. I told that to empty gray eyes and a blood-drenched body crumpled in death.

I meant it. But when the blood began to dry on him

and he drew not another breath, my frenzy passed. The guilt stayed, but no longer could I fool it with a crazed hope that Patroclus could do what I asked. Patroclus was dead, and the dead did nothing.

I'd not been fortunate enough in life for any of my bouts of madness to last, mercy that it would've been.

Achilles was not me.

His mind left him and it did not return.

His last words to me remained, ". . . you swore to keep him safe." I'd been surprised he didn't try to finish what he'd started in killing me. I didn't know what I'd have done if he had. Handed my sword over to him and let him do his worst? I thought I might very well have. It hadn't been put to the test. To Achilles I no longer existed. His mind had fallen away to nothing, his sanity washing out and disappearing like the tide. He'd given Patroclus his funeral, kneeling by the pyre as empty and blank as a doll, and then he'd gone into Troy to die. But what he'd done before he died . . . the inhumanity of it, the savagery . . . I hadn't forgotten. *Paien* had a much different opinion of right and wrong than humans did, less restrictive, yet even so I'd shut my eyes that night in Troy. I hadn't wanted to see what Achilles had become.

Homer was a drunk and a liar and sometimes a coward. In his epic writings, he lied when he didn't know the truth, and when the truth was more than anyone could bear, Homer left it out altogether.

Achilles was a hero. Achilles died. No one needed to know what else Achilles could be or what he would be when pushed to the edge.

I closed my eyes to block the sight of the crimson running down the screen . . . as if it were on the computer and not in my mind and memory, forever engraved. Pucks do denial as well as anyone else when they want.

"I had to do it. Cal was right. Grimm was here," I said

with the weight of truth on my side. It was convenient when truth actually worked for you. "Cal was hurt. He couldn't have held his own. Grimm has sworn to him not to touch any of us. It's only Cal he can tear to shreds if he wants to keep playing that psychotic game the Auphe play."

The game of: I make you bleed. You make me bleed and who's still standing when it's all over? The Auphe had played it with each other since the dawn of time.

"He would've hurt him or, worse, he would've taken him. Gating away was the only option I could think of. I didn't tell Cal to take me, as I could've been the straw that broke the camel's back." That was true as well, in its way. If Cal had to gate three people instead of two, his chances of survival would've gone down radically.

The fact that I'd wanted to talk to Grimm alone didn't make that any less true.

"How did you get away from Grimm?" Niko asked with suspicion. My boy. I was proud.

"Retreat is the most valuable skill one can use in a fight. I reminded him of Cal's promise to blow his own brains out if Grimm killed one of us"—Cal's family—"and then I ran like a cowardly bat out of hell." Not at all true, a complete lie, but it had been half a million years at least since I cared between truth and lies or that I'd thought the divergence between them anything more than cosmetic.

Seizing my attention with several low tones, I opened my eyes to see that several e-mails on my computer appeared worthwhile and I answered them with promises of rewards and a reminder that if the world couldn't be saved, a single dollar bill would mean nothing to them.

"Is he gone?"

I shut down the computer and rubbed a hand down the leg of a set of finely woven bleached cotton pajamas.

I told Ishiah they were my monk-wear, available at all the finest ascetic monasteries. I had preferred to sleep in the nude, but a deceased housekeeper who'd later tried to murder me and Cal and Niko both had all made their preference known that walking about naked in the living room or kitchen while they were around wasn't acceptable. After the murder attempt, which often makes you stop and reevaluate, I decided this once I might be in the wrong. That was so unlikely, however, me being in the wrong, that I decided to go with the odds: fifty-fifty. Now I slept sometimes in pajamas, and sometimes only in the skin that no god was skilled enough to make, pity them.

Unless I was drunk. I always slept in the nude when I was drunk.

"Grimm? From your place, yes. I sent a minion around this morning to check." I had and was pleasantly surprised not to lose a minion for once, although I had to pay the fee and that was annoying. Sherlock Holmes and Arthur Conan Doyle acted as if street kids and the homeless worked for pennies. That was a laugh. "Does he remain in the city or gate in and out regularly? I have no idea. He must have been wondering all this time why Cal stopped gating again. It is unlikely, although that he knows anything about Cal's electrocution via serial killer and how that threw him offline, so to speak."

I'd given much consideration to asking Niko if we could turn Cal off, then back on again. My tech support hadn't failed me with that advice yet. Deciding I preferred to live, I didn't mention it, but I had thought about Grimm and what he was thinking when no gates pinged in his brain woven of barbwire. It wouldn't be good, I did know that.

Grimm hated Cal.

Grimm wanted to be Cal.

Grimm knew he was better than Cal.

Grimm knew that Cal was better than him.

Grimm wanted Cal to be with him, the founders of a new Auphe race.

Grimm had no idea what he wanted from Cal, but he knew he wanted something.

Grimm would kill Cal without hesitation if he thought Cal had become somehow lesser—such as losing his gating ability.

Grimm might kill himself as well, out of boredom and lack of competition.

Grimm was fifty gold ingots of crazy in a five-gold-ingot bag.

I left the computer and wandered into the kitchen, checking the refrigerator for whatever my new, less murderous housekeeper had left me the afternoon before. Ah, feta cheese, raspberries, blackberries, and grilled chicken on a spinach salad. With the plate and a fork I'd taken from a drawer, I settled in at the granite kitchen island. "Cal is stable, yes? When he first started gating, just one would knock him out for hours. He's basically starting over again. I'm not surprised he won't wake up yet. Give him a few hours before panicking."

My fork hovered over the salad as I thought, for the first time, I wasn't telling all I knew—what if Niko was doing the same? Me lying was a given, but what of Niko? He could lie. I'd seen him do it. He'd learned well from his con artist mother. He didn't like doing it, but he was quite, quite good at it when he had to be. What if this was a "had to" situation?

What if Niko was lying and I hadn't thought to listen, *actually* listen to him? What if he was buying time on his way to kill me or to kill himself because Cal was . . . gone?

"He *is* stable, isn't he? You would take him to the hospital if he was otherwise. Penny-pinching Charon, he's not *dead*, is he?" I didn't care that that would mean Niko was coming for me with vengeance in his heart and hands ready to bathe in blood. It made no difference in this life that Niko might hold on to a fraction more sanity than Achilles, enough to avenge. I cared simply that if Cal was dead, then Cal was *dead*. And Niko would soon follow him, and I'd sworn that wouldn't happen this time.

Not this soon.

Not again.

"Niko." I'd lunged to my feet, the breakfast plate gone sliding and spinning off the granite to shatter on the floor. "No. *No*. Put him on the phone. Hades, he's not awake, you said. He can't speak. You're lying. You're lying. Niko, tell me. Tell me he is alive. That he's not . . . *tell* me!"

My panic was enough to have Niko's restraint solidifying, returning to normal. What I lost, he regained in equal measure. "Robin, he's all right. He's asleep, but he's not bleeding and his vital signs are normal. Here, listen." Niko's voice vanished and for several seconds I heard the soft in-and-out pattern . . . the inhalation and exhalation of someone sound asleep. Cal.

"Robin?" It was Niko again, sounding considerably more worried than he had before.

I sat with a clumsy stumble, none of my customary grace, on the floor, berries flattened and smeared beneath my bare feet. "He wasn't in your armor." It was randomly said. I didn't mean to say it, but I couldn't stop. It appeared to be the day for reliving Troy . . . the nightmare war and cursed city. I could not let that one life go, much as I'd tried; I couldn't be at peace with it.

"That part of the story wasn't true," I continued dully. "You had matching armor or not quite, but close enough. Matching armor for the cousins." Matching armor that had been a gift from me. That sort of irony was a blade sharp enough to slice into your gut all the days of your very long life.

"But the Trojans didn't know that. They thought he was you. There was a plan. We all knew it. So he went, but he went too far." Patroclus then as Cal now inevitably went too far. Older than Achilles, he was a man with the heart of a boy, wildly impetuous with no grasp of his own mortality. "He was supposed to pull back when the ships were protected, but he didn't. He chased them all the way back to the gates of Troy, and that's where they killed him." Stupid, *stupid* boy. "I was following him, trying to catch up, but I wasn't soon enough. You and I were with him when he died, and his words were blood." I was numb, but the memory was sharp. "He spoke in blood."

"Goodfellow." The name buzzed in my ear, but it had no meaning.

Air that bubbled through thick scarlet. What had he tried to say? I never knew. The floor was cold beneath me, but all I saw, all I felt was red-soaked sand and an unforgiving white sun in a painfully blue sky.

"You wouldn't let anyone take his body. Not our men. Not me. You said he wasn't dead, and killed two of our own soldiers when they tried to pry him from your arms. He couldn't be dead, you swore. It was all lies, lies, lies, but he was. You fought us off for an entire day. Finally you let us take him. You cut off your hair to mourn."

How unlucky was I to have seen that tradition twice in my life now?

"You helped us build the pyre to burn him." His eyes had been a gray as empty as the dead ones of his cousin as he watched him burn. Cousins with the matching eyes and matching armor and legends in their own time, but now they were gone.

"The funeral games lasted days." And he didn't say a word to me or acknowledge me again. The only words I heard him speak after fighting off those who came to prepare Patroclus's body for funeral rites were when someone asked couldn't our patron god Pan, he who fought by the cousins' side, bring Patroclus back from Hades and the Elysium Fields? His response had been cold and flat.

"Pan? There is no god Pan. Gods do not exist."

He was right. When it came to me, that was the truth and nothing but.

"All those days and you wouldn't speak or eat. I pushed you and I goaded and I begged. I told you Patroclus wouldn't want this. I knew you would fight. To fight and die in battle was an honor then, but you didn't choose honor. You didn't choose to fight. You chose only to slaughter and die, taking every man, woman, and child of Troy that crossed the path of your sword with you."

"Robin, stop this. Stop it now."

Patroclus died and so did Achilles without once thinking of how they left me behind. It was the one end of days I hadn't let myself wallow in or give in to self-pity over. I didn't deserve that release, as their deaths in that life had been entirely my fault. I should've known what Patroclus would do. I knew him, *knew* him perhaps best in all the lives I'd known him, and knew how reckless he could be.

Resting my forehead on one knee, I saw a blue sky cloud with smoke and thought of how I'd stayed until the ashes of Achilles were mixed with those of Patroclus. Then I left. I hadn't returned to the site of Troy again. I never would.

The Great God Pan.

I'd been such a fool.

"Goodfellow? *Robin*?" Niko said it sharply and with a worry that indicated it wasn't the first time he had been calling my name.

I jerked my head up at the strong voice in my ear, leaving the haze of sand, salt, and smoke behind. "Niko?"

"Cal is fine. He's asleep and once in a while the brat even snores. Here. I'm sending you a picture." There was a click and thirty seconds later on my phone was a picture of Cal with a small bandage on his temple, his mouth hanging slightly open, and a definite darker, damp area of drool on the pillow. There were still pale strands of Auphe-silver in his dark hair, but it was Cal. Breathing, drooling, alive.

I touched a finger to it. Bewildering how in these modern times you could keep what you lost. There and ready at the press of a button. I thought, considering all those I'd lost, it made it all worse. It made forgetting impossible.

But Cal wasn't lost yet and I could see that for myself. He'd looked nearly identical to this before in Pompeii other than his eyes being dark brown. He'd painted then. Frescoes. When he wasn't brawling at any and every House of Bacchus.

"It's like the one time we went to a *lupanarium*, a whorehouse, in Pompeii and he had forgotten his coins. I told him they'd make him work it off in trade with whatever disease-ridden gladiator that slimed in off the streets. I laughed so hard it took three of the ladies of the house to get me back on my feet. He ... Never mind." I shut up. No more memories today, not even good ones.

Plus, Cal was fine. But Cal might not stay fine if I had to keep hypnotizing him whenever I told the harmless part of a story from a former life and the Auphe racial memory kicked in to let him recall it. Including the bitter and bloody endings that he wouldn't appreciate any more than I did. The stories I did tell would have to be very carefully chosen.

"Goodfellow?"

"Cal is fine." I repeated his words, in control again. If we were going to survive, I didn't have a choice there. "Good . . . that's good. Come home when you can." I hastily added, "Don't tell him what I said about Achilles and Patroclus. Troy is a memory that won't fade for me. It's always there. It was not . . . it wasn't pleasant and I wish I hadn't told you. You didn't need to hear that and he doesn't either. You know Cal. Chronos curse us all, it was a different *lifetime*, but martyr that he is, he'd find a way to blame himself." I was desperate enough to use a word incredibly rare for me to voice. "*Please* do not tell him." I swore silently to myself at the truth that was. Neither of them needed to hear it, especially after having lived it, but I'd spilled the nightmare of it over Niko nonetheless.

"I won't and we will be home whenever he wakes up." Niko hesitated and added, "Robin, are *you* all right?"

It struck me then, for the first time.

After Troy, I had not been all right again. I didn't think I could be. A handful of years out of a million, and those few years had changed me forever.

Wasn't that strange?

Was I all right? I laughed. What a funny thing to worry about. And, worse, the wrong time to worry about it. I laughed again and it hurt my throat in a fashion laughter wasn't meant to. Turning off my phone, I kept laughing—laughing was a better word than for what it actually was—until I slammed my arm against the cabinet I leaned against, knocking a butcher's block of knives to the floor. The blades scattered like a school of sleek silver fish in a shallow creek. Seizing one, I laid on my side, the floor colder yet, and vegetables, fruit, and pieces of plate scattered all around me. Continuing to laugh, I carved the polished wooden floor until it read συγχωρέστε με in wide letters with the painfully jagged teeth formed of bloodstained splinters. "*Syncho_réste me*. Forgive me,"

I had no expectation of it happening, but I had to ask all
the same. The problem was that I was asking it of the
wrong person. Achilles was gone and if he wasn't, there
hadn't been absolution there. I should be requesting it of
myself, forgive myself. I let the knife fall. I was less likely
to do so than Achilles at his most insane. My arm tired
from the inscribing of my guilt, the memories that refused to fade thousands of years later weighing me with
exhaustion, I slept on the floor. Unconsciousness was the
place where I could be more honest about the sounds I
made when I dreamed.

And what those sounds really were.

Delilah was nude and ordinarily I would've enjoyed
that . . . for hours or longer. I'd have used my phone to
record the image for posterity. I might have excused myself to their bathroom for an exceptionally inspired time-
out.

This was not ordinarily, however.

And I was not, inconceivable as it might be, in the
mood.

"I am not paying two point five million dollars for you
to let a Vigil assassin shoot Cal *before* eating said assassin,
see clause B, subsection twelve. This is exceedingly clear
in the contract. Eating the assassin comes first, and Cal
does not get shot at all," I snarled. Snarling, growling, and
violence were all the Kin understood. Luckily I had a
sword I'd stolen from a museum in Russia in one hand
and a 9mm I'd stolen from Cal in the other. I couldn't
decide which to use first. I was angry enough to bring out
the man-made weapons instead of my words. The last time
that had happened Rome fell. Not all my work, but I had
lit the fire.

Unimpressed with my weapons or my words, Delilah
sprawled on the wine-colored sofa with a wall of glass

behind her to show the skyline to best effect. Her place was enormous with marble and large silk pillows spread in piles on the floor for the Wolves to curl on. Silken dens. I could barely see her kitchen from where we sat, but I did see the size of the refrigerator. It was large enough for three people to comfortably fit inside, six if you didn't care about their elbow room, and I had not a doubt that if I took a look there would be at least one person hanging in there. Delilah had wasted no time in spending the Kin's money and didn't seem inclined to keep an office at the docks or the falling-apart Kin warehouses. The other Alphas had. They'd gone home to luxury, but they toiled in the filth with the pack—most likely as they didn't trust their pack. There's only one way to become an Alpha, and that's by killing one. Keeping your eyes open paid off.

On the other hand, there had never been an Alpha such as Delilah. She was a criminal ruler, a political ruler, and a religious ruler all in one. She'd started with one pack, her Alpha, killed them all, and hadn't stopped. Her Wolves worshipped her for it. She was the unforgiving teeth of female rage at being denied their chance to lead. She was nature's jaws ripping out the throat of the Wolf with pure genes—the ones that thought they were superior as they could be both entirely Wolf and entirely human. Delilah hated them: the ones who chose to live as human, as *sheep*, instead of trying to find a way back to their first form.

The perfect form.

Delilah had also risen in the ranks by a common method in ancient royal families: assassination. She'd started the Wolf way by taking out Alphas, but she'd moved on to high breeds and males. You didn't have to be an Alpha to die. She'd destroyed the Kin as it had been and remade it to her liking. She had come at them from three different directions and three different ideologies. She started a revolution and she brought a crusade to their doorstep. It had been a thing of beauty, the entirety of her manipulations. She was brilliant, cunning, and her strategies were exquisitely bloody and effective. No other Wolf could've done it and they all knew it. I could see why she didn't run her empire from all-but-collapsing places of filth. Delilah had nothing to fear from any of her Wolves.

She was their goddess.

That didn't imply that admiring her flawless exhibition of Machiavellian warfare didn't make me any less furious. I could be impressed and enraged, both at once. As I was now.

She extended her right leg to examine her boot. It was all she was wearing: a pair of knee-high, dark-cider-tinted leather boots. "Heels or no heels. Cannot decide."

"Heel height slows down speed unless you entirely shifted to Wolf and lost the boots altogether. Lower heel height increases number of prey brought down without loss of footwear. Stay with the low heels. It's more true to your heritage." I leaned back against the couch, chocolate brown, that I'd claimed and wondered how anyone in the whole of the world, save me, survived with what little brain power they had. Running quickly, away from or toward, depending on your need, was the top skill to possess. Then again, the past had shown Delilah had nothing to fear.

Nothing save me.

Curving her lips, wild and wanton, Delilah stripped off the boots, waved a hand at her Kin second standing between us to continue our business, and turned into a white Wolf. The amber skin and eyes with the glorious Asian tilt were gone and the Wolf rolled on her back to shove her muzzle between the couch cushions. With paws drooping over her fur-covered chest, she was either asleep or ignoring me or both. Wonderful. You get so much bang for your buck when dealing with the cream of the criminal element these days.

"The Lupa Alpha," her second began, her straight black hair a waterfall to her hips.

Lupas were what Delilah had called her female pack before taking down the Kin. Lupa had meant she-wolf in Greece and Rome long before Delilah was around. She could read; that was a point in her favor. Most Alphas in the past had thought books were drink coasters.

Still . . . how patronizing on her part, turning into a form that couldn't physically speak to me at all, whether either of us wanted her to or not.

Patronizing and not subtly so either.

"The Lupa Alpha," I interrupted. "She took over the Kin, a male-dominated organization, not to mention a high-breed organization, not one All Wolf allowed in a position of power. She killed every high breed she could find. She slaughtered every male Kin Wolf who didn't run his furry nuts out of the city and she needs a special title too? Just 'Alpha' doesn't express all she's done, the fact that you have a furry Amazonian hold over millions in the city, although you're up a sperm-free waterway when it comes time to have a cub? 'Alpha Delilah' simply doesn't get that all across? You had to add to it?"

"Lupa-Alpha Delilah," her second continued serenely, moon-round eyes blue pale enough to almost be silver and fixed on me with nothing but hunger in their depths. If it weren't for them, she could've passed for human. She had a nice business suit with short skirt and heels that were the same shade as her eyes. "Lupa-Alpha Delilah is aware of your concerns and finds them both boring and tedious." She examined her nails, pale blue to match, demonstrating her boredom and tedium as well. I wondered if she had them done each time she shifted. The upkeep on her mani-pedis must be a *boring* and, oh yes, a *tedious* strain. It must be destroying her life.

What a pity.

That was it. I didn't care that this was a penthouse more exclusive and overpriced than mine. Or that there were Kin Lupas everywhere in here and in the outside hall. I was shooting Delilah between her eyes or chopping off her head, depending on what hand I decided to use. Crime was crime and I understood that, but this was *business* and to any puck, business was sacred.

We had a contract and it would look ideal framed in her white fur and hanging on my wall. I knew a cleaning service that could get blood out of anything. "She'll find it massively more boring"—the sword, without a doubt, I was using the sword—"and infinitely more tedious when I stop payment on the check or, worse, let it go through and have my banker deal with you if you default." I put the gun away, hefted the sword, and stood.

Delilah pried her muzzle out of the cushions, aimed it at me, sighed. It was an odd sound as it went from lupine to human as she shifted back. She braced one elbow and propped her head up as her silver hair covered her shoulders and breasts like winter's first snow. Winter's first snow didn't conceal very much. I was grateful for that. Exceedingly grateful and felt no shame. I was a puck. I couldn't help myself by my very nature.

"No sense of humor." That was the only thing that gave Delilah away as an All Wolf, nonhuman vocal cords. Slightly rough, like a purr, and fooled you into thinking she had an accent, instead of noticing she was a werewolf. "What happened, little goat? You used to see the fun in everything."

Sometimes yes, sometimes no, but I'd been good at faking it all my life. At this particular moment in this particular life, I couldn't be bothered to fake humor, fun, or anything else that fell in that category.

"I have too many other things to deal with, all more important than you. My banker is Midas, and you know what he'll do if the contract isn't met." Every *paien* knew of Midas. Most creatures had a tiny amount of gold in them, many trace elements in fact—Midas only cared about one. It was less than one-fourth a milligram in his entire body for your average individual. If the contract wasn't satisfied, Midas would take that back from the one paid, from everyone in his family, from everyone in his extended family, from everyone in his business, to finally everyone in his *species*. It was such a small amount that you wouldn't miss it at all if it weren't for the fact that Midas killed you when he took it. That's why I banked with him. Everyone tended to think that as a puck, a born con man, I didn't deserve services for payment given. Midas kept them . . . honest.

I grinned as I did when I was one up on the competition, which was always, and pointed the blade at where her heart would beat under soft skin. "This wouldn't be my first extinction, nor my second. Are you bored now? Is this all too tedious for you? Because I can call my banker any time of the day or night. He's available twenty-four-seven and he loves his work." It would take all the Wolves in the world drained and dead to have a hope of recouping two million. You worked with Midas when you wanted to keep someone honest, but you also worked with him when you felt you had nothing to lose.

I was feeling both of those.

I was feeling a little homicidal madness as well. I'd fought with Vikings. When I'd lost my temper then, their infamous Berserkers had feared me. Live as long as I have and vacations from reason were not unheard-of and in some of us, the norm. There was no therapy for

•

lives millions of years too long, no mental institute capable of curing that. Although Freud had told me that I'd end up in one. Rude, quite so. That rudeness was why I'd talked him into a phallic obsession he'd take to his grave. Quite the competition.

I won.

"The Vigil?" I prodded Delilah with the tip of my sword, a crimson teardrop falling free to the carpet from between a pair of perfect breasts tipped with mouth-watering apricot. "Are we going to do better now? Fulfill the contract? Behave as good puppies should or do I let my banker foreclose on your life and the life of nearly everyone you know and every Wolf that ever howled?"

She flipped to all fours and growled. The position was more intimidating, oddly enough, in human form than it would've been in Wolf. Amber eyes stared at me through the rain of white hair that half hid her face. "Go." The growling became the grind of gravel in her throat. "Contract will be kept. When it is over, I will split your ribs and eat your heart."

"My heart? Good luck finding it. Bring a microscope." I laughed and there was no denying it. It had nothing to do with humor or the slightest grasp of reason, and she could hear it.

Her claws extended to pierce the leather of the couch and she growled, *"Rabid."*

At this particular moment, to a Wolf, I was indeed rabid as they understood it. "Temporarily," I bared my teeth to match hers, "but do as the contract says, and you have no worries. Don't and I'll kill you before Midas can and let him have the rest of the Wolves." I put the sword under my coat after saluting her with it and left.

I did snap a quick nude picture of her on my phone, but anyone I knew had to have seen that coming.

9

Caliban

I'd slept for two days straight, which hadn't made Niko happy. Steering my sleepwalking self to the bathroom hadn't made him any happier, but I hadn't ruined the bed. Kudos for me—even as ruined as it already was.

Niko didn't leave. At the deepest levels of unconsciousness, I knew he was there. When you spend your life waiting for a monster to explode through the window and take you to its personal hell, you get a sixth sense about not having someone watch your back when you can't do it yourself. Nik watched my back while ordering pizza and Chinese food when he grew hungry. It smelled so bad that I didn't want any part of either—and I ate New York hot dogs, which probably contained actual dog and a few victims of the Mafia. The human one. The Wolf one too; it could be. What did I know? Nik, I guessed, didn't care, and wouldn't take no for an answer.

It's hard to chew when you're basically unconscious. I had tried. It meant a great deal to him, asleep or awake, I could tell. That all he was giving me was foodlike and not-so-much-foodlike meals to eat meant there was nothing else available. If tofu or soy was available for delivery, he'd have been forcing that down me instead. I stumbled with his assistance into the bathroom, and I slept. Eat, piss, and sleep—that was the cycle. The other issues were fine, eating and toilet breaks, but sleep was what I craved most. I slept hard, deep, and in spite of that, I dreamed.

I'd dreamed of him for the past few days—the boy who ran over misty green hills, who laughed when his brother chased him, who tried to ride sheep and ended up panicking them all, and who despised shoveling manure over the garden as punishment. The boy who existed but didn't exist because I was supposed to forget him—forget and obey my guardian. Obey Goodfellow. But the boy didn't agree and he wasn't playing that game or any game—not this kid. The one with the darkest of red hair, almost black, and eyes darker—the color of a night's sky before the moon and stars came out. Sometimes I thought I saw his throat covered in blood, but then it was gone. It didn't seem to bother him. I followed his lead and didn't let it bother me. His name was Cullen and he took no crap, then or now. He didn't even take Goodfellow's shit, but he thought we could trust whatever he was planning . . . for now.

There had to be a plan. Robin was always scheming.

Since Cullen was a kid in the know and this was nothing more than a dream, I had no problem with going along with him. "Lot of sheep in Scotland," I mumbled. "Lots of sheep shit. Don't blame you. Wouldn't want to shovel that either."

"Cal." A hand was on my shoulder, shaking me. Someone . . . Nik was saying my name. I opened my eyes to see a stained and cracked ceiling, immediately identifiable as a no-tell motel anywhere in the continental United States. "You were talking in your sleep," Niko said, resting his hand on my forehead. "About riding sheep." He sounded tired but pleased. "Is there anything about your sex life you want to tell me about?"

Sheep? Oh, the dream. Green and blue and the red of genuine ruby, the exact wet shine and hue of blood. It was all a jumble that meant nothing now that I was awake.

"Awake? Yeah, I'm awake." I yawned until my jaw ached and ignored the sheep remark. Niko didn't need more ammunition to use in mocking me. I lifted my head from the pillow and glanced around, cataloguing the broken TV, the bent lamp, and a chair stained in enough ways that a CSI team would have a frigging orgasm or coronary, one of the two. There was a sharp pain to one temple and a sear of lava heat across my back. Shot. I'd been shot. We'd been fighting a *Bakeneko* and not doing that great a job of it when someone . . . the Vigil, had to be . . . had shot me. I'd gated us. We'd been back in our place and . . . nothing. It was a blank. I had no memories after that. I sat up, oddly stiff and achy. "I feel like I'm ninety. How long have we been here? Hell, where is here?"

"Arkansas." Nik didn't sound happy about it as he cracked open a bottle of water and handed it to me.

"Arkansas?" I shuddered. "Why? Who hates us that much?"

"I suppose this could be considered Sophia's fault, as we were working in a carnival here when you were thirteen. The field we set up in is behind this motel. Or it could be Robin's fault for not asking me if I wanted you gating when you were too out of it to know what you were doing, in addition to being shot and having burned through the epinephrine you'd already injected. But with Grimm in our apartment, things were moving quickly, and I doubt he thought he had a choice if we were going to survive. I will make him understand in the future that if we have even a spare second and you're down, he's to ask me about gating. I'll also give him a list of ages with better homes to return to, such as any of them were, should he feel the need to make suggestions again."

Niko was pissed. I could see that Robin had a long, long talk in the future about suggestions and who was allowed to boss me around. It was one person, Nik, and Nik didn't have any problem taking it to hand-to-hand or sword against sword if someone wanted to argue that. In any event, I'd gotten bossed by someone. I would've minded more, but the fact that I couldn't remember much of anything after gating to our place and before doing the same to Arkansas had my choices at pretty much nil. If Robin hadn't told me to gate, Grimm might've eaten me by now . . . or worse.

Didn't you have to love a life where being eaten was the least objectionable entrée on your goddamn menu of "I'm screwed with a side order of roasted fuck"?

I tried sitting up to discover I was suddenly ninety years old. "Jesus, I know I was shot, but what the hell?" I winced and tried again, this time as stiff as I'd been in a three-year coma. With Niko's assistance, I made it and tried moving my upper body at least to loosen it up.

"You most likely feel muscle pain, as you've slept for two days, other than letting me take you to the bathroom. The food you ate in bed, which wouldn't reduce the arthritic feeling in the least. But you were stubborn. You refused to go to the table and eat," Niko said with less sympathy than I thought I deserved.

"Big brother." I turned my head away from the table

by the blind-covered window and tried to control my gag reflex. "If you could smell what is on that table, you wouldn't eat there either. I hope you didn't. If you did, you probably have syphilis. If you were a woman, you'd be pregnant and have syphilis. Do me a favor. Stay away from the table."

He slanted a glance of disbelief at me but opened the door to our room and shoved the table out before moving to sit on the edge of my bed. No one knew when I was or was not kidding as well as Nik did, and no one wanted to deal with pregnancy *and* syphilis. "How do you feel now, besides sore and stiff?"

I closed my eyes and roamed around my brain. My body was nothing. As long as I had all my limbs and wasn't pinned under something that weighed roughly the same as a building, I could stay in the fight. It was a matter of how far you were willing to go. I'd been willing to go as far as necessary for my whole life. But the gating . . . that was different. No matter how determined I was, it could knock me down and keep me down, depending on the circumstances, one of the circumstances being when I'd first done it. When it was new, and I was younger, lacking in experience. If I was unconscious for a day and no more, I'd been doing exceptional.

"I'm good. I'm not sure why I slept so long unless it's the same when I first started gating." I yawned again. When that had happened, it took me down and out. One little gate could knock me out for a day back then.

But that didn't seem right, did it? It wasn't the same feeling of exhaustion. It was almost like I'd been drugged.

"Do not come back until tomorrow at the very soonest."

"Odiemus."

"Obey."

Okay, that was weird. Weird instructions, weird foreign languages, more freaky dreams I couldn't remember or shouldn't remember, and my life was full of enough similar weirdness that I was going to ignore all of it. Whatever this was, if it was anything at all and not my brain cells being destroyed from the gating, I didn't want to know.

I sincerely did not want to know.

Instead I went with what made sense. That when I'd started gating in the past, that gate would knock me out for hours. It took a while, but I'd improved until it was no worse than walking up a flight of stairs. If that was the case, I'd improve again. I opened my eyes, tangled a hand in Nik's long braid, and held on. I'd started doing this when I was around fourteen, as soon as his hair was long enough, to get on his nerves, as little brothers do, but it had ended up as a reassurance, a habit to check that he was with me.

Neither of us missing, neither of us dead.

"If there's a drugstore we can rob," I offered, "I can gate us home no problem."

Niko tapped a finger on my forehead. "I suppose the concussion you gained from being shot in the head is nothing?"

"It was a graze." I yanked at his braid with less strength than I hoped, but that didn't mean anything. "I gated already twice with this." I dropped my head back on the pillow. "The first Vigil shooter was much better. The second one with a night scope should've dropped me like a bag of dirt. I hope they weren't paying him much. He wasn't worth it."

"He was being attacked by a Kin Wolf while shooting at you. I think he should merit some respect. Shooting, and that close to accurately while being gutted by a werewolf, isn't the same as serving Slurpees at the 7-Eleven," Niko responded neutrally. He was torn between hating the guy for shooting me and having respect for him for doing it while basically being eaten alive. Niko did value commitment. I didn't blame him. I'd have the same respect for the guy who'd shot me if I had Niko's standards: duty first, dealing with the gnawing of your intestines second. I wasn't Nik, though. If I was doing a contract for hire, I would be fee-first. If a Wolf showed up wanting to chow down on my internal organs, that would have me shooting the Wolf or running away— I would've already been paid, so screw the target, and the Wolf. The Vigil were not me, no proper sense of priorities, and wasn't that too bad? The Vigil were too motivated for their own good.

There had to be easier jobs out there for an assassin.

If the Vigil had any sense, they'd hire me instead of trying to kill me. That was quasi-military organizations, like the Boy Scouts, for you all over. They couldn't see the bigger picture. If they could, Boy Scouts would be selling cookies too, not getting their asses financially kicked by the Girl Scouts, have more money, afford more camping trips, up their training, and then the Vigil could've outsourced this job to them.

Okay, maybe not. The Vigil wasn't thinking things through, not as much as they could have. I was hazardous to the extreme, but like the Cold War of the eighties with the nuclear policy of Mutually Assured Destruction, wouldn't you rather I was on your side? Wouldn't you want me as your fail-safe? Your Last Strike? Instead they'd come for me after I'd shown I was blatantly out of control. Who wants an out-of-control nuke? Not many people. Who'd piss off an out-of-control nuke?

Not many people. Stupid people. The Vigil. Apparently.

I was thinking about that, not happily, when I noticed I didn't have a shirt.... Niko must've cut it off back at

our apartment to bandage my back. I was considering
stealing his when I felt the gates open. Three of them.

"Shit." I catapulted out of bed, grabbed my pants
folded over the CSI chair, and pulled them on before going for my boots, which were neatly lined up beside the
tiny table between our two beds. "Gates. Three gates."

Gates were no good. Gates that weren't mine were
extremely bad, but I had pants, which made the situation
a little less of a nightmare. I didn't see Nik's katana anywhere in the room, nor did I see my shoulder holster or
guns. I didn't remember it, but it looked like I'd probably
gated us out while Niko was doing some first aid on me,
our weapons in a neat pile on Niko's dresser. His anal-
retentive neat fetish would get us killed yet.

"Grimm?" Niko yanked his shirt down—aerodynamic
for the coming fight. It was the one that I wished I had
the opportunity to swipe, a gray one I remembered from
the *Bakeneko* hunt. It had been washed in the sink, was
my bet, but still showing the faded brown bloodstains
he'd gotten from me bleeding all over him. He snatched
at his boots, gray to my black, just as quickly as I'd seized
mine.

"No." I slid my feet into my ten-year-old combat versions I'd bought at a military outlet place, broken in
perfectly, and felt for the knives normally sheathed inside. They were still there. Fucking A.

"This feels different. Weaker, stranger, not Auphe.
Bae." Bae, the offspring of the half human/half Auphe
Grimm and succubae, who if given the choice would
have nothing to do with Grimm. Succubae hated the
taste of the energy of the Auphe, part or whole.

A succubus had been the only one to gag after kissing
me. At nineteen, that does serious damage to your ego. I
didn't know if the fact that it *was* my Auphe-tainted life
energy was corrupted and disgusting to her delicate pal-

ate and that it had nothing to do with halitosis made me feel less revolting or more so. I would've been able to buy mouthwash, but there wasn't anything I could do about having a dark and not particularly tasty life force.

Was this the time to be thinking about this?

No. Not so much.

"How did Grimm know to send them here? Robin sent us here by picking a random age. If they did catch him he wouldn't be able to give us away, because even he wouldn't know where we were. That was brave of him. I shouldn't have threatened to kill him." Niko pulled his own two blades from his boots. Italian poniards, sleek, narrow, and silver—they could slice you before you knew they were in the air and swinging at all. "But the fact remains that we don't have any idea how Grimm knew where we went."

"Buy Robin a fruit basket. It'll be forgive and forget, and Grimm has been gating for twelve years, since he was eighteen." My knives weren't as pretty to look at. They were KABARs, combat knives, large and thick, black matte, and serrated to slice flesh from bones. "I couldn't gate at all five years ago, and then I learned." Slowly. "When I finally picked up on it, I became psychotic as hell when I started gating all the time. You remember." Psychotic barely covered it. That's when Niko had Rafferty dial me down, let me gate twice a day with the third one giving me a burst vessel in my brain.

An explosion in your brain is the ultimate deterrent. Rafferty was the healer who had now twice tried his best to heal his cousin Catcher and to heal me and to end up doing us both worse in the end.

"After that, when Grimm came along I couldn't afford to be limited in any way." I cured myself of gate limitations with the balm of an ancient healer, who no one had equaled present or past, not even Rafferty. Niko's father, what a homicidal dick, had carried it with him until he died. As I was the one to make certain he was dead, seconds ahead of Niko doing it himself, I wasn't sorry about the balm-stealing.

It had worked and, until Jack toasted my brain, all was good. As good as it could be. Lots of gates, minor amounts of psychosis but controllable. "In all those times," I said hurriedly, "when I started gating, I could detect a gate from a block away, two blocks, and finally after a few years at my best I would've known if a gate opened anywhere in the city." At my best. At the end. That had all been before daily shots of epinephrine as if I were a combination of diabetic, anaphylactic, and junkie. I had no idea how far I could feel them now.

"Yes, Grimm has more experience in gating—some anyway—than you," Nik admitted with more concern than impatience. "What does that mean?"

I finished tying my boots by feel as I sat on the edge of the bed to stare at Nik. Incredulous . . . incredulous and disturbed as shit, because I knew what this meant if no one else did. For all that I hated him, no one knew Grimm as I did.

That was the bitch about relatives. As much as you hated them, you also *knew* them. And that I'd have given anything for Grimm to not be related to me, he was. DNA does not lie.

"A year or two, that's what it took me to pick up a gate in the city," I emphasized. "Grimm has been gating for twelve years. Twelve. He could probably detect a gate anywhere in the *world*." I bent over and unsheathed both knives from my boots, one for each hand.

"There is no place I can gate that he couldn't find us. We—Auphe, I mean . . . Bae too, I guess—have to see or know intimately where we're going when we gate—except when we mature to a nice grown-up predator, when we perfect the skill, and then we can follow someone else's gate. The Bae are too young, but Grimm could open gates for them and he did. Grimm followed us here, and he can follow us anywhere. Anywhere at fucking all."

Even Tumulus, there was a good chance, but I didn't want to test my sanity on that one. "I think he always could. When he first appeared in New York to mess with us last year, I think he could easily have followed us to wherever I gated." To the places I'd thought safe, because I'd underestimated Grimm. Mistake. Big mistake. "I'm guessing he let me think I could escape him because he liked playing the game too much to make it easy for him. He wanted it to last." I shrugged. "After all, I am the only one left to play it with him. Once I'm gone, he'll be one bored son of a bitch."

I stood, wished I had a shirt, but let it go. We were doing this B-movie action hero–style. When you're the furthest thing from a hero, it's almost funny. I'd once played a drinking game with Robin, who wasn't a *Star Trek* fan but knew William Shatner personally—who was this century's cover identity of Bacchus, patron god of wine and theater. Wasn't that fucking ironic? Whenever his shirt was ripped or torn off completely in an episode, which was a damn lot, we drank.

I wished like hell we were playing it now.

"At least Grimm only sent a few Bae after us," I added. "He didn't come himself." Grimm was the type who'd fold a winning hand to keep the game going as long as possible. It wasn't the pot that he cared about; it was the game itself.

Grimm wanted to see me bleed. Grimm who was lonely. Grimm wanted to see me scream.

Grimm who wanted a brother or cousin or any family who was like him. Grim who wanted to see me burn and beg.

Grimm who wanted me at his side. Grimm who wanted me to join him in taking back the world, because games aren't as fun with the boring, the subservient, the humble Bae children who would lick his feet in gratitude.

I'd told him, but Grimm wouldn't admit it. His Bae offspring, his new hybrid Auphe race, they were nothing compared to the real deal no matter that he bragged they were more evolved, better in all ways. Grimm was lying to himself. A pure Auphe would've kept them as pets on leashes, as they weren't even worthy enough to slaughter.

Grimm wanted me, the last of the half Auphe—the last like him. But if Grimm couldn't have me, and he couldn't, he'd see me die in the most terrible manner there was to die. Grimm didn't like rejection. For now he stayed in the courting/killing as a compliment stage. Sooner or later, though, he'd figure out I wanted nothing to do with him. It wasn't because I didn't know him inside and out that I rejected him; it was because I knew him *too* well.

If I'd spent eighteen years in a cage, feral and tortured daily, like Grimm had before he'd escaped, I would *be* Grimm . . . or Grimm to the tenth power . . . and that was why I understood him as much as I did. I knew him, because I knew what I would be.

I twirled the knives in each hand and gave Niko a sharkish grin. "Two or three Bae at the most. One of us can handle them while the other one sits in a lawn chair and drinks a six-pack. Which do you want to be?"

Niko, the dick, flipped his poniards up in the air a bare half inch from the ceiling, spinning at least ten times, and then caught them on their way down without even glancing at their progress once. "Let's be nice and share. One for you and two for me."

In case my concussion or the two days of near coma from gating or unknown origin slowed me down, that's what he was thinking. "You're no fun," I grumbled as I headed for the door. "It's daylight, you know. If someone sees us, the Vigil will be more cutthroat than they were before, and that is a shitload of throat-cutting." As the door opened, I spotted a truck that must belong to the motel's maintenance mań. "Fuck me running with a smile on my face, that's a shovel."

"I have no desire to know what expression you would have if someone were to fuck you while you were running." Niko, at my shoulder, peered out the door, and confirmed it questionably. "But yes, that is a shovel. And that means what exactly?" Niko with his precise language, planned maneuvers, and knives he could flip ten times with such skill that he didn't have to pay attention at all—Niko needed a shovel in his life like he didn't know. I was happy to demonstrate.

I grinned and sprinted toward the truck. "That's right. You played soccer in school." Before he'd had to get a very off-the-books job at twelve, *twelve*, to keep us fed, Sophia included. It was wrong and unfair, but right now it was going to pay off at least once. "Let me be the first to tell you," I offered with fond recollection from when I was nine years old, before I'd been kicked out of gym. "Big brother, 'Batter's up.'"

Wherever the maintenance man was, as difficult as it was to believe from our room that they had one, he wasn't hanging around his truck. I tucked one knife back in my boot, wrapped my hand around the wooden handle of the shovel to pull it free of the rest of the junk in the truck bed, and headed around the dingy motel at a dead run into the field Nik had told me about. The one behind the motel, the stretch of nearly shoulder-tall grass where we'd once lived in a carnival. I remembered, but it was faded enough that it barely qualified as a memory. We'd lived in at least ten carnivals as kids. This one didn't stand out.

Except maybe for that asshole guy.

Yeah, the guy. Suddenly I remembered him.

I'd forgotten about him, forgotten about that night at the carnival, until I was running through the same field. Then it was there, the sharp smell of the grass and that dead oak tree that looked as if it gobbled up kids there at the back, same as when we'd set up the tents and rides.

I'd worked a booth in the carnival. Everyone worked in the carnival. Unless you were too young to know how to walk yet, they had you doing something. One of my jobs was running the dart and balloon con. I didn't remember if business was slow that particular night, but it had to have been for me to rip him off without thinking twice. Hell, he'd ripped himself off. Without any prompting from me he'd bet me fifty bucks, under the table naturally, that he could pop all five balloons with only five darts. The game was rigged—they all were—and I was a thirteen-year-old who'd been swindling for years. I knew how to take care of business.

The guy had missed not one, but all the balloons, which, rigged or not, was odd, but he'd smiled, a little sadly, I'd thought, but if losing fifty bucks was going to throw you into a pit of depression, don't bet. Simple as that. He forked over the fifty bucks as promised, eagerly enough that I thought that he wasn't as glummed and bummed as he acted. I'd talked to him some—that was part of conning, talk the talk. I didn't remember much of that autumn, but for some reason this had stuck with me, although I hadn't known it until I was in the same field . . . with the same smells . . . the same creepy tree. He hadn't said much, no way was a con man despite the big bet. I could spot one of Sophia's kind quick, and he wasn't one

of them. He hadn't talked the talk. Not a con man, so
what was he? He didn't seem to be a perv ... and the
carnivals were full of those. I could zero in on one a mile
away. This guy hadn't looked like the type to be in a carnival at all. Too high and mighty. Too clean. Too wary of
getting sticky cotton fingers wiped on him by kids who'd
pound past. He looked like, I hadn't known, something.
A soldier, not from the way he dressed, a blue silk T-shirt
and brand-new jeans, or his hair, but he was big, had the
muscle, stood straight, and walked with his shoulders
back. There were lines of wariness and tension in him,
the kind you get when you're watching for the enemy. I
knew that because both Nik and I had them. The wariness and the enemy.

But this guy couldn't have been a soldier. His hair,
light blond, had been longer, to his shoulders—definitely
not a military cut. It had looked strange, the pale color
combined with his dark eyebrows. His eyes ... hell if I
knew. Those were the days I'd checked eyes for molesta-
tion potential and homicidal serial killing urges. That's
all I cared about then. Color didn't register. He might've
had a scar on his face, seemed like he had, but it was too
long ago. Who knew?

He'd handed over the fifty dollars discreetly so I could
shove it in my pocket and no one would know I had it,
which meant no one would try to take it from me. "You
lost on purpose," I'd told him, frank once the money was
safe in my pocket. "Why? You're not pinging on my perv
radar, but it's still weird as shit." And at thirteen my perv
radar never failed.

Wincing a bit at my cussing, he'd shrugged. "We have
the same ... acquaintance. Robin. He doesn't have any
idea I know about you, I don't think. He didn't ask me to
keep an eye on you. He'd never ask me for anything at
all, I don't think. He doesn't trust me." He dropped his

gaze to the ground, not happy from what I could tell, and seconds later his eyes were aimed at the sky and then finally back at me. "But this acquaintance of ours would be pleased to know that I gave you assistance when I could." He looked back up at the sky, uneasy if the way he was shifting from foot to foot said anything. "And I still like to do God's work now and again, retired or not. But sometimes I'm uncertain that I know what God's work is."

I didn't know any Robin and I didn't care to know any God that had given me this life, but money was money. My brother, Nik, would've been offended at that—at the thought of charity. He hated it. Niko was too proud for our lives. I knew better. Charity was a few steps above me waiting in the back of an alley with a broken beer bottle to get our rent or food money any way I could. Charity was fantastic. No one had to spill blood for charity.

"Then . . ." I'd lined up the darts on the counter and given the intentional loser a smile that felt dark and curdled before it made it to my mouth. "You aren't doing it for me." I'd switched the darts around to make a circle with all points in the center. "You aren't doing it because you care that kind of money will let me and my brother eat actual food, and not just the spoiled hot dogs and barbecue that stinks of food poisoning, all that's left at the end of the day." I'd picked up a dart and nailed a balloon head-on. The game was fixed, but I was the one who fixed it. That made winning easy for me.

"You gave me the money for *you*. For your *acquaintance*, which, yeah, we all know what that means. Get out of the closet already." I'd rolled my eyes. "He doesn't know, but you're hoping he finds out, aren't you?" I was wrong there. He blanched at the thought. Anonymous do-gooder, but why anonymous if he could score points with his generosity, such as it was? I wasn't going to let that rest. "You aren't getting any now, but you *do* want to get some of that. And look, you gave me fifty dollars, right?"

My smile split into an abyss, and like Niko read to me at night: Do not look into the abyss, lest it look into you. I was an abyss of hunger, homelessness, fear, terror, rage, the target of human monsters with cold grasping fingers and nonhuman monsters with claws, red eyes, and a thousand metal teeth. This guy had given me fifty dollars and thought he was a humanitarian. I'd laughed and thrown the other four darts, each popping a balloon.

"Go on and tell your friend what a great guy you are. Or get someone else to tell him since you lack the sac, and it'll look better that you weren't bragging on yourself. You know, a little less like the self-centered dick wad you are." There is no one more caustic and hateful than a bitter thirteen-year-old; that is a guarantee.

"Tell him how you gave a kid fifty bucks and didn't ask him to suck your cock." He'd flushed an angry red. I'd guessed he wasn't around a lot of pissed-off thirteen-year-olds. "You're a fucking saint, aren't you?" I hissed. Niko was due to cut my hair and it was long enough to hang far past my eyes when I dipped my head forward, strange and wild, as if I'd been raised by wolves. I might have been more social if I had been raised by wolves and not Sophia.

Sophia could raise rattlesnakes and they'd end up needing therapy.

Thank God for Nik—what would I have been without him?—but this asshole hadn't needed to know that. "Fifty bucks should take care of me and my brother for a month."

I'd straightened, tucked my hair behind my ears, and leaned to grab a tiny yellow teddy bear from the wall. "A whole month of eating real food. I hope that warm and fuzzy feeling lasts you as long." I'd studied the bear cradled in my hands, small hands. It seemed I'd never grow sometimes, always be small and slender like the father who'd spawned me. Not birthed me, but *sired* me. "There you go. We don't have a stuffed animal that means self-righteous dick, but the yellow is all you."

I'd tossed the bear at him. "You know what yellow means, don't you?"

He'd caught the toy without meaning to, I thought. His reflexes were too good to not snatch it out of the air. "Coward," he said, so low and ill that I barely heard him.

"Too right!" I'd grinned blackly. "But don't feel bad. You fed me and my brother for almost a month. What a hero you are! Once your 'acquaintance' finds out what you did for the needy, starving boys who pick their next year's school clothing out of garbage cans, I'm sure he'll hop in bed with you. You're a miracle waiting to happen, aren't you?" I'd snorted. "And if it doesn't work out for you, my mom charges twenty-five bucks for a BJ. Fifty bucks for the weird stuff. I could hook you up."

He bent a bit at the waist as if he might toss his cookies then and there. "No. *No*. That's not what I meant to ..." He'd swallowed and I remembered the scar then, thick and running along his jaw. "I might be able to save you. I don't know, not for certain. Your mother would be simple to go around, but your father and the rest of them ... they would try to kill us. They would probably succeed." Hands clenching the bear tight enough to rip it open and his shoulders slumped. The weight of the world or just two boys. It'd been too much and his tune changed. "And where I live, I'm not allowed to kill them. It's against the law for my kind. We can't have a hope of beating them if we can't kill them. They're too strong. They never give up." This time when he met my eyes I didn't remember the color again. I was too goddamn pissed to register it. "I hope that you can kill them. I wish you good fortune. I swear that I do."

Cold and full of disgust, because he *knew*—I hadn't known how—he was probably another supernatural creature. Our personal monsters weren't the only ones we'd seen, especially in the past few years. I stared at him. "You're no different from them. They'll do anything they can to get what they want. You'll do anything you can to get what or *who* you want. Wait—you are different because you won't get involved. Good fortune to me? That's what you said earlier, right? You know, but you won't commit. You'd leave us sitting ducks because you're even more afraid of them than we are. You hope I'm strong enough to fight them when you aren't? I'm a fucking thirteen-year-old kid. I hope your 'acquaintance' knows that, because he wouldn't give you the time of fucking day if he did. You leaving kids to run from monsters. You, a guy five times my size, says he can't fight them but good luck to me. As for God's work, either your God sucks or you're not doing him much damn justice."

I'd slammed the metal shutter closed to the booth and locked it, but not before I saw the guy walk away, pale blond hair washed out under our dim lights. He was walking slow and grim as if his dog had been run over. Fifty bucks to get on someone's good side and here was hoping we lived long enough to spend it. Asshole. I hadn't thought about him again beyond giving the money to Nik to feed us, clothe us, and keep Sophia in the dark about it. Out of nowhere there was an explosion of white and gold light around the guy as he kept walking, and then he was gone. Vanished. Supernatural dicks. I cleaned the money out of the booth, including the fifty bucks. Fifty bucks and sorry about your impending doom, kid.

"God's work, my ass," I'd snorted, and stomped a white-and-gold feather into the mud as I'd left to find Nik and get supper.

The recollections became so sharp and real that I stopped running through the waist-high grass to swear. Light blond hair, gold-and-white wings, following after an acquaintance of ours named Robin, throwing a little God's work in there.

"Ishiah, that worthless son of a bitch." Fifty goddamn dollars to get on Robin's good side, fifty bucks to get laid by a puck. Fifty dollars were his thirteen silver pieces. I was glad that hadn't worked out for him at all and Good-fellow haven't given him the time of day for twelve more years. Ishiah had known about the Auphe, which Robin hadn't when we were young, and Ishiah had left us anyway. Angels and peris, neither were worth a damn. They'd saved us once when it was easy, but when it came to the Auphe—the truest of monsters—they hid behind excuse of rules and fake ignorance.

Robin would've taken us if he'd known about the Auphe, but we hadn't known enough about him or them to tell. As far as we knew, he was human and that wasn't any help. And as far as he knew, the Auphe in me much harder to sense at that age, we were human kids that needed to live their lives until they were old enough to have the stamina and legality to hang around with him. He'd been waiting for us, ready to find us when life decided the time was right. If he had known about the Auphe, he would've hidden us from them immediately. He would've died trying to save us if he'd known. He'd said so when finally admitting to the reincarnation bizarreness, and I believed him as I believed only Nik in this world. Robin hadn't known and so had walked away to let us grow and develop as this life demanded until he would see us again, grown and ready for more adventure.

Ishiah . . . he had *left* us and had walked away without
a backward glance. Ishiah, who had known that the Auphe chased us, and had given us fifty bucks. Two twenties
and a ten, and good luck surviving the entire Auphe race
who is after you. Fifty bucks, but you might be able to
bribe the totality of the Auphe nation with that if you
bargain wisely.

"Ishiah, that worthless son of a bitch," I growled.

That had to be out of nowhere for Nik, but he was
used to that from me and kept going. Beside me, he
pushed me back into motion. "That's your customary
opinion of him, but not pertinent right now."

He had no idea what I was talking about, and with the
situation we were dealing with, that was for the best.
"Yeah, it usually is. Duck!" I yelled.

Niko hit the ground and rolled over onto his back as
I swung the shovel and half decapitated the Bae leaping
out of the grass at us, fast and strong as the lion I was.
With transparent, glittering scales, eight-inch fangs from
a snake meant to pin and rip flesh, inherited from their
succubus mothers. The white skin beneath the scales, the
metal composition of the fangs, if not the dark color, the
crimson eyes, the slippery white hair cascading down
their backs like a waterfall made for hypothermia and
death—that was Auphe.

"Home run," I crowed.

The Bae staggered. Grimm called them the Second
Coming, an improvement on the Auphe. I would have
thought he'd learned some after the last time he'd sicced
them on us, which ended up in their death. Gruesome
and bloody, like one of your better sparring sessions, it
was saved in my mental scrapbook. We'd killed them, but
that didn't mean that was all of them unfortunately, and
not one who fought us survived. Once you'd fought a
real Auphe, a Bae . . . a Bae was *nothing*. If Grimm knew

any other half Auphe besides me, I'd tell him he needed to invest in peer review of his Frankenstein lab work. If he didn't have peers, as I was not at all willing to help, then he should review and rethink his own work.

However you saw it, Grimm had never fought an Auphe or he would've known his Bae weren't going to do the trick against those who had fought them and *won*.

I gave our attacker a vicious grin or maybe it was my I-just-won-the-lottery-grin—sometimes I didn't know the difference since both put me in a good mood—as it weaved back and forth, trying to keep its cervical spine from fracturing in half completely. It held on to its head, handfuls of hair, with both hands and was washed chest to waist in black blood. It bared its enormous curve of titanium metal fangs and hissed at me, little garter snake that it was.

I leaned closer and hissed in an exact echo back, "It's an old saying, but Grimm should've taught it to you anyway. 'There's no crying in baseball.'"

I'd played sports when I was young. Niko thought it would help run off my excess, more than human energy. And it had worked for a while, until my lack of comprehension regarding rules became more of an issue when a dodgeball in your hand had not been as effective as a baseball bat. I'd never understood rules and I didn't to this day. If you were playing to win, you'd do absolutely *anything* and rules didn't count. Winning was winning, and did I get that?

Yes, I did.

That meant I carried my bat with me after hitting the ball to take down a second baseman before he could tag me out, or I tackled a kid before he made it to home plate, banging his head into the ground until I was sure that home plate was the very last thing on his mind. I didn't hurt anyone that badly, didn't put anyone in the hospital, as that would draw attention, which we didn't do. That had been Nik's rule and that one I understood. Attention was bad when you lived life on the run. No, no hospital—I'd been careful while doing as I had been told by the gym teacher: Win. It didn't stop me from getting labeled with "rage issues" and daily visits with the guidance counselor. She couldn't understood no matter how many ways I explained it to her: If winning is the goal, rules have to be ignored. You can have one or the other but not both. That's logical. She hadn't seen it that way and written "sociopathic tendencies" in tiny cramped letters in my file. I didn't care. She was a human and except for Nik, humans had no idea about the world, not the real one. She could label me a sociopath if she wanted, but I wasn't ashamed. I'd guarantee I'd survive longer than her with that label.

Winning is all. That's what the coach told us. It was one of the few things I had been told in school that made any sense. That was what resonated throughout me as nothing else ever had.

Win.

"Batter's up!" I gave a warning call.

I swung again and while the Bae's head didn't come off completely, its body did fall to the ground, where I bashed in its skull with the shovel. It only took three or four times. I had to say, it was a good shovel. It was a little rusty, but the head was solid and heavy and as much a weapon as the guns I'd left behind in our apartment. If I needed a shovel in NYC, I'd take this one with me. I might take it anyway for decoration and the occasional beat-down of whatever broke into our place.

When we were young or even in our early twenties and we'd faced the Auphe, we'd been . . . shit . . . terrified. Killing one of them . . . only one . . . with Nik, Robin, and me, it was doable but not guaranteed. Every time you

faced one, you were flipping a coin as to whether you'd
live or die. Killing the entire race of over a hundred
seemed impossible. I was more afraid of them than death
a thousand times over. Death was easy. The Auphe were
a nightmare you couldn't imagine no matter how hard
you tried, and with them there was no escape unless they
wanted it. They were monsters to the other monsters.
They were crazed, bloodthirsty, sadistic, insanely cunning, and you could not win against all of them unless
you were willing to die and take them with you. Unless
you were lucky enough that they missed your plan and
let you *die* when you took them with you. Auphe didn't
understand sacrifice and giving your life for something
else. They couldn't predict that.

Yet that's what we'd done . . . but it'd worked out better than I'd hoped, although the suitcase nuke the Vigil
had provided us with, ah . . . the irony . . . had contrib-
uted quite a bit.

It *had* worked though and that was all that mattered.

Then Grimm, a half-breed like me, who'd been running free while I hadn't known and while the Auphe
themselves hadn't known, had captured succubae and
made these things—these Bae. One-fourth human, one-
fourth Auphe, and half succubae.

They were . . . curious and interesting.

At first.

Grimm had been different. He'd lived life in a cage
for half Auphe failures, those who couldn't gate, for eighteen years with a part-Auphe caretaker/torturer watching, and tormenting him and the others. That would drive
anyone insane—until he had learned to gate and escaped, carrying insanity and a grudge so massive that
King Kong couldn't have lifted them with both hands.

But I'd spent two years with the real thing, *living* as
the real thing, the Auphe in Tumulus, with all they could

say and do to me. I didn't remember it, but I knew I fought as they fought, I ate what they ate.... I still couldn't even approach that thought sideways without lunging for the bathroom without quite knowing why, except it was something so bad, so wrong that I thought I'd sooner die than remember.

And I learned to gate as they did. While I knew that had happened—the Auphe wanted me as their weapon, and that meant they had to make me the same as them or at least think and act the same, what else would be the point? It might have worked. I didn't know anything other than when I left through my gate I was naked and covered in blood. It hadn't been my blood either. It had been Auphe blood, and it was my sire's blood—I'd never call it a father. I'd torn him to pieces to make my escape.

It was one more thing I knew, although I couldn't picture any of it. All my memories of Tumulus were buried in my subconscious. My conscious had built a wall ... a door ... something that couldn't be breached or open between the two. I didn't complain. You tend not to when your brain comes up with methods to keep you sane. It hid the specifics of those two years away to let me hold on to my sanity. I knew about them in the way you know of your first Christmas. You could guess what went on, what had happened around you at the time— Santa, a tree, presents—but you couldn't dredge up a mental picture, a memory of the genuine event. In this case, I didn't want to remember, because if I did ... Grimm, wouldn't he be fucking pissed?

If I remembered those two years, Grimm would watch me take his place—as an Auphe—true and the worst of the worst.

Insanity and slaughter made flesh—and one who would consider Grimm an insult to the Auphe race, an abomination born only to die.

Watching the Bae come after me the first time, seeing the speed of their moves, how quickly they could gate. I thought that they could fight just enough to be a challenge, but could they take a half Auphe like me? Were they capable? Who knew? That's what I'd wondered at the time.

I found out.

No. Nope. Don't bother calling. I wasn't rolling out of bed for anything less than ten of the snakes. And I'd have to think about it long and hard at even ten.

I'd gone from entertained at the challenge to pissed and offended when Grimm sicced his babies on me. Grimm could take me or I could take Grimm, depending on how much of my humanity I had left and was willing to sacrifice. Grimm and I, we were matched. We could battle to the death easily—winner or loser but most likely a tie.

Grimm's Second Coming, on the other hand? His Bae? His kiddies he said had evolved beyond the now-gone Auphe? No way. Maybe in fifty years when you have a few hundred of them and they've matured enough that they might have a chance. But a one- to five-year-old Bae, physically mature but not in the hunting sense, gating and claws aside, it couldn't spell predator much less be one . . . not to me.

I did know that the three Grimm had sent couldn't. Three of them, what was he thinking? I could handle three while fighting with one hand and jacking off with the other. I was insulted as hell.

Feeling the gate open behind me, I threw myself to the side and hardly saw the twin silver streaks in the air. Sitting up, I saw another Bae down, crushing the grass beneath him, each eye socket pierced by Nik's poniards. "Nice. Blood, no matter the color, always looks better on silver."

"It does, I agree." Niko went and retrieved his blades. "And thank you for the fashion advice."

My KA-BARs were as effective if not as sleek and bright. I got to my feet enough to crouch, no higher. "We can't all be about the aesthetic like you, Nik."

"Finding out that you know the word 'aesthetic' makes this whole ordeal almost worthwhile." Nik turned in a slow circle without seeing the third Bae. His eyebrows formed a disappointed V. One more kill, they said, was it that much to ask? "You said two, maybe three. You always underestimate to keep things interesting. Where's the third?"

The third chose that very moment to gate onto my back. He hit me hard enough that I went facedown for half a breath, the grass smell unimaginably green in my nose and lungs; then I flipped us over and somersaulted off the Bae, losing only a few stripes of skin to his ebon claws. I was back on my feet, crouching by his head and staring down at his face—white, scarlet, titanium fangs as long as my hand. "Hey," I greeted cheerfully (the glee inherent in it carried such a shadowed psychosis I wasn't certain I could admit it to anyone. I'd told Niko days ago I felt fine, hardly homicidal at all. I hadn't lied. But now I wondered if homicidal was so normal for me that it did *feel* fine).

"You fucked up, didn't you?" I could see a faint reflection of myself in his eyes. "I don't know what Grimm told you I was, but"—I laughed and snapped my teeth at him—"he left something out, didn't he?" I knew Grimm had seen enough of me before I'd gated us away. Grimm didn't miss a trick, and I knew he didn't miss the physical changes in me.

"Don't you hate it when Daddy lies?" I leaned in even closer. "You're Bae, right? But what do you think I am?"

The crimson eyes were frozen on me while his arms and legs twitched, but they didn't move at all beyond that, not aggressively at the least. "Your hair. Your eyes."

His black claws scrabbled at the bent strands of grass beneath him. "You are becoming the first. You will be Auphe." For a Bae, he was pretty smart. "Father told us we were better, more advanced, the apex predator. Better than Auphe. He said it and so it must be."

I didn't look away. Survivors don't take their eyes away from their enemy . . . or their prey . . . but Nik said quietly, "Your hair became one-third white after you gated, while you slept. When you woke up your eyes . . . they shifted, from gray to red and back. They're red now. Completely." Too bad I hadn't checked the mirror in the motel. I could've saved Nik the grief of having to tell me. I knew he wanted to say it less than I wanted to hear it. Saying it or hearing it, it didn't change it, and that was how it was.

Shit happens.

"Yeah, I'm more and more Auphe these days, but forget that, as the true Auphe would've thought you Bae nothing but *mongrel* dogs. Nothing more than walking abortions." My attention was immovable from the last Bae as I said that with all the philosophy in me—not my philosophy, but the Auphe one. Then again, mine too, except I had much more respect for a mongrel dog than I had for a Bae.

I had one combat knife left in my left hand and it fit with artistic perfection in his ice white forehead. My movement was fast enough that while I was the one who'd made it, I didn't see it, which meant I doubted the Bae did either or he would've gated. Through his forehead and into his brain, the metal blade was embedded, instant death and less than a spoonful of blood.

"Shit does happens little snake," I murmured out loud this time, to the limp body. "You should've known that. Daddy isn't teaching you right."

Removing the knife, with some crunch of bone, wasn't

entirely pleasant to hear, but you had to deal. That's how our lives were. "Ready to go home?" I held a hand up to my brother and he pulled me to my feet. "Drive or gate? If we can hit a pharmacy, I'm more than ready. No lie."

"We're stealing a car and do shut up about gating unless you include your concussion and too many gates turning you green and vomit-prone." Niko, he was too observant, not for his own good, but for my own good. It was hardly fair.

Niko stole a once turquoise but now faded blue Toyota? Why? They weren't fast. The sound system was crap. They weren't anything you desired in a stolen car, I thought. Nik said, ignorant criminal that I was, that Toyotas were the most stolen car there were. That meant much less chance of us being pulled over with one. Everyone had a Toyota. There weren't enough cops in the world to pull them all over. Then he jammed a screwdriver into the ignition and twisted without mercy.

Who was I to argue? I was expert at killing, less so at stealing.

When we were in the car I tried to get the quickest of glimpses in the side mirror. It was for a time too small to barely measure, but I saw white-streaked black hair, at least a third white as Nik had said, and eyes that changed from red to gray and back to red. They were staying red longer and longer, gray less all the time. I hadn't minded when facing the Bae. Now was different. The reflection in the mirror, it was not me. Yes, me. Not me. Yes, me. No.

No. Not yet. I always thought I'd have more time. I'd fight for that time.

Nik's hand, warmer than mine—enough so that we couldn't be the same species. It wasn't possible or was it too possible? Did he care? I don't think so. The heat of his hand slid into mine and passed over a pair of sunglasses, dark enough to hide whatever color my eyes decided to be at the time. "Thanks," I muttered, putting them on.

"Thank me for something like that again and I'll kick your ass," he said, calm and sincere.

I couldn't help elbowing him sharply in brotherly affection and appreciation. Nik, brother to a human, brother to a half-breed, and brother to an Auphe. He didn't care which of the three.

"Let me tell you something about Ishiah," I said, the vivid and angry flashback of what had happened here twelve years ago circling in my head like a whirlpool. How could he do that? How could he do that to kids? Just . . . how? It kept going round and round.

"Me? Why? He's your boss." He steered the car onto the interstate. "I wouldn't say we were friends. His and my low tolerance for annoying personality types makes us too much alike."

I put my feet up on the dash in revenge of that remark, aimed solely at me.

"He's helped us before with Spring Heeled Jack. Saved Robin once when he was shot in the throat. He let us back in the bar after an Auphe killed one of the other peris to piss us off and terrorize us. He forgave us for it. All in all, without him, the three of us would be dead." He slapped down the sunscreen and gave me a considering glance that meant he might steal my sunglasses. "I suppose I trust him. What else is there?"

Trust him, I thought, and he had saved us from Jack. He, as a peri/ex-angel, could've died doing that or been expelled from NYC for killing a pagan storm spirit. It was in everyone's best interest that Jack go down, but rules were rules whether I understood the concept or not. Ishiah understood them, but had fought against them. That time. I'd given him more truth than I thought he was prepared for in that carnival long ago. All the truth and then some. I imagined that he'd ignore it except when it came to Robin, but there had been Jack. And there had been Danyael, the peri who had died for no other reason than I worked at the bar with him, and the Auphe were making certain I knew no place of mine was safe. Danyael died because of me. Nik wasn't wrong in saying Ishiah had forgiven us ... forgiven me. I didn't think I'd be that forgiving.

I might've been wrong. People can change.

"Never mind," I said, elbowing Nik in the ribs again. "How about some fast food? I'm starving."

People and creatures and peri and angels, they do change.

Helping us kill Jack and save Nik was one point chalked up to Ishiah to demonstrate he may have.

One point. I wasn't sure the thirteen-year-old in me would consider one point enough.

I'd watch.

We'd see.

10

Goodfellow

The brothers called to let me know they were embarking on their twenty-hour road trip, during which Niko absolutely refused to stop and let Caliban rob a pharmacy for epinephrine so that he might gate instead. Neither would he steal a faster car with an improved sound system. He also ignored all the more tasty of the greasiest food establishments. Following all that, the brothers made it home . . . or to my home.

I was stretched out on the contoured sofa and glared at them when they unlocked the door and came in, Cal wearing a T-shirt that said I (HEART) PIG WRESTLING and carrying with him a bloodstained, brain-spattered rusty shovel that had clearly been used to beat someone or something to death — the condo board, cooperative when enough money passed hands, would have no difficulty if anyone had spotted that. A filthy gardening implement carried by what could only be a mass murderer who enjoyed wrestling pigs while not out and about on a frenzied, shovel-waving killing spree. I suppose those all would cover the entirety of Arkansas's statewide hobbies, true. Perhaps someone on the condo board was originally from Arkansas and would slide this under the rug in a fit of nostalgia.

After leaning the shovel against the wall beside the door . . . for the latest in my string of housekeepers to see to, I could only imagine . . . he walked over to drop onto my chest a bag of what had the stench of grease-laden chicken parts compressed into deep-fried lumps and then fell on the sofa and my feet. "Eat up," he drawled. "Even zombies wouldn't mob that stretch of the highway. If this wouldn't turn a zombie vegetarian, nothing would."

At my further investigation of the temperature with one fastidious finger, they were approximately twelve-hour-old stale chicken parts compressed into deep-fried lumps. Much more thoughtful. Fourteen-hour-old ones would be impolite. "Your gift giving astounds me." I picked up the bag gingerly, hoping my shirt hadn't been contaminated by the film of grease, and let the faux-food drop onto the rock crystal of the coffee table. It was the only safe surface to face what was soaking through the bag. "Also, calling me over ten times during a car trip because you are bored and wish to whine about all the things your evil brother won't do is enough that I now consider you a seven-year-old girl."

"Yeah, I went to voice mail a lot after the first ten hours. I'm hurt." He went for my phone and swiped it with what appeared to be mild interest off the table. Niko, who had dropped into my overstuffed recliner, gave me a subtle, close-to-invisible concerned shift of his shoulders. That was Niko for *He's traumatized. I'm letting*

him do as he pleases to distract him from it. Save me. The
man could say a considerable amount in a shrug

I switched my gaze back to Cal. The streaks of white
in his hair had definitely grown—soon it would be half
white—and his eyes weren't gray with red specks now
and again any longer. They were either completely gray
or completely red and I'd already seen them change
twice in the two minutes since they arrived.

"I know," he said when he caught me staring. "I knew
it might happen some day, but . . ." He took a deep breath
and gave his familiar snarky grin that did little to hide
the darkness within. "Can't do anything about it and I
guarantee no one will 'forget' to tip me at the bar now."

I gave Niko credit for recognizing whose skills at distraction were more advanced of the two of us. My view-
point when it came to trauma was to offer a different and
more horrifying trauma to put things into perspective. It
hadn't failed me yet.

I'd distracted Socrates from his refusal to slavishly
follow the rules of his death sentence, his hemlock-laced
state punishment. His annoyance became another rant
at finding that same hemlock-poisoned goblet empty
hours later after I'd poured it out during one of his several previous frothing rants as we discussed the ridicu-
lousness of moral philosophy. One argument and he was
teaching yet in Greece today . . . if under a pseudonym.
Cal would be less of a challenge to preoccupy.

"About my phone you're smudging with your plebian
fingers, word to the wise," I warned carelessly as Cal
found the pictures on the phone and began scrolling
through them. The warning was far too late, of course.
How else would I inflict twice the trauma if the warning
was in time? "Do not look at the pictures."

"Why?" it was an idiotic question, but generally those
were the only kind I could manage to pry from Cal if

he'd had less than twenty-eight hours of sleep. The man was a sloth, more so than I was, which I'd thought impossible.

"They're mostly nudes and not the tasteful kind either." I arranged a brocaded cushion under my head, then folded my hands across my stomach and waited for the trauma.

It was bound to be intriguing, especially if he saw the several of Ishiah and me together, in all the ways there were to be together. And there were hundreds. Ishiah, for all his observance of human nature over his time spent in service of his God, once had no idea whatsoever what humans and particularly pucks could get up to when they put their mind to it . . . or their genitals. Or their minds and genitals when combined with kitchen appliances.

For Cal personally the one of his brother might be best. That might scar him for life, especially if I didn't reveal that it wasn't voluntary and had cost me five hundred dollars to the cleaning company that worked Niko's dojo, including the dojo gym shower. I definitely considered that five hundred well spent.

"What's that?" Cal turned the phone from side to side and then upside down. His eyes narrowed and then widened in a phrase I like to pull from one of the more recent wars: Shock and Awe. He fumbled the phone and then tossed it back on the table as if it were on fire and singeing his practically nunnery produced hands. "That was . . . and you two . . . in fucking midair! In midair, I mean! Just midair!"

"No, no, you were correct with the term 'fucking.' Wings aren't simply for transportation." I gave him the slowest and most depraved of smiles.

I didn't have to see the battle of curiosity against the profound desire for denial of this subject. I knew it was there. I knew Cal. "Ishiah doesn't mind?" he asked dubiously. "With the whole used-to-be-an-angel thing? Because that was perverted. That was seriously perverted, and I don't think possible if you have a skeletal system at all. If you're not a jellyfish, that shouldn't be . . ." He ran out of words to explain his own apparent lack of flexibility.

Ah, naïve youth. I shrugged. "Do you honestly believe there is a creature alive I could not convert to my wild and wicked ways if I chose to? Why do you think the temple virgins of Rome and Greece disappeared? They did so long before the temples themselves did. It was something of a mystery at the time." I crossed my ankles, which wasn't easy while Cal was sitting on them, and tried on an innocent expression. I hadn't pulled that one off . . . ever, I thought. "A mystery until now. It was me. You can't have temple virgins if there are no virgins left."

"But there were other people. In the pictures. On the phone." It was if he thought he kept the comments short, the situation would be easier for him to deal with. He was oh so wrong. "Who the hell else do you have naked pictures of besides Ishiah and the two of you while you were all . . . ?" He put his hands together in a twisted convoluted ball that I had to admit was fairly accurate of one of the pictures he must've seen. "Doesn't Ishiah mind it's not just him?"

"It'd be easier to ask whom don't I have nude pictures of." I flashed him an amused smirk. "And Ishiah is of the opinion that if I merely look but do not touch, all is well. The ones of myself naturally don't count."

He regarded the phone on the table as if it were a cobra about to strike, then gave me a look ripe with even more suspicion. "You? You take them of yourself too? Holy shit, that one that I thought was the Loch Ness Monster?" He was off my feet now and sliding down the couch.

"The Loch Ness Monster is smaller, but yes." I raised my eyes to a sky that lurked beyond my condo ceiling. "Did you think I wouldn't have hundreds of self-portraits? I am my favorite subject."

"Niko? Tell me I didn't scroll past Nik," he asked in the way people do when they have no wish at all to actually know the truth. Cringing and wan.

"So you didn't get that far. Pity. A very nice shot. Artistic really. The wet hair falling to just above buttocks of marble, a true work of art." Niko would take it as a joke in the ongoing effort to transfer Cal's trauma, although it might be best for me to also do some transferring off my phone in case he, untrusting soul, checked.

Cal glowered at me, for the first time since coming through the door not avoiding my eyes, not wanting me to see what he was becoming. That was progress. "And me?"

"With your prudish fear of nudity in front of the same sex, you'd think not." I met his crimson eyes with a sly Cheshire grin and said while fetching my coffee off the table, "But you'd be wrong. The time the Titan injured you and you were bedridden, I obtained at least ten pictures off that. Then there's the spy camera I planted in your bathroom. Niko invariably covers it up with a washcloth, but I'm thinking he didn't feel as if telling you about it would be in his best interest. I have a Web feed on that one. Fifty dollars a hit, and five dollars each minute after. You should consider lengthening your shower time, paying thorough and exceptional care to certain areas." I sipped the coffee. "And if you could get your brother in there with you—"

"I don't know if I can fit that whole coffee cup down your throat," Cal growled, "but I'm willing to try." The fact that he hadn't noticed he'd met my eyes with the currently Auphe ones of his own made the rather sad threat worthwhile.

I slid a glance at Niko, who was far more relaxed now that Cal had different non-Auphe problems on his mind. With his eyes half-shut, he gave me a small, thankful nod before asking, "You said Grimm was at our place before Cal gated. What did he say after we left? He did send a few Bae after us, but that was the same as trying to take us down with the equivalent of attack Chihuahuas. Did he say what he wanted?"

Ignoring the question, I raised an eyebrow and sat up with my cup. I pointed at the whipped cream on it, then to Cal or more specifically his crotch, and finally to my phone. "If you happen to be in the mood, I'd be interested to see what sort of artistic composition you could come up with."

He moved away from me again, nearly a foot this time, but wasn't touching that topic except for "You drink coffee with whipped cream? Not very manly. Or puckly."

"I've lived a very long time and I have slept with more women than currently live in the continental United States. Whether or not I like whipped cream has nothing to do with where I put my cock, how often I put it there, or that there isn't a woman in the world who would choose you over me if I put my mind to it." I took a finger scoop of whipped cream and sucked it off my finger, hoping he was thinking that *I* was thinking of Ishiah as I did it—which I hadn't been, but was now. Hmm.

"Which isn't to mention the equal number of men I screwed over the years," I continued, regretfully saving the fantasy for later, "and in a time when most did have to follow certain societal guidelines or end up constantly fighting instead of having sex. I personally did not mind the fighting when it was for a good cause. If I am forced to kill someone to save him from his own prejudice, I will give in and do the necessary work. I'm giving that way."

I bared my teeth in the same grin I'd given hundreds of bigoted dead men. There'd been a staggeringly high turnover rate for priests during the Spanish Inquisition when I happened to travel through Seville sometime in the sixteenth century. Or would it be considered a turnover if that included turning them over to flip into their grave? That was an excellent question. "I've not killed quite as many as I've fucked over the years, but if you could resurrect any of those I did, I doubt they'd have comments whatsoever on how I take my *coffee* these days."

Cal was my brother in any life, this one included, but that did not mean I would accept a lack of respect. I had slain thousands for trying to force me to be something I was not. Women, men, and all the *paien* sexual flavors in between, I would do what I liked, fuck who I wished, and no one should dare try to stop me.

Or mock my fondness for whipped cream . . . whether it be on a beverage or an intriguing body part from so many of which there were to choose. Ah, and I was back in another happy little pornographic fantasy. I might need to take a personal break in my bedroom for a short while. Hmmm.

Cal slumped. "Yeah, sorry. I forget sometimes that I'm fucked up in the sexual arena and that you're the gladiator that rules it," he said ruefully. "So, did Grimm say anything?"

Sadly, Cal was correct. He was fucked up quite severely in the sexual area, but that wasn't his fault. The fact that he incredibly feared anything that might tempt him at all to be less so was his sacrifice. There would be no more Auphe, he'd sworn, and if he hadn't once found Delilah, whose uterus had been clawed out by her high breed Alpha who had no tolerance for All Wolf cubs, and if I hadn't found him nymphs who pollinated and couldn't possible breed his get, then I had no doubt he wouldn't have any sex. He didn't trust condoms against Auphe sperm or vasectomies against the Auphe body's ability to repair itself in peculiar manners, and I could not say he might be wrong there.

He did have that horny history of his throughout all his other lives, and it was a shame he was thoroughly heterosexual in this life, as even an Auphe couldn't impregnate a human male, as opposed to some of his other lives when both sexes were fine by him. He'd preferred women, true, but he hadn't been limited by them. Of course Greece, Rome, Macedonia, and many others he'd grown up in had been much more flexible when it came to sexuality during certain eras. What he was doing now was against his former natures, if only considering the part that had often been exceedingly oversexed—by human standards. By my standards he could've fit in more orgies, but on the whole, for a human, he'd been impressive. I should let him bitch. I shouldn't call him on it. Aphrodite knew whether or not it was a sacrifice I could've made. She didn't need to know. I knew. I couldn't have made it.

I handed Cal my coffee. "Try it. You'd be boggled what truly expensive whipped cream can do for one's mood." And mine made Bavarian cream churned by milkmaids in erotic push-up bras seem cheap. "What I've already told Niko. He's back to play the game. That would be the game where he tries to slaughter you in some horrific manner while simultaneously trying to get you on his side to create his improved Auphe race. He's schizophrenically optimistic, isn't he?" I tapped his knee with a sharp finger. "It is a valid vetting process, I must admit. If he can kill you, you're not worthy and the position goes to Bob-the-intern." I tapped again. "I know you don't want the position, terrible pay, long hours, becoming the epitome of soul-flaying evil, but do try to be worthy. I prefer you alive. I'm positive that killing Grimm will be a succinct thanks-but-no-thanks for the opportunity that his corpse won't be able to ignore."

"Kill Grimm. What a concept. All that time I spent stabbing him and shooting him, that never crossed my mind. Thanks for the tip." Cal was attempting to pretend he didn't enjoy the whipped cream while I casually leaned forward, slid my phone over quietly, lifted it quickly, and took a picture.

"I like this one." I showed it to Niko. "The cream on his nose is highly suggestive. I may have Ishiah hang this in the Ninth Circle as 'Pervert of the Month.'"

There was some squabbling after that, but always had that been their way since, Zeus, since beyond when I could remember. Back to the time when the two of them bickered over which fleas belonged to which of them. It was reassuring in its own manner. While it went on, I considered the actual problems, not that Grimm wasn't an actual problem, but not exactly as I'd told the brothers. I needed more information on him before coming to a conclusion. I had another problem located, so to speak, and en route to not being a problem. Then I had the problem that interlocked with *that* problem and damn Canada for being so large. I had my entire network on it, tricksters and nontricksters. I had psychics, but when your problem is on the move and quickly, most psychics aren't that gifted or that helpful. If I could get that in order, then most should be solved or as solved as they could get in my world.

I did need that one piece of information from Ishiah. He said he could get assistance from those he'd spent time with a long time ago, but I hated to depend on that. Peris I could handle, but angels—full-on, still holier-than-thou, still willing to smite anything that wasn't good and right with Heaven, which was everyone I knew and everything I did ... those angels I had problems with to say the least.

While I was on that thought, self-righteous angel bastards, I called Ishiah. When he finally answered, making me wonder how high he was flying, I exhaled harshly. I did have worries that the angels now would not want to have anything to do with former angels, or worse, want to smite them for their desertion of Heaven. They wouldn't bear goodwill toward former angels who had learned free will after their long time on earth.

"Ish," I said, relieved, "any word yet? Grimm has shown up here and things are in motion. It would be good to know how much in motion that would be."

As luck would have it, he and several hundred angels, who had despite my expectations put aside their prejudices to hunt a common enemy, had found the Bae hidey-hole out West in a desert string of caverns. Not that the location mattered, as they gated here, there, and everywhere. I was certain they wouldn't be stuck in one spot as a sitting target. Ishiah gave me the information, his grim worry, his sorrow, his affection, and his promise to be home soon.

He was afraid—for me, the once warrior angel and yet still a warrior. He had reason to be. He knew from watching over several thousand years that I didn't ever keep to my own business no matter what versions of Cal and Niko I found in whatever centuries I found them. I wouldn't leave them, and he knew better than to ask me to do so.

I stared blankly at the phone. Finally I hit DISCONNECT and put it down very carefully. If I hadn't, I would be tempted to shatter it against a wall.

"You had Ishiah looking for something about Grimm?" Niko asked, doing his best to hide his own concern at what I'd said to Ishiah. He wasn't successful.

Running my hand over my face, I said slowly, "One might say that. Remember when Grimm and his Bae first showed up? How we guessed that Grimm probably had fifty or so Bae considering he'd been free for twelve years and the rate at which succubae reproduce and with one egg at a time?" I repeated it. "Fifty Bae. It seemed logical, but I thought it best to check, as logic isn't, well, as logical as it should be at times."

"And he found them?" Cal questioned, putting down the coffee, which was probably an excellent choice right now. Cal's tendency to throw things was much worse than mine.

"With assistance, he did," I said distantly, caught up in the overwhelming now and the long-gone past where I'd had this moment time and time again, life after life, when I finally opened blind eyes and saw the end rushing toward us. But not *us*, them, and wasn't that the problem? I was forever left behind. "Not that they'll stay there, the Bae," I added, "I would think. Grimm is too intelligent for that."

This was how it most often started—heading into war without the full information or knowing full well we faced overwhelming odds. Neither one gave us pause, careless fools we were.

It reminded me of one life and one war in particular, so much it did.

"Pan." The arm slung over my shoulder. It had been night then, the stars as numerous as pebbles on a beach. There were skies more beautiful than that of Greece, but none I worshipped more. "Some asshole prince stole some other asshole king's wife. We're off to Troy to burn it to the ground for the insult. Like we give a giant goat's crap, but the pay is good. And it sounds like a banquet of blood, guts, and an entire promised shipload of whores. Want to come?"

When I'd pointed out I was already in a whorehouse, I was promptly dragged out of it by a laughing Cal ... Patroclus.

"You can get whores anywhere, especially as you're a god," he'd pointed out without stopping with the laughter. The single time I'd seen Patroclus not laughing was when he was dying. "With this you get gold, battles, and whores." His arm tightened around me and shook me roughly with good cheer and excitement. "Achilles is coming. I've seen you looking at his ass too many times to count. He's bound to get drunk enough sooner or later during a war to get a little curious. You might get your chance." Patroclus had been one of the more devious humans I'd known. The most devious of the Cals to be sure.

Until Troy killed him.

"How many Bae, then?" Niko appeared worried. I could hardly see him in the here and now—Grecian stars and the uncontainable joy of Patroclus at the thought of battle—but that didn't mean he shouldn't be worried. He should.

And damn Patroclus, who'd dragged me along to that death-in-the-sand. Not once during the Trojan War had Achilles gotten as drunk or bicurious as Patroclus had hinted he might. But drunk was a good word for this moment, this life, with Troy long, long gone. I got to my feet, walked around the rock crystal table, and returned with six bottles of wine and a corkscrew.

"It's only two apiece to start with, but I have more, and yes, we'll need more." I sat back down and began opening the bottles. I passed the first two to Cal. It was fair. Patroclus had died first then and he most likely would do his best to achieve the same here. Between Grimm and the Bae, Cal would be in front, leading the way. "You used to drink like a fish," I told him solemnly, "and every whore knew your name in the old days. Drink now and remind me of better days."

Before he drowned in his own blood by the gates of a city thanks to politics he hadn't given a damn about.

His eyes flickered scarlet and returned to gray. He moved over until he was next to me, leaning against me in an uncommon lapse of Caliban's normal personal space. It had grieved me for years now, what I saw in him—he didn't touch for fear of being hurt and for the equal fear of being the one to inflict the hurt. He took the bottles and put one between his legs and drank half of the other one before he lowered it. "It'll be all right, Robin."

So unlike this Cal to say that—as I'd thought days ago, this Cal differed a great deal from all the others. He used to be the optimist of the three of us, at least seventy-five percent of the time. Biting and sarcastic, that was a constant, but with more humor and far less of the bitter streak that fed it now. And he laughed; whether he was cheerful, savage, mocking, horny, drunken, with his teeth painted in blood, loud with adrenaline, or uncontrolled with the thrill of the ordinary act of living, he'd laughed.

This Cal didn't laugh like that. When this Cal laughed, blood would definitely be involved. In those lives Niko had sometimes . . . often, now that I thought on it . . . implied it was as he'd been dropped on his head as a baby. I missed that about him. I wanted the old Cal back, the one who got us into more trouble than even I could manage, but entertaining trouble. I hated this black and grim life of theirs, and as much as I tried to change it for them, I couldn't change Auphe genes to human ones. This life next to Troy's end often seemed the worst of all. But it was all I had for now and I didn't want to relinquish it. I wouldn't. I gave Cal a faked curve of a smile and then opened two more bottles to pass to Niko.

Niko took them but asked without more than holding them, "How many Bae?"

I ignored him and opened my bottles. "Robin, how many?" he demanded again.

"Drink," I ordered, and drained half a bottle myself.

Sighing, Niko raised a bottle and swallowed a third. Very notable for Niko, who in this life barely drank at all. In appreciation I clinked one of my bottles against his and then against Cal's almost empty bottle now. Good for him. For this life, I was impressed indeed.

"Now," Niko said, leaving his chair and sitting beside me on the couch. With one bottle on the table and one in his hand, he laid an arm across my shoulders . . . as Patroclus once had. Immediately Cal slung his arm on top of his brother's, and the weight and warmth of them both resting on me gave me the courage to say it.

"Tell us," Niko coaxed. "How many?"

"A thousand."

I drank again, then bowed my head. "A thousand Bae, more or less. A thousand for which Grimm has to play his game. A thousand when we thought there could be fifty of them at the most, and we'd thought defeating the hundred Auphe in the past with a *nuclear* bomb was a feat unheard-of. And the Vigil won't be offering us any suitcase nukes for our use any longer, will they?"

This time when I bowed my head, I let it go all the way to rest on my knees. I cursed in over a hundred languages, vicious and hateful, curses capable of killing entire fields of crops or forests of trees if I meant it. When I gave in to the ugly, jagged choking that passed as weeping in a creature who after the gates and pyres of Troy had forgotten how, Niko's and Cal's arms tightened over me.

I wouldn't have been ashamed if I could remember how. If I could taste the salt in shed tears, as there was no copper-drenched blood to spill as a substitute.

I'd wept when Patroclus died and then when Achilles died. I had tried when Caiy and then Arturus died ... when Hephaestion and Alexander died ... when Phelan died and I'd mourned even for Cullen, although I had never met him and hadn't seen his blood rush free. I mourned, but Troy had broken me in several ways. I would not feel the dampness of despair on my skin again. Those were only four—now five—lives and there were hundreds, perhaps thousands, more in which they were human, save this one, and in all they had died while I lived on. When I had them left to give, I would've killed the man who thought a single tear was wasted on any of the lives and deaths of these brothers ... these cousins ... these comrades in arms.

I would kill the man.

I had done so before.

And I'd enjoyed it.

After drinking all the alcohol I had in the condo, which was a great deal, and they let me have the lion's share, I'd told stories of their ... our past. I no doubt shouldn't have for fear of waking more of Cal's past selves, but at least I'd been alert enough to leave Cullen and Phelan out of the stories. Cullen was in Cal's subconscious at the mere slip of a tongue already. I didn't want to bring him out to play. When I wavered near unconsciousness, they had supported me to my bed, stripped me to my boxer-briefs, and let me sleep. Let me escape into a darkness thick and muffling—in which I could've stayed forever if I'd been allowed. For thousands of lives I'd had my companions, but for thousands of following years I'd been left alone in the dark.

When was enough enough?

Morpheus knew how long later, I clawed my way out

of sleep and I heard them. They had left my door open, either accidentally or to be able to hear if I choked to death on my own vomit in an alcoholic stupor. That wasn't heroic but more often true.

Once I'd thought Cal had also put that death to the test after we'd ridden war elephants over several mountain ranges, causing widespread motion sickness and prayers for death from all, to finally reach Italy. The celebration when we eventually arrived before the fighting there had begun was extensive. None of us had cared to see an elephant or a mountain again, drinking the memory of the sickening and wholly unhygienic journey away. When I had staggered awake the next day, it was to find the body of Canno—Cal—in the dirt outside our tent, surrounded by vomit while yet clutching an empty amphora stained the purple-red of the cheapest wine. His eyes half open, fixed and dull—I could not believe it. All the lives I scrambled to keep his scrawny, malnourished ass from death's ever-waiting grip and he did this to himself? He did *this*?

Regardless of his idiocy, I would've shouted down the sky at his passing . . . eventually, but I indulged myself . . . for the first and only time. "I do all that can be done to keep you alive, you ignorant, self-destructive son of a pox-ridden whore and a blind, one-balled donkey." I kicked his body. "I endure your flatulence whenever you devour cheese as the milk of goats is too much for your delicate organs." The second kick was as swift and hard. "I laugh at your inane and filthy humor." Which I had to admit to myself I enjoyed thoroughly as mine was the same. It simply made me kick him repeatedly and more furiously at the pure idiocy of him dying in such a manner.

It was on the fourth kick that he had bitten my ankle as viciously as a rabid wolf but with far worse breath drifting up to my nose. A night of bad wine and worse pork. "You are a demon to bring this morning upon us." He'd snarled up at me in Phoenician, a magnificent language for insults. "And you sucked the cock of the donkey that mounted my mother." Then he was gone again, sound asleep and content in his bed of dirt and vomit with his eyes closed this time against the sunlight.

One cannot pick their family or, despite the saying, often cannot pick their friends when fate is involved, and one definitely cannot pick their karmic-bonded idiots.

The proof was in my living room.

"Arturus and Caiy?" From there Cal sounded tired as well as if he too had only woken up with enough alcohol in his blood system to regret it.

"King Arthur and Sir Kay. It wasn't as legend and movies have you think. There was much more horse manure and body odor than gold and legendary swords. Arthur was no more than an illiterate chieftain and Kay a soldier and foster sibling with a noted acid tongue. Yes, that would be you, Cal. Your heroic death was probably closer to being kicked to death by a cow. A Roman cow, maybe, to keep you British and 'noble.' Caiy died fighting a Roman conqueror, bovine conqueror. I'm guessing they left out the bovine part of the tale. There was also a Myrddynne who could do things that men found to be 'witchery.' That would be Merlin and Robin, I'm quite certain. He could pass off pulling rabbits out of hats and coins behind ears as 'witchery' in those days." Niko sounded equally exhausted.

It hadn't been rabbits. It had been frogs and the occasional hedgehog I'd made magically appear in that stupid hat. And for the maidens, it was a given, it was my cock that materialized within. It wasn't as if I wore that ridiculous hat, which was not pointed or be-starred as idiot fiction would claim, for the things it did for my hair.

"Then there was Alexander and Hephaestion," Niko went on. "They died months apart. For all that we seem to have what most would call an unhealthy attachment to each other and cannot live an entire year alone, we don't seem to do any service to Robin, who does go on alone and who knows for how many hundreds of years before he sees us again. You heard him. He has spent thousands of lives with us and yet we keep leaving him, which might not be so bad if we were old and withered and he'd be glad to see us depart in our decrepit stage. He could find others to drink with if that happened and stop paying village women to change our medieval diapers, but if that has been the case but once, he hasn't mentioned it."

"Phelan and Cullen," Cal said, low and not meant, I don't think, to be said in a place here or now.

"What did you say?" Niko asked, with the same weariness, but, praise Mnemosyne, no genuine comprehension of what Cal had said.

Cal's voice went on as if Phelan and Cullen had not been said aloud, had not happened, and I kept hoping Cal wouldn't know, not consciously. Subconscious was a lost cause. "Achilles and Patroclus. Alexander and Hephaestion. I didn't give a crap about history or any of the other subjects you homeschooled me in, but I remember that those two pairs were close. Like, really close. As in closer than brothers and more into . . . you know. Oh, shit. I think I need to put my head between my knees." Ah, poor Cal . . . if he remembered what he'd done in other lives, including orgies that offered men, women and, not to forget, hermaphrodites . . . would combust.

"I imagine . . . no, I *know* . . . that Robin spread those rumors and laughed while he did so." Niko was right to say that. I had lied, I had spread rumors, and if it was because Achilles wouldn't give me the time of day, in a sexual sense, and Patroclus had given me false hope, the bastard, of his cousin to drag me into a long, drunken war. They deserved the rumors.

I tossed aside one of my pillows and thought of the foul-tongued Persian mercenary who'd made malicious comments when I clawed the ground until blood stained my fingers at Patroclus's funeral pyre and then he had laughed outright, saying I wasn't a god—I wasn't even a man, when I'd knelt at Achilles' own pyre and begged his forgiveness. Of course the dead can't grant forgiveness.

The Persian had laughed, yes, but only once. He had no time for a second as I'd instantly taken him to the ground with a vicious slice that opened his guts. Knee on his chest pinning the thrashing, screaming garbage in place, I considered what gift he could make to the pyre in apology for his disrespect. It was an easy decision. He thought I wasn't a man for mourning my comrade, my family. I knew without a doubt what he'd prize the most in proving himself a man. I relieved him of them, and I did not do it quickly or mercifully. When done, I let him continue to scream and struggle for a while. Why wouldn't I? Surely a *man* could take a little pain.

Finally, I tired of the noise and the mess as his attempt at flailing about caused his intestines to begin to pour free from his abdomen. With my dagger, I indicated his cock and balls lying in the dirt and sand beside his head where he could turn for an excellent view. "Not a man, you say? How much of a man do you feel with your manhood itself gone?" I hissed. While the day was warm, I was cold—a creation of ice. "What? No answer?" Nothing he could say now would move me, not that he didn't try. The screams had faded to moans and now became begging. I hated when those as worthless as him begged, and today wasn't the day to spend much time on this son of a whore. This was Achilles' day.

I was crouching beside him now, and I rocked back on my heels for a better look at the display I had made of him—the pageantry of what precisely was *not* a man. "I'm going to kill you, but first you watch. If you don't, you won't die for as many agonizing days I can drag from you no matter how you whine and plead."

The pain already had his skin tight against skull, as if he'd been dead for years. He did watch as told, as I knew he would. First I reached down and hefted his cold and shriveled prick in my hand to hold before his eyes. "The merit and value of a man . . . I hope for your sake it isn't measured by the length of your dick. You would fall short to say the least." I tossed it on the funeral pyre. "What you thought made you a man, I sacrifice to one who was born knowing with his first breath what truly makes one." Bravery, courage, loyalty—that was what made men.

"As for these. . . ." I ignored his whimper as there was a faint sizzle when his flesh entered the fire, "These shall be for Patroclus." I showed my teeth in a rictus of a grin I knew couldn't possibly reflect the current insanity inside me. I picked up the testicles and whistled. All the camp dogs came running and I tossed the Persian's balls to the nearest one. "Patroclus liked dogs. I think he would've appreciated you giving them a scrap, no matter how tiny, of meat."

He was crying and had been since the first cut to his stomach. So much for that portion of his definition on what defined manhood. The base coward was not an offering worthwhile of Achilles here now or of the ghost of Patroclus days gone. I hoped they took it in the spirit in which it was offered. Defeat of the dishonorable and a laugh for Patroclus who had genuinely loved that pack of dogs.

I'd exhaled, abruptly too exhausted to care if I took

another breath. My dagger slashed, cutting the mercenary's throat deeply enough that his head tilted back to show bone cut through. It was only the few strips of flesh and tendons that left it attached to his body by the scarcest of tethers. Unimportant. The only thing of importance now was the silence.

There was quiet and it was good. Not a sound could be heard but the crackle of the flames. No one laughed. Not that they didn't want to learn the lesson the Persian had—that wasn't the reason. They too knew and fought with Achilles. They were his men and they mourned as well.

There were no more gathered around who lacked respect for the greatest warrior of his time.

The rest of the body I left for the dogs to devour. They'd had the smallest of tastes, they were ready for more. It was a good day to be a dog. I turned back to kneel again by the pyre. There I would stay until the fire burned to nothing, until the last charred splinter of wood was cold.

The Persian had known nothing.

If you've never wept at the funeral of a friend, then you have never had a friend.

Memories. They were but memories, that was all. I pushed them aside with long practice to return to the present in time to hear Cal's next words.

"He's gone through too much for our sakes." I heard the rattle of empty bottles against one another. Cal cleaning up? That was unlikely, but it could happen. Unlikely as the sun turning purple, but vaguely possible. "We're not like him. Haven't you noticed? All those people we were or the ones we know about, they died young and who knows how long it takes him to find us to begin with? He was careful not to let us know anything about this reincarnation crap when we were kids in this life. That means he did that in all our other lives. He waited for us to grow up and become whoever the hell we were supposed to be."

There was the shattering crash of glass. Cal was cleaning then, in all his carelessness, which made me appreciate the effort more. "In all our lives he waits until we're adults and then, to thank him, we up and die after hanging around with him ten or fifteen years at fucking best. We leave him after fifteen years, and he spends hundreds alone until we can be bothered to be born and found by him again. A *thousand* lives or more that we've come and gone, a thousand, he said. How he's not crazy as hell, I don't know. I would be. This life right now with the Auphe by itself is too much for anyone. Hell, I wish he wouldn't torture himself like this. I highly fucking doubt we're worth it."

"He chooses this. He doesn't have to find us and go through life after life at our side. He could ignore us if he crossed our path. He could not seek us out." That was Niko, and Niko most often knew what he thought, but he didn't sound certain this time. He wanted to believe what he said, but I don't think that he did.

"Nik, shit. If we lived forever and Robin died and lived and died over and over again, do you think we'd let him do that alone? Particularly if he had a death wish like we seem to have?" Cal snapped. "Hell, no. There's no choice. He's family. For all that he's done for us in the only life we remember, imagine what he's done for us in the thousands we don't remember. If he did that for us, we'd do the same for him. I know I come first with you the same as you come first with me, but maybe that's because we don't remember Robin each time we're reborn." There was the explosion of glass this time. A bottle hitting the wall. Cal's typical reaction to what he couldn't fix, and it made me that much more fond of him, as I was that accustomed to it now. "He talked about Patroclus and Achilles and he didn't say how we died, but as much I wish I had ignored your history lessons, I *didn't*, because I know how it happened."

I stood at my bedroom door now. My penthouse was large and the hallway long and I could barely see a bare slice of Caliban, his now black-and-white hair hanging down as he tilted his head to stare at the floor. I watched as he combed fingers through the strands. He was worrying about me when day by day he became physically more Auphe. He wasn't thinking of himself, desperately compromised . . . but of me. Could any god have created a more true friend? No.

"I know Patroclus died first," Cal asserted quietly, hoping the breaking bottle hadn't woken me or because he was tired. That feeling I knew very well. "And I know Achilles freaked the hell out. Killed that prince and desecrated his body. I remember that because you taught it to me. That's what I know from the history books, but what I *remember* now that I've heard most of the story from Robin." Except for the end, for the dying part I refused to talk of, not a word. No one could convince me to do that. But my silence had been pointless. One would think after Cullen that I'd know that not telling the entire story wasn't protection enough with Cal's Auphe-enhanced memory. I'd been a drunken fool.

"I remember a sword cutting my throat and then again, stabbing into my chest."

I saw Cal's head fall even lower. "I saw you and Robin above me, talking, yelling." Not yelling—screaming. We had screamed, Achilles and I. "But I couldn't breathe," Cal went on. "I tried, but I couldn't fucking breathe. I felt like I was drowning, but I didn't taste salt from the sea. It was copper. It was blood. I drowned in my own blood."

I heard him clear his throat as if he could taste that blood still. "You looked mostly like you. Your hair was a darker blond, you had scars on your face, but your eyes were the same gray." Not surprising as Achilles had managed to fast-talk his genes into what would be the Leandros clan. "Robin . . . Robin was exactly the same." There was a choked laugh. "He'd have to be the same, wouldn't he? And I don't remember that from any history lesson you taught me. Goodfellow, Puck, Pan, at the battlefield."

Cal's words became louder, stronger. "You said he was to keep me safe. You said, 'You are the Great *God* Pan and you swore to keep him safe, oath-breaking bastard.' You blamed him, cursed him, hurt him, almost killed him. I think he would've let you. I know he didn't try to stop you, and I *couldn't* stop you. I couldn't breathe through the blood or say a word and I couldn't tell you to *stop*. I died and fuck knows what you said to him then." There was a ragged exhalation. I heard it and saw it in the heave of his shoulders, but when he spoke, it was unbreakable steel. "Nik, don't do that again. Don't ever put that on him. He can't keep me safe. You can't keep me safe. That's what being human is about, and even if I'm only half human now, it doesn't matter. I will never be safe and my life will always end. Don't blame Robin for that. He does all that he can and more. The same as you do."

There was a long pause and Cal didn't raise his head. "I said that?" Niko questioned quietly, the remorse blatant, but I didn't want that. I didn't want his guilt. I didn't deserve it.

Why this? Why now? Cal remembered Cullen and now he remembered the sands of Troy. I sighed. Auphe-human racial memory or not, why was it only the worst things he remembered?

"Yeah." Cal straightened and I backed away from the door. I didn't want him to see me and I didn't want to see any more. "And I know in this life you would never say that. In this life you wouldn't blame him. But every life is different, isn't it, every time is different, and we are different, at least a little. Just . . . if I die first this time and with a thousand Bae, hell, we're both probably going to die, but if I do go first, don't blame him. It's not his fault. It's not your fault. It's no one but Grimm's fault. Feel free to take it all out on him if you get the chance."

I heard the smile. I even somehow heard the crooked, boldly wicked nature of it. I smiled myself, whether I meant it or not, and went into my master bath to wash off the residue of wine and the sweat of old and new fear.

When I was done, we'd think of somehow to fix this.

We would.

I'd accept no less.

Not this time.

"For the love of all that is holy." Niko aimed his scrutiny toward the kitchen, almost opposite from me. "Buddha, help me concentrate on Nirvana and cast aside these earthly dismays."

Cal blanched and twisted around to head rapidly toward that filthy shovel he'd brought in with him the day prior. "Has a puck been killed by a garden tool before? Would I be the first? Is there some sort of award that would go with that?"

I shook my head and turned to go back to my bedroom. "This is my home," I called over my shoulder, naked shoulder—naked everything actually, but as I'd said, this was my home. "I could walk about naked or worse all day long, especially if I was hungover, and that would be perfectly in my right." It was true. I could walk about dressed in whatever could be paid for and delivered via the Internet, no matter how disgusting I might find it. That wasn't the issue. The issue was "my home, my right to walk about nude or in whatever made you wish I were nude." And if I had to walk about in something revolting to prove it was my right, then I would. I was obstinate in that manner.

Plus, I'd been drunk, and sleeping drunk and naked was invariably the rule. But until something horrendous could be thought of and delivered to prove nudity wasn't a quarter as shocking as they thought it to be, I came back out in brown slacks and a green shirt. "I expect breakfast is ready. I provided several thousand dollars of alcohol last night. The least one of you could do is cook. Oh, and watch out for the hole in the floor." Where I'd ripped up the wood I'd carved a plea for forgiveness. Niko could read Greek and I had not been in the mood to explain my small break from this current reality. "Termites."

Cal released the shovel and it thunked heavily against the wall. "I don't cook. It's boring."

"You appear to be living with me with no invitation that I recall, and I do not customarily give out keys unless the person I give them to makes sexual areas of me thrilled to exist. Specifically my cock. There is that option or you can cook." I pointed at the refrigerator. "Pancakes. Blueberry. Now." I began to undo my belt. "Or there is this. . . ."

Hopeful my temper and sexual demands in exchange for keys would subside, Cal dived into the refrigerator muttering the foulest of filth under his breath. I'd come up with far worse ones to spread across various continents. Less than impressed, I gave him a wolfish grin, refastened my belt, and sat at the island to wait for the feast to be delivered unto me. I tapped fingers on the granite and glowered at him. I'd not seen a mostly Auphe hurry about to cook breakfast to prevent inducing further ire in me. Then again, my ire was fierce. It was entertaining to view his reaction to it.

"Robin." Niko had sat on the stool next to mine and

kept the conversation quiet and low to avoid Cal's attention. "What of the Vigil? We have too many problems to name, but the Vigil has made two runs at Cal. We need to solve that in some manner or we won't have a chance of surviving Grimm and the Bae."

"Orange juice," I demanded loudly, and Cal had it poured in a glass for me within moments. That was nice. I approved of that service. I hope it lasted long enough for a meal before Cal decided strangling me with my own belt would be less embarrassing. I took a swallow of the juice, full of pulp and tartness. "Don't worry about the Vigil, Niko," I advised, passing him my glass of juice. The man was uptight to an unfathomable degree. Perhaps juice could aid him. Did vitamin C reduce anal-retentive behavior? I would have to research it.

"The reason the Wolves are attacking the Vigil is that I paid them to do so." I yawned and took my juice back, as Niko was only staring at it and then me, confused. "I paid them a great deal. They will do their best, not that I'm saying that is the highest effort in the world, but given what they have to work with, they are offering their paramount endeavor."

Cal started to turn from the stove. "What . . . ?"

"Pancakes!" I snapped.

He reverted immediately to a cooking position. I saw him glance at the knives in the butcher block before deciding against taking me on. That was wise. I could give him a buzz cut with one of those knives before he had a chance to twitch.

"You paid the Kin to stop the Vigil from killing Cal?" Niko asked, more quiet than the pop and sizzle of the grease Cal was using to cook my pancakes.

"Yes, although to be politically correct they are called the Lupa now." I could smell the blueberries and they smelled amazing. They'd smell better with bacon, I thought. "Caliban! Bacon!" He lunged for the freezer. "I rather enjoy him like this," I murmured, low enough that Niko could hear, but not his brother. "Terrorized by my sexuality *and* guilted into a cooking frenzy."

"Should he feel guilty?"

"No." He clearly did or my belt would've been around my neck fifteen minutes ago, but he shouldn't. "Neither ought you. All lives are different. Achilles had an inexcusably abusive father I would wish on no one, and that bastard instilled a sense of perfectionism in his son that was not achievable by anyone, human or no." I rested against Niko's shoulder. "In this life you carry Cal. In that life, he carried you. That didn't turn out well when he died, but I couldn't save Patroclus. You couldn't save Patroclus. Patroclus couldn't save himself. It was no one's fault. Let it go."

"You heard us." Niko didn't comment any further on something that was obvious. "You heard that Cal is remembering things he shouldn't." He wouldn't want anyone to know that he raised his eyes before looking away at the sight of the spreading silver in Cal's hair. He wouldn't want anyone to know, and that meant I didn't say anything. He behaved as if the moment hadn't happened, his face a mask of flat determination before speaking again. Niko was Niko. All things were to be borne, and buckling under their weight wasn't acceptable, not to him. "Then let us pay you back for what you gave the Lupa." He changed the subject. Niko was excellent at that when he wanted to divert his train of thought. "What you paid to stop the Vigil."

I shook my head, drank more juice, and laughed. "No."

He was offended at that. It was Niko. I knew he would be with his unbending pride. He and Cal had both taken showers as I had. Niko's blond hair spread around his shoulders and down his back to his waist. It was damp yet, but that didn't stop him from gathering it up to braid it. I'd noticed Niko did that when irritated. He would either unbraid or braid his hair to keep his hands from fastening around your throat to choke the life from you. It was a polite coping mechanism. I approved. Cal would simply have, once again I mention it, just strangled you. "Why?" he demanded. "We don't want to take advantage of you."

Finishing my juice, I propped my elbows on the island counter and smiled winningly. "Niko, first, it's kind of you to not want to take advantage. If I were less manly, virile, and brimming with machismo, I'd go so far as to say it's rather adorable that you think you could."

That anyone in the world could. I was the first and then the second trickster born and the oldest left alive. I did not get taken advantage of . . . unless it was sexually and I wanted to be, of course. I had no qualms about separating irritating people from their lives and their money. No regrets, not one. That's who I *was*. If you warranted death, and regrettably most humans did, and could be convinced to hand over your fortune as you "passed on" with my assistance, I was more than happy to usher your wealth unto a better place. Such as my offshore Cayman bank account.

"Alas, adorable isn't in my vocabulary and I'll have to remain comment-free there. Second, no. No. You cannot pay me back. You never live long enough to earn almost three million. If you were like me, if you had hundreds of thousands of years at the very minimum to realize what is valuable and what will be valuable"—and then accumulate mineral sources that all short-sighted individuals would have assumed to be worthless—"perhaps we could talk. That is not the situation, unfortunately. If it weren't for Ishiah, however, sexual payback would be on the table, but regrettably . . ." I gave a classic European shrug, which meant *I lust for your ass, but it cannot be*. The Europeans had a wonderful system of body language.

Cal whirled and slid a plate of pancakes and bacon in front of me. His eyes were gray this morning. "You paid that bitch Delilah three million dollars to keep me alive and the Vigil off my ass? You could've paid me that and I would've gone off to live in Antarctica with the best ruby-encrusted entertainment system made by man. They never would've found me."

He didn't fail, of all those in the world—not once, Cal didn't—to make me feel as if I were the responsible one. That was rare for me, excepting the lives of the brothers, and it made me feel good about myself. Smug. I truly enjoyed feeling smug. "It was only two point five million, and I couldn't be responsible for what an Auphe-penguin hybrid evil overlord might perpetrate upon this planet."

Opening his mouth, he considered, and then sat on the other side of me, sulking. "It would have to be consensual penguin sex. Adult consensual penguin sex."

"Yes, I'm certain. There was not a doubt in my mind." I poured on maple syrup shipped from a tiny farm in Vermont and took a bite of his breakfast efforts. It tasted like charcoal combined with blueberries and syrup. It was inedible. I chewed and swallowed with effort. "The best I've had, Caliban. You've ruined me for all other breakfast foods." He looked pleased, then suspicious and then pleased again. No matter the color of his hair or eyes, he remained Cal yet. I patted his shoulder. "As it stands now, the Vigil is mostly not our problem. I'm not telling you not to be alert. That would be idiotic. I'm certain the Lupa will slip up now and again, as they don't care if you live or die and their refund policy isn't the best I've come across to say the very least. I have heard, however, that the Vigil are going down like the firstborn of Egypt and the Wolves are enjoying themselves greatly. But never trust rumors. You aren't free and clear with the Vigil yet, simply better off than you were with them. Mainly, however, we need to think about Grimm and his thousand children who do not fit in any story tale shoe. Or rather you need to think about that."

I let my hand fall to squeeze his wrist tightly enough to have his eyes flash from gray to red with surprise at the command in my grip. "I have other problems to deal with, as important, I promise you. But you, Caliban, you need to decide how you will deal with Grimm and his Bae. All of them. You are the only one who can predict what they might do." He was the only one who thought as Grimm thought. That was half the truth, but it was all the truth he needed to hear now.

The scarlet of his eyes flared and his lips curled into the nastiest of grins. I recognized it. It was one he'd picked up from me five or six thousand years ago. "You're right. I've outthought them twice before. I'll think of something, something to make them the sorriest bastards on the face of the earth. Trust me."

"I do." That was true of him and Niko. I'd trusted them with anything and everything. I trusted them forever.

Except their own lives.

On that, I'd learned better.

11

Caliban

Robin had gone out to handle something; what it was, he wouldn't say. Hell, I'd just discovered he had someone take over his car lot days ago, before Nik and I had a remote clue that shit was going down, until this mess was cleared up ... or we were dead. I was leaning heavily toward death. But we weren't dead yet and he asked me to stay and wait on the delivery. What was I going to say? Nah, I don't do favors for friends for less than four million dollars? Take your measly two point five million and shove it?

Worse yet, I had the feeling the delivery was for me personally. Dropping a few million to save my life, having Ishiah call in favors from Heaven—which I was no fan of, but I did get it was a very big motherfucking deal and more reason to forgive him, to double-check how many Bae there really were. Something Nik and I hadn't thought about since the "yeah, it's probably fifty" discussion that had lasted maybe five minutes, because we were idiots. Not that Robin hadn't cautiously agreed at the time, but neither had he forgotten. And he'd done something to verify its goddamn staggering lack of reality. Now he was working on other problems he waved off every time we asked about them. We'd died so many times on him, it was a wonder he hadn't reached the point of if you want to keep them alive, do it yourself because they can't be bothered.

Could I say that wasn't true?

I seemed to repeat the same mistakes over and over. I didn't need memories for that, only history books.

Patroclus had definitely gotten himself . . . myself . . . whatever . . . killed. Ignored orders, ignored common sense, ignored what it would do to those he left behind because he was a bloodthirsty idiot who hadn't come across a fight since birth that he didn't want a piece of. It might've been all right, that kind of stupid behavior, if he'd been half the fighter Achilles or Robin was, but when I asked about that, Robin said promptly that naturally he was, a warrior unsurpassed, and hand me another bottle of wine, please.

When he'd said that, I looked quickly at Niko for confirmation. Nik had a great poker face, but he wasn't Robin; he wasn't a trickster. I saw a flicker of truth before he hid it behind his own wine bottle. Nik studied great warriors . . . and their sidekicks. He knew who was brilliant and who couldn't fight off a toddler with an axe and a mace. Patroclus had been okay was what Nik's expression had said. Just . . . okay. From how Robin had talked more openly, he'd been ruthless and fearless. I'd bet that part was honest, but in the middle of a battle gone bad without superior skills to back it up or the plan he'd tossed aside, Patroclus would be in deep shit if he didn't have Achilles or Robin at his back.

Had been in deep shit. It doesn't get deeper than dead. He . . . I'd gotten myself killed and then, while dead, I'd gotten Niko killed — wasn't that impressive? I didn't have to be alive to do enormous damage. I could be deceased, gone, the beat of an owl's wings in the twilight, and do it all the same. I'd also given Robin what seemed like one of his very worst memories. The guy had lived millions of years and I was the one to give him his worst fucking memory.

Wasn't I special?

Was I selfish enough to wish the new "gift" of Auphe-human racial memories would go screw themselves and let me believe Robin's lies and misdirection at the end of all his stories about the three of us? I was. I admitted it. I wanted to believe the legends, not the truth. But that wasn't happening. And while Robin was trying to spare us on what really had occurred, I was busy giving him new shit, like last night with the Bae, to add in his giant memory book of Cal-fucked-up nightmares.

A thousand Bae, why were we trying at all?

A buzz from the lobby and then a few minutes later a knock at the door distracted me from the image on Robin's face when Ishiah had told him about the thousand Bae on the phone. I couldn't hear it, but I could see him and I couldn't imagine what could be that god-awful to make the eyes of my endlessly wicked asshole friend go so goddamn desolate and flat that I could see him wishing he actually were dead. That being dead would be better than this. That Hell would be better than this.

So the knock was a distraction. And it was one that I needed desperately, as I absolutely didn't want to relive in my mind the lack of life and hope on Robin's face again, not now. Hopefully not ever.

I could kill whoever was knocking if they deserved it. I was good at that. Emotions I didn't do so well with, but if death and destruction was needed, I was your go-to guy.

My luck was the same as usual and the person knocking didn't deserve or require death. Didn't that suck? It was one of Robin's people, and he had "people" for every damn thing under the sun. The guy was a big and overly muscled gym jock with bleached blond hair—no surprise there, Goodfellow, Mr. "I certainly can look even if not touch." He handed over the box, hovered as if waiting for something like a tip. As if that was going to happen. No one ever tipped me at the bar. I gave a friendly glance at the shovel leaning next to the door, and the guy bolted. Closing the door, I investigated the delivery box. Inside were fifty bottles of epinephrine and enough syringes to supply a hospital. They weren't the EpiPen kind, but I'd have to make do. It'd be like a flu shot—one damn big flu shot. I'd gone to one of the guest bathrooms to put the box down on the countertop beside the sink and was unwrapping one syringe to "gate up" for the day when I took in how much epinephrine fifty bottles was. It was a helluva visual. So many bottles, so many syringes . . . a few were big enough to inject a steer or a horse.

I raised my gaze up into the mirror and this time I studied my reflection for the longest I had in years. I didn't bother with looking at what hair I had that remained black, ignored when my eyes flickered gray. Instead I saw only the silver-white strands and the crimson eyes that went perfectly with the Auphe pale skin I'd been born with. I'd known I'd change someday. Grimm had said so and Grimm was the same as the devil in fiction . . . all his best lies were the truth. I'd thought, though, that the change would be a gradual sort of thing. There would be a silver hair that would show up here and there every few years and a speck or two of red that would do the same. But of course not. On the inside, it could be a confused macabre mess that I couldn't predict from day to day. On the outside, it was different. When I started to change, there was no holding it back. At the rate I was going, I'd look mostly Auphe in a week or less.

I should've minded. I should've minded a great goddamn deal, but I didn't. It was more . . . honest. When I went Auphe in my mind, I never knew.

Was I all Auphe? A little Auphe? Halfway? Would I come back? Be human again ever? I couldn't tell you. I didn't have any way of knowing. This was better. This I could measure. This I could *see*.

"There you are," I muttered. "Finally come out where I can see you when we play." I traced a finger over my silvered image, smudging the glass. "I've carried your ass around so long, now it's time you do something for me."

Dropping my eyes back down to track from bottle to bottle of epinephrine. One, two, ten, twenty, forty, fifty. It was an incredible amount.

Where could you gate with all this?

I smiled, twisted and triumphant.

For that matter, where *couldn't* you gate?

Nik was in his bedroom—guest bedroom Robin would emphasize if he were here—when I asked if he was ready to go back home to pick up some weapons. He'd borrowed a clean pair of clothes from Goodfellow and was sliding his katana into its sheath on his back that had been converted from a double shoulder holster before pulling on his coat over it. "You're feeling well, then?"

I slapped the top of my leg where I'd injected a gating dose of epinephrine. "Juiced up and good to go." I was wearing a pair of Goodfellow's jeans and shirt as well, but I wasn't lying to myself by calling them borrowed. They were stolen and that was the fact of it. He was not getting them back. This wasn't the first time this had happened and I didn't feel at all guilty, as Robin had planned for it. The evidence was the T-shirt I was wearing under the also stolen leather jacket. I'd found it in the dresser of my designated guest room, the one with the least furniture to damage.

The shirt was black with small red letters that read IF I CANNOT MOVE HEAVEN, I WILL RAISE HELL. The trickster would sooner be found dead in superhero spandex than a common cotton T-shirt. Armani could have virgin sheep sheered of their wool by virgin sheepherders and woven into cloth by blind virgin nuns to be sold by virgin strippers in diamond-covered thongs and that wouldn't change the fact that he'd find it unworthy to wipe his puckster ass. That meant intentional present for me.

Straightening his duster to hang long and smooth to conceal all his many borrowed knives, Niko took in my shirt and cocked his head before shaking it in mock despair. Or I hoped it was mock. The guy did have reason for true despair. Hell, didn't we all? "How appropriate. If you recall, Virgil was the one who—"

I cut him off as quickly as I could. Nope. Didn't recall. Didn't want to recall. "Nik, don't ruin the shirt for me, okay? If you force literary knowledge into my brain, I won't be happy. Can we go pick up our toys now?" We'd decided with Grimm showing up that there was safety in numbers and we would stay with Robin, as Goodfellow refused to stay at our place. Or . . . wait. Had we decided that or had Robin decided that and talked us into it despite the fact that we didn't want to risk his life too? He did, I knew he did, but how had he managed that? What had he said . . . ? I didn't bother following that path of reasoning any further. I knew my limitations. If Goodfellow had talked us into it, we wouldn't find a way out.

I pulled out a pair of sunglasses from the jacket pocket. As they were Robin's, they probably cost more than Nik's car, not that that was saying much. I shouldn't need them if I could gate us to and from our apartment, but better safe than sorry. "I can gate us in and out of our place, no problem. I don't feel Grimm, but as I can't sense Auphe more than a few blocks, that's not what you'd call reliable. He could be in the city. Hell, he could be in our apartment, but if he is, I'll gate us back out."

"He can follow us you said, so that's not especially reassuring," Niko said dryly.

"True." I put on the sunglasses, which were too retro and Terminator-cool for Goodfellow anyway. "But he only sent three Bae to Arkansas, and that was after I'd recovered enough to wake up and fight. He's playing the game, but he's not playing it with much enthusiasm." That worried me. I didn't want him dumping a thousand Bae on my head, but that he was barely trying wasn't a good sign. Losing interest in me was as terminal as wanting me dead—they were, in fact, the same thing. "Let's hope he ups the ante some."

Niko reached over to lift my sunglasses up and check my eyes. I didn't know if they were red or gray, and his face told me nothing. "Your pupils look fine." He let the glasses fall back in place. "Normally after Arkansas and the fact that you were shot in the head"—he gave me a grim frown as if I'd forgotten that—"I'd say we take a taxi, but if Grimm is in the city, I know you need the gating practice with the epinephrine." His finger aimed and stabbed me rather painfully in the *Hell* on my shirt. "But if you get the slightest twinge of a headache, you stop. Understand? Are we clear on this? If you gate us home and I find one fleck of blood on you anywhere, I will flush the epinephrine and we'll have to make do until I think you're ready."

The bastard would and do his damn best to keep between me and a gate-happy Grimm—never mind that was impossible. "All right. Okay. Jesus, such a crybaby. Shot in the head like I have anything up there worthwhile." There wasn't much Nik could say regarding that, as he was the one who continually reminded me of how empty my skull was ... he'd once compared it to a beyond-empty void that went on into the astrophysics realm of black holes, sucking in all useful information to be crushed, destroyed, or spat out into an alternative universe depending on if I was aware what science fiction, with its differing levels of accuracy, was and how certain B-movie-esque theories operated.

"It's enough to keep you house-trained. Let's hold on to that, shall we? As I've had to do that for you twice now, I'd be grateful to escape a third time." He rested a hand on my shoulder. "I'm prepared. Let's go."

Twice?

That meant when I came back after two years in Tumulus that Nik had to house-train ... wrong. That was wrong in too many layers of embarrassment and outright humiliation for me to begin to try to deny it. That was why he said it. True or not, he knew that I wouldn't be able to question him about it. "You are such an asshole," I said with a growl before gating us back home.

There was no headache, no nosebleeds, no adverse reactions at all. Epinephrine was my new drug of choice, overriding caffeine for the first requirement in the morning. I took a look around the living area where I'd brought us to check for overall damage, but that was my cover-up for what was much more essential.

"Grimm's not here," I said.

"No Bae either," I added. There was nothing and no one here I could feel. A relief, on the Grimm side of it. On the other hand, he did have a thousand Bae. The three in Arkansas hadn't been any kind of challenge, but if he threw a hundred at us—one-tenth of what he had—it was damn doubtful we'd walk away from that. They weren't Auphe, but they weren't nothing either. More dangerous than Wolves several times over, a hundred would take us out easily enough. Easy for them, that is to say, if not at all easy for us.

Don't forget the game, Grimm, was all I could think. He was what I could handle now. I was working on a plan for his Bae, but it would be a trick and a half to pull off. I'd have to put Grimm and Bae in play when I needed them and where I needed them. Difficult, incredibly fucking difficult. The plan was half sketched out at best, which wasn't what you'd hope for either. I knew what I was going to do, but I didn't know where . . . where we'd leave and where we'd come out . . . and that made my plan somewhat lacking at this point.

I gave it all a rest for now and headed for my bedroom. "Lock and load, Nik." He followed me, steady and smooth. The first time that I'd gated him and Goodfellow, they both came close to puking. They'd both gotten used to it after a while, being yanked through a hole in the world. I had mixed thoughts on that. It was fortunate they had adjusted to it, as I used it often when I could to escape with our lives. And unfortunate they had to become used to something they found intrinsically disturbing despite it often being our last chance at escape. That's how unnatural it was—that you'd consider dying first, that was how sick and abnormal everyone else found it when pushed through. Everyone else, but not me.

I liked it.

Hell, let's be honest, I *loved* it. It made a hundred continuous orgasms boring in comparison, and I knew what that said about me.

Nothing good.

A stray piece of silver hair fell across my eyes to underline faithfully who and what I was, and I pulled the whole mess of it back with merciless competence into a ponytail—Robin even kept the elastic bands around for that or they were Ishiah's, which I wish I hadn't considered. Second chances or not, I persisted in staying pissed about what the peri had done or not done when Niko and I were kids working the carnival, but I wanted my hair out of my face and my sight more. I couldn't win. Giving up every thought I currently had that didn't involve weapons as a lost cause, I knelt beside my bed and began moving metal storage boxes from beneath it out into the light.

My Desert Eagle and SIG would be in Nik's room where he'd cleaned up the blood and did his version of first aid, incredibly more detailed than your basic version, before I gated us to Arkansas. I didn't go for them. That was if I'd managed to hold on to them after being shot. I couldn't remember, but it was a rare thing indeed that I lost my guns no matter what condition I was in. They would be three days fired and not cleaned. That wasn't anywhere near a problem, but as I had many guns—one might categorize the number as a shitload—I didn't have to take the chance. I had several Desert Eagles, matte black and chrome, several SIGs, several 9mms, and beyond that several guns that long-past, if classic, Dirty Harry would've found to be excessive in size and firepower.

Dirty Harry was a pussy in this day and age when a six-year-old could smuggle a gun illegally converted to full auto with five hundred rounds into his juice and cookies. A pity that was, I knew, but I had paramilitary organizations, werewolves, part Auphe and full-on Bae to take on. I armed myself as needed. What ordinary people, who didn't know monsters were real, much less were fighting them, were arming themselves for, I didn't know.

The collapse of Walmart maybe? That would be more destructive than any zombie apocalypse.

There were too many video games and bad movies in the world, I thought absentmindedly. I opened one last box that held a glove. The box held a considerable amount of hypocrisy as well, but that didn't stop me from grinning viciously at the sight of it.

When I first met Grimm, face-to-face, he'd worn a glove, black leather and supporting a set of three long metal claws attached. If he made a fist, those claws would be six inches of steel extending past his knuckles and capable of ripping out throats. It was his answer to lacking Auphe true talons. They'd been born with them, long and black and sharper than any razor. Grimm had the silver hair and the scarlet eyes and even a second set of metal needle teeth that dropped over his human ones when he was annoyed, but he didn't have the claws. Grimm was smart. Grimm knew what he wanted, and Grimm had his own made. I'd seen them and I should've been disgusted and outraged, but ... I was Auphe too. After all was said and done, as in I kicked his ass and he ran home for Mommy—except half Auphes don't have mommies, as they're all *deeeeead*—I hadn't been able to forget. And knowing he'd come back ... it didn't seem strange to me to want to be well matched for him when he did.

Wanted. Wanted. Wanted. Wanted for yourself, no one else. Not for Grimm. For you. Liar, liar, liar.

That would be the epinephrine and gating gathering

all the Auphe parts of me into one. I'd been missing a part of me without the traveling, but now I had it all. I was whole. That wasn't desirable. I'd been doing well when my genes were working on fixing my absent gates, less homicidal in every way. Did I wish it could be different? Maybe. But Grimm had come, which meant I had no choice, and that was all there was to think about that situation. I let the pushing and prodding of my vindictive and partially fiend/freak subconscious range free—I had no time to think about it. I had a sight before me now that deserved more of my thoughts.

I slid my hand into the glove I'd had made by an artist of weapons, the man who most often obtained or forged blades for Niko. He hadn't failed Niko and he hadn't failed on this one. The glove fit perfectly and when I made a fist, the matte black talons, which were the same color as those of the Auphe, proved in a weird fashion I was more true to them than Grimm with his unnaturally polished metal ones. Like his in one way, however, they extended those six inches that would take out throats, guts, or anything else I could reach. I liked guns. I liked the distance of a kill when you were forced to it. I'd taken that into account when I had the glove made for my nondominant hand. I was good with knives too, excellent, you could say, thanks to Nik's constant drilling, but I'd always preferred guns and distance when it came to weapons.

Until now.

I continued to smile at the glove-and-claws, thinking of all they could do. Who they could do it to. How efficiently as well. I now regretted I hadn't had it made for my dominant hand, saving that hand for a gun. How boring, guns, compared to this. The smile turned into a jagged twist of lips that felt beyond vicious and into something actually alien on my face, but I didn't care.

Claws were for those who weren't afraid to fight close and personal.

Claws were for the Auphe.

Weren't they?

I was made by the Auphe.

Wasn't I?

"I like the T-shirt. Shall we trade?"

Grimm squatted on my bed above me, his grin as feral as mine. His gate came and went with such speed it was as if he'd always been there, for years and then some, and I hadn't noticed. It wouldn't be that surprising. In some ways he belonged to this existence more than I did. He knew what he was and he didn't have any reservations about himself for an instant.

Grimm was Grimm. That was all he needed to know. He was his own creation. He knew himself inside and out because he'd *made* himself. Half Auphe, and he'd shaped out of himself something more. Smarter, swifter, more deadly than the original Auphe in some ways. It would've been unimaginably remarkable . . . you know . . .

If he hadn't been wrong.

"Mutt," I greeted him with a bored tap of my claws on the floor. "Sire of mongrel beasts not worth pissing on." My grin stretched wider into less than sane proportions and it felt good. I was a lion raised by sheep, raised to be docile, *domesticated*, but that hadn't taken, not as much as I sometimes fooled myself into thinking it had. "How ya been since I last shot your ass?" And shot him, I had. Several times.

Good times.

Aside from the bullets, he was the same as before: Auphe silver hair, Auphe crimson eyes, but skin more human in color than mine, black jacket, T-shirt, and jeans and the glove-and-claws I'd had twinned. I didn't feel bad about that, the claws. He dressed like me, carried the

same guns as me; he copied me intentionally to screw
with my head and had said so—I was allowed one deadly
glove to make up for it. Not to mention my claws were
fashionably black and invisible in the night.

So fuck him.

"Your shirts are ever entertaining with their quaintly
murderous quotes." He stretched out his nonclawed
hand to rest on the top of my head, touching silver hair,
no black left now, I knew. I didn't have to see it reflected
in a mirror or window glass, not that there was neither in
my room, or to have him tell me.

I just knew. When he appeared, it had been a matter
of seconds before the last of my visible humanity had
disappeared.

"So bright and beautiful—the color of an ice-frozen
carcass." His hand grew heavier, then smoothed its path
along my hair until it cupped the back of my skull. "I told
you what you'd become. I told you what you would be,
but did you hear me? Did you pay *attention*?" he said in
a ground-glass croon. "I think not. F for effort. F for execution."

Grimm was judging me. Grimm with his GED, I
thought he'd be a monster with his master's by now.
Grimm who assumed that I hadn't paid attention.

That pissed me off.

Too much to measure.

His lips lifted farther to reveal the metal teeth that
fell into place over the human ones. "But any execution
is a good execution no matter the grade." He leaped,
somersaulted over my head, and ended up crouched on
my Salvation Army dresser behind me. I moved almost
as fast, aiming a gun with one hand and my claws up and
ready with the other.

Dressed in human clothes, *my* clothes for all I could
tell, he was settled in the predatory position of a hungry

beast ready to leap and attack whatever living creature that dared pass by. Did you smell of blood and meat? Then he would be on you, one would think ... but he appeared so human—if not for the hypodermic teeth and not your entirely average coloring. At this point he might appear more human than I did. He had the teeth of an Auphe, but I ... laughter seeped out of me uncontrollably ... I *was* an Auphe.

"Poor Grimm," I mocked. "I lived in the caverns and slept on red sand, learned to survive on air with half the oxygen, hunted naked under a sky the color of diseased urine, ate whatever ... *whoever* I found, and fought for the scraps with all the others. You'll never know the truth of that life. You who eat flabby security guards and go to school like a good little monster."

I remembered. Being torturedbeatentrainedsubmitchangedAuphekillinghunting*free*.

I wasn't supposed to—someone had told me that, to bury Tumulus and not remember it again—but I did. I did remember. Grimm thought himself better. Grimm had gone to school, gotten an education, planned the demise of mankind with mankind's own teachings. Grimm aped their behavior by wearing clothes and planning genocide—the human equivalent—using their own flawed history books to plot against them. Grimm who was so very smart according to human standards. Grimm who ate people, probably with a napkin at his side and floss for his metal teeth, and created Bae, but remained trapped by his half he didn't acknowledge existed.

Yawn.

How stupid.

How very stupid of him.

I laughed again and it sounded wrong, if you were in this world, but if you were in the Auphe home, how it sounded in the thin, thin air would be unmatchable music, songs screamed by the dying and pleased to die they had been. Hymns of the devoured and damned.

"Grimm, my cousin, my not-brother, maker of the Bae-abominations of weakness with no will of their own, it is time for *you* to listen." The trigger was pulling tight under my finger, but I knew that wasn't how it would end. Grimm was wary and too quick for me to catch him off guard with a gun again. I didn't mind, as I didn't want it to end in such a mind-numbing fashion.

"Grimm," I said; the absurdity of it all hadn't faded. "I am Auphe, your disgusting offspring are useless Bae, frail little snakes who can only do what they're told, but you . . ." I couldn't stop laughing as much as I tried. "You are worse." I let the gun fall from my hand to the floor and laughed on. "You went to *school* on purpose. You wear my clothes. You cannot speak Auphe, you cannot go to Tumulus." Unless I took him there, and I wouldn't—he hadn't *earned* it. "You use human methods of warfare."

I sat on the floor and reclined against my mattress with the dark hilarity that wouldn't cease. "Human, Grimm. You model your war to come after their wars of the past. You listen to human prey as if their words have any wisdom at all. You write down the bleating of *sheep*. Of *cattle*. Why would I join you, Grimm? You are lower than the mutts you conceive. You play dress-up with your hair and eyes and teeth and think you are Auphe because you look like them. You think you are more than Auphe, as your thoughts of killing and how to protect your army never stop, but your thoughts mean nothing. You *think* like a human, Grimm, how to survive."

He loved killing, but he wanted to continue to keep breathing along with that. For an Auphe, that was illogical, incompatible thoughts to hold simultaneously. A lone Auphe hadn't thought how to survive. A lone Auphe knew he couldn't fall. Prey fell; prey died, not Auphe. "That is what prey thinks, no-brother-of-mine. 'How do I protect my army?' If they need protecting, you should kill each and every one yourself. 'How do I stay alive?' That's what your next meal thinks, not an Auphe. You, cousin, you think like *prey*."

That did stop my laughter. Auphe as prey, disgusting. No Auphe had thought how to live, only how to make others die. I choked on genuine bile that it would be any other way. Unnatural. Defective. I spit my disgust on the floor. "I never did. I never thought as sheep do. You are more of a human than I ever was from my first day, bathed in birth blood. You're a born if not bred victim. Nature didn't make a better Auphe in you. Nature made a better *human*."

"Cur." This time I said the last insult in Auphe, which Grimm wouldn't understand and wasn't that the point? How could you think yourself more than Auphe if you were but the weakest imitation of an Auphe to begin with? It wasn't a lie what I told Grimm. He was closer to human than I was—than I'd been.

Sorry, Nik, but that's how it is and how it has been from when I could first crawl. You knew, didn't you? It was why you watched me that closely in school. Not for who might hurt me, but for who I might hurt. Or both. It didn't make a difference. I hadn't ever been anyone's definition of human and I wouldn't ever be, but you're my brother. My being the bogeyman didn't change that, and my genes could scream forever in denial of it, brother to a human, but I wouldn't listen to them. Not about you. You don't have to *runhideflee* from me.

Niko was safe from me.

Grimm . . . I didn't give him a warning as I threw myself at him, my claws eager to bury themselves in his flesh. He was prey. Prey didn't warrant words. It was time to end Grimm. He was about to be roadkill scattered two miles long.

Grimm was the one who should run.

Grimm was the one who should hide, as my claws were now inches from his skin.

Grimm was dead fucking meat, and I couldn't *wait*.

Unfortunately, thanks to Nik standing in the doorway aiming a gun, it turned out that I didn't have as much a choice about waiting as I'd have liked.

And the thing about it? About waiting?

It sucked.

12

Goodfellow

A phone call from Niko led me to the brothers' apartment. Urgent as it sounded, I wasn't as quiet as normal about picking the lock and running through the place until I found them. Even so with me at my most careless, Niko didn't hear me as I came to a stop in the doorway of Cal's room. That meant Niko was not having the best of days. Blond head bent, his back to the door . . . back to the Zeus-forsaken *door*—Niko who couldn't have been born breech, as he wouldn't leave his back unprotected in fetal stage . . . he was oblivious.

"Niko?" I tried cautiously.

"I shot him." He didn't look up or back at me. Too tired to take the most basic of precautions and that was worse than the phone call had been.

"He was attacking Grimm and they looked the same." He stumbled verbally, murmuring "not the teeth, not yet." As if he'd said nothing, he surged on. "Robin, they looked the *same*." Niko was sitting on the floor of Cal's room. "When I saw that, I shot him." He had one hand resting on Cal's chest to make certain it continued to rise and fall as smoothly as it should. To make certain that Cal continued to breathe despite what had been injected into his bloodstream. Niko's other hand was white-knuckled around the grip of a tranquilizer gun modeled after one we'd used on Cal a long time ago when he was possessed by a Darkling. This one I'd had made with the strength of the sedative taken up past "horse" to "herd of elephants." I had known when the time came to use this that Cal would be Caliban and Caliban would be as Auphe as he could be.

End-days Auphe.

End-days Auphe would come with a metabolism to match, and I wanted to know that once hit he would go down without killing one of us, as I didn't know if he'd know what that meant any longer—to be one of us. I'd had the gun made after Cal gated in front of all the world, for what he cared, gated in the light of humanity's eyes and then killed a basement full of murdering humans with a single thought all because of that murdering Jack who had taken his brother. I'd given the gun to Niko this morning after insisting Cal take the trash to the incinerator, as he'd created so very much of it making breakfast.

There had been massive rumblings about my lack of gratitude, but I'd gained the few minutes necessary to give the gun to Niko and do a great deal of convincing in a very short period of time. I knew, however, he wouldn't have accepted it any sooner, not while I was seeking my assistance with the Vigil. That hadn't been threat enough to cause Cal to lose himself.

But there had been Cal's physical transformation, and

while that itself hadn't done it, there had been Grimm, then the thousand Bae, and finally Niko couldn't deny it . . . End days.

The transformation that was all but complete now.

I sighed and sat cross-legged on a floor Cal apparently hadn't cleaned, not once, after they moved in—slovenly infant. I sat beside Niko—whose phone calls, by the way, were beginning to rattle what was serving as my most stable grip on sanity lately—and a crumpled Cal. I traced a careful finger along a length of silver that had come free from the younger brother's ponytail. The strand bit at my finger with invisible barbs and I absently sucked a drop of blood from my skin. There wasn't a single black thread remaining in his hair now. I lifted one of his eyelids to see a scarlet iris and drug-dilated pupil. White and red. He was all Auphe save, as Niko dreaded, for the teeth now. His sedated breathing remained slow and he didn't move under my touch. "You knew you might have to," I said. "You doubtlessly saved his life."

"I'm not sure. I think I might have saved Grimm's instead." A little gray behind his olive skin, Niko clenched the hand on his brother's chest, fisting a handful of a T-shirt I'd bought as a joke not so long ago that seemed much less humorous now. "I think I might've saved them both. I think they would've killed each other. Grimm is Grimm and Cal . . . I heard Cal. He was talking about Tumulus. He remembered it. The worst parts of it"—he swallowed harshly—"and he was laughing. Robin, he was *laughing*."

Not like the first time at all, then. Not like when I had hypnotized him to remember and he'd screamed until I thought his throat would bleed. The Auphe had taken Cal at fourteen and they had kept him two long years before he escaped. There were times, great stretches of it, where a boy that young would give in and be what his tormentors forced him to be to escape the pain and horror of all that was being done to him. Maybe forget who he'd once been altogether.

"Niko, he was fourteen when he was taken by the Auphe and sixteen when he escaped. That is not the type of kidnapping to which Stockholm syndrome can remotely be applied. There was a time at the beginning when he would've been Cal, but it wouldn't have lasted long. Fourteen and at the mercy of the Auphe"—a joke as they'd had none—"he would've done and been whatever he had to be to survive what the Auphe were doing to him. He didn't have any choice, and some parts of that will always lurk in him. Unfortunately Grimm happens to bring them out. But they are not the whole of him and not in any measure his fault."

I could not imagine what he'd gone through, and wasn't that an amazing lie, even for me, that I had just told myself? Unfortunately, I could imagine it. I could imagine too much of it, and I knew I wouldn't have survived it. Two years? After a week I would have chewed through my own wrist to bleed my life away. I could kill a true Auphe. Cal had been with over a hundred. A fourteen-year-old boy had survived what a million-year-old puck couldn't have.

"You are the bravest son of a bitch I have ever known in the whole of time, kid," I said to his closed eyes and still face. I lightly slapped his cheek with affection; pucks had no brothers save for me, and my brother in Cal could not be equaled. I would fix this. Ishiah's God was not my god, but if he had been I would've been his right hand of justice or, more appropriately, his sinister left hand of bloody vengeance. Watch me. I then said briskly to Niko, "Did you shoot Grimm as well?"

"I had to. As I said, they would've killed each other. But the bastard gated away as soon as I hit him."

I groaned in spite of myself. "He would. As persevering as Cal when it comes to clinging to life. In many ways I almost wish we could save him as well."

Niko replied with an immediately wary tone to his accusation, "He's evil."

"He was kept in a cage from birth until eighteen years of age. He was treated in a manner I don't care to think about." Electrocution, branding, starvation—both Cal and Grimm had let those slip, Cal in moments of self-doubt and Grimm in battle.

"He's what the Auphe made him. He's not evil in that he chose it, but he is too far gone." I tsked at the claws on Cal's hand, unfastened and removed the hateful glove. "Of the three of us in this room, none of our hands are lily white or free of blood in this life. If you count my long one and the stream of lives of you and your brother . . ." I smiled carefully. I'd seen Grimm's Auphe metal grin. I could make him seem as a toddler if I wanted with what I could exhibit in a show of my teeth, pearly white though they were, but I held back. ". . . Grimm is but a babe in comparison to the combination of who we are and what we've done throughout history."

Niko frowned and I could see the protest forming on his lips. I tapped his temple before he could. "You don't remember, and I'm glad of it. I would have it no other way, but do know, Niko, this life *is* one of the true episodes of karma I've seen you show. This life wipes away a few others you have lived." I let it go, as it made no difference, not in the end. How Grimm came to be was horrific, who he was inevitable, but no matter the why, the how, or the sympathy he might deserve, I wouldn't hesitate to kill him and I wouldn't regret it.

I'd consider it compassion.

I'd mentioned Grimm to Cal once when he was half-asleep after one of my smaller, but still quite alcohol-laden parties. Grimm and the other half Auphe kept prisoner in those cages, tormented by a sadistic jailer, more animal than Auphe or human. Unable to gate to escape. And Cal, who wouldn't remember saying it now or wouldn't have remembered it the next morning after the party, had said, "What is done cannot be undone. What is made cannot be unmade." It sounded as if he'd said it before, if only to himself.

It was true.

Grimm could not be unmade. No matter how he came to be, he was here now and he had to be dealt with. "I brought the car. Let's get Cal out to it and home." Not that Grimm couldn't find us there once he woke up from the tranquilizer wherever he had gone, but if he did, he did. We would deal with it if it happened.

Niko's hand wrapped around my ankle, gripping it tightly. "Thank you for this. There aren't many people I know . . ." He shook his head. "There is no one I know at all who would come when I asked them to help me with my full-on Auphe psychotic brother with no guarantee he wouldn't try to kill them. Promise would come, but take the time to arm herself thoroughly. More and more she passes the chance to see Cal." I could see him wondering, unsure whether she feared his brother or feared the end. I thought it was both. "So . . . thank you." He rested a hand against the side of my neck briefly and then he stood, bent, and managed to get the deadweight of his brother slung over his shoulder.

"Someday I'll tell you how you rescued me from a drunken Caligula in his stables with his brand-new stallion." I grinned and slapped him lightly on the back of the head. "You probably would not consider us remotely close to even."

"You're not joking, are you?"

"Oh, how you wish that I were," I answered gleefully.

Niko walked, footfalls heavy, toward the door. Cal wasn't too much weight to bear, but neither was he light, in all ways.

Make of that what you will.

"I never joke about the occasions when I am able to genuinely scar your psyche for a lifetime, Niko. Who do you take me for?"

"The devil?"

Please.

The devil wished he had half my style and a fourth my schemes.

My phone beeped as I sat beside Cal still sleeping in the bed in his personal guest room. Niko was also asleep on the living room couch, as I might have drugged his tea — not enough to knock him out completely in case we were attacked, but enough to let him sleep if he needed it or I needed it for him. I was excellent in judging those sorts of measurements.

I had taught the Borgias everything they knew.

The number came up unknown, but I had all my sources working day and night and sources I didn't personally know, difficult as it was to believe there were any of those left, so I took the call. "Goodfellow. The reward is still guaranteed, but my patience is limited and your life even more so if you don't deliver. Go."

"Robin, you confuse me, and that really is something. It is!" There was a familiar voice and the laughter that is tears that is laughter again of someone who knows all that is to come and has no surprises left in their future. Wouldn't that make you cry and laugh all in one?

"You are the best of friends with Cal and Nik and the worst of enemies to anyone else and then you cover that up with the face — handsome — and words of a walking, talking, living celebration. You're a party, Hob the first, one that will kill the moment someone's back is turned with a knife in their spine, a smile on your face, and a song on your lips." The girl laughed again, a little more full of cheer this time. "I should've read you much sooner, but I was naïve and young." A soft-voiced exhalation that reminded me of ice cream ... sweet and buttery on the tongue. I could picture her light brown skin, dark chocolate eyes, and curly red hair that fell to her shoulders.

And yes, naïve and young she had been.

"Georgina." Now, here was a psychic worthwhile, not like the others. A psychic too good, in fact, as she served fate and fate had no mercy. The fact that she knew I came from Hob showed how good ... and merciless she could be. I had been Hob, in a manner of speaking—the first puck who would've given any Auphe at least a small run for their money. Even after Hob had made a second puck, me, in our race's parthenogenesis reproduction, I was still Hob, identical in thought and memories, as well as desires as twisted and murderous as those of any Auphe. It was only through time after Hob and I separated to roam opposite sides of the world that I eventually developed a personality of my own. To become Robin Goodfellow with more pleasurable and decadent desires. Who sought companions, good food, alcohol—I was a different puck. It didn't change the fact....

Once I had been Hob.,

To know that indeed made Georgina the Oracle of this generation. But she was one who refused to interfere with intended fate or assume it could possibly be interfered with at all, which made her not very useful. All the power in the world and she refused to use it, refused to think it could be used or that anything could be changed

I gave Cal a quick check, but he was still under with no signs that the love of his life ... one life, spare me ...

had pulled him to consciousness. "I thought you did not believe in the destiny that could be changed, that you spat on the history of Delphi, the Oracle you could be now if you truly cared." If Georgina were more like them, I'd have spent the past few years with less pulling out of my hair and killing not quite so many people who might have only questionably deserved it.

"Those were the days, weren't they? But do you not remember the strife and chaos they caused with the simple truth?" She sounded wistful and far away, mentally if not physically. "And you know I don't mind meddling in the smaller matters. Do you know that I met Grimm? Actually I did," she exclaimed. "He's scary, isn't he? But so much like Cal I almost couldn't believe it when he tried to kill me." The laughter had gone to nostalgia to a faint giggle and then to a deep sadness. "I changed his thoughts. I was his teacher, not in New York. I couldn't stay there anymore, not when I couldn't do what Cal asked."

Look at their future and tell him it was safe for them to be together, safe for her. She simply would not—and her philosophy that fate was fate didn't make me any more forgiving of her for it. And Cal couldn't live with that, the thought that she could die because of him and his life, but she refused to give in. Genuine, holy psychics are a true pain in the ass.

"But who shows up in my classroom no matter how far I go but Cal's brother? Isn't that the way it always is?" She didn't sound surprised.

"Grimm is *not* his brother, and you changed his thoughts?" I questioned, which wasn't what I wanted to know, but the chances of George calling again were remote. I had to take what I could get.

"I know. You couldn't care less that he tried to kill me. Your heart has room for only three people, and I'm not one of them." Now she was amused and too accurate, as always she'd been. "Moving on, Grinch, I was teaching GED students and I told him I knew who and what he was. I didn't have to look. If anything, he impacts this world so strongly that he forced the visions to look into me. I knew how that would end." Not well, I knew myself. "But he is so like Cal that I told him anyway that I knew him and was sorry for him, but . . . it didn't matter. He remembers the illusion of killing me vaguely, but not who I was to Cal or where Cal lives due to some meddling with his thoughts on my part. As much as I could meddle and don't ask if I could do more. I can't. I do what I can do, and if I can't, I can't."

I truthfully thought that an enormous load of bullshit, not that I would say bullshit aloud but I would think it. Instead I passed it all by and asked something important, for once in this conversation, "He found Cal regardless as is our luck. What can you tell me, then?"

"Oh." She was quiet a moment. "Will you tell Cal I miss him?"

"No," I said flatly. Would I tell Cal the love of this miserable life determined to kick him in the testicles at every turn that she missed him? I knew the Marquis de Sade, but that did not mean I was a sadist. "You love him, but you do not love him enough to give him what he needs." Reassurance. "Would you really want me to?"

"If I was kind, I'd say no." She was quiet a moment. "I'll be kind. He deserves that, doesn't he? Some measure of peace?"

"More than that," I said.

"You're right." I heard her let it go. Let Cal go, as it was the most thoughtful thing she could do for him. Let the past be the past. Now, "I have an address for you. One in Canada I've sensed you need. Do you have a pen?"

I had a photographic memory, not always, but when I needed it.

Gods damn the pen.

"I'm listening."

Cal woke up.

It was approximately half an hour after Georgina had called, not that I would ever tell him about that. He coughed once, blinked, opened his eyes to stare at the ceiling, then slant them in my direction. I'd rather hoped he'd be confused, but he wasn't. "I fucked up, didn't I?" he asked with complete misery.

"You did . . . a little." I'd removed the elastic band from his hair as efficiently as I did for Ishiah most nights, and had spread out the ponytail to a messy halo of his newly quicksilver hair on the pillow. I ran my fingers through it now in comfort and then commanded, "*Audite me.*" *Listen to me.*

"*Audio vobis,*" he replied. *I am listening.* His eyes and face had gone blank, and did I feel guilty about that? Yes, I did, but it was done and it had to be done. Guilt was irrelevant.

Audio vobis.

Cal, who had thought English and Auphe were the only languages he could learn, had learned Latin quite easily under hypnosis. But that was my burden to bear and no one else's. "*Et Tumulum non record abitur ultra non erit.*" *You will not remember Tumulus and you never will again.* It was a patch, at the very best, and one I could only hope would hold until Grimm was gone. "*Obedite.*"

Obey.

Cal's eyes were on me, red without a hint of gray. "*Ní bheidh mé ag déanamh.*"

Gaelic, before it had made its journey from what

would be Ireland and Scotland. Gaelic, not Latin, not my hypnosis, and no, he was telling me, I will *not* obey.

It was Cullen again and Cullen who had died at five years and yet was worse than any version of an Auphe Cal. Who could think it? Cullen was relentless. "We are done and over—*Bhí muiddéanta.*" The kid was hardcore as ever a kid had been. But then this kid had traveled lives until he'd landed in this one, a life where he would be Cal. I shouldn't be shaken over it.

"Mura bhfuil tú ag éisteacht le domunless."

Unless you paid heed to me. Unless you listen. Cullen was a bossy little shit too, no denying that, but I wasn't surprised there either, was I? Hardly. No, I was not, and good for him, I thought reluctantly with my own rebellious trickster respect.

"I will listen, Cullen," I said. "I am a trickster, but tricksters need help now and again too. I will listen. I won't discard what you have to say. This I swore, as before, times three over."

The unbreakable oath. This kid had me on the run, Robin Goodfellow, and wasn't that something to put you in awe?

"Grimm is better because Grimm cares for no one or nothing," Cullen said, which was when my slightly optimistic mood faded somewhat, although I'd known it to be true. I'd been of the opinion that Grimm wasn't better, that he and Cal were equally matched, but that could only be factual to a certain degree and I'd known that. If Cal considered Niko worth saving and not fair prey, which was true or he would've attacked him at their apartment with Grimm, then Cal had weaknesses he wouldn't give up. In that Cullen was correct. Grimm was better, as he had no Niko, no weaknesses. The only mindset Cal could use to defeat him would involve denying his family, denying Niko, denying me, ending both our lives, and he wouldn't do that.

Could not do that.

"Yes, Grimm is better, but it's not the best who always wins. Not when I'm around. Not when I cheat. Trust me when I say that no one has cheating abilities are quite close to mine." Normally I would've sounded smug when I said that, but now I sounded desperate. Never had I had so much riding on someone believing me. I could double-deal like no one that had ever been birthed or born. I had been banned from Vegas and Atlantic City forty years ago, and that was gambling and me not trying hardly at all at what barely qualified as a game. It had been nothing close to what we were playing here, and yet I could cheat all the same. I cheated in every aspect of life and always came out on top. I knew that. Everyone knew that. Cal knew that. I hoped Cullen trusted his future self to give me the benefit of the doubt.

"Then cheat and make it work. Without you, they are dead. Niko and Cal are as dead as the one you called Phelan and me." Cullen's voice drifted to the higher birdsong pitch of a young child out of the grown mouth of Cal, but it didn't stop the next words from being a killing frost. "Unless you stop it . . . *this* time."

As I hadn't stopped it in his time.

Or all the other times.

As I had never stopped it.

"Cullen . . ."

He paid no attention. "Cal has a plan." The Auphe red eyes turned to the dark of a starless sky. Cullen's eyes. I'd not ever seen them, but I knew. "His plan will kill him. Him and Niko. If Cal dies, if we die"—as they were in many ways one and the same—"that's all right. But my brother cannot die. Will *not* die. No more of this. No more following me everywhere, even into death." His voice was getting louder and more fierce. The last thing I wanted was to have Niko wake up in the middle of this.

"No," I insisted. "Trust me, Cullen. Cal can predict Grimm, but I can predict Cal. I know what his plan will be. I know it, I swear to you. I will do whatever it takes to make it so that Niko and he survive it."

"You said you were my *caomhnoir*," my guardian, "and you swore three times over. . . ." He paused, his exhalation a child's fear for his brother and himself . . . a child, five winters old fighting to keep another brother alive. "Keep your promise, please. It hurts to die and I'm . . ." It was Cullen who said it, but it was Cal's chin that lifted stubbornly with a voice unsure." . . . afraid."

"Three times three," I promised again, and felt my stomach lurch. He was afraid. Cullen and Cal both, the same person in one way and yet not in another, but they were both afraid whether both would admit it or not. "I will give my life for his, but, Cullen, stay hidden, please, and keep Tumulus hidden too, if you can. This is Cal's life this time around. I know yours was short, but he deserves to have one of his own. Tumulus would rip it from him. Push it down as far as you can."

"I will. Keep your promise and I'll keep mine." The eyes stayed on mine and a hand snapped out snake-fast to clasp mine. I twitched but held on to it as the dark eyes flooded back to Auphe red and Cal, back in all his profane if now woozy glory, repeated, completely confused, "Where am I?"

He looked around the room again as if seeing it for the first time. "Oh, shit. I fucked up . . . didn't I?"

I felt my bones shift under the hold he had on my hand, but I cared not at the pain, and laughed in relief and renewed faith. "You did. You fucked up.

"But would you be Cal Leandros if you did not?"

*   *   *

I fetched Niko into Cal's room and ignored any scowls or accusations that might have been made regarding foreign sedatives substituted for honey in my hospitably offered tea. People could be unaccountably suspicious when they cared to be. Wasn't that a shame? Especially when I had done it and did not care one bit if I were caught out in such a thing?

Humans. They did make me laugh.

Niko had replaced his hand in Cal's where mine had been, and that was fine. If there weren't cracks in the smaller bones of my hand, it wasn't for lack of effort on Cal's part. "How are you, little brother?" he asked.

"For shit. That's how I am." He sat up under the covers of the guest bed, no less dejected than he'd been before. "I'm sorry. I don't remember it exactly. I don't remember what I said or did, but I know I went Auphe. I know I fucked up. And I'm goddamn sorry."

"But you didn't try to hurt me and here you are now. You're you, so what have you to be sorry for?" Niko pushed it all away as if it hadn't happened or, if it had, wasn't important. It was so well done that I honestly was in wonder of it, how dismissive he was of not one, but two Auphe right there ready to slaughter anyone and everyone.

Except Niko.

Everyone save Niko. I didn't know what an Auphe-Cal would do if I'd been there. When you don't know things, there's one way to find out. Ask. "Cal, if I'd been there with Niko and Grimm, would you have killed me?" I plopped on the end of his bed in a casual slouch with a curious countenance and something hidden behind my back.

"No, Robin. Shit, you don't believe . . . no. Not you. You fought and destroyed the Auphe with us. You were at the gates of Troy, you fought against the Romans when

I was Caiy, you who stood with Alexander when I passed, you're always there," he answered, shocked then retreating behind one of many walls. Miserable that I would ask that, angry that I would doubt him when I'd worked years to gain his trust. "You're the one who guarantees that Nik and me aren't alone . . . ever. If I don't remember it, the fucking history books tell me that," he finished flatly from behind the wall. Angry at me for my uncertainty, angry at himself for causing it.

Ah, children. So faithful. Ah, me. So cynical.

I should've known better than to question. I didn't know if he'd have that kind of control, but he thought he would. He wanted to; he wanted to stay with us as long as he could. That was all that mattered. Every—Maat cursed—one of us needed to believe some things, whether we were lying to ourselves or not.

"I am sorry. I know you wouldn't." I gave one of his blanket-covered legs a pat before adding. "Especially as I'd defeat you easily and spank you for the naughty half Auphe that you are." He gave me a wary sideways glance but the wall crumbled somewhat. I felt his formerly tense leg relax under my hand. It was a good start. "How about Promise or Ishiah?"

"Promise and Ishiah . . ." His eyes went from a thoughtful scarlet to a bitterly angry crimson, and what was written on his face was not an indication of certainty at all. "Hmm. Let me . . . fuck . . . think . . . who? Bloodsucker-leech-Promise. No, Niko loves Promise. No. Yes. Maybe. Ishiah . . . bad . . . bad. Pigeon who left us to die. I remember him. I know him. Coward. But Robin feels for him. I don't know. . . ."

I didn't know what he was caught up in with Ishiah. Ishiah hadn't known of Cal and Nik until the past few years, but Cal was sane, relatively sane, honestly as sane as I could hope for at this time. I'd have to go with that.

I stopped his Auphe-ish drifting by moving my hand from behind me and slamming his glove-and-claws against his chest with a hard toss. "Here. Use it as you wish, but make certain you know who you use it against."

Cal caught it with surprise and an edge of guilt, as if he knew he'd done wrong with it but couldn't recall how. That was right and I didn't try to reassure him there. He was dangerous and I wouldn't try to convince him otherwise. That would be idiotic. "You're sure?" He lifted the glove as if he wanted to put it on but feared it at the same time.

"No." I could be honest. It didn't happen often, but it wasn't impossible. "I'm not, but you had better be before you put it on again. Do you understand me, Cal? Niko and I might be safe from you, but there are more than the two of us out there, and you and Grimm hooking up to share a buffet made up of human homeless at the nearest shelter isn't an option."

I straightened, leaned in, and had a blade at his throat before he or Niko could register the movement. My family, they were, and I loved them, but they were human or Auphe-human, and while the second was worthy of fear, he wasn't me. He had been born *of* the first predators on earth, but I had been born the actual first *and* second predator long before dinosaurs had hatched to see the sky. It made a difference. A horde of Auphe were undefeatable, true, but one incredibly young Auphe like Cal? One Auphe did not have my speed or my ability to take a life one on one. I loved Cal, I loved him as my brother, but that meant I had a responsibility to end his life as my brother if he didn't have it all in check ... before he could do what he would always regret.

I had told Cullen I would be there for Cal, but being there had so many meanings, mercy in life and a mercy killing, a child couldn't know.

"Cal, I will tell you this only once: If you put that glove on again and lose control, I will kill you." He said Niko and I were safe, sacrosanct, but Ishiah and Promise he was less sure about. Then there was the fact that Niko had said he'd remembered his time in Tumulus, boasted of hunting and eating in a way that defied any measure of humanity left in him. And he'd laughed. He'd laughed at the memories of that Auphe-hell as if it were fucking Disneyland. That wasn't the control I needed from him.

"As much as it would hurt me—and it would hurt more than you could comprehend—I would do it all the same. I would end you. Do you understand?" I questioned as I watched the small rivulet of blood course down the skin of his throat.

He nodded, unmindful to the steel at his throat and his attention on me alone. Silver-white hair, lava red eyes, but Cal through and through. "Fuck, of course I understand, Robin. I'd do my best to let you. I mean it. Three times three." An oath that couldn't be broken. A promise he had no idea what meant now, but knew at a subconscious level, Cullen's level, what it had once meant. That was enough for me.

Three times three.

I smiled, put away my dagger and surged forward to rest my forehead against his. "Put it on, then, cub, and let us go kill as many Bae as we can find."

13

Caliban

Niko had lost his shit, which hardly happened.

I was a little more than in awe of it as I watched Robin and him shout at each other—and there was a huge amount of shouting—with the artfully tarnished silver and copper hand-painted design of the bedroom wall as a background. The colors wavered in and out, as my head wasn't quite right yet. Whatever Nik had shot me with had left me dizzy and with a sharp headache.

The shouting didn't help any of that. I slid on my glove-and-claws and felt a fleeting disappointment that it wasn't the disemboweling sort of shouting and wasn't that too bad?

What was worse than the "too bad" that skittered through my head was the fact that I thought that at all.

It was that secondary thought, that recognition that had me pulling it together. I kept my promise to Robin and held on to the human Cal, claws and all, and not the Auphe Cal. Three times three. Whatever that meant. I had no idea, but it seemed important. Like one of those old historical oaths, the rare ones that people used to keep. The ones you didn't break. Considering the other things that had gone through my head today, not knowing why a bunch of threes equaled an unbreakable vow was nothing at all in comparison. It was also nothing at all in comparison to the fighting.

Not that I cared when Goodfellow and Niko sparred, mock fighting. But this was real. They were fighting like dogs in a pit. It was wrong. They didn't fight like that. Not for dead and gone and that's all there was, but I could see in Nik's set and cold face that's where he was now.

At first I thought it was about what I'd done. I knew I'd lost something of myself back at Nik and my place when Grimm had shown up. I didn't remember much more. The claws, Grimm, Tumulus, maybe, although that was gone now, Nik in my bedroom doorway with a gun. Nik with a gun—that was unreal no matter how you frigging looked at it. But there he'd been. Nik with a gun. My brother who considered anything not a sword as disgusting and lazy and, well, me all over. Him with that attitude the majority of his life and yet he'd shot us both. Grimm and me.

But he'd shot me first.

I knew why. He was *saving* me first. I'd been shot with a tranq gun before. I recognized one when I saw it, although the Auphe in me didn't. That had been lucky, that Auphe ignorance, or things might have turned out differently . . . and far more bloody.

That wasn't the issue currently. Keeping my brother and best friend from killing each other . . . watch me prioritize.

I put my hands up, one clawed as deadly as you could

want, and shouted, "Stop! Jesus Christ, just . . . stop. I was Auphe. I'm the one who fucked up and yeah, I'm the one who needs to be put down like a rabid dog if I can't hold it back, but I am holding it back now. I'm Cal now, not Auphe. So, fuck, just stop!"

Robin looked at but not out a window, as it was covered with blinds and a curtain, both so muting that there might not have been any light at all from outside. His shoulders were set with anger and regret because it was his back to the wall, wasn't it? Before it had always been Nik alone who had accepted the responsibility of taking me down if it came to that. Now the puck was throwing his money into the pot and showing his cards. If Nik couldn't do it, and for all the years he said he would—I didn't think he could—but Robin would. "I'm fine with who you are and who you might be," Goodfellow said, guttural, and not from the shouting, I didn't think. "And I know what I'll do in either case." What he was saying was unrelenting and reassuring all at once. I had no problem with it. As he said, he would do whatever needed to be done no matter who I was.

Cal or Auphe or both.

Mind? Hell, I was grateful he could be that and do that for me. And he'd be doing it for Nik as well. If Nik didn't have to do it himself, I'd be thankful. I didn't want to put that on him, to kill his own brother, and it had been on him for a long time now. Goddamn grateful didn't cover it.

"Nik." I looped fingers around my brother's elbow, fortunately within reach, and jerked him back down to the chair beside my bed. "He'll stand behind me if I fight Grimm, and he'll stand against me if I fight the world. What more could I ask? Nothing. He'll put me down so you don't have to. That's a *gift*. He's a goddamn saint for that, okay? Now calm the fuck down, would you? Please?"

Niko, who sat on the bed beside me as alert and ferocious as any guard dog, was so many levels of screwed up, fucked up, and a thousand times done with this shit. I was surprised he had words for it all. He bowed his head, exhaled, and let it all go. Much more calmly, he offered, "He's doing what I should do. But what I don't think I can do, as often as I promised. I am the one who should apologize, to both of you."

Nik, who'd been my brother, my father, my mother. He had seen me take that first breath, and that was no exaggeration at all—how could I expect him to be the one who made sure I took my last? Whether he thought it his duty or not, whether I needed it or not, I couldn't expect it.

"Do not say you are sorry or I'll swat you again." Goodfellow sounded serious on this one. "That is why I am here." Robin gave me another pat to my foot and then rubbed a hand across the top and back of Niko's head, pretty much destroying his braid. "To do what you cannot bear to do for each other." He stood and gave a full-body shudder. "Now this is becoming sickening. Embrace or hug or whatever perversion one must do between brothers. I have to leave before I must vomit at the sight of so much emotion. I'm off to the living room and wine to wait for Ishiah."

He was gone and I smeared carelessly at the few drops of blood that I could feel pooling at the base of my throat. "He'll do what has to be done, Nik. I'm not sure it's fair—hell, I'm sure it's not—but he'll do it. That's better than you having to do it. Let him, all right?" I swung my legs out of the bed. "You shot me and you hated that, didn't you?"

"You have no idea." I felt his fingers automatically wipe away the blood on my throat, on a bathroom cloth that wouldn't be seen again. "Despite that, you don't know what I could do if I had to."

But I did. I did know what Nik could do and what he couldn't, and Robin knew that as well as I did. Niko couldn't kill me.... Whether it would save the world and all humanity or not. He'd had to once make an attempt at killing something that was not me but lived inside me. At the last second he'd turned an attempt at a mortal wound into near-mortal. That, combined with the desperately good fortune of getting me to a healer we knew in my last moments to bring me back, had given him a taste of what he'd sworn. He wouldn't be able to do it again. That's the way it was, and I was glad of it for the both of us. My brother couldn't kill me, but Robin, my other brother, could. He could remember me in every life and knew, painful as the passing years were, I'd return. Niko knew that, believed that, but he couldn't remember it. As the ultimate agnostic, I knew: If you couldn't see it, you couldn't believe it. It was difficult to kill your brother on faith alone.

Robin had seen it, lived it. Robin didn't need faith; he had fact. He could save humanity from Grimm and me by ending us both, and that was more than I'd hoped for.

"I'm starving. Since I made breakfast, you can make lunch." Twenty-five years of protein shakes and vegan casseroles caught up with me in a hurry as I thought better of that and what he would make. I slid out of bed, taking off the claws. They weren't practical for eating ... not what humans thought of as food. "We'll scrounge in his refrigerator. He usually has a buffet that would boggle Vegas in that thing."

On the living room couch Ishiah had arrived and sat giving Robin an oral report of his findings. If you think oral means his tongue was down Goodfellow's throat, you'd be right. I groaned but went with relief it was only his tongue. I didn't believe it—all right, didn't want to believe it when Robin said I'd once gone to orgies thousands of years ago. I had no problem waiting on my next life, human again, to see if that were true or not. As I headed for food, Niko was giving them the same look he gave me when I fondled my guns a little too much during cleaning.

"Maybe he can tap out in Morse code with his dick if he learned anything else about the Bae," I suggested with bite. I hadn't forgotten Ishiah and the carnival yet, whatever he'd done for us since. "Or spell it out in saliva."

"Ask me," came a voice far more familiar than I wanted it to be.

Grimm crouched on top of the refrigerator. "I can tell you all about your one thousand and twenty-five brothers and sisters. That is what your sickly flying rat was looking for, right?" Once again, his gate came and went so damn quickly I didn't see it and barely felt an uptick in my pulse at its presence. How the hell could he be that good, better than the oldest of the Auphe had been? Could he be right that he was an improvement over any Auphe? If in gating only?

"Ah, but look." There was that silver grin. "I have a phone now, as communication is important, even to us monsters." Yeah, the motherfucker did. He took it from the pocket of his leather jacket and held up the screen to face me. There was a mass of white serpentine coils in which I couldn't make out one Bae from another. "That is the last litter. Precocious. They ate their mother five minutes after they were born." His tainted silver grin mocked me. "A family moment. Should I text so that you can see the next birth? Sometimes they eat each other as well. Those Hallmark moments always deserve to be commemorated."

I had already heard Nik's katana come out and was pissed as shit someone had taken off my holster with my guns or that I thought I couldn't eat a goddamn bologna sandwich without being armed with claws. "Are we going to get down to the business of killing each other or what?" I snarled. "Because that would be infinitely less painful than listening to your shit."

But at least someone, or a few someones, was excessively armed, as no fewer than five knives were slicing through the air toward Grimm. All disappeared with the faintest of dark shimmers before they reached him and he paid no attention to the attempt. Why would he, something so easy that he hadn't needed to *think* about it? I'd killed people with gates and a thought . . . but it had taken at the very least that one thought. With Grimm it was as automatic as breathing.

Holy shit.

It was true. A thought I'd considered, but I hadn't let myself believe it. Not wanting to believe didn't change what I was seeing. Denial couldn't defeat the truth, and the truth was right there.

"Getting down to business. Is that what you want?" Grimm sounded mockingly doubtful but agreed. "Then we will. One of us will die. Maybe both. That was always meant to be. But will that be now or a hundred years from now when we tire of chasing herds of humans in a world once ours again?" He shrugged and I swear to God I recognized the dismissive, bored sentiment as a mirror image of mine come back to bite me in the ass.

"We will fight, however. For fun first, and you know how fun it will be, and to prove yourself worthwhile, because you are far from showing that. Definitely. We will fight. Anytime, anyplace. You name it, Caliban, but only between you and me. Understand? The first rule of Auphe Club." He made a movie reference. His grin, metal ripping through gums to drop over his human teeth, was so destructively elated that I could see his own blood coating his teeth; he cared that little about death and life that he'd made a movie reference. I didn't know if that was more disturbing or the fact that he was a monster and could *make* movie references. "Call me." He held up his other hand and made the universal sign to go with the words and that was somehow worse than the blood dripping from his mouth. Such a casual human gesture. My control between human and Auphe was sketchy, but Grimm's . . . his was ironclad on both sides. His bloody grin widened as he tossed me the cell phone and was gone the moment it left his hand.

I caught the phone, furious, full of adrenaline that had nowhere to go because it was now clear that while Grimm could follow my gates, his gates were far beyond my abilities. Worse, I was more than a little confused. He was much easier to deal with when I was full-blown Auphe who didn't know doubt or fear. This . . . I dropped the phone on the granite kitchen counter as if it were a face-eating Amazonian spider. "He left us baby pictures and quoted *Fight Club*." And he'd bled while he did it, showing his teeth, thinking nothing about it. Blood to Auphe, whether of others or even your own, was to be savored, never feared.

"You're not fighting him alone," Nik said adamantly.

I sat on the island and put my head down after picking up the phone again to toss to him. "Here. Look at some baby pictures. I'm going to think about how Auphe I need to be to survive this fight and how much Auphe will have Robin cutting my throat. Complicated balance. Oh yeah, and a plan to get Grimm and all his little fucking snakes together to take them all out at once, because if we do it one by one, we'll be drowning in them in five years."

"His gates seem much more advanced now. From an

eye toward scientific observation only." Robin sounded speculative, not accusing, but I couldn't let that go all the same.

"His gating is a fucking sight more advanced, thanks, Mr. Spock. I think he was holding back on me last time. Getting me to underestimate him. He still hasn't decided if he wants me dead or not, at least not immediately. Then there's the fact that he has been gating about twelve more years than me, and no matter what I tell him about being less than an Auphe, he isn't. I thought ... but shit, he isn't less. He's more. He's better than them, better than he even thinks he is. Evolution. I lose sight of that when I go ... you know ... insane, because to an Auphe ego there can be no one better. But we wiped out their asses, a human, a half human, and a puck, so they were wrong, weren't they? And when I'm all Auphe all the time I'm wrong too. I think like them. I forget my weaknesses. Don't accept I have any."

Ishiah had taken a step back. "Better than an Auphe? More? That cannot be."

Goodfellow wrapped one hand around the peri's wrist and squeezed. "Faith. You had it once. Remember it again." He'd stolen the phone from Nik with his other hand. "He does have one number in here. Apparently he was serious about you calling." He quickly copied the number into his own phone.

"What are you doing?" I sat up. "Don't fuck around with him, Robin."

"I have never fucked around, as you so tastefully put it"—like he hadn't said more than four hundred synonyms for fuck one night on a stakeout to prove he could and to drive Nik onto the verge of a stroke—"with an Auphe yet, but perhaps we can share movie reviews as he seems to be a fan." He continued to fiddle with the cell. "Who doesn't love *Fight Club*?"

"Yeah, he's a triple threat. Killing, gating, and movie watching." I put my head back down on the counter and growled. "Go ahead and call him. Tell him I'll meet him in four hours where Ishiah located his nursery of man-eating monster snakes." I wouldn't be alone, but Robin would know better than to say that. "Nik, could you print out the location on Google Maps, as magnified as you can get, so I can see it and get us there?"

I stayed down on the counter, exhausted. It'd been a long day.

Mumbling, I added, "And, Christ, someone call for pizza."

The pizza was naturally delivered by a member of the Vigil.

How he—as a pizza guy, not an assassin—got past the front desk slash security of Goodfellow's building, I didn't know. They had a strict list with descriptions and photos of who was allowed up, and pizza men were not on it, although Robin's more illegal delivery people were. Nope, they left the pizza at the front desk where the building's occupants were so intensely wealthy that they paid the salaries of not one, not two, but five runners to be there at all times for occasions such as food delivery among hundreds of other deliveries a plebe like me couldn't begin to think of.

That meant when I opened the front door at the soft and respectful knock and saw a pizza uniform, a shiny plastic name tag that read Gerry Martin, I knew better. Hell, the Wolves knocking last time had taught me better for life.

"Pizza guy!" I shouted; it was warning enough. I had my guns back after Grimm's visit and shot the guy before he could shoot me. Unfortunately I went for a center-of-mass shot, much easier to hide from your neighbors than brains splattered on the wall, which knocked the guy down, but he was right back up ... fucking Kevlar vest ... with a full-auto AR-15, finger on the trigger, that might have killed at least one or two of us before I could get him with a head shot.

Then he didn't have a trigger finger to use any longer. He had a bloody stump, a ripped-out throat, and a large plastic-lined suitcase he was bundled into with the efficiently vicious breaking of bones before the lid was snapped shut. "Thank Fenris you have the basest common sense to use a silencer," was delivered in a bored, familiar voice. The woman who had achieved all this in less than twenty seconds calmly licked the blood off her claws as she checked up and down the hall. As Robin was one of only two occupants on the floor and the other was a deaf old lady who hadn't noticed when Salome slaughtered her equally old and feeble Great Dane to leave on Robin's pillow, we were probably good.

Claws cleaned, they reverted to human nails. "I suspected that type of work would be hell on your mani-pedis," Robin said cheerfully, handing several hundred dollar bills past me. "Accept my condolences, as it was an excellent nail job"—he glanced down at the suitcase—"in all senses of the word. Allow me to cover the replacement, Roma."

She had hip-length straight black hair and eyes as inhumanly round and pale blue as the mythically named moon. Same as when I'd seen her before. "Not to be pissy, but she tried to kill me a few days ago."

She gave me the look given to most idiots. "But I did not try very hard, did I?" Looking down at the suitcase that contained an assassin she'd killed in seconds, I saw she had a point. "It was a test. Lupa-Alpha Delilah wanted to know if you're still worth her personal touch in your death ... after the contract is completed, of course.

"I did not tell you my name," she then countered with suspicion aimed in Robin's direction, but she took the money despite it. She must really enjoy manicures ... a Wolf. Jesus, who knew?

"You are Delilah's Beta, her second. Of course I know your name. But I also know the names of each and every Lupa in the city. Isn't that what they're starting to call it all over the city instead of the Kin—the Lupa? It was only a matter of time. It seems prudent on my part regardless, especially as I hear Delilah is moving into other cities and their Kin may soon be Lupa as well. She's quite the furry female Robespierre. *Liberté, égalité, sororité.*"

He clapped his hands once to get things in motion. "But enough gossip. Kudos on an execution well executed, although it would've been somewhat nicer had you gotten to him before he obtained access to the building. On the other hand, Demeter of Grain and Harvest smiles on us, as we have pizza." He bent and picked up the three boxes the man had been carrying, miraculously unspilled. "Thank you, Roma, for your impeccable service. Good day." With that, he closed the door.

"I am famished. There is only so much death and destruction in one day I can be expected to handle without sustenance." He placed the boxes on the coffee table, opened the top one, and started to dig in. "Hmm. I wonder if poison was a backup plan, should shooting you fail." He handed the piece to me. "You try. You have all that Auphe resistance to most poisons and venoms. Somewhat. Enough that you'd probably survive. Hurry, would you? I'm starving."

At that point I honestly wouldn't have minded being poisoned, and I snatched the pizza, taking a bite. Swallowing, I said, "Still alive, no poison, and, seriously, is this how you've handled all your would-be killers, assassins, murderers . . . you know, anyone who's *met* you . . . in the past before Niko and I came along to try to buy a car from you the first time? Hire someone to kill them for you because you're lazy as shit?" I held up my hands, one still holding a gun and one with half a piece of pizza. "Hey, no judging, as this time it's saving my ass and I know you spent shitloads to do it. I'm just curious."

He took a piece for himself and smirked at me. "You wish you were rich, don't you, kid?"

Sometimes I liked the fight, but sometimes . . . "Hell, yes," I said fervently, sitting on the table and waving over at Niko, who appeared either mildly stunned by developments, comatose, or most likely hiding behind a stony mask a desire to kick my ass for eating possibly poisoned pizza. "Come on, Nik. Pizza courtesy of assassin delivery. Assassin times two, I guess."

"I have fought when rocks and my hands were the only weapons available. I've fought with spears and stone axes and bow and arrow and swords. I have fought with every weapon conceived against too many *paien* to classify, humans, angels, demons, you name it." The puck ate with one hand and used the other to gesture for emphasis. "In every life that I've crossed paths with you two, I've fought and to be fair, in those times, wealthy or not, king or not, you would be in the battlefield slaughtering. Way of the world back then. But since the eighteen hundreds, I did get a bit tired of it. I thought why not take a break and let someone else who needed the money do it for me?"

"We weren't around in the eighteen hundreds, I take it?" Niko asked, finally accepting a piece from another box, a white pizza with spinach. Naturally.

Robin shook his head. "No. The last I saw you before

this life was the sixteen hundreds." He brightened. "Musketeers. Brilliant fun, even more so than the books or those idiotic movies would make one think. Constant duels, wine everywhere—I think I was inebriated for an entire decade. And the corsets and breasts. It was a sea of powdered breasts wherever one looked."

"So almost four hundred years before you saw us again," Niko persisted before reconsidering. "You didn't . . . I apologize. That would be a painful topic . . . I'm sorry."

Goodfellow gave a breezy smile that didn't seem as genuine as I thought he might hope. "At least you show up at the more interesting times in history."

"You've killed angels and demons? Other than what became Jack?" Ishiah asked, uninterested in the pizza or the Musketeer story, and I gave him a narrow-eyed stare I suspect was worse than any of mine in the past, as this one was bloodred. It appeared to confuse him.

Not stopping with his dinner, Robin dismissed him. "All tricksters do. We don't throw the first punch, but it's a given that we will throw the last. You know what goes on in Vegas. You were involved. I heard Azrael finally got his just deserts. Angel of Death, my flawlessly shaped ass. He'd kill anyone, sinful, pagan, or not. Ha! I wish I'd seen that. Or had the opportunity to party with the first Angel of Death, current Duke of Hell, Eligos. If he doesn't shred you to small gobbets of flesh, Eli's one entertaining drinking companion." He shoved a slice into the peri's hand. "Let it go, Ishiah. You, Eligos, you were all the same once. You might still be the same if God had been more a fan of free will in the early days."

"Vegas," I said. "That's one place I haven't been. I'll bet it's like one big carnival." If my eyes hadn't been red before as I glared at Ishiah, I knew they were now.

His jaw tensed while the rest of him froze until I

looked away and in the periphery of my vision he finally
began to slowly eat. I'd not noticed before in the few
years I'd known him that he'd been searching for something in me. Behind his glares, annoyed expressions, the
unbelieving ones when I blew up the back wall of the
bar, he'd been searching for recognition.

He'd finally gotten it.

Asshole.

Speaking of . . . I wiped a greasy hand on my jeans
and put the gun down. "I have to fight Grimm. Whatever
plan we come up with"—I had already come up with one
except for a single detail—"we can't lead him into a trap
if I don't play first. With Auphe there's no payoff if there's
no play-off."

"Think hard," Robin cautioned. "You think he wants
you alive, mostly, sometimes yes, sometimes no, at this
point, but Icarus thought he could fly as high as he cared
to as well. Yet when he reached the sun, he burned to
ash."

"That's not remotely how the legend goes," Niko said.
"And not poss—"

"Do you want to discuss dusty mythologies and the
true and false nature of them, Niko, or would you like to
keep your brother alive?" The question was brusque,
completely unfair, as all Nik and Robin did was talk
about dusty mythology and history ninety-nine percent
of the time, but I was distracted from the back and forth
by the thoughts of Icarus flying toward the sun.

Huh. I did remember the legend.

Icarus had never touched the sun.

But I could.

It was several hours before we came up with the best we
could do for now, planwise. Not the end game, but a step
to get us there. I wouldn't tell anyone what the end game

was . . . not yet. In the meantime Ishiah had cornered me while Nik and Robin were off squabbling. I was beginning to think all this forced togetherness was making the two of them worse than Nik and I could be . . . which was staggering to contemplate.

"Cal."

I kept my eyes on the bundle of glove-and-claws I tossed from hand to hand as I sat on my temporary bed. I couldn't decide if taking them with me would make things better or make me worse. "Yeah, Ish, don't bother asking. I remember." I didn't want to look at him when it came down to it, not until I had to. "You don't have to sneak around it trying to find out if I do or don't. I've remembered for a couple of days now since Robin told you where I gated. Since I woke up in Arkansas."

"You can't know what it's like for the rest of us." He closed the door behind him with determination behind his eyes, his face, his white-knuckled hand on the door handle. I knew the emotion was fake. I wondered if he did or if he was fooling himself. "Niko, Robin, and you . . . the three of you were unique in being the first to put aside your fear and fight what others couldn't. Fight the Auphe. When they lived no one fought the Auphe. No one dared." My boss, gruff and hard, who'd not let me see a moment of vulnerability in him on the job, in fights too numerous to recall, in two genuine battles, and here he was, afraid, if hiding it. Not crawling, not yet . . .

You could make him. Worthless pigeon. Make him crawl.

Auphe thoughts, but not necessarily wrong in this situation.

"I never had met you face-to-face before then," he continued. "I watched you now and again through your frequent lives because Robin was with you. I've not told him that I watched even when listening to his stories of the three of you. You were important to him, I wanted to know why. I was more angel then, less understanding of how emotions felt. I knew what they were and meant, but I didn't feel them . . . except I knew I was drawn to Robin. To follow him. To speak to him. He only laughed and mocked, as the only words I knew were the Words of God and they do not apply to pucks." For a second his face changed, lightened at the memory of Goodfellow's laughing ridicule. Then his face fell again. "In the past hundred years, I finally had learned how to feel, peri, not angel. I followed Robin still, saw him find you as children. That's when I began to check in on you and Niko now and again, to understand Robin better, and that's when I saw the Auphe following you for the very first time, knew you weren't entirely human, knew what you were. . . ."

"A monster?" I asked, cold and not at all surprised of his opinion.

He turned and punched the wall. It was a sturdy wall, but that didn't stop him from creating a crater in it. "No! A *child*. I felt like the worst sort of cowardly shit, but I knew the Auphe, and I knew standing against them was death guaranteed. I wanted Robin to live because I'm selfish, and I knew against the whole of the Auphe he wouldn't. I knew he had no idea they were there and . . ."

"And if he did know, he'd try to hide us, try to save us." I put the glove down and let the Auphe thoughts go with them. "Promise fought with us once against them and she's a vampire, not an angel. Robin fought with us and he was the swiftest sword in action to this day. You were just a coward," I said, matter-of-fact. "You were a bastard and a coward who left two kids under the hand of the Auphe. You gave me that bullshit about how your kind wasn't allowed to kill *paein*, but that's only in New York City. Hell, you could pick a bridge, go over it, and kill the first *paien* you saw if you wanted and you were in fucking Arkansas. You were in Arkansas and you left us there like, I repeat," I hissed, "the fucking *coward* you were."

"He would hate me, if he knew what I'd done, though I did it to save him. He'd hate me and repudiate me." Guilt, anger, fear, loss; Ishiah knew all the emotions now, didn't he?

"Repudiate? That's a fancy word to say he might fucking *kill* you," I growled, then cocked my head, hair falling loose that I'd not bothered to pull back up. "After all, he's known us a lot longer than he's known you. Thousands of years more. He's known us before *you* were even created. We're his family. And family trumps sex and fuck buddies every time."

He had nothing to say to that.

I thought about it before saying in casual dismissal, "Yeah, you were a coward and worse. Hell, maybe you still are." But this was the time—the Grimm time—for second chances. If not for Ishiah, then for Robin, who could need someone very soon, someone like Ishiah, to be at his side as the future of Niko and I was nothing but a bleak and rapidly approaching ending. Absently I noticed the taste of blood-tainted copper pennies in my mouth.

The taste of blood, the taste of tomorrow.

"But I'm going to give you a break," I said flatly to the ex-angel. "You helped us with that serial-killing bastard Jack. You helped save Nik's life, but that's not why I'm letting this go, because now I don't know if you risked anything on that at all anymore. Ex-angels and compromised angels . . . you could be the same. Here's your break: I'm not going to mention this to Robin, any of it—how you knew the Auphe were after us when he didn't, how you were a craven chicken-shit with wings.

And how you fucking left us to die or worse ... and it was *much* fucking worse than dying ... but I'm not telling that to him. Not for your sake; don't think that for a god-damn second. It's for him. It would hurt him, and after what he's done for us, I won't do that. I won't hurt him."

"I fought Jack. I helped to fight that storm spirit *paien* and then thought I'd be banished from New York by all *paien* for doing the forbidden, of killing it. I did that because Robin, Niko, and you had taught me what true courage was. In the past five years I've learned more from all of you about bravery and honor than I ever learned in my four thousand years." He raised his eyes, closed them, and his fist twitched as if he wanted to punch the wall again. I was thinking Heaven had disap-pointed him. But that was his problem, not mine. "I wish I'd known those qualities earlier, at the carnival, but I didn't. Or I had them, but not enough of them," he ad-mitted gravely, opening his eyes. "I can't change what I did then, but I will not let you down now, Caliban. Yours and Niko's and Robin's. I won't betray you again."

Blah, blah, blah.

He could be telling the truth; he probably was. Did I care? Not so much. Redemption didn't come as easy as he thought it did. For what he'd done, for my two years in Auphe Hell, redemption might not come at all.

I lifted my ass off the bed to reach my wallet and pulled out two twenties and a ten to wad up into a ball and toss at his chest. "There's your fifty bucks you gave me then. Thanks for the loan. And, no joke, my mom really would've sucked your dick for twenty-five." I gave him a grin, because my gift of silence to Robin or not, forgiveness wasn't in my nature. The grin, ferocious and warped, was less lethal than ripping out his throat, which I did consider. That's when I felt the metal teeth, all one thousand of them, drop over my human ones.

Like Grimm's.

There were triggers and then there were triggers. Leaving a thirteen-year-old me at the not so tender mercies of the Auphe was one damn big trigger.

I tasted the metal and blood of my smile and I didn't care. I kept going. "I hope you kept the bear I gave you at the carnival." My voice was the Auphe guttural rock slide of the shattered glass when they deigned to speak human. "After all, you and your fifty bucks *earned* it."

He gave up, bright guy that he was, and disappeared nearly as quickly as Grimm—although Ishiah used the door. I felt the teeth slide back up and I licked the blood from my human ones where my gums had been punctured. Ishiah could be a better person now.

He hadn't been with Robin then, over a decade ago. He'd been an admirer at best, not that he would admit that to Goodfellow's face. Then again, maybe he would. And Robin would make you a better person if you ignored the stealing, lying, conning, whoring, and tricking and concentrated on the loyalty, bravery—suicidal bravery, especially as he wouldn't be reincarnated—generosity, and willingness to do anything for his friends.

Not that I minded the stealing, lying, conning, whoring, and tricking, as that's who my friend was: Robin Goodfellow, once the Great God Pan, and once Hob the first and worst. He was a puck and I liked him for all the parts of him. Ishiah was an ex-angel, though, and maybe Goodfellow had improved on Ishiah's past rampant self-preservation skills and willingness to let children be eaten by Auphe, changed him with what the nonjudgmental would consider the puck's finer qualities. Anything was possible. And as I'd told Ishiah, I wouldn't hurt Robin that way, hell, in any way, not after all he'd done for me.

I would hold a grudge, though. I might lose my mind, my soul, but never my grudges. They were something I'd

forget. If one day Robin tired of Ishiah on his own with
no influence from me, huh . . . we'd see.

Hopefully the peri was a higher creature than he had
been. I didn't know that I'd be able to see it or recognize
it if he were—my conscience had never been completely
functional and shiny—and gauging his path was something that I could barely hope for at the most, right?

You could hope.

Niko and Robin, both had taught me that. I did genuinely hope he was, Ishiah, what I wished for because
Goodfellow deserved that. I wished the universe would
get off its ass for once and make sure that he got it.

"Time to go?"

I grinned at Niko in the doorway, a proper grin . . . human teeth, no blood. A good grin. Slipping on the glove,
I stood. "Grimm agreed to the time and place. What am I
saying? Robin got through to him on the phone. Talked
to the potential conqueror of the world on the phone?
That's . . . freaky. Yeah, pretty fucking freaky." I decided
not to think about it. Better for my sanity. "Then off to
see the Bae kiddies? Should we get some balloons?"

"Only if they're filled with acid," he said, face grim
and eyes dark.

For the grin I bestowed on him this time, I had to
make a conscious effort to keep the second layer of hypodermic needle teeth up and out of sight, but I managed. He had to see the hair and my eyes. The teeth too,
no. Other than skin color, there would be no difference
between me and Grimm . . . physically. I'd hold back on
that sight as long as I could. "Acid and baby Bae. You
made my day. Think we can get some before we go?"

He snorted. "Just be ready to fight, little brother. I
have your favorite weapon ready to go with us. Let's not
get cocky."

"You had to say it, didn't you?" I drawled seconds

before Goodfellow popped his head in and said, "Cocky? Cock-meister? Did someone call me by name? Want a demonstration? I have a pair of Velcro pants somewhere that come off with one yank. Ah, let us talk about the word 'yank' for a moment. . . ."

Going to see Grimm in the far-off desert wasn't that bad, if one thought about it, not in comparison.

Was it?

Hell, no.

14

Goodfellow

I'd called some friends in Canada, thanks to Georgina's tip, to track down some other friends. I'd called an RV full of fur and dander and sent them in that direction, although they were close already. I knew Canada and I'd made a few educated guesses. The fact that I'd had to talk to Canadians . . . unholy. Human or *paien*, they were good-hearted and good-natured and everything good. Hearing a wendigo say "aboot" was horrifying all on its own.

There had also been a call made to the Lupa that for three million more, I would pay them to take down every member of the Vigil in NYC. That was for Cal, yes, because they wouldn't stop coming after him, not as long as he lived. Every member of the Vigil agreed his control was gone and he had to die. I'd been told that by an informant, gone by now from the city. My mole in the Vigil,

Samuel, was a man who took no money for what he told me. He owed a debt to Cal but especially to Niko, who had made clear that debt would never be paid, but Samuel had best keep trying.

For Cal and for Niko, I'd paid the money, but it was for the *paien* as well. We could police ourselves on whether humans knew about us or not. If one of us ran amuck among the humans under the bright sun to be seen by all, we would make the decision of who could be saved and who could not. That was not for a human organization to do. I'd had enough of it, and helpful as they'd been in the past, they'd been so for their convenience . . . not ours.

The Vigil could play their games in all the other cities, but we had made New York an angel-free, demon-free zone, and we would make it a Vigil-free zone as well. This could be *Paien* City in time and if I had a legacy, if I died during all this, that would be it. I couldn't save Rome from falling, but I could raise up New York to a place for our kind to be more free than anywhere else on this world.

"You seem pretty damn happy," Cal said suspiciously, as of course Cal in the here and now was always wary of happiness . . . or drugs, sex, and rock and roll.

I bounced on my heels. "I wish I could've seen you at Woodstock. That would've been memorable." I searched for the word. "*Epic*. Jimi Hendrix was a fan of fire too, as you probably do not know, as you are an ignorant fetus."

"All right. Pizza makes Goodfellow high. Keep that in mind. Niko, you have the baby ready?" Cal asked. "She's temperamental. Treat her right."

" 'She' is a flamethrower. They are sturdy, I promise you," came his brother's exasperated reply as he hefted the tanks on his back. He could only carry one katana now, and I did not imagine he was content with that.

"Be grateful I didn't name her. Sylvia. That's what I didn't name her. Sylvia, and if she has problems with fuel injection, whisper that non-name to her and she'll come around."

Grimm's location was in Arizona. Cal had been confident about finding it and had gone off to the bathroom to give himself an added boost of epinephrine and I saw him put several more syringes in his jacket pocket. I hoped the combination of the extralarge box—the way I like my condoms—I'd obtained for him and my not so subtle hint early of a poorly told legend would do the trick.

When he came back out, he already had Grimm's phone in his hand and was halfway through punching in his number. When it connected, he said immediately, "I'm on my way."

He'd told us that he wasn't about to let Grimm open a gate for him and let us walk through, but there were a few desert locations he'd been to as a kid and a few he remembered well enough to get to combined with the Google Map Nik had printed for him.

That and the call I'd make to Grimm later should we survive this.

Flipping the phone shut without waiting for a comment from Grimm, he said, "Let's go jack this motherfucker up. I'm opening the gate about six feet up in the air. Figure it wouldn't hurt to drop on them like the Wrath of God—if they're aboveground first."

Frowning at the phrase, Ishiah had his sword out and seemed ready. I'd given consideration to telling him not to come, as, if Cal did lose his grip, I wasn't at all positive he wouldn't consider Ishiah simply another Bae. But Ishiah had been determined and Cal had absolutely no comment one way or the other than to say with a peculiar curve of his lips, "If he wants to roll the dice, his choice."

That? That in no way was reassuring. "Can you be at all sure that you won't get ... uh ... excited, think of him as a Bae with wings and kill him?" I asked.

"Nope, I can't guarantee that at all." The peculiar stretch of Cal's lips widened and I thought I saw a glimpse of silver.

Wonderful. He was already excited and not in the manner that I favored best.

Before Ishiah could argue, I ordered, "Close it behind me, Cal. Don't let him through."

"Robin, no," Ishiah refuted fiercely. "You need me and you need me fighting with all of you. You can't—"

Cal meanwhile was shrugging over Ishiah's outburst. "Gotcha. No God in the Wrath of. Here we go, boys and girls." He went on to open the gate in my living room, saying, "See you on the other side." He walked through the tangle of colors I didn't know he could see. Mixed in with the purple, gray, and black was the indescribable color of the world bleeding with every gate he opened. With everyone he or an Auphe had opened, it was as if you saw a little slice of the world wither and die.

Looking back at Ishiah, I exhaled, "His control isn't ideal. He could kill you, Ishiah, with a single thought. I'll be back. I promise." I had learned long ago and particularly at the gates of Troy not to make promises in war. "My tongue betrays me," I said ruefully.

"It most often does." Ishiah watched me go, but there was hope in his eyes, a clear light of faith. Both were what angels did best, but this hope and faith wasn't for Heaven. It was for me. I took a handful of his shirt and pulled him in for a quick kiss. Faith and hope. I was a trickster. I had faith in myself and hope was for the unprepared.

"And don't listen to Cal. It's this side I'll see you on again." I turned and, carrying my own sword, was on Nik's heels as he went next.

I'd rather stab myself in the stomach than pass through a gate, but I was doing it more and more often. At least I no longer vomited. One took one's blessings where one could.

They had shown up on time. That did surprise me. Grimm and forty Bae. That was less of a surprise. I landed hard on top of the back of one Bae and reached around to slice through his throat with the dagger in my other hand. Not far from me Cal had done the same, except with the use of his man-made claws. Grimm stood off to one side on a small swell of sand, wearing his own claws and carrying a gun in his other hand. Letting the muzzle dangle toward the sand-colored twilight as the sun dropped beneath the horizon, he said to Cal with approval, "You said you'd come alone. You lied."

"I'm a killer. Did you think I'm not a liar too?" Now Cal was grinning and I could see why his smile had been so peculiar earlier. He had his teeth now, a legion of needle-fine metal teeth covering his human ones. He had not a single strand of dark hair left and his eyes were the same red as Grimm's were. This gate had taken the last slivers of his physical humanity. The single difference between Grimm and him was their features, perhaps an inch in height, and Grimm's darker, human-toned skin.

"What are you?" Cal questioned with a scorn that couldn't erase that hideous grin. "The audience? Aren't you going to play?"

Grimm's grin was a twin to that of Cal. "You have to earn my participation. Let's see if you can."

Between the two of them, myself, the Bae, Niko was the only human. I didn't know how that felt to him, as I was used to being the single puck wherever I went, but I saw how his gaze fastened on Cal as he hit the sandy ground and it wasn't different from any look he'd ever given his brother—full of confidence. Then Niko, knowing the first rule of combat, struck the first blow. There was no honorably patient waiting for the Bae to attack as he swiveled, triggered, and sprayed the flamethrower back and forth, setting several Bae on fire. It was the closest batch of crouching Bae, who'd had the sense or the Grimm-ordered sense, to spread out for more difficult targets, but when it came to what Niko was armed with, the gift of Prometheus, their precautions made no difference.

Cal had always loved that flamethrower and it was useful, but Cal was loving something much more now. He was in the midst of the Bae. He'd put his gun away and beneath his claws their black blood fell like an unhallowed rain. Three leaped and took him to the ground. In less than a second he was back up, tossing the head of the first with a cleanly sliced stump of neck down at the second one, who was still on the ground, its arms amputated to soak the sand around it. He then wrapped an arm around the neck of the third, which had been on its way back up, and tore through the scaled white flesh down its back to reveal the gleaming bone of its spine. It was instantly cut in half with titanium talons. The Bae collapsed, the upper part of it twitching and the bottom dead as a graveyard.

I'd been the one to give Cal back his clawed glove, but I wished now I'd hidden it and let him use his guns. He enjoyed his guns, and savage grins showed occasionally when he used them. His grin now with black gore dripping from his leather-and-metal-covered hand wasn't savage. It was feral, wild, and the color of the silver cupped in the hand of Judas.

Niko had said Cal had mentioned how they hunted in

Tumulus. Packs of Auphe like packs of wolves ... and Cal with them racing across the ground and killing anything they came across. Whether he was remembering or not, I thought Cal considered this a hunt.

Fire, blood, bone—less than a minute and it was already heading toward a massacre.

I thought the Bae would start gating away, out of range, then gate back to take you from behind. That's how they'd fought before, but not this time. It hit me abruptly why that was so.

Once Cal had said that if you could gate, then you could stop others from gating. It wasn't a matter of who was stronger than who to do it. All Auphe could, although when it came down to stopping more than the one to equal you, strength and will, especially will, did enter into it. Cal had done it before, even stopped other Auphe, although not as many as forty, the number of the Bae here, and it had nearly killed him. But Bae were not Auphe, not in their ability to murder, and not in their ability to gate. They weren't Auphe, only pale shadows of them, and Cal could hold them much more easily. *Was* holding them.

The Bae—lesser in all ways than the Auphe—and his belief in them, was Grimm's first true mistake.

Cal and Grimm were different. They were an improvement on the Auphe—astonishingly enough, they could do things the Auphe hadn't been able to do. Cal could open a gate inside someone and turn them into a geyser of flesh and bone. No one else could do that. The Auphe, definitely not the Bae, and if Grimm could, I had yet to see it. It was a new skill that had come with the mixed human/Auphe genes in him.

Grimm was a different story. I knew Cal couldn't do that with him. He'd tried before and failed. Grimm had stopped his gate easily. When Cal had then tried to keep

Grimm from gating and failed, it was then a fact. Cal had been able to stop Auphe from gating, but he couldn't do the same to Grimm. Grimm's ability to build gates was inconceivable, unstoppable, and better than that of Cal and the long-dead Auphe. Perhaps that was *his* newly bred skill.

Interesting.

The Auphe had created more than they had ever known.

The Bae, confused, were growing more murderous at what Cal had done to them. Enraged at the loss of half of what they were, that their fighting was limited in a manner that was close to neutering them, they grew more vicious or more desperate—sometimes the two are the same. No vanishing and returning to snap your neck from behind. And wasn't that terrible they were held to the same rules as Niko and me? While my sympathy for them did not overflow in the slightest, Niko continued to burn them alive, and I fought as I'd fought on so many battlefields. The sand beneath my feet was the same as the sand I'd stood on for too many wars to count: It soaked up blood with the same efficiency.

I took one Bae's head, to whirl and slice the one leaping from behind me from sternum to pubis, and stepped over the guts that spilled free. I skewered one with a dagger through the eye and sliced through the throats of two more who'd crouched a little too close to each other. I felt claws rake across my back and twisted to the side and buried the dagger in one pointed ear to scramble what little brains it had.

In the next second I had one of them on the ground . . . the trees here were horrid, twisted things, vegetation scarce—I didn't see a vacation here in my future . . . as I rammed my sword through its stomach. "You are . . . not human. Not . . . sheep." It drooled black froth with its last gasping breaths. I tapped my dagger on the tapered snout on his spade-shaped snake head. "No, child. I am not. And you are not an Auphe or anything close to one."

Poor snake. If there weren't a thousand of them, moving as one beneath Grimm's command, they would be little in the way of a threat at all. Yet there were a thousand, and as magnificent fighters as we were, or at least I was, talent and ability didn't matter when the three of you were smothered under the weight, teeth, and talons of a thousand.

Rolling to one side and leaping to my feet, I avoided the hissing, slithering charge of three more, taking two heads and then the third with a sweep of silver. Four more came and I started to lose track. White scales, the shine and curve of long metal succubae/incubi fangs, the sheets of night-shaded blood, the screams, and thuds of falling bodies.

Work, work, work.

A fight, yes. It could be considered a small battle. They weren't Auphe, but they were incredibly more adept, dangerous, and deadly than human warriors.

It certainly was not a war, though.

Rather dull, considering that I'd once kept company with Ares, God of War.

I heard the barest shift of sand behind me and had my sword at a throat before they could move—standing thirty feet away was hardly good enough to evade me in the midst of a killing dervish.

"Goodfellow?"

"Ah." I let the tip of my sword fall. "Apologies, Niko. I tend to lose track with busywork. I wish Cal had let them gate. That would have been more interesting." That was a lie. If they had been able to gate, one or more of us might have died fighting forty of them. But I did have a reputation to maintain, didn't I? I moved about to nudge the nearest body with the tip of my sword. "This isn't enough to stop me from allowing myself to be distracted thinking where I might next vacation. This desert landscape depresses me."

"You're . . ." He moved his hand in the air in front of him from his head to wave at his feet. In the purple light he appeared to grimace if only very slightly. This was Niko after all.

I knew what he was referring to. It wasn't the first, hundredth, or thousandth time I'd been covered head to toe in blood. It was why I was wearing some clothes I'd, this time for once, borrowed from Cal instead of the other way around. I wasn't ruining any of my clothes this way. "Yes?" I raised my eyebrows in question. "It does go with the territory. You most often fight with a sword. You know this."

"I am guessing I never fought quite as you do." He was disappointed in himself. I could see it.

There'd been many and I'd put more effort and speed into it than was customarily needed. We fought skirmishes these days, but many other times we'd fought wars, fought against hundreds of thousands in a single battle. I patted him consolingly on the shoulder, leaving a bloody, wet black handprint on gray cloth. "Niko, did you actually think that you did?" I stepped back farther and scanned for Cal and Grimm. "I am your teacher, though, in as many lives as I can be. If you didn't die after thirty or so years and rest between incarnations for hundreds of years, you would be much closer to me in ability, I swear."

The frown evident in his voice told me I hadn't done the job I'd hoped in improving his mood. Or to be honest, hadn't hoped that much: Did he truly consider himself one with he who had been Hob? I thought not, lifelong companion and war-birthed family or no. All this time and the two remained far too young for that in experience or general comparison of my incomparable fighting skills. I saw little need to sugarcoat that. I had my own ego to think of, didn't I?

"They are there." He pointed.

One hundred or so feet away, past the mounds of dead Bae. Some were burned. Some were bloody from my sword, Cal's claws . . . and some torn at with teeth. Cal's teeth, and that was a good sign that lucidity had left the building and sanity was a stain in the sand.

Cal was surrounded by seven Bae and I knew he had let that happen. He had his gun holstered but wasn't using it, and in no world would Cal let himself get encircled by the enemy. If nothing else and there were too many, he'd find a rock and put his back against it. He wasn't trapped. He was playing.

Playing. Ares himself would be alarmed.

He was also laughing as if he was having the time of his life. And, Hades help us, perhaps he was. "You." He pointed at one Bae. "Boom."

It exploded, spraying blood and pulped organs in every direction. That would be Cal opening a gate in him with that special talent I'd thought of before, but hadn't thought how the bile would rise in my throat to see it in action. I expected him to do the same with the other six. I was wrong.

They couldn't gate, as he wouldn't let them, but he could and gate he did. He was here, then there, then behind, beside, and in front of them all. He ripped heads from bodies, flesh from bone, tore out abdomens with his teeth—his *teeth*—used his claws to cut arms and legs free. Finally, although "finally" was barely a minute if not less, he let the last Bae fall, spitting a large chunk of its throat onto the ground. The worst part was he left half of them alive ... suffering. For some it would be minutes; for some it might be hours.

His mouth and the metal in it were dripping black with blood. It was easy to see despite the approaching darkness overtaking the twilight, as his grin was that wide. Almost too wide for his jaw and far too wild for reason. I felt Niko's hand tight on my forearm, but he didn't say anything. I didn't think he had any words for this. "Do you still have the tranquilizer gun?" I asked quietly. If he didn't, I had another hidden under my shirt, not that I'd felt the need to share that information.

It was strained, hoarse, but he did manage at least one word. "Yes." When we had come through the gate, Niko was calm at the sight of a completely physically changed Cal. He was less calm now, but he was holding on and he was not broken. "But he said he would stay with us, and he will." More words, kudos to Niko, but they were naïve ones.

We puck had a saying: O ye of too much faith.

Grimm had stepped across the ground, smooth and silent, without the warning a rattlesnake would have the courtesy to give. He stopped to stand beside Cal. "Look, Caliban. Look, my brother. They are afraid. They are afraid of you."

For all Niko had that faith and for all I wished I could, Cal and Grimm looked much closer to brothers now, same clothes, same hair, eyes, teeth, and the shadows of approaching night hid the difference in skin color. And they were both staring at us as identical amusement and reflection, cold and beyond lethal, flowed over their faces. I imagined the reflection was at what they might make from our intestines when they pulled them, the difficult way, out through our mouths. Cat's cradle would be no challenge at all, would it? Details, details.

"Afraid? Is that what you see?" Cal watched us with a head cocked, curious. "They do smell afraid, don't they? And maybe they are. Maybe they have their toy gun with them so they can put me to sleep again. Maybe Goodfellow-Hob-the-younger will kill me for the world's own good or maybe he'll just try. Or just maybe I'll slice off the dick he never stops talking about and give it to your other Bae as a toy or take it back to his pigeon as a present."

He licked the blood thoughtfully from his lips and teeth. Either he had no problem with the taste, the ingestion, or he might not have noticed he was doing it, but he kept at it until the metal shone bright again. All the while he contemplated us and our fear, because it was there—that fear. Impossibly his grin went wider. "And maybe ... just maybe I get tired of repeating myself when I say you're *not* my fucking brother!"

He buried the dark claws low in Grimm's abdomen and ripped upward. Red-black blood gushed, intestines began to spill, and Grimm was gone. He left nothing but air and falling blood behind. Not dead, that I doubted. Grimm had shown in the past he could survive horrific wounds, but he was gone.

I approved of that. If he could be more gone, as perhaps from existence and memory, I'd approve of that more.

The metal teeth slid up out of sight as the blood continued to drip from the claws mounted on Cal's glove to dapple the sand in a cheerful spring shower, and Cal's grin stayed in place, but human now and pleased as he aimed it at us. "Good game, guys. Damn good game. I should make you honorary Auphe."

I'd lived long enough that there wasn't much left that could startle me, and surprising me I would have thought to be close to entirely out of the question. That didn't stop me from answering Niko's comment in the manner that I did.

"I think I may have pissed my pants," he said, his voice low and absent of life.

"You are not fucking alone," I replied honestly.

15

Caliban

"You were really afraid?" I asked.

Goodfellow threw a statue of a mermaid and a horny dolphin at my head. The thing was the size of a basketball and shattered against the wall as I ducked. He then continued pushing Ishiah out the front door of his condo as he'd been doing since I gated us back. The statue had once sat on a table in the foyer. Convenient for tossing. I wondered if he planned it that way while having the place decorated.

"But I stopped all the Bae from gating, and without that, they're nothing like the Auphe to fight. Nik had the flamethrower, and I saw you taking them down, Goodfellow. You went through them like a Stephen King possessed-from-Hell lawn mower. I was impressed." And a little jealous. "It was a downpour of blood wherever I looked. You couldn't have been afraid—" This time it was a bronze bowl, small but deadly, and it bounced off my shoulder.

"Ow, you shithead. What the hell?" I complained.

"Absolutely not, Robin. I am not leaving you to face this Grimm and Bae situation alone." Overriding my complaints, Ishiah was refusing to go, and Robin, the puck of all the words, had not one to say to any of us. Ishiah was bigger than Robin, but the trickster was older, wilier, with some sneaky moves I hadn't once seen Nik use, and that meant they were sneakier than hell. He had Ishiah out the door with it slammed and locked quicker than the eye could follow.

Finally he did have some words, but not many. "Don't bother trying to break it down with your sword," he said through the door, "or I'll call security." In other words, he'd let the humans see, and Ishiah, unlike me, was sane, followed the rules, and wouldn't risk that.

"It was barely a game at all," I said to Niko, who was on the couch . . . sprawled on the couch.

I had not in my life seen Niko sprawl, not a single time, and he had a thousand-yard stare that a troll and a boggle combined hadn't been able to give him. Robin stalked past us without a look, covered as literally as a person could be in blood, black blood, but blood was blood. I'd seen him fight many times, but not against forty at once. It kicked his game up a notch. He'd been lazing a lot in the past apparently, but I didn't think now was the time to bring that up.

"It wasn't," I insisted. Robin's shoe hit me in the side of the head from twenty feet away. "Jesus Christ." I backed away from him even as he kept moving in the opposite direction. "Was it Grimm?" Fuck knew I was wary of him when I was in my right mind. He could be death incarnate when he wanted. To non-Auphe he had to be scary as shit. "It was Grimm, right?"

"It was you."

I whipped my head away from Robin's retreat to the shower, I was guessing, to Nik. "What?"

"We were afraid of you," he said it as blankly as his eyes stayed.

Not Goodfellow was afraid. We. We were afraid.

My stomach lurched. No. That couldn't be right. That couldn't be true. "But I was in control. I told you I'd stay in control." I did too, and I was proud of that as it had been close to impossible. "I was able to get the drop on Grimm by pretending I was Cal, but Caliban. That I couldn't hold out, that I was the same as him like he wanted." Because the Bae weren't the point in the game. When we played, Grimm and I were the pieces that mattered. "I faked it ... you didn't know? You thought I meant what I said?"

Nik shook his head, but before he could answer, Robin discovered words again. Out of sight, he yelled them down the hall, "It wasn't only the words! It was the words about my *gamou* cock combined with the *gamou* metal teeth and you killing *gamou* Bae and spitting out their *gamou* flesh with your *gamou* metal teeth and the *gamou* licking of the blood from your *gamou* metal *gamou* teeth, you *gamou* idiot!"

Shit. Shit. Had I done that? I remembered the waves of white scales and black blood that would go flying as I sliced with my claws ... and then ... then I'd bit with my teeth, my jaw locking, and the ripping-away motion as I'd jerked my head. Damn it to hell, I had. I had torn open throats with my teeth. I'd licked off the blood like if was leftover ice cream, and I hadn't thought once about what I was doing. It was natural. It was instinct. It was who I was. God. I promptly puked black vomit on Robin's billion-dollar antique rug.

"Hades, take me now! Why do I try?" Robin didn't

bother coming back down the hall to follow his frustrated shout, and I didn't know if he would again. If anyone could drive a wildly partying puck to become an agoraphobic hermit, it would be me.

"To be fair," Niko continued, a face so lacking in emotion that it freaked me out, "I believe it was your threat to cut off his penis that disturbed him as much as the killing with your teeth and lapping up of the blood."

"Do you *gamou* think that might be the *gamou* case? Or that he said he'd *bite* it off with his *gamou* metal *gamou* teeth, piece of *skata* that he is! Zeus, strike me dead. Lift me to Olympus. Save me from this horror of an existence." His voice was getting louder, but I had the feeling he was getting further away from us and not physically.

I stared dully down at the dark vomit at my feet. "I think I broke Robin." I stepped backward and looked up at him. "Did I break you too?"

The blankness was replaced slowly with a solemn study of me before he said, "I've told you before you could speak, Cal, I will always be with you and I'll never give up on you. If that means dragging you back from the brink, then I will. If it means going with you over that brink, that I will do as well. Whether I'm afraid that most of you might already be gone doesn't matter. I'll be on your heels bringing what's left of you with me. Fear can't stop me. That the Cal I grew up with now has silver hair, scarlet eyes, and bear-trap teeth that come and go can't stop me. That will be true until the day we die." The twitch of his lips was more reflex than anything, but I'd take it. "All the days we die, which as Robin keeps telling us are many. Now would you step over your vomit and bring me two bottles of Robin's most dusty and expensive-appearing wine? I'm in an unaccustomed mood." Drinking, he was drinking again. My brother who thought tea with caffeine was the equivalent of Jägermeister.

I had done this. The Cal he'd known with the black hair and eyes the same as his was gone, and the image of an Auphe was in his place. Anyone else would've already killed me. Would've been justified in killing me when the words of an Auphe came out of the mouth of one, but I expected Robin and him to not be afraid? To know I was pretending when all the times in the past there had been no pretense.

Idiot me.

An hour later I'd cleaned up the puke, although the stain would stay, I thought, for eternity. Salome and Spartacus the zombie cats regarded it with feline disgust, and if they'd had working bladders, no doubt would've pissed on it. I was sitting on the couch. Niko had forced me to. After a bottle of wine, he'd ended up with his head in my lap. He hadn't passed out; he wasn't that much of a lightweight. No, he'd gone to sleep, exhausted. I was too, but every time I closed my eyes I saw myself as I must've looked to Nik and Robin while I'd stood with Grimm, threatened them, and now I understood. To see two Auphe, one your brother but maybe not any longer when you see the way he'd killed with metal teeth and claws, how would you know what to think? I'd kept my promise. I said I wouldn't go Auphe, and I didn't. But I hadn't entirely been Cal either, tearing Bae apart like an animal would. Like an Auphe would. I couldn't sleep when I relived that each time I started to doze.

Robin came out finally. I wouldn't have been surprised if he hadn't come out for days. He was clean of the head-to-toe blood, wearing a long dark green bathrobe of some material so expensive whoever made it had to charge by the inch. He had his sword and a tranquilizer gun with him.

Dropping into the chair, he took in his stained rug, the empty wine bottle, a comatose Nik, and spoke with utter disinterest, which was wrong. Robin always had an interest, in one direction or another—always had an opinion for or against. This . . . *lack* . . . wasn't the Goodfellow I knew.

"You've destroyed my life, my belongings, my ability to get an erection . . . at least for another hour . . . and my relationship temporarily, as I had to send Ishiah away, as chances are high that you might eat him for drinking the last of the orange juice." He tapped the oddly shaped muzzle of the gun against the arm of the chair. "Your work is done, Cal. You have done what no other creature could claim. You've driven me to the edge of insanity and removed all willingness to live from me entirely. Bravo. If I had two free hands, I would applaud you."

But he didn't have a free hand, as both held a weapon specifically for me. If I hadn't broken him, I'd done a damn good imitation.

I didn't say I was sorry. That would be one helluva insult in view of what I'd done. All the things I'd done. I didn't say I'd make it up to him, as, if I lived to be ninety, I couldn't, and I wasn't going to live to be ninety. I'd be lucky to live ninety more hours, much less years. "You deserve better." That I could say, because that was true.

He deserved better and Niko deserved better. "Next life toss me in a volcano the minute I pop out. Make sure Nik never sees me. Force-feed my mother birth control." But that was all impossible, of course. He didn't find us that young, didn't find us when we were still cooking in the oven. Didn't find us in time to save Nik. "Hell, Robin, at least save yourself. Don't try to find us anymore. And if you do accidentally, walk away. I'm a curse. I might as well be your and Niko's personal fucking curse. All our lives sound as if they end in blades and blood. You have only one life. Just . . . walk away. Walk away and enjoy your life, because it would fucking kill me if you died thanks to me. And unlike Nik and me, you wouldn't come back."

He sighed, deep and full of the sound of resignation, and with that he was back. Not a Robin-shaped manikin, but the genuine deal—real, if ruefully that way. "I couldn't. I'm a hopeless case, kid. Damn you for reminding me." Propping the sword against his chair, he offered, "And you wouldn't say that if you remembered the good times. Try. Think about the time you were Patroclus and we were in that one *chamaitypeion* that had a statue of me depicting me as far less endowed than I actually am. You were so offended on my behalf . . . and drunk . . . that you—"

"Pushed it over and shattered it, then set the whorehouse on fire," I finished, because *chamaitypeion* was Greek for whorehouse or brothel, and I knew that although I'd never learned it. I knew it because I'd lived it.

"Or when you were Caiy and that one chieftain caught us with his daughters."

"And I stole all his horses," I said, the memory suddenly so clear. The twenty shaggy horses, the white crescents that shone in the rolling of their eyes, the aggressive stomping of large hooves, the annoyed bugle that came from velvet muzzles as we moved them into a gallop.

"After setting his tent on fire. Of course you were nice enough to clear everyone out first," he said. "That was considerate of you. And when you were a musketeer . . ."

"I tried to set *Paris* on fire," I said with horror and, all right, a little pride in having high goals. That was nothing but a blur. If Robin had spent a decade in a drunken state, I'd been right there with him.

"You can see why I'm not surprised by your love for a flamethrower these days," he responded with a fond forgiveness I didn't think I could've managed in his position.

"I don't want to know where I was for all of this. Tell me and I'll destroy you both," Niko said with his eyes still shut.

I yanked lightly at his braid. "Paying bail? Breaking us out of prison, the gaol, stopping the execution, whatever they did to ... um ... high-spirited people back then?"

"High-spirited," he repeated with palpable scorn. "My entire existence spent as a babysitter."

With a snort he sat up. I thought about that: how he'd rested his head in my lap without a thought for metal teeth, silver hair, crimson eyes, and flashes of homicidal mania. It was an unbelievable trust and an equally unbelievable lack of survival skills when it came to me.

My brother, and there was nothing more that could be thought or said to encompass that.

Robin laughed; it wasn't his usual one, but it was a laugh and that counted. "I love how you assume you were some sort of Mother Teresa with a sword. You helped burn down that brothel and then disappeared with three of the whores. We didn't see you for a week. You've always been an excellent warrior, but you do not get to be Achilles or Alexander or Arturus by wiping the foreheads of the sick and delivering food to the hungry. In many lives you were rather power-hungry and ruthless ... *nobly*, of course." Goodfellow's straight face did nothing to hide the mockery beneath. "As nobly as you can be when visiting whorehouses before washing your enemy's blood off you. Oh, and Arturus didn't get his sword from a stone. He pulled it out of the gut of his primary rival, but with a very noble flourish as he did so, if that makes you feel more principled and honorable."

"You should've left the vomit on his rug," Nik growled. "And I know my history. Allow me my illusions if you please. And while we speak of illusions, what are we to do about Grimm?"

"I know." The shadowed blight on the rug didn't shatter any of my illusions as I focused on it, but then again I hadn't had any. It was a confirmation of what had to be done. "I've known for a while what to do about Grimm and all his Bae, every last one."

Niko wouldn't like it, but he would see the necessity of it and the inevitability of it. Robin wouldn't care for it at all, as much effort as he'd put into keeping us safe and alive in the past week or so. It would've been better if he hadn't begun to forgive me for the *gamou* metal *gamou* teeth incident barely an hour ago. I hid a mental smile, rueful and tasting of regret. I should've left him fearing for his true love: his dick. He might not object to my plan if I had. He most likely would've packed us a lunch and taken a nap or called Ishiah back to make up for all the screwing he was missing thanks to trying to take care of us. Money, sex, and almost his life—Goodfellow had pulled out all the stops on this. I wished he hadn't.

In the end, it would be a waste.

"Pine Barrens. New Jersey. Delilah dragged me out there once in the sexing days to look for the Jersey Devil or Cthulhu, I don't remember. But there's a fire tower on Apple Pie Hill that's high and isolated enough for a thousand and one Bae to swarm and no people to see them." Or get eaten by them, which I thought those hypothetical people would appreciate that.

Robin's mild leer let me in on the fact that he knew what Delilah and I had been doing out there and it wasn't looking for the Jersey Devil. "It's been an incredibly wet fall. The fire tower would be unmanned. That is a positive. What do you plan on doing with Grimm and the Bae when or if they show up?"

"Gate them away, someplace they can't come back from. With all that epinephrine you had delivered, I can make the biggest gate the world has seen."

"And where will you send them from which they can't return? You can only gate to places you've been to or seen," Niko said. He was suspicious and it showed in deepened lines beside his mouth and the millimeter narrowing of his eyes. "Any of those including Tumulus they could make their way back."

I pointed up.

They didn't like it. I told them I could gate all the Bae for certain into the sun and with a chance I'd survive. It wasn't a substantial chance, I noted, but it was one. Grimm was the problem. Grimm could gate like nothing I'd seen. He might escape my gate, but he wouldn't be able to take all the Bae with him, four or five at the most. That was something I, and my box of epinephrine, was sure of. And a handful of Bae he could save, we could kill easily enough. Grimm himself should still be weak enough from the gutting I'd given him, if given a few days or not to duct-tape himself back together, that we'd have good odds of taking him out as well.

They still didn't like it. Niko, because he knew I was lying, but he knew the same as I did that the time had come and this time there'd be no escape. Robin took my word that I'd survive. His problem was I didn't want him there. There was nothing I could do about Niko. I hated it and I hated that I was fucking cowardly enough to be comforted that I wouldn't be alone. But this was a lifetime of eventuality in motion. It was our time and that couldn't be changed, thanks to Grimm, and we'd be back . . . someday. If Robin didn't make it, he wouldn't. I didn't know what *paien* paradise he had picked out. He said there were hundreds upon thousands, but he had a good life here. He wasn't ready to die and I wasn't ready to know that when Niko and I eventually did come back in fifty or a hundred years, he wouldn't be here. He'd tell me I was an idiot and that I wouldn't know he wasn't there with the new set of memories I'd make.

But I knew he was wrong.

Getting my brother killed with me was . . . fuck . . . it was enough. I wasn't letting my friend die with us. That was why I called Ishiah. I wasn't any more happy with him than I had been, but when death is half a breath away, you gain priority. What he'd done, he'd done. He couldn't undo it, couldn't go back in time and change who he'd been then. But since I'd known him in New York, he'd backed us up every time, he'd saved our lives, especially Nik's, risking his own to do all of it, and he'd saved Robin's life. The last was most important, as I needed him to do that again. I let my anger go—there was a first—and told him my plan and when and where I needed him to be then forced a promise from him to not tell Goodfellow. That was the easiest part. If he told him, Robin would die and Ish didn't want that any more than I did. He wished me good luck and sounded sincere, which was ironic, as I was going off to die, but angels, ex or not, they were weird.

And then it was a waiting game. I had gotten Grimm with a good shot, but he was tough, he healed fast, and he would duct-tape his gut together before backing down from this kind of invitation to play—that hadn't been an exaggeration. I called him with the place and the time. "I'll give you five days to find the place and teach your Bae to either follow your gate there or take them in field trips of fifty to get it fixed in their mind." I was lying on the guest bed and staring at the ceiling. Robin's condo was like the Sistine Chapel. All the ceilings were painted but with far less biblical images . . . unless you

counted the one in the corner of this room where Eve
and the Serpent were doing some pretty unspeakable
and hopefully illegal things with each other under an apple tree. "It'll also give you time to scoop your guts back
into your belly and staple it shut. I think me killing all
one thousand of your Bae snakes should make up for
how pathetic your own performance will be. You didn't
even touch me yesterday. That, you Auphe-fucking-
wannabe, is pretty goddamn pathetic."

"I touched you." Auphe wannabe or Auphe wannabe
better, he had their voice. The screech of metal and shattering of glass that come from the most catastrophic of
car wrecks, where blood turns the paint job red and no
one walks away. They're pulled out in pieces. Whenever
an Auphe had spoken, whenever Grimm did, that was
what you heard . . . or worse.

"I saw your teeth. I didn't put a hand on you, Caliban,
but since I first saw you, I've touched you every single
day. Haven't you looked at yourself? You and I, our first
game, I triggered this in you. I turned you from a member of the herd into the Second Coming. No more graz-
ing with the cattle for you, *brother*. Only eating them."
He laughed, an avalanche screaming down on you to
sweep you away. "I saw that my Bae you killed were
missing a few mouthfuls of flesh. Did you really spit
them all out or did you savor one or two bites? Do you
think your friends, your so-called cattle family, will taste
any different? More meaty? I'll bet you're wondering
right now, aren't—"

"Five days," I interrupted, shut off the phone, and
threw it against the wall. I hadn't eaten any of the Bae.
The blood, yeah, I'd licked that off my teeth and it was
probably a good thing I was going to die because I
wouldn't fucking forget that otherwise. But I hadn't

eaten any of them. I didn't believe it. I refused to because it had *not* happened.

Your Honor, I bit but I did not swallow.

I turned over and buried the less than sane laughter in the pillows. Behind and above me, Eve, her thoughts as reluctantly dark and twisted as mine, rained commiseration on me and the Serpent sneered and smirked, welcoming me to the Big Time.

The five days passed and I don't know how they did or what we'd done. We couldn't clean out our apartment and give everything to the Salvation Army. Robin would've known what the true plan was if we had done so.

Niko spent the nights with Promise, and I couldn't bear to ask what he told her. I knew he didn't tell her good-bye, as she'd have told Goodfellow within seconds and double-teamed us in an effort to stop us. I'd taken that away from my brother as well as his life—the chance to say good-bye to the woman he loved. The days he spent with me. We didn't say much, I don't think, as we'd had our entire lives to say it all. But if I sat on the couch, he sat beside me shoulder to shoulder. At breakfast at the kitchen island, he did the same, although he had to move the chair over by nearly a foot. Robin had started to say something about that, but at the last minute didn't.

Instead he told us more stories of our numerous pasts, but only the funny ones and the happy ones. I was a little surprised at how many of those there were. I was not surprised to learn that Robin as Myrddynn/Merlin pulled his dick out of his hat instead of a rabbit. At Robin's goading, I *did* remember, on first seeing him do it as Caiy that I'd tried to beat the giant serpent to death with an axe handle, then fallen on the dirt floor of the hovel we were in laughing myself sick over it, followed by sulking the rest of the night at how I did not measure up. Caiy, I was thinking, drank a great deal, more than all the rest of my incarnations combined.

I did practice a little with the epinephrine, measuring the rise of my heart rate, which grew less and less each time I injected myself, the Auphe immune system at work. I had hoped it would work that way; otherwise the epinephrine could kill me before the gate did. Good to know that I was going to die and take a thousand monsters with me and not just shoot up to drop dead of a heart attack while the Bae and Grimm finished off Niko. That was not a heroic way to go. Not that I counted what I was doing as heroic either. It was a last resort, as I wasn't smart enough or good enough to do anything differently, as Grimm had been smarter and created an army. He who disdained the Auphe and had been right in all he told me. He was a smarter, more efficiently lethal monster than the Auphe. The Bae fell short, but sheer numbers couldn't be beaten. He'd make more and more and more until he ruled the world and drenched it in blood, just as the Auphe had tried to use me to do. He was the better monster and I could compete with that only by being the more insane one.

That would be my obituary. Caliban Leandros, Crazy beats smart every time. Free porn collection at this location if a puck doesn't steal it first. See ya, would've liked to be ya.

But monsters didn't get to pick who or what they would be.

However we passed those days, they did pass, and finally we were in the Pine Barrens after a silent drive and a long trek though trees and grass-covered muck masquerading as ground. The fire tower was easy to find, right where I'd remembered it being. I hadn't gated us, as I wanted to save all that up. We climbed the stairs and took a look around at our last stand. It was nice, brisk, cool breeze, and the smell of pine needles sharp and astringent. Taking a last glance around at the world, I turned to the small duffel bag I'd carried with me. I'd been injecting epinephrine the entire ride, and once we were up in the tower I had several last of the horse-sized syringes to go. I unzipped the bag and reached for the first one.

"Directly in the heart might be the way to go," I said. "Just in case."

"Just in case you want that much fluid pressure to explode your heart, yes, certainly. Niko, you failed at teaching him biology, anatomy, physics, and how much water fits in a glass." Robin knelt on the floor of the tower, swiped the syringe in my hand, and cheerfully jammed the needle through my sweatpants—he'd insisted I wear them over jeans and now I knew why—and into my outer thigh. "Come to Daddy," he said as he hit the plunger home.

"Motherfu—" I didn't have the breath to finish, as he was already injecting the next one and then the next one, switching thighs with each one, and with a speed that had several near-orange-sized lumps swelling at the top of both my legs before slowly being absorbed.

"And you wanted all that injected into your heart." He gave my jaw a light slap. "You barely have a heart, Cal, and one the size of a basketball? I think not." Straightening, he discarded the last syringe. "Time to be all the Auphe you can be, little sociopath."

First, I wasn't little. I was his size if not taller. Second . . . "I'm not a sociopath. I love Nik. I love my brother, and I have vague feelings for you that aren't necessarily hatred or disgust. Ergo, not a sociopath. More like a generalized, family-oriented lovable psychopath." I massaged my legs and felt the epinephrine disperse further and go to work. "Okay, occasionally lovable," I snapped as Robin crossed his arms and yawned in the face of my sincerity . . . or as close to it as I could come to sincerity.

"My heart is warmed. Truly. You don't inevitably hate or are disgusted by me. It's every comrade-in-arms' dream come true." He had moved to again stare out over the trees, but he reached behind to pat me absently on the shoulder.

Niko had his sword ready as the sun started nearing the horizon. "We should've waited with the epinephrine. Until we were certain they were coming."

"They're coming right now." Robin kept his gaze out to the green that stretched below us and infinitely into the distance. "It's like smelling the ozone of an approaching lightning storm. The rumble of Vesuvius at Pompeii. Can you not feel it?"

I could. I didn't know how I missed it. Grimm's gates were too quick for me to feel now. The gate of one or forty Bae I wouldn't feel until a second before they appeared. But a thousand Bae all gating here. It was like a storm or a tsunami. You felt your stomach fall, your ears pop, your heart stutter in your chest, and your brain curl up into a knot and pray not to know. Earth-shattering. Unstoppable. That was the Bae. That was the Second Coming. Or so they named themselves. So they thought.

They were wrong.

"Ishiah!" I shouted. "Now!"

He came flying in at a speed I'd not seen him reach before, tackled Robin, wrapped his arms in tight imprisonment around him, and was out and flying again in less than the blink of an eye. Goodfellow was screaming, "No!" Not shouting, but screaming as if he'd been gutted on the battlefield and it was horrible to hear, but it didn't stop me from shouting at Ishiah again. "More than a mile! Go more than a mile! I'm taking it all with me!" White-and-gold wings beating, and I'd denied it before, but I saw it now. Wrath of God in every wing stroke. In that moment I forgave Ish completely. He couldn't save my brother Niko, but he could save my brother Robin. I didn't know if the puck would forgive us, not in this life, as we'd be dead. Not in the next life either, I didn't think. He, for once, could do the sane thing and avoid us for the rest of eternity. I wouldn't blame him.

They disappeared from sight just as the Bae appeared. I grinned at Nik, wishing the metal teeth wouldn't fall into place, but they did. "Our own personal Bolivian army." I peered over the side of the rail to see white everywhere. White serpentine bodies, scales glittering like snow on fire in the failing sunlight. The eyes were fire and nothing else. Thousands and thousands of metal fangs were bared, and the hissing was louder than a hurricane.

"You're not smart enough to be Butch or handsome enough to be Sundance," Niko had to shout in my ear to be heard, but he was smiling.

"We'll just be ourselves, then. That's more than good enough for me."

I didn't see Grimm, but the Bae were climbing the tower now. They could've gated up, but there wasn't room for more than a few at a time and I'd planned on that. They couldn't suffocate us with their sheer numbers. Niko sliced the throats of several and the heads of a few more who tried to climb over the rail and I leaned over myself and gated my voice to a hundred locations, for miles, over a thousand heads to be heard by every last one of them.

"Grimm, I know you're out there somewhere, watching me and your children." Then I saw him perched at the top of a tree less than fifteen yards away. He was grinning the same as I was. Matching metal smiles. He rested his chin in his hand as if he were a teacher observing a student. I didn't doubt he thought he was. Even over the Bae, I could hear him, "Show me, brother. Show me, Caliban. Show me how you plan to win this particular game." He hissed in laughter and anger, "But you can't. You can't win and you'll throw away the world we could make. You'll throw away your family, my family, the only family the two of us will ever have. You'll throw away all the bloody games we could've played. Selfish *bastard*. Make your choice. Choose death. Isn't that what all cowards do?"

He was furious—that I would deprive him of a conquered world, a new race, and the games that were all the Auphe ever truly lived for besides murder and slaughter. Furious I would leave him alone when murder is more entertaining with two.

The Auphe, the original ones, all the half-breeds they created—they'd destroyed. Even the successes, Grimm and me. They had more to answer for than I'd known.

But it was too late now.

"Your children. Your Bae, your snakes, not mine," I said with disgust and derision. "Then there's Tumulus. You've never been to the homeland. Can't get there. Never seen it, never will. Never seen your true world." I grinned, savage and proud, too much at the taste of the metal of my teeth. "But I have. I lived there for years, and doesn't that eat you up alive, cousin?" Not that it mattered that he craved what I'd had when I'd have given anything in my human moments, my soul if I still had one, to have never seen that hell. "And here? Earth, that's only the Auphe feeding ground. They were the first murderers to walk this place, but this place wasn't the first they walked, was it?

"You're a Second Coming without the Promised Land, without Tumulus. And while you're supposed to treat this"—I threw my arms wide to indicate anything and everything in the world—"as a hunting ground, a buffet, a vacation house that belongs to you, fight to the death with anyone who tries to take it away, including the natives—you don't *live* here with the cattle. You own it ... you come and snack as you please. Low-maintenance massacres. But staying here, mingling with the herds, stinking of the sheep, the cattle, and the bleating *paien* who are no more a challenge than humans? You might as well be their shepherds. It's pathetic. That's not the Auphe way. And your Bae? They have no way of their own, no instinct, no home, *nothing*. All of you, you don't belong. Not here. Not anywhere.

"You're trespassers but you won't goddamn leave!" I was all taunting contempt as I saw the blood drip from his sliced lips where teeth were buried to keep him from screaming in rage. "You're tourists. That's all you are. Fucking *tourists*. And I'm kicking your asses out ... permanently."

Then I let it go—all of it. Everything I'd been saving up all my life, building and growing inside me, too much to hold in one half-human body. God, I thought I'd known, but I hadn't. I'd had no idea all that was in me. So much. Too much, until I cracked here and there and everywhere, but I held it down. I trapped it in mental chains that were on the verge of shattering, held on until all I saw was a haze painted the same dim glow of a thousand long-dead stars. It tried to push its way out of every part of me, out of every single pore in my skin, piggybacking on every thought, carried on my pain-racked insanity-driven scream. It pushed and fought to be free with a force that turned me into a bomb with a timer vibrating on zero.

Now was the time.

Now I was free, but so was everything I'd fought so hard not to be.

The gate—a living, carnivorous thunderstorm of rage and hunger—exploded around us. It did as I'd told it. It obeyed. Why wouldn't it? It was starving. It wanted to be fed. Shredding and tearing through the glowing dusk around us, it opened in the very air itself: a jagged wound that I could see no end to. I felt reality recoil and rush away. I heard the world wail at the unnatural horror that clawed at it until it was ripped open. I also heard the hissing screams of the monsters surrounding us as they tried to retreat—too young and unpracticed to tear free of my gate with one of their own. They were trapped and they weren't getting out.

Amateurs.

I laughed, and then hummed silently to myself.

Anything you can do, I can do better.

Anything I can do, you can't fucking do at all.

Kiddies shouldn't play with grown-up toys. Too bad for them. I was Ground Zero and there was no escaping the shock wave of the implosion that was designed to trap, not blast free. The gate was an inescapable tsunami that swept wave after wave over the thrashing lengths of white-scaled nightmares—it covered them in deepest blacks, glowing grays, and painfully bruised purples, all of which was ringed with a whirlpool of lightning made to burn through flesh.

It was light and the absence of light. It was a gangrenous wound of the veil that stood between here and there. It was a door.

It was the end.

That's what happens when you show up to a fight with claws and I show up with an evolutionary-created one-way trip to thermonuclear Hell.

Top of the food chain, bitches. It's the only place to be.

"Buckle up, time to go, boys and girls!" I laughed, and if it was a little dark and a shitload more than a little crazy, it wasn't like anyone was going to be around to tell the tale. At least no one who would hold it against me, I knew, as I felt Nik grab my hand and hold it high in victory. In life together, in death together—why had I thought that was wrong? With my brother always, what could be more right?

The door was open and I didn't hesitate when I picked the destination.

Then I died.

I didn't mind. That was, after all, half the point.

I died when I took the gate to the sun, dragging with it a thousand screaming monsters, two humans, more or less, and a big fuck-you to the murdering army of assholes that thought they could take me down.

I died, making certain every monster in a one-mile radius went with me.

I died on my own terms and denying the darkest part of me with my last breath even as I used that darkest part to make it happen.

I died with my brother at my side. I died free. There are worse ways to go, but there are no better.

I died, and it was slow and painful, but that was a price I was willing to pay.

Nik and I took our last look of the world as our hearts began to tear themselves apart, gripped hands tight enough to feel the blood drip, raised our eyes to the descending sun, and took our last ride of this life as I took us into the fire. It hurt. It hurt more than anything could, that gate. I was dying cell by cell and I felt every one of them go. That was all right, though. There would be other lives and they'd be as good if not more so as we'd stay family. Death couldn't change that. I should've known that before Robin had told us.

We rode into the sunset in a life where that meant dying.

No happy ending.

But that was okay. I was with my brother. I got to save the world.

There'd be other endings.

They would be better ones.

So yeah, as I said, shit does happen.

But sometimes . . . sometimes it's not that bad.

There was one last thing, one last thought. From me to Grimm and the Auphe and Bae nations.

I played your games, all of them, and fuck you. . . .

I *won*.

16

Caliban

I wasn't dead.

That wasn't life. It was a stupid thing to think—death isn't life—but it was true. This wasn't life—life didn't work this way. Not my life. There was no happy ending. No riding off into the sunset, not while I was still breathing. I didn't get to live after gating a thousand Bae into the sun. That shit didn't happen unless being alive meant something much worse than death was waiting for me. And what that could possibly be, I didn't want to know. I could imagine many things, too many and then some, but I did not want to know. Period. End of story.

Shivering, I could feel the cold around me. Maybe I was back in Tumulus. The Auphe had somehow resurrected from the dead and were going to keep me there for years of torture until they had a hunt across the red sand with me as the rabbit. That would qualify as worse than dying. Yeah, you could say that. That would be no real surprise with how my life had gone up until now.

But . . .

I smelled the bite of snow and pine trees, the distant musk of what I was guessing was an elk or a moose and Wolves, the were kind, and I smelled Nik and Goodfellow. I smelled Grimm too, but as if he'd been here and gone, not that I cared. What I did care about was that if I was alive, Nik would be too. He had to be. I couldn't have gotten him killed but not myself. That was not fucking acceptable and I'd take Tumulus over that. I'd take any fucking form of hell and be goddamn happy with it over Nik being gone without me.

I opened my eyes and it was light. There was a blue sky with the sun only now sliding toward the top of the trees and the horizon, and they were tall trees, very tall, dark green pines with snow clumped on them. There was a warm weight on my chest, a bare hand, and I followed the arm it was attached to up to a familiar face with shaggy reddish hair and predatory gold eyes. "Rafferty?" Rafferty, the healer and Wolf who'd saved my life twice now. He'd saved me when Niko had first thought years ago he could keep his oath, kill me if that was the only solution. He couldn't and had taken me to help. That had been Rafferty then, and he was here now. How? Damn, I hurt. Fuck. *"Nik."*

"Here, little brother."

I turned my head to see him next to me, flat on his back as well and with Rafferty's other hand resting on his chest too. His braid was nearly buried in the snow we were lying in and he was shaking from the cold the same as I was, but he was alive. Fuck. He was *alive.* "You're not dead. We're not dead," I said, stunned.

He reached out a hand toward me and I stretched

back to grip it as hard as I could. Relaxed and as peaceful as I hadn't seen him since this all began, he let his lips edge into a smile that came close to being astounded as mine. "No, we're not. But I applaud your grasp of the obvious."

"Yeah, not dead now, but you were," Rafferty snapped, as irritable as he'd always been all the times he'd healed and helped us through the years. "Dead as they get, both of you. You don't build a fucking gate to the sun and expect to live through that. I'm surprised I was able to get all your blood back into you. Show a little respect and gratitude to the guy who kicked the Grim Reaper in the balls to yank you back from his bony fingers."

"You healed. . . . How the hell did you know? How'd we get here? Where is here? And how the fuck did we get out of the gate?" I had more questions and a great deal more pained cursing to go with them, but that's when someone cleared their throat. It sounded so damn smug that I didn't have to look up to see who it was, but I did. I was an idiot that way. Robin stood behind the crouching Rafferty. His arms were folded as they'd been in the fire tower, there was snow in his hair, and the smirk on his face combined with the bright gleam in his green eyes was that much more arrogant.

"You," I accused.

"Of course me. Who else could pull this off, kid? Did you buy into my screaming when Ishiah 'saved' me? I thought that was Oscar-level acting there. You should be appreciative I pulled out all the stops on that performance. As you bought in to it, so did Grimm." The smirk grew. "Before you ask why I couldn't tell you, think about it. Long and hard." His smug smile transmuted into something stark. "As it became apparent over the past, I don't know, five hundred incarnations of yours

that you two were utterly incapable of keeping your-
selves alive, I thought I'd finally better step in and fucking do it for you."

Niko slowly sat up and Rafferty let him, but when I
tried, he shook his head and held me down with his hand
remaining on my chest. "I'm not through with you yet.
Freeze your ass off for a couple more minutes while
Curly tells us all how goddamn amazing he is."

Robin scowled at the back of Rafferty's head. He'd not
been fond of the nickname the first time they'd met.
"Scruffy leg-humper. If you owned a cell phone like every
other creature walking, flying, or swimming the earth, I'd
have found you sooner. And we're in Banff, Canada, by
the way, if Niko and you were curious."

"He's still healing me here," I protested. "Could you
not piss him off, which would waste all your work? Not
to mention that I kind of like being alive—there's that to
think about."

Before he could decide on whether it was worth it or
not, Nik asked, "How did you get us out of the gate?"

"I didn't. Grimm did. We have discussed how Grimm's
gates put the true Auphe and yours to shame. If anyone
could pull you out of your own gate to another destination, it would be Grimm." Goodfellow was in his element now, so self-satisfied and impressed with his own
cleverness that he could barely stand it. "When Cal was
first shot by the Vigil and Grimm showed up in your
apartment—"

"And you had Cal gate us away," Nik interrupted,
"while you said you ran, but you didn't run, did you? You
stayed to talk to Grimm. Goodfellow, he could've killed
you."

"Yes, I lied. No, I didn't run. And kill me?" Robin
snorted, a plume of icy vapor filling the air. "I can talk
anyone into anything as I've told you too many times to

count. When will you believe me? I suppose it's my own fault. The greatest trick I ever played was convincing the world that I didn't exist."

"That's about the devil, you conniving asshole, with your stolen prose. Stolen and a lie as you take every Fenris-blessed opportunity to tell anyone who'll listen that you exist," Rafferty grumbled, the heat of his hand beginning to burn through my clothes and tingle almost painfully against my chest. "Get on with it."

"You could ruin a weeklong marathon spank-fest," Robin growled. "As I said, he didn't kill me. We talked, had a little discussion. We made a deal." He might not have been the devil, but the grin on his face now would've fit the devil perfectly as you signed away your soul. "I bet Grimm that Cal would beat him *or* his thousand Bae *or* both. And should Cal win in any of the three ways, Grimm would let him walk away for good. The game would be over. Finished. It was the ultimate move in that fun little kill-or-be-killed, maim-or-be-maimed Auphe game you so love to play. Naturally as it was *I* who was the one who was selling that move, Grimm went for it."

"You bet Cal's life?" Nik accused flatly, trying to get to his feet somewhat unsteadily.

"Cal was already dead," Robin retorted cuttingly. "He was already dead. You were already dead. Your hearts merely hadn't stopped beating yet. These were the end times, and Grimm was appropriately the Reaper. I obtained for you a chance to live, as you can't ever be bothered to do it yourself, and made Grimm no longer a threat, not one to us at least. Not to mention that as it was a chance that I created, it was ninety-nine point nine percent foolproof." He paused. "Although I admit when I found out it was a thousand Bae and not merely fifty, I had a moment where I entertained a doubt or two."

He paused, face still and frozen. It wasn't long, a second maybe, but it was long enough. I had seen it in the past days in the shadows that followed him, the faded green of his sly eyes, the constant drift of his thoughts to mostly memories of better times—it hadn't been a doubt. He'd very nearly given up. Robin, who didn't know of anything he couldn't get out of with fast-talk and faster hands, he'd almost lain down to die with us.

The hesitation disappeared and he was as smug as ever. "But never has a doubt defeated me, which means here you are. Alive. Unmutilated. No better endowed sexually than before, but one can't have everything. Healers aren't miracle workers. Bringing you back from death is one thing, enlarging your penis to a passably normal size would require the selling of your soul. As Rafferty said, show him some respect."

For once Nik was a little abashed. I could tell, as the tips of his ears turned pink, or that might have been frostbite, but I was going with embarrassed. Whether it was at the thought of rudeness or that Robin had somehow gotten a glimpse of his dick, I didn't know. With Nik, rudeness would be my pick. He was weird like that. "I apologize," he said. "You're correct. We're alive and we shouldn't be. Wouldn't be. But technically Cal lost. We died in the gate."

"Ah." Goodfellow unfolded his arms to hold up a superior finger. "No. He killed all the Bae. That was the deal. He defeats Grimm or the Bae or Grimm and the Bae. That it would be a kamikaze suicide plan was beyond easy to predict. All Cal's plans are. He just usually somehow survives them out of sheer dumb luck."

"Hey," I protested, surging up. Rafferty smacked me back down with his other hand to my forehead and Wolf strength. "Fine. Whatever. How'd you save me from my idiocy this time? How'd you even know what it was to begin with?"

"It's as if I'm playing chess with preschoolers, it truly is." He held up a second finger. "A giant box of more epinephrine than you could possibly need for the next entire year, enough that you could gate anywhere."

"You mentioning Icarus and your false telling of him flying to the sun instead of near the sun," Niko added. "You planted the idea."

Robin nodded and held up a third finger. "It was the one place you could be certain the Bae wouldn't survive. And once I found out Grimm's gating powers are advanced enough that he can do virtually anything with them, I knew it was safe enough to nudge Cal in that direction. Once Cal opened the gate to send the Bae and you both to the sun, he had won, and as he had won, I told Grimm the equivalent of letting him walk away was plucking you both out of the gate before the two of you made it to the sun."

"But that large a gate killed me when I activated it. I *felt* it. I felt myself die. And Nik wouldn't have survived it either," I reasoned. "You had to know that."

"Which is why I'm sitting on my ass in the snow," Rafferty rumbled, finally dropping his hand to dust them both off. "Curly lit up the entire worldwide trickster network a week ago to find me in the wilds of the Great White North so I could have the probably unpaid privilege of bringing you both back to the land of the fucking living." He shrugged. "If possible. If you'd been exploded balls of meat, I couldn't have swung that, but you weren't. Damn close, but not quite. It worked. That's all that counts."

"He sent me track him down when he have location. Give healer cell phone. Listen to them yell for hours at each other. Someone *will* pay me."

I sat up hurriedly and twisted around to see a beat-up RV that I remembered as brand-new and expensive as hell and also stolen from Goodfellow. An albino Wolf, of the All Wolf Cult variety, stood in front of it. "Flay?" Flay, with his lupine claws, white hair, red eyes, mouthful of wolf teeth, and not-especially human vocal cords, had helped me infiltrate the Kin five years ago and saved Niko, Georgina, and my life. After his betrayal to the Kin, to get our help in rescuing his kidnapped son, he'd fled New York in an RV stolen from Goodfellow, pissing the puck off to no end, and hadn't been seen or heard from since. He was also Delilah's half brother. Which is how I met Delilah . . . and there was no reason to think of that now.

"Your sister took over the Kin," I said, rather mindlessly, but I couldn't think of what else to say. My brain was as frozen as the snow I sat in. Robin had planned all this? Finding Rafferty, who apparently didn't believe in owning his own cell phone, using Flay to chase him down for some communication and to get him to what I was guessing was the spot Robin picked closest to the Wolves or to at least stay in one location.

I couldn't picture it, but it had to have happened—then Robin giving Grimm GPS coordinates, which was why he'd copied the half Auphe's cell number from me, and telling him to make certain he could get our bodies there should I win. It was more than a little unbelievable. Yet he had. I knew that he had, as that was exactly what Robin would do to have all prepared for being on the winning side of a deal. He could've talked Grimm into bringing him here as well or more likely had Ishiah pull in another heavenly favor from an angel that didn't have to actually use his wings to go long distances. And when I'd called Ishiah to "save" Robin, Ishiah had already known everything—Goodfellow's entire plan.

Robin had gotten a retired angel to lie to me. What couldn't that son of a bitch do?

Flay shrugged in his parka. "Not surprised about Delilah and Kin. She always bossy when pups." Speaking of
pups, the RV door was pushed open and a half-grown
apricot-colored wolf jumped out.

"Slay." Flay's son. I'd been the one to get him back
from the kidnapper, although him biting a chunk of flesh
out of my side had been my only thanks. But what the
hell? At the time he'd been only three years old, and a
damn deadly three he'd been. Flay shrugged again but
grinned this time with those overlarge sharp teeth. "He
likes rabbits. Easier hunt this way." Slay bounded off into
the snow to kill a few Thumpers.

Someone else came through the door. His hair was
reddish too, although it was one shade darker auburn
than Rafferty's and his eyes were one shade lighter to
full gold. His disposition was lighter too; his grin was
happy as hell. "Looking better, Cal. You still remember
how many cocker spaniels you have to skin to make a
pimp coat for an Auphe?" That was the same god-awful
joke Catcher had told me once, using a pencil to type it
out on his computer because Catcher was a Wolf and a
wolf. He'd been sick in college and Rafferty had healed
him, but he'd had to go to the genetic level to do it and
he'd done it too well.

Wolves, werewolves, weren't people who'd evolved
the ability to turn into wolves. It was the other way
around. Wolves had started out as wolves and Rafferty
had cured Catcher only to start him on the path to de-
evolution. He'd been stuck in wolf form and, worse,
slowly losing the higher intelligence werewolves have in
any form. The last we'd seen them had been in Yellow-
stone Park when Catcher was a wolf in form and mind,
finally lost to the wild, and Rafferty had joined him to
live out their lives as wolves.

"Holy fuck." I grinned back at him. It was the first

time I'd ever seen him in human form other than in a
picture on the dresser of his bedroom. "Doesn't it feel
weird not to be on all fours after so long?"

"That's what she said," he laughed, shoving hands in
the pockets of his jacket.

"Damn," Robin muttered. "I wish I'd said that."

Niko was staring at me and that was odd because here
was Catcher, not back from the dead, but improbably
back from something equally difficult. He'd been stuck
in wolf form for seven or eight years before his mind finally went. "Rafferty," he said, "you told us you couldn't
fix Catcher. You couldn't undo what you'd done at the
genetic level."

"I couldn't. No healer, shaman, half trickster, no one
could help." Rafferty was, as far as we knew, the best
healer alive in the world today. We'd brought him in to
fight the antihealer, Suyolak, Plague of the World; that's
how talented he was. If he needed help with Catcher, his
chances of finding it had been extremely low. "But I finally found a full-fledged god who'd made a short jail-
break and was running around northern Canada. Our
god, god of the wolves, Fenris. He heard me, he saw my
offerings of meat and blood. He came when I asked." He
looked up at the sky, refusing to be ashamed if his stubborn scowl meant anything. "Wolves do pray too."

Even I knew Fenris was the Norse wolf-god and son of
the trickster god Loki. "He showed me a few things about
genetics and shape-changing. He's back on the chain gang
again." He lowered his eyes back to the ground and
shrugged as if the loss of his god were nothing. . . . Nothing
he was willing to show us was more likely. "But I got my
cousin back. My more mouthy version of him anyway," he
amended. "And at least he remembers to flush now."

Catcher rolled his eyes as he stepped down into the
snow, bent down, came up again, and nailed his cousin

with a snowball. "The love, it's almost embarrassing." He grinned cheerfully.

Niko reached over and took a handful of my hair to hold up for me to see. "Is that how you were able to do this? Genetics?"

It was black. My hair clenched tight in my brother's hand, it was black again. I swiped a tongue across my gums and didn't feel the ridge of receded metal teeth any longer. "My eyes?"

"Gray." Niko smiled. "Plain boring gray. Do you think you can survive that? Is that not exotic enough for you now?"

"Is it permanent?" I turned to Rafferty, who was brushing the snow out of his hair. "If it is, I'd think about kissing you on the mouth if it wouldn't give Robin ideas. Maybe even tongue."

He grimaced. "Yeah, I think I'd rather be paid, thanks. And yes, it's permanent. Okay, not the eyes. You can still give a flash of red to scare the shit out of whatever you're fighting at the time. I know you're ass enough to enjoy that and a little Auphe cred goes a long way. They're wired to your emotional responses, your evil temper, same as they were. You'll have to practice not making the cabbies piss themselves if you get annoyed at being short-changed."

"Please keep the tongue and the ideas to yourself," Catcher added. "I'm as laid back as a Wolf gets, but I'm not a saint."

"As if I don't always have ideas." Robin reached down a hand and pulled me to my feet.

Rafferty followed us up. "You're not human. I still can't remove half your genetic material without you turning into a puddle of fleshy goo. But I've taken you to as far back as I could, your birth DNA setting. You're still half human, half Auphe, but now you're frozen that way. The Auphe genes won't take over. It can bite my healing ass. This once Auphe genes *don't* win."

The closest to human I'd been . . . but not a part of humanity. I had been different since the beginning—from the first beat of my heart in the womb. Everyone who'd come into contact with me, child, kid, or adult, had known it. They'd known I wasn't like them. I might look like them, but on the inside, I wasn't. They sensed that I was other. Not human. Not Auphe, as they didn't know what an Auphe was. My own species—mine and Grimm's.

That didn't mean it wasn't a fucking miracle. As a kid I'd been a lion doing his best to behave in the middle of a herd of sheep, but in the past few years, I hadn't been a lion. I'd been a rabid *thing*. While homicidal rage came in handy once in a while, I'd make do without—because, hey, fucking goddamn miracle. "What about gating?"

He made a so-so motion with his hand. "Not sure. Gating isn't a physically cosmetic attribute like the eyes. Can newborn Auphe gate? I don't know. I really don't want to know. It could go either way. Don't try it here, though. It's fucking disgusting to see or feel for the rest of us. I hope you have to walk like the rest of us clowns."

Robin's hand was still gripping mine from pulling me to my feet and I yanked him into a hard hug. "You saved our lives, you ass, lying from start to finish. Hell, you always save us in some way we don't know about, but this was an outstanding con job from the beginning. A thing of beauty." It had been. Sophia would've clawed out his eyes with envy. We'd been manipulated by him for months now if not an entire year, and as much as I chafed against being scammed, he was the only reason Nik and I were alive. I, for once in my life, was not going to bitch about things being kept in the dark.

"You have every right to brag, you son of a bitch." I smacked the back of his head just as Nik had taught me by example. *"Go raibh maith agat"*—*thank you* in Gaelic—"from Cullen," I whispered at his ear. "Also Cullen kicked out your hypnosis when Rafferty healed us. You saved our lives with it, I know"—the only reason I wasn't pissed as fucking hell he'd manipulated me into it to begin with—"which is the single excuse I have for not following Cullen's example, but by kicking a sensitive body part of yours instead, asshole. Don't try that again, not without asking, lifesaving or not." I smacked the back of his head again. "But thanks all the same from me, too. This me."

Robin twitched in surprise when I mentioned Cullen. Then he grimaced at the mention of the hypnosis. He kept hoping, I think, that Cullen would sleep again. I thought he would now, that part of me, but he'd waited around to see the end, after popping up here and again to look through my eyes and tell me the lengths that Robin would go . . . including the whole Svengali thing he'd pulled on me.

"Brat." He tried for scathing, but he didn't come close to making it. "Besides, a promise made three times three. What could I do but save this new life for you? *Nil a bhuiochas ort, Cullen,*" he told Cullen, and as he did I felt Cullen slip away, satisfied. Resting once again. "You're welcome."

The words were painted with melancholy. Robin and Cullen, in real life they'd not had the chance to meet. I wish they could've. The two of them, both devious as hell . . . my descendants would still be kings or queens of an independent Ireland and the rest of the U.K. would be huddled as far from the drunken and nuclear-enforced border as they could get.

I'd once been devious. Hadn't thought shooting someone in some area of the body other than the face was as sneaky as you could get. Who'd have thought?

"It's too bad reincarnation doesn't go backward. Imagine what we could do then knowing what we do now," I said, slapping him hard on the back to pull him into a rough embrace before turning him loose.

"Funny you should say that. There's an artifact I've heard of for thousands of years now. It is said to manipulate time in some fashion. No one's quite certain what the result of its use is, but . . . it's a thought. I was thinking of looking for it. Achilles and Patroclus could live long enough to get erectile dysfunction. I would find that hilarious." He slung his arm over my shoulder and both of us grinned at the sight of Nik dropping his face into his hands.

"You should have let us die," he said, muffled and heavy with grim morose, the complaint aimed at Rafferty. "It would've been more merciful. Never mind. I'll do it myself. Someone hand me my katana."

I laughed, a real laugh without a hint of cynicism, and it was one of the first I could remember being that fucking pure, before throwing my own arm around Niko's neck and reeling him into a pile of three—three times three times three. Niko, Robin, and me . . . death itself hadn't been able to change that no matter how many times it took two of us. We came back each time and each time Robin was waiting. "You said you were ready for a new game, a new ride." I gave my brother's braid a yank.

"How about we live our life, perhaps even a whole one, this once? I could use the rest." He gave a doubting groan, but I knew a fake one when I heard it.

"I think we can do that." I grinned at him. It was a genuine one. Despite the earlier laugh, it didn't feel any less odd on my face. Wildly rare and beyond bizarre. "We made it, Cyrano."

He swatted the back of my head lightly as I'd done to

Robin as Niko had done to me and on and on. "We did, little brother." His smile was small but ... at peace. For Niko the smile was equal to my grin, and the peace ... this was a first for that.

I'd thought right before I died that shit happens. I'd thought it every hour of every day of my life and it does. Shit happens. All the time. All my life. But sometimes, while I wouldn't have believed it until I saw it here, miracles do happen. Even if a trickster has to make one out of thin air. Sometimes you do get to ride off into the sunset, whole and alive, even if ironically enough you have to die and be brought back to life to do it.

All we had to do was saddle up.

And watch us ride.

17

Goodfellow

Niko and Cal were talking with Rafferty, Catcher, and Flay, who were all quite complimentary to Slay when he trotted back with a plump dead rabbit. The brothers hadn't asked me how I'd been positive Grimm would let Cal walk away. You'd think they would be more than curious, as they would be and then some, had they a gram of sense.

Cal had said about himself: He was a killer; why wouldn't he be a liar as well? That was the truth. Yet they weren't thinking about that truth. It could be that they didn't want to offend me to insinuate that after saving their lives, I would then risk them all over again on the belief and my word that Grimm wouldn't keep his. That he wouldn't be the same as Cal—a killer and a liar. They would want to have faith I had him in a bind, to have faith in me instead of what they knew of Grimm—liar, cheater, killer. They would want to believe that I'd gotten the better of him and somehow forced him to keep his word. They would want to believe in me, as I'd not given them the reason to think otherwise.

That I was the same as Grimm . . . liar, cheater, killer . . . they didn't mention. Family members are like that, aren't they? Always thinking the best of you. That was quaint. They shouldn't have worried about my emotions. My *feelings*.

I wasn't the same as Grimm.

I was so much worse.

I only needed the opportunity to prove it.

The Wolves had kept quiet as I'd asked them to, which I appreciated. I'd have to tip them, despite the fact that Rafferty's bill would be exorbitant. His always were. Barkers without Borders was a myth to him. He charged more than a concierge doctor who came with a complimentary bottle of aged scotch. Not that it mattered as long as he kept his mouth shut. What did matter was the fact that I thought it was best like this for Cal and Niko. That they trusted that Grimm would hopefully keep his word to me, but staying alert and sharp for him to attack out of nowhere nonetheless.

Alert, sharp . . . safe.

With their history, it wouldn't do any harm at all for them to stay vigilant and observant. Whether that particular bogeyman showed up, they had to know, there'd be others. Better safe than sorry.

I felt a hand on my shoulder as Ishiah returned from deep in the woods where he'd dragged the body. "Hidden away?" I asked.

"Hidden away," he confirmed. "Until the wildlife eats it or it rots."

Earlier with help from some still current angel companions, Ishiah had been able to bring me here. We'd

beaten Grimm's gate and I'd watched at a distance alone
as Cal's and Niko's bodies had been dumped out of midair to lie dead in the snow. Unmoving in the crystal
white, they'd been as unmoving as gravestones of flesh as
blood seeped seemingly from every pore, covering them
in a blanket of crimson, staining the snow with death. I'd
seen their blood time and time before . . . in the dirt, in
the sand, in the grass, drifting in the salt water of the
ocean. I hadn't wanted to see it again. Instead I'd shifted
my scrutiny to the one beside me.

Grimm.

I had stood by him but not too close. No, not close, as
I was not a fool. He would've thought me one if I had,
and it would've been true.

But I was anything save a fool.

"He wins this round, little goat," he'd said to me as
Rafferty began to work on restarting their hearts, repairing the infinite damage that Cal's killer gate could've
done within them . . . putting them back together, cell by
cell. "But this is better as there will be more. He lives and
I get to torture him over and over until he gives in or
dies in agony." He gave me a mirror/metal-bright smile
of murderous anticipation. "Wasn't that the *deal*?"

There had existed no deal in which Grimm would
willingly let Cal walk away forever. That would be a
dream and a fantasy and a lie. I hadn't bothered to bring
it up in our earliest negotiations for the waste of time it
would've been. That white lie was one I'd created for the
brothers. White lies are always better than the truth. I
frankly couldn't believe that they'd bought it, all in all.

"More, Grimm? Why?" I wouldn't have stood even as
near him as I had if I hadn't seen Cal rip him open from
navel to sternum with his metal claws. I didn't know how
fast an Auphe could heal, but it wasn't this fast. Grimm
was standing with his intestines either held in with surgi-

cal or duct tape, pure will holding him up. Add to that the gate he'd promised and delivered, which had pulled the brothers out of Cal's own gate long before they reached the sun, separating them from all the Bae—that would've drained him to the dregs. He was weak, weaker than he'd ever been, slower than he'd ever be, at his most suscep- tible, and blind to his vulnerabilities. That was conceit for you. His ego wouldn't let him believe it, and he thought I didn't know it.

He'd been mistaken.

A puck was *made* to spot weaknesses, and I was noth- ing if not a product of my race. I didn't have the power of a god. I didn't need it. I was a *trickster*, and we had gods bowing at our feet with the force of our words alone.

"Honestly, why?" I'd repeated. "Aren't you tired of it yet? The never-ending killing. The game. World domina- tion. All of it. It's dull after a while. I've done it. Trust me. I have ruled and I have rampaged. I've been the throne and the power behind it. I know," I'd said, and meant it. I had done it all and tiresome it had never failed to be- come.

"It's all we have." His metal slice-of-hell grin that chilled all that breathed and lived widened into a night- mare where you could see a thousand of your reflections. "It's what we are made to do whenever we gather to- gether. What we were born for, Caliban and I.

"Caliban said it himself. We are something new and something old and something unlike anything on this earth," he'd finished with his grin twisting with vicious spite, scornfully annoyed at my questions.

Impassioned in his dark belief.

Distracted by the thought of future games.

Was that opportunity knocking?

I thought that it was.

Distraction is for children.

I'd barely had time to think what a naïve child he truly was when Ishiah's sword had cut through his neck from behind with a swiftness that left Grimm grinning yet when his head hit the ground, followed a fraction of a second later by his body falling onto the snow. Perhaps I hadn't been as alone in my distance as I'd seemed, but I was a liar too as I'd said, in words and impressions. I'd felt no obligation to emphasize to Grimm what he should have already known.

I had been careful to give Ishiah that necessary swing room for his blade, but I thought I felt something splash my chin. I'd bent down and studied my reflection in Grimm's gleaming silver teeth as his decapitated head tilted to one side on the frozen white beneath it. Ah, there it was. Wiping the drop of blood from my chin, I echoed, "Mmm. Whenever you gather together. Pity there is only one of you left. No more gathering now."

I'd straightened and inhaled the pine and glacier scent in the air. It smelled good. Fresh and clean, like a new beginning. I wouldn't mind one of those.

"Something new and something old and something unlike anything on this earth." My laughter had been superior, yes, and condescending, somewhat, but I'd *earned* that attitude. I'd then given his separated head a contemptuous kick into the depths of the thickly growing trees. "Actually you're the same as everyone else, and guess what. There's one of you born every minute.

"Sucker."

ABOUT THE AUTHOR

Rob Thurman lives in Indiana, land of cows, corn, and ravenous wild turkeys. Rob is the author of the Cal Leandros novels, the Trickster novels, the Korsak Brothers novels, *All Seeing Eye*, and several stories in various anthologies.

Besides ravenous wild turkeys, Rob has three rescue dogs (if you don't have a dog, how do you live?)—one of which is a Great Dane/Lab mix that weighs well over one hundred pounds, barks at strangers like Cujo times ten, then runs to hide under the kitchen table and piss on herself. Burglars tend to find this a mixed message. The other two dogs, however, are more invested in keeping their food source alive. All were adopted from the pound (one on his last day on death row). They were all fully grown, already house-trained, and grateful as hell. Think about it next time you're looking for a Rover or Fluffy.

For updates, teasers, music videos, deleted scenes, social networking (the time-suck of an author's life), and various other extras such as free music and computer wallpaper, visit the author online.

CONNECT ONLINE

robthurman.net

ALSO AVAILABLE

SLASHBACK

A CAL LEANDROS NOVEL

by *New York Times* bestselling author
ROB THURMAN

Taking on bloodthirsty supernatural monsters is how Caliban
and Niko Leandros make a living. But years ago, the brothers
were almost victims of a (very) human serial killer.

Unfortunately for them, that particular depraved killer was
working as apprentice to a creature far more malevolent—the
legendary Spring-heeled Jack. He's just hit town. He hasn't
forgotten what the Leandros brothers did to his murderous
protégé. He hasn't forgotten what they owe him. And now they
are going to pay...and pay...and pay....

**"Thurman continues to deliver strong
tales of dark urban fantasy."
—SF Revu**

Available wherever books are sold or at
penguin.com

facebook.com/AceRocBooks